Praise for D. B. Reynolds's
VAMPIRES IN AMERICA

" . . . another can't-put-down book, so clear your schedule and hunker down for a terrific read."

—*La Deetda Reads on RELENTLESS*

"This is a power read, and fans will not be disappointed in the latest installment of Reynolds's tantalizing series. Top Pick! 4 1/2 Stars!"

—*RT Book Reviews of LUCIFER*

"Captivating and brimming with brilliance, CHRISTIAN is yet another defining addition to the ever-evolving world of Vampires in America created by D.B. Reynolds."

—*KT Book Reviews*

"Did I mention that the sizzling sex factor in this book is reaching the combustible stage? It is a wonder my Kindle didn't burn up."

—*La Deetda Reads on DECEPTION*

"D.B. Reynolds has outdone herself with this exhilarating story; and VINCENT is a worthy addition to Reynolds' always excellent Vampires in America series."

—*Fresh Fiction*

"Terrific writing, strong characters and world building, excellent story-lines all help make Vampires in America a must read. Aden is one of the best so far." A TOP BOOK OF THE YEAR!

—*On Top Down Under Book Reviews*

"In one of the most compelling vampire books I've read in a while, Reynolds blends an excellent mix of paranormal elements, suspense and combustible attraction."

—*RT Book Reviews on LUCAS*

D. B. Reynolds
Vampires in America

Raphael

Jabril

Rajmund

Sophia

Duncan

Lucas

Aden

Vincent

Vampires in America: The Vampire Wars

Deception

Christian

Lucifer

Quinn

The Cyn and Raphael Novellas

Betrayed

Hunted

Unforgiven

Compelled

Relentless

The Stone Warriors

The Stone Warriors: Damian

The Stone Warriors: Kato

Quinn

by

D. B. Reynolds

ImaJinn Books

This is a work of fiction. Names, characters, places and incidents are either the products of the author's imagination or are used fictitiously. Any resemblance to actual persons (living or dead), events or locations is entirely coincidental.

IMAJINN

ImaJinn Books
PO BOX 300921
Memphis, TN 38130
Print ISBN: 978-1-61194-875-2

ImaJinn Books is an Imprint of BelleBooks, Inc.

ImaJinn Books was founded by Linda Kichline.

We at ImaJinn Books enjoy hearing from readers. Visit our websites
ImaJinnBooks.com
BelleBooks.com
BellBridgeBooks.com

10 9 8 7 6 5 4 3 2 1

Cover design: Debra Dixon
Interior design: Hank Smith
Photo/Art credits:
Background (manipulated) © Burben | Dreamstime.com
Man (manipulated) © Anatol Misnikou | Dreamstime.com

:Lqws:01:

Dedication

To everyone who made Dublin 2017
such a wonderful adventure!

Prologue

Dublin, Ireland
5 years earlier

THE AMBULANCE rolled through the gates of Dublin Port, winding through stacks of huge containers before zeroing in on the blinking lights of the Harbor Police patrol, the two medical technicians unclear on what they'd find. The report had come in on two victims—one distraught female, one wounded male. Which could mean just about anything.

They slowed as they drove by an old warehouse and onto an older part of the dock. The woman came into sight first—slender, young, with long red hair that obscured most of her face as she hunched over the much larger man. He wasn't moving. But then neither was she.

The passenger-seated paramedic jumped out of the ambulance first, ignoring his partner's cautioning advice. "Slowly, lad." But it wasn't in his nature to go slow. Hell, it wasn't his *job*, either. He hurried to the woman's side, quickly drawing close enough that he could see she was alive. If just barely. He dropped to his knees and laid a careful hand on her shoulder. "Miss, are you hurt?"

Her entire body jerked at the touch, and she scrambled away, moving in a quarter circle to escape him, while remaining hunched over the man, as if protecting him. But there was nothing left to protect. It wasn't an official finding, but the paramedic could see the truth at a glance. The man was dead, his throat a gaping wound so far gone, it wasn't even bleeding anymore.

The woman stared at him from across the body, her brown eyes, red-rimmed with tears, devoid of expression.

"Are you hurt, love?" he asked again, gently.

Her hands clenched on the man's jacket, but there was no other response.

The paramedic looked up when his partner joined him, along with a Harbor policeman. "We'll take 'em both," he told them. "He's"—he

glanced at the traumatized woman and chose his words carefully—
"severely wounded. She's in shock. Let's go."

The woman cried out when they tried to pull her away from the
dead man, hanging on to him as if she could hold back the truth. The
paramedic exchanged a quick look with his partner, then slid a syringe
into the woman's arm. She collapsed into his arms without a word.

"JUST TELL ME WHAT happened, lass. Whatever you saw."

Eve gazed around the hospital room, picked fitfully at the tape
securing the IV line to her arm, and tugged the sheet higher over her
chest. Anything to avoid dealing with the police officer's very polite
request. She snuck a glance at him, her heart pounding a drumbeat of
fear in her chest. She could tell him what she saw. Every tiny detail.
Every time she closed her eyes, she was right there all over again. The oil
and brine scent of the port, the giant trucks spewing diesel fumes as they
powered by, carrying stacks of containers. The weather-worn wood of
the warehouse that had left splinters in her trailing fingertips. There'd
been bright lights beyond the warehouse, and she'd hurried toward
them, knowing that her brother, Alan, was waiting, knowing she was
late.

And then she'd heard men's voices, arguing. The ugly sound of a
fist hitting flesh. One voice rising above the others—just as angry, but
with enough fear to raise the normally deep pitch of his voice. Alan.

She'd run forward, panic drying every ounce of spit from her
mouth. But this was *Alan*. His safety was everything. She'd crouched
down to peer around the corner. And had bit back a gasp of utter terror.

Eve blinked back into the reality of the hospital room and stared
fearfully at the kind policeman. Had she spoken any of that out loud?
Told him the truth? She didn't think so. If she had, he wouldn't be
looking at her with such calm patience. He wouldn't want to hear the
truth of what had killed her brother. Wouldn't want to learn that when
she'd peered around that final corner, two men had been standing over
her brother's motionless body, men with eyes that had burned as red as
the very fires of hell. And in their mouths . . . fangs, just like in the
horror movies. Not men at all, but *vampires*.

Everyone knew vampires existed. It was hard not to these days,
what with paparazzi stalking them like rock stars. But that didn't mean
people wanted to deal with them, especially not normal people like the
Harbor Police.

"I'm sorry," Eve said, the words coming out on a choked sob of guilt. For being late, for getting her brother killed, and, finally, for betraying him with her lies to the police. "It was already over when I got there. My brother—" Her voice broke, and she had to start over. "Alan was already on the ground, bleeding from everywhere. I held him. I tried . . ." Hot tears filled her eyes, and she looked down at her hands, surprised to find them clean. "There was so much blood," she whispered. "I tried, but I couldn't stop it."

"It was a serious injury, love. There was nothing you could have done on your own. I'm sorry to put you through this."

She swallowed hard, rubbing away her useless tears, as she fought for control. "What happens next? When can we—" She couldn't say it. The cold words that would seal her brother's fate.

"You have a mortuary? Someone your family uses?"

Eve blinked. A mortuary?

"A priest?" he prodded gently.

Oh. Oh, God. She nodded. She didn't go to church much, but her mother went every Sunday.

"Call him," the officer urged. "He'll guide you."

"Do you know . . . do I have stay here?"

"Not at all. They're just waiting for the doc to sign off on your paperwork, but you needn't stay for that, if you don't want to. Is there someone I can call for you?"

"No," she said softly, then saw his look of consternation and knew it was the wrong answer. "I called my boyfriend," she lied. "He'll come for me. Does . . . does my mother know?"

He nodded. "She was informed."

Did he wonder why her mother wasn't there with her? Why she hadn't even called, much less rushed to her daughter's bedside? Eve would like to have been surprised by that, but she wasn't.

"Thank you," she said, and meant it. If the police hadn't informed her mother, then it would have fallen to her. And she couldn't deal with that right now. She swung her legs over the side of the bed, grabbing the sheet, embarrassed by her bare thighs beneath the hospital gown.

"Careful there. Let me get the nurse for you. She'll remove that IV."

"Right," she said absently. "Thank you. Um, my mobile?" she asked.

He stood, then opened a long, narrow cupboard, and handed over her purse. "It's there."

She gave him a smile. He was so kind. But she didn't want him to hear her phone call. "I need . . . my boyfriend," she said, gesturing with her phone. A silent plea for privacy.

"Of course," he said quickly. He even blushed a bit, before handing her a business card. "My number, in case you remember anything more. Or if you need . . . anything."

She glanced at his name as she took the card, certain he'd already told her, but she couldn't remember. She made a point of meeting his eyes. "Thank you, Desmond."

"Des," he corrected quickly.

She smiled. "Des. If I think of anything, I'll call."

"Or if there's something I can do. I'm happy to help."

"I'll remember."

His blush deepened. "I'll be going, then. The nurse should be in shortly." He jammed his hat on his head and rushed out the door, closing it behind him.

Eve waited until he'd been gone a few minutes, then called for an Uber. She'd have rather used a cab, but if anyone saw her, the Uber service could easily pass for a friend picking her up. The app said 7 minutes. Perfect. Pulling out the IV from her arm, she slapped a piece of tape over the wound, then stripped off the hospital gown and got dressed.

By the time she was climbing into the Uber guy's plain gray sedan, she was back to her usual self. Except for the bloody, gaping wound in her heart, where her brother used to be. There was not enough tape in the world to make that better. But she knew what would.

Justice. No more university for her, no more exams. The guilt was so thick, she could barely breathe. That's why she'd been meeting Alan last night, to celebrate her acceptance for graduate school. He'd been so proud, and she'd been so happy.

No longer. She was a hunter now, a killer. She was going to take from the vampires what they'd taken from Alan, and from her. Their bloody, fucking lives.

Chapter One

Kildare, Ireland, present day

QUINN STEPPED OFF the helicopter, bending slightly as he hurried out from under the blades, shielding his eyes against the dust to look around. He'd thought Lucas Donlon was bullshitting when he'd talked about his Irish "castle." Turns out he wasn't. The damn vampire really *did* have a castle. A gray stone monstrosity, complete with a fucking turret clinging to one side of the two-story main building, and a wall around the whole thing—at least twelve feet high and crenellated, for fuck's sake. As if anyone was going to be firing off arrows to repel invaders. The place had to be a few hundred years old, but the warm light spilling out from perfectly clear glass windows gave away the modernization inside.

He couldn't fault Lucas for making improvements. Castles were drafty affairs, with vermin in the walls and bad plumbing. Quinn had never lived in a castle, but his mother had grown up in one, courtesy of his grandfather who'd been the head groundskeeper for a property that had been turned into an expensive hotel—a fate far more common to old castles than what Lucas had done to this one. It took serious money to upgrade an old building of this size. That Lucas had done so spoke to two things, only one of which mattered to Quinn. First was that Lucas Donlon had a lot of money. No surprise there. All vampire lords had money, especially the old ones. But, second, and most importantly to Quinn, the money and time that had gone into the renovation told him that this castle *mattered* to Lucas. He'd been up front with Quinn about that, and about his intention to reclaim his lands, no matter who became Lord of Ireland. Quinn had a feeling Lucas would have claimed it long ago, if not for the consideration of vampire politics that had been pressed on him by Raphael. Even his brief acquaintance with the two vampire lords had made it clear to Quinn that Raphael was someone— maybe the *only* one—whom Lucas listened to. Of course, Raphael was also the guy who'd blown vampire politics all to hell just a few days ago, when he'd flown into France and taken out Laurent Pierre, the Lord of Nice, along with every vampire who'd been sworn to him. Apparently, even Raphael threw politics out the window when someone tried to kill his people and blow up his house.

Ostensibly, Raphael's French incursion had been designed to draw attention away from Quinn's far more discreet arrival in Ireland. It had worked. No one had paid Quinn any mind when he'd flown into Dublin and then on to Kildare, even though he'd been traveling on Lucas's private jet, which should have drawn at least a cursory notice. But the vampire grapevine had been buzzing like a Wall Street banker on a cocaine high, and all they'd been talking about was Raphael and France.

As the helicopter lifted off behind him, Quinn noticed a woman striding through the open gates and walking with purpose toward him and his cousin Garrick, who was the only vampire he'd brought along on this journey. The only person he trusted absolutely.

The approaching woman, also a vampire, headed straight for Quinn. He reacted as a vampire first, weighing her power against his own. It wasn't a particularly aggressive move—that comparing of powers—it was simply the way things were done in the world of Vampire. Power was everything. Quinn had it. Most vampires, like the female approaching him, didn't. But what she lacked in power, she made up for with a killer body and the unconscious seduction of a woman who knew her own appeal.

She was slightly above average height, dressed casually in skin-tight jeans over long legs, and a red sweater that hugged the swell of full breasts. She walked effortlessly over the uneven ground, despite a pair of high-heeled boots, and gave Quinn a smile of warm welcome.

"Lord Quinn," she said, offering a slender hand. "I'm—"

"Imogen Cleary," he said, meeting her eyes with a return smile. "Lucas's . . . *butler*, I believe."

"I'm flattered, my lord. As for the title, it's somewhat dated in this day and age, I know. But it fits the task." Her head tilted as her smile widened, and Quinn knew he was being charmed. It was no accident that Lucas's only female staff member was the one greeting him. He grinned, deciding to play along. Who was he to spoil a good seduction?

"Quite the opposite, Ms. Cleary," he said, raising her hand to his lips for a courtly kiss, and adding a touch of Irish lilt to his words. "A good butler is an invaluable asset, especially when combined with such beauty and grace."

She blushed right on cue, betraying a genuine fluster. She could fake the charm, but not the heating of her skin.

"Tell me," he said softly, stepping in close enough that she had to look up to meet his eyes, close enough that if she breathed too deeply, her breasts would brush his chest. "Does Lucas demand every moment of your nights, or are you free on occasion?"

"Lord Quinn," she breathed, her fingers clenching against his. "I . . . yes. I mean, no. Lucas, that is, Lord Donlon is generous with my time."

"Excellent," Quinn crooned, holding on to her hand and steering them both toward the castle. "You'll have to come visit me in Dublin, then. So I can return your . . . hospitality." He layered so much sexual heat into that single word that her breath caught, and her heartbeat jumped.

She leaned into his side, pushing her breast against his arm, her head touching his shoulder. "I'd love that," she murmured. "How long will you be staying with us. I don't mean to pry," she added instantly. "But I'd love to show you around Kildare. I have a small flat that I keep in town, for when I need . . . privacy."

"Great." His cousin's dry voice interrupted what had been a perfect seduction, albeit not the one that the lovely Imogen had intended. "I'm Garrick, by the way."

"Oh," she said, sounding startled. She dropped Quinn's hand and turned to greet Garrick, as if surprised to find him standing there. "Imogen Cleary," she said, offering a businesslike handshake. "Lord Donlon's—"

"Butler. Yeah, I heard. And I'm Lord Quinn's lieutenant."

"Of course. You're both expected. Please, follow me."

She took off for the castle's open front door, while Quinn held back long enough to gain a semblance of privacy against vampire ears. "Nice cock blocking, cousin."

"Please," Garrick murmured, rolling his eyes. "You were playing her. She was trying to seduce you, and you beat her at her own game."

"I would have let her win eventually."

Garrick snorted. "I'm sure. Nice castle, yeah?"

"If you like that sort of thing." Quinn looked up with a smile when they reached the waiting Imogen. She tried and failed to hold his gaze, her blush even more visible in the lighted doorway. "You've done wonders with this place, Imogen," he said warmly.

"You're very kind, my lord. But I only supervised."

He brushed the back of his fingers over her cheek, feeling the heat of her flushed skin. "Lovely," he murmured lazily.

"I'll take it from here, Imogen," a brisk male voice called.

Quinn raised his eyes slowly, as Imogen stepped back. He'd sensed the other vampire's approach and knew this was Ronan Ivers, the vampire who handled Lucas's business interests in Ireland. Quinn was sure those business interests were wide and varied, but that would change once he solidified his hold on the country. He didn't mind Lucas's claim on this modest plot of ancestral lands, but everything else would belong to Quinn once he was Lord of Ireland.

"Ronan. It's good to meet you in person after all those phone calls."

"A pleasure, Lord Quinn. And at least the phone lines are good over the Atlantic these days. Not so long ago, we might as well have been shouting into tin cans."

Quinn's gaze followed the sway of Imogen's shapely hips as she hurried away, but he laughed gamely at Ronan's comment about overseas communication. At 89 years old—32 human, 57 vampire—Quinn was young enough that he'd enjoyed modern tech for most of his life. Not so for Ronan, whose age had weighed on Quinn's soul when he'd shaken the vampire's hand. He was at least 200 years old, and Quinn wondered idly how long he'd known Lucas. Hell, it was possible, maybe even likely, that Ronan was Lucas's child. There was no question that his allegiance was with Lucas, and not the recognized Lord of Ireland. But he didn't ask for specifics. Vampires could be quite sensitive about their personal histories. It was always better to get to know a vampire well before digging too deeply.

"Was your flight . . . I won't say good," Ronan said, smiling. "It's a long fucking way from America. But was it at least uneventful?"

Quinn laughed. He liked this vampire. "You're right on both counts. We wanted to arrive in darkness, which meant flying too many miles in daylight. Not my first choice, but unavoidable given the distance." He glanced over at Garrick, then stepped back to include him. "Ronan, this is my lieutenant, Garrick Owen. We appreciate Lord Donlon's generosity in lending us his jet for the journey," he continued while the two vampires shook hands. "Having a ride that's properly outfitted for vampire passengers makes all the difference."

Ronan grinned. "Lucas hates flying in daylight, as well."

"I suspect we all do." They walked a few steps in silence while Quinn studied the castle. "It's completely renovated inside?" he asked lifting his chin at the structure.

"Top to bottom. It took for-fucking-ever, too. Every time we'd finish an upgrade, a better way of doing it would be invented, and we'd have to start all over again. This latest round should hold for more than a few years, minus a technology re-do every so often. But those at least don't involve tearing out walls anymore." He gestured toward the stairs. "We've plenty of hours left in the night. We'll get you settled upstairs, then I've prepared a brief on the situation here. I'll answer what questions I can, and find answers for those I can't."

Quinn and Garrick were ushered upstairs and into a sumptuous three-room suite—two bedrooms and a sitting room—that was worthy of a true Irish lord of old, an *An Tiarna*. Apparently, Lucas Donlon had a direct bloodline to precisely that title. The castle and lands had been his grandfather's over 200 years ago. Quinn didn't know all the dirty details, but he knew Lucas hated his grandfather. He'd bought this place from a bankrupt cousin to make a point—that he was the direct heir, not some twice removed cousin—but he'd also done it in hopes that his grandfather would spend the rest of eternity spinning in his grave. Old hatreds died hard, and since this one had cost Lucas's mother her life, he was determined to keep it very much alive.

"You plan to live this way, Q?" Garrick strolled in from the bedroom he'd chosen at random.

Quinn snorted. "Hell, no. I'm not gentry enough for a castle in the countryside, never mind one as old and titled as this. I'll take the big city and good plumbing any day. Not to mention air conditioning and lights that don't flicker every time it storms."

"A good generator can fix that. You never did understand how things work."

"I know enough to hire people who do. Why the hell do you think I became a lawyer?"

Garrick laughed. They both knew the real reason for Quinn's career choice had been his compulsive need to control everything and everyone around him. It was good that he'd awakened as a powerful vampire. He'd never have tolerated being someone else's flunky. He'd probably have walked into the sun first.

"Ronan seems like a decent sort," Garrick said with deliberate casualness.

Quinn looked over and caught his cousin's meaningful glance at an ornate table lamp. Ah. So, they were being monitored. Not entirely unexpected. He gave a smug smile and flicked a finger in the air, creating a short burst of power that wiped out every electronic device in their wing of the castle. It was an effort not to laugh out loud as curses traveled up the open stairway. Quinn thought he'd been quite considerate. He could have wiped the entire estate. He might be young in vampire years, but he was powerful as hell.

There was enough moonlight through the windows that neither he nor Garrick felt the need to search out a flashlight. Or, for that matter, bring up the app on their cell phones. Because, of course, their own devices remained unaffected by Quinn's zap of power. He and Lucas might be nominal allies, but that didn't rule out a little friendly spying. Anticipating the possibility of electronic surveillance, they'd carefully shielded all their own sensitive gear before boarding Lucas's jet in New York. Quinn might not know plumbing or HVAC, but he damn well understood power. And he'd never doubted that Lucas would do everything he could to spy on them, not only during the trip, but after they arrived in Ireland. Electronic surveillance was the easy part. The more difficult task would be ferreting out Lucas's spies from among the Irish vampires Quinn would have to rely on as he built his power base from within the country. Lucas was Lord of the Plains back in the U.S., but he'd been born in Ireland and seemed determined to control her destiny. Or, at least, the destiny of the vampires living within her borders. Unfortunately for him, Quinn had no intention of sharing.

At the sound of a soft knock on their door, Garrick walked over and opened it to reveal Ronan Ivers.

"Sorry to disturb," he said, handing over a flashlight. "We've had a power surge of some sort. You'll want to check your phones and all. Bringing modern tech to these old places is always touch-and-go. I swear sometimes, I think it's ghosts who dislike the changes."

Quinn laughed on cue. "I was just telling Garrick that I preferred the city for those very reasons. Give me a new build with no ghosts any day."

"Those can be hard to find, even in Dublin. We're a country of ghosts."

"So I've heard."

"I'll be waiting in the library whenever you're ready. Go left at the bottom of the stairs. You can't miss it."

Quinn lifted his chin in acknowledgment. "A few minutes."

Ronan gave a respectful nod and walked away.

Garrick waited until they heard his footsteps on the stairs before closing the door. "You think he suspects you were behind the power surge?" he murmured.

"Oh, he does more than suspect. He knows. But if he brings it up, he has to admit they were eavesdropping, which is a violation of traditional Irish guesting laws, if nothing else. And what's he going to do about it, anyway? Challenge me?"

"Good point. Are you ready, my lord?"

Garrick's use of the honorific wasn't lost on Quinn. He drew a deep breath. Up until now, this entire venture had been theoretical. Sure, he'd met with Lucas and Raj, and then the incredibly powerful Raphael. And, yeah, he'd helped Raphael fend off a fucking helicopter gunship attack, after which they'd gone back to plotting the invasion of Ireland, because Raphael and the rest of the North American vampire lords had grown weary of fighting off repeated European attacks on their soil. Rather than waiting for the next attack, they were bringing the battle to Europe in a strategy that would force the European vampire lords to defend their own territories instead of attacking North America. But Quinn knew that the larger plan was to change the European vamps' strategy once and for all, by killing off the vampire lords who were pushing it.

Ireland was the vanguard of that strategy. Once Quinn seized the country by eliminating the current lord, Orren Sorley, Ireland would serve as a staging point for the North American invasion of Europe.

He met his cousin's steady gaze with a short nod. "Let's do this fucking thing."

They found the library easily enough. It was a large room that took up a significant chunk of the building's first floor, and, despite its name, had very little to do with books. Sure, there was one wall of shelves filled with a mix of modern and old titles, but a cursory glance told Quinn that none of them appeared to be rare or unusual. The absence made sense, given the truly exquisite collectibles adorning the room's three other walls. Weapons. Ancient bladed weapons of every kind and era. Quinn was a scholar of sorts, a man who loved books and learning. But he was also a powerful vampire who'd quickly understood the nature of his new reality. Vampires were of all ages, but many of them, including some of the most powerful, were old enough to have come from a time long before sub-machine guns or even six-shooter revolvers were the norm. Quinn had set out to study ancient weapons, in general, but he'd been particularly taken by the huge variety of blades in the world—a variety well-represented by the collection on Lucas's wall. Arranged by nationality or culture—some of which no longer existed—they were in excellent condition, lovingly restored, while not destroying the fine patina of age that blackened intricate designs, and retaining a lethal gleam on every sharp edge.

"Beautiful," he said, half to himself.

"Lord Lucas is a man of war," Ronan commented.

Quinn glanced over. "So I've heard."

"And you, my lord? What is your preference?"

Quinn let the "my lord" go yet again. Better for Ronan to start thinking of him as the Lord of Ireland, equal to Lucas. Hell, *above* Lucas in this country.

"My preference, Ronan, is for victory. I do whatever it takes, use whatever *weapon* it requires, to reach that end."

Ronan gave him a tight smile. "Then let's get started, shall we?"

TWO HOURS LATER, Quinn was thinking that flat out violence might be the way to go. Bloody, efficient violence exacted on Ronan Ivers and every one of Lucas's people, including possibly Lucas himself. It would be an even match, but Quinn thought he could take the Plains Lord, if it came down to it. Either way, it would be better than sitting in the *library* listening to *Lucas's* plan for Quinn's takeover of Ireland. Which, naturally, included a great deal of influence for Lucas himself.

Did the guy never give the fuck up?

Quinn pushed away from the table impatiently. He was getting a headache. A fucking *headache*. Vampires didn't get headaches. It was all those beautiful blades hanging on the library walls. The damn metal was ionizing the air. Or maybe it was just listening to Ronan detail, for what felt like the 5000th time, how he and Lucas's other loyalists were going to *facilitate* Quinn's takeover of Ireland.

"Facilitate, my ass," he muttered under his breath. "Yeah, fine," he said more loudly, intending to be heard. "Look, Ronan, I appreciate all the work you've obviously put into this, and we'll certainly be studying it in detail." He jerked his head in Garrick's direction, signaling it was time to make their exit. "But I intend to go in small first. God and Garrick know I'm a man who believes in research, but I need to get a feel for the country itself. And the only way to do that is by working from the ground up." He stood, and his cousin followed suit. "Garrick and I will leave for Dublin tomorrow night. Just the two of us," he added, reiterating what he'd been saying for the last hour, despite Ronan's repeated offers and assumptions that he'd be sending a team along with them.

Quinn didn't need Ronan Ivers's permission or approval for whatever he chose to do next. Lucas had been generous with his resources, and Quinn was grateful. But Lucas needed to step aside now. Ireland was Quinn's, and it was time for him to step up and seize what was his.

Chapter Two

Howth, Ireland, present day

EVE SAT ON THE bed to pull on her leather stiletto boots, the final component of her vampire hunting costume. That's how she thought of it—as a costume. She didn't dress this way on what she considered her off time, those rare nights when she met with old friends from university, or when she wasn't hunting anything other than a hot cup of tea and a warm bed. The boots had cost too much money, especially for someone without a real paying job, but they were necessary. She spent long hours walking and running in those boots when she was on a hunt, and they had to be comfortable, as well as sexy. She stood and surveyed herself in the full-length mirror on the closet door.

"Sexy as sin," she told her image. She stared a while longer, until the familiar sadness began creeping in, and she turned away. "Stop that shit," she hissed. That was another familiar thing of late, talking to herself. She lived alone in this closet of a flat, a single room with a small bathroom, and a microwave and sink that passed for a kitchen. Most nights, she was out on the streets, tracking vampires, killing the ones who deserved it. She didn't kill every vampire she came across. She killed the ones who abused humans, the ones involved in crimes, like the smugglers in Howth, who imported guns and drugs, the ones who killed without a thought.

It wasn't easy for her, and it wasn't without risk. She wasn't a large woman, and she sure as hell didn't possess any superpowers, like strength or speed. She had brains and determination going for her, but, if she was honest, it was her looks that got her close enough to do the deed. She hated it, but mostly she seduced her targets, getting them away from their friends, into a dark alley, or behind a building. She'd fill her thoughts with sexy images, wait until they were distracted by her breasts, and then go in for the kill.

It sounded easy when she thought of it that way, but it wasn't. In the beginning, she'd spent more time running away than killing. Even now, it wasn't easy to ram a wooden stake into a person's chest, even if that person was a vampire. And it wasn't squeamishness, either. It was physicality. The human chest had all sorts of safeguards meant to protect vital organs, like the heart, which wasn't just sitting there waiting to be stabbed. But Eve had studied, and she'd improved. She knew just where to slide the knife. Because, yeah, that was another lesson she'd learned. The fatal blow didn't have to come from a wooden stake. That was a myth. Anything that destroyed the heart would do, and a knife worked a lot better than a wooden stake. It sure as hell penetrated more easily, anyway. A gun could, potentially, wreak even more destruction in a shorter amount of time. And from a distance, too. Of course, guns made noise, even the silenced ones, and she preferred not to draw attention her way. But that wasn't her biggest problem with guns, since she typically hunted in or around noisy pubs and other public places where vampires hung out looking for a meal. No, her biggest problem was that guns and ammo cost a lot of money. Something she didn't have, obviously, or she wouldn't be living in this dump of a flat.

She'd bought a small Smith and Wesson revolver from a black market seller. It had cost more than she could afford, and it hadn't been worth it. Not for killing vampires. She suspected a different type of ammo would be more effective, but she could hardly walk into a shop and ask what it would take to blow a vampire's heart apart. Vampires had rights in Ireland. It would be the same as if she'd asked how best to kill her husband, or her mother. There might even be some law that required them to report that sort of thing. Besides, she doubted the local gun shop owner either knew or *cared* to know how to kill a vampire. Vampires were public and all—not only in Ireland, but around the world—but they were also discreet. Most people preferred to pretend they didn't exist, which was easy enough, since most would never, in their entire lives, encounter a real vampire.

So, she turned to the internet. But though Eve was a whiz when it came to online research, intel on killing vamps seemed to be missing. It was as if the vampire community had teams of people whose only job was to make sure there were no helpful hints about vampire hunting on the internet.

So, a knife it was. A big, very sharp knife that she carried in a specially made sheath down her right thigh. The black leather blended seamlessly with the black of her skirt, and most people, including most vampires, never saw the blade until it was drawn. She made sure of it. Like males everywhere, vampires liked to get up close and personal with women, and Eve used that against them. While the vampire was pawing her breasts, she was slicing his throat. It didn't kill him, but it weakened him enough that she could stab him in the heart with the same blade.

As for the paying job part of her life . . . Well, vampires had money, especially the criminal types she mostly had contact with, and they tended to carry a lot of it with them. Once they were dusted—which was a whole 'nother category of disgusting—they had no use for that money, and, sure as hell, no heirs to claim it, even if she'd bothered to go looking. She thought of herself as a modern-day bounty hunter, and the money as her reward. Combined with her side job of writing research papers for unmotivated university students, she had enough income to provide food and clothes, and to pay for this flat, which, ratty as it was, at least let her live on her own and not with her mother, Brigid. As if the thought conjured her up, Eve's mobile came to life with the theme from the movie Halloween. It was Brigid's ringtone and couldn't have been more appropriate if it had been written specifically for her. Eve doubted Brigid would ever understand the not so subtle message that ringtone sent. Mother and daughter had never been close. Eve's brother, Alan, had always been their mother's favorite child, mostly because he was male, but Eve thought it might also be that the young Brigid and her husband had still been madly in love when Alan was born. By the time of Eve's unexpected birth, unfortunately, economic reality and the hardships of years spent working on the docks had taken the bloom off the rose of their love. There was also the fact that Eve and her da had been close, something Brigid had bitterly resented. And when her da had died, Brigid had come right out and told the 8-year old Eve that it had been her fault, that if she'd never been born, her da wouldn't have had to work so hard and been so tired that he'd had the accident that killed him.

Alan had been 17 at the time. He'd been outraged on her behalf, defending her against the unfairness of their mother's accusation, even amidst his own grief. He'd stepped in, time and time again after that, becoming the only parent Eve had really known. But then he'd died, too. And this time Eve *knew* it was her fault.

She and her mother never talked about Alan's death, except to agree it was Eve's responsibility to get revenge for his murder. Eve had never told Brigid that it had been vampires who'd killed him, and yet Brigid had known. It made Eve suspect that her mother had known, long before Alan died, what he'd been up to. That he'd been flirting on the edges of some criminal activity or other that had included working with vampires, and Brigid had gone along with it. Had he done it because they needed money for Eve's university tuition, for books and all the other supplies? That's what Brigid had told her. That's why she said it was Eve's job to avenge his death.

Eve didn't know if Brigid was being honest with her, and doubted she ever would. Her mother had only two expectations of her daughter— one, to kill the monsters who'd murdered Alan, and, two, to solve all of Brigid's problems for the rest of her life. Eve tried, and sometimes failed, because that was Brigid's deepest, sickest, wish. And yet, Eve kept trying, even as she recognized that she was really trying to win her mother's love. Even as she knew that it would never happen. Pathetic.

She sighed and let her mother's call go to voicemail. She'd pay for it later, but she had a job to do tonight, and she didn't need her mother's demands distracting her. Killing vampires had become second nature, but she never forgot how dangerous it was, how easily *she* could be the one who ended up dead. Or worse.

Pulling her skirt up over her thigh, she slid her knife into its sheath. She smiled, remembering her first efforts, and how she'd carried her knife down her back. Her long hair had become so ragged from the blade that it had taken years to regrow. That sort of thing didn't happen now that she'd switched to a thigh sheath. In fact, she'd become quite the expert at killing vamps. The thought should have made her happy. When it didn't, she realized how tired she was, and how much she'd rather stay in with a hot cup of tea tonight. She chastised herself for that kind of self-pity, and reminded herself that she did it for Alan. That he deserved justice. And when a tiny voice asked what that meant, how many vampires would have to die before his ghost was put to rest, she shut down every thought except one.

The sun was down, the vampires were out, and it was time to hunt.

QUINN STRETCHED in the uncomfortable bed, reminding himself, as he had every night since they'd arrived in Howth, that he needed to buy a new one. He'd bought the house partially furnished. It was a convenience, though none of the furnishings were to his taste. As he'd told Ronan Ivers, he was a modern man through and through. He appreciated the beauty and value of old things, but he didn't want them in his home. Bad enough that *he* was becoming an old thing, he didn't need to be surrounded by them. Even if he'd never look any older than the 32 years he'd lived as a human.

"Garrick!" he called as he opened the bedroom door.

"Yeah, I know." His cousin's dry response came from down the hall. "Remind you to get a new bed."

Quinn growled and headed for the shower. The house had four bedrooms and three bathrooms. More than enough for two bachelor vampires, but, spoiled American that he was, he would have preferred an ensuite bath, so that he wouldn't have to step into the hallway in all his sleep-disheveled glory just to take a piss. So, call him a grouch. He'd never been a morning person. It was a personality trait which had apparently transferred itself from sunrise to sunset upon his rebirth as a vampire. And on top of *that*, he really missed the caffeine rush of morning coffee. Vampires didn't benefit from caffeine. Their bodies were no longer able to metabolize it, but like many vampires, Quinn still drank it for the taste. It was a holdover from his human life, especially the years he'd spent in law school, and then, even worse, the time he'd spent climbing the corporate ladder at the big law firm who'd recruited him right out of school. He'd claimed a generous salary, even as junior associate, but the hours had been killer. This new coffee routine stabilized him, but he really missed the thrill of that first caffeine jolt.

He leaned into the shower and turned on the water, letting it run hot. The shower, at least, had been updated, along with the rest of the plumbing in the old house. It was the reason he'd bought the place. Well, that and the fire sale price, because the previous owner had been promoted to a position on the continent. He'd been eager to sell, and Quinn had been offering cash. It was a match made in heaven. Or hell.

He stood under the pounding, hot spray and considered what to do with his night. Garrick would be driving over to Dublin proper to do some light scouting, under clear orders not to engage or endanger himself in any way. His cousin was good at blending in, listening while others talked, and stepping into the shadows, despite his substantial size. People, humans and vampires alike, tended to underestimate him, mistaking his preference for silence as an absence of thought. In reality, Garrick was quite brilliant, his mind sharp as an edged blade, his body a honed weapon. All of which made him an excellent scout.

And while his cousin would be prowling the streets of Dublin, Quinn would be doing the same here in Howth, which was one of Dublin's outer suburbs. To all appearances, it was a quiet fishing village on Dublin Bay. It claimed a fair number of tourist attractions—old castles, beautiful hillsides, lovely bayside location, and the like—but at night, the sidewalks rolled up and the vampires took over. Few tourists, or even residents, seemed to be aware of just how many vampires there were in Howth.

Quinn, on the other hand, had made it his business to know exactly that. Orren Sorley, the current Lord of Ireland, was into a lot of shady commerce, just as his predecessor had been. Sorley had done very little to change or improve the vampire economy of Ireland, taking on the various businesses he'd inherited with the title and letting them carry forth with barely a notice by anyone, other than the former lord's closest allies, all of whom were now dead and dusted.

Quinn had been surprised to discover just how much illegal trade came through Howth's small port on the average night. During the day, it was a thriving fishing village. At night, it became a smuggler's paradise. A *vampire* smuggler's paradise. The ships that slipped into the harbor after dark wouldn't be recognized by any of Howth's hardworking fishermen. The smugglers started arriving around midnight and were long gone by the time the early rising denizens of Howth were beginning their day.

Quinn had assumed, based on everything he'd been able to discover from the official police files, that Dublin Port, in the city, was the center of Ireland's drug trade. After all, Dublin was Sorley's home base. It made sense that he'd want to keep his cash cow close at hand. But that wasn't the reality. Not to say there weren't plenty of drugs coming in through Dublin Port, but there was also a lot of competition. Ten gangs controlled the vast majority of the drug trade coming into the main port, and only two of them were Vampire. Not long before Sorley killed him, Lord Tiege had decided he'd be better off establishing a new route, rather than trying to compete in Dublin Port. And once he'd added guns to the smuggling business in Howth, Ireland's vampires had a nice, profitable income stream, albeit an illegal one. But then, there had always been, and would always be, a lot of money to be made in smuggling. Today it was drugs and guns, tomorrow it would be something else. Quinn's only decision was how much he wanted to invest in smuggling as a major source of income for Irish vampires. The answer was not much, but he couldn't change it overnight, either. Too many vampires derived their main income from smuggling and were either unqualified or unwilling to try anything else. But over time, Quinn intended to bring his new territory into the light, so to speak. Not the light of the sun, but of legitimacy. He'd made a hell of a lot of money during his years as a corporate litigator, had made even more investing it over the years since he'd been made a vampire. And now, he was willing to put his money where his mouth was, willing to invest his own wealth into Ireland's future.

But first, he had to become Lord of Ireland. And to do that, he'd have to sink into the depraved depths of the current vampire economy. Which was why he now owned a home in Howth.

"You ready?" Garrick asked, sometime later, when Quinn descended to the first floor.

"No," Quinn replied sourly, then grinned. "Yes. Remember what I told you. No heroics. You're there to reconnoiter only."

"Yeah, yeah. You worry too much."

"That's because you're the only family I have," Quinn said in a moment of seriousness.

Garrick paused with his jacket halfway on and studied him. "It's going to be okay, Q. You can do this, you know."

Quinn grinned. "Don't I know it. All right, we meet back here two hours before sunrise to compare notes and decide what's next."

"Yeah, yeah, I got it. You're like an old woman."

"That's *Lord* old woman to you, asshole."

Garrick laughed and pulled open the front door as Quinn followed him outside. Garrick scowled at the nondescript mid-sized sedan sitting the driveway. "You could at least have gotten me a decent car."

"This one will blend, which is your job, remember?"

"Yeah, yeah. You sure you'll be okay on your own here?"

Quinn gave him a dry look. "I'll manage."

Garrick punched his arm hard enough to hurt. "See you in a bit." He pulled open the car door and slid into the driver's seat, and then cruised down the drive and onto the street without another glance.

Quinn rubbed his arm. He'd never have to worry about becoming too arrogant in his lordship. Not with Garrick around. His cousin would always see him as simply Quinn, the cousin he'd known all his life. Though he always treated Quinn with careful respect when anyone else was around, because appearances mattered.

He contemplated the simple sedan he'd rented for himself, no happier with it than Garrick had been with his. If appearances mattered, shouldn't he be driving something better? An elegant and lethal bullet of a car, maybe. "But not tonight, boyo," he muttered to himself. Tonight, he was haunting the docks of Howth like one of the many ghosts that supposedly plagued the place. And by morning, he intended to be in control of a good part of the district's illegal trade. It was his first step. Tonight, Howth. In one month . . . all of Ireland.

EVE STEPPED CAREFULLY as she cut through the old graveyard

and over to the steep stone stairs that dropped down to the next street level. She'd been taking that shortcut all her life. She and her mates had played in the graveyard when they'd been too young to understand the superstitions of their parents, and had then defied those same superstitions as teenagers, proving their courage by drinking and making out among the old gravestones. When she'd left Howth for university, she'd never intended to return. She'd had big plans for her future, and none of them included the small fishing village where she'd been born.

But then her brother had been murdered, and her plans had changed. She'd come back at first just to stay with her mother for a bit, to set her on her feet since Alan was gone. He'd left Howth for Dublin, too, but he'd been a far better son than Eve had been a daughter. He'd come home every week to visit, sometimes more than once. Of course, his visits with their mother had been far more pleasant than Eve's. He was the son, the favorite. The only child Brigid Connelly had ever loved.

With her brother gone forever, Eve had stepped up and done her best to take care of her mother. The old woman didn't give her so much as a smile of thanks, but Eve did it anyway. For Alan's sake.

At the same time, she'd started researching vampires, reading everything she could find about them online, in magazines and books. From lofty academic tomes to the paparazzi's gushing reports, she'd read it all, studying every word, scrutinizing every photo. After nearly a year of that, she'd felt ready to return to Dublin and start hunting. But fate had intervened, with her very first hunt.

Howth, 4 years earlier

EVE STROLLED ALONG the deserted dock, hugging herself against the cold and damp night air. She hadn't intended to walk this far or this long. She'd argued with her mother. Again. They couldn't be in the same house without going at each other. Hell, they couldn't be in the same city. Tonight, Eve had informed her mother of her intention to return to Dublin and the university. That last part was a lie. She had no intention of going back to school, but she wasn't going to tell her mother that, any more than she was going to share her plans to start hunting vampires.

As for tonight and her big announcement, she'd half expected her mother to be relieved that she was leaving. She should have known better. It didn't matter that Brigid Connelly hadn't a single kind word for her own daughter, that no matter what Eve did, it was never good enough. Brigid demanded attention, and since Eve was the only child she had left, Brigid's needs became Eve's obligation. An obligation she couldn't fulfill if she lived in Dublin, because they both knew that once Eve left Howth, she'd never come back. Brigid would be on her own, and that was unacceptable. So, Eve's mother had laid into her tonight, telling her what a thankless daughter she was, comparing her to Alan who'd reached sainted status in their mother's memory. She'd even gone so far as to predict her own early demise as a direct result of Eve's neglect. Eve knew her mother far too well to buy into the guilt trip, but it troubled her all the same. She'd long ago stopped expecting affection, but shouldn't a mother want her child to succeed? Even if only for bragging rights among her friends? Shouldn't she be happy that Eve was going back to school, making something of herself?

She felt a brief flash of guilt, reminding herself that that part of her story wasn't true. She *was* going back to Dublin, and she *was* going to make something of herself. But it wouldn't be as a barrister or an accountant. She was going to avenge her brother's death by destroying as many vampires as she could . . . before they killed her. She had no illusions about living a long life, but she'd take a lot of them with her before she died.

She stepped off Howth's concrete pier and onto the wooden planks of the dock, wishing she'd worn something other than her new spike-heeled boots, but she needed to become accustomed to walking in them. She'd also taken to wearing the revealing clothes she'd purchased as part of her costume, wanting to get a feel for the way they moved, wanting to be sure she *could* move if she had to. These were vampires she was hunting—faster, stronger, and probably a whole lot wilier than she was. The outfit showed a lot more skin than was normal for her. It was sexy and form-fitting, and it made her look like vampire bait, which was exactly the point. Everything she'd read said that vampires liked to seduce their victims, that when a vampire fed, it was the best sexual high in the world. Eve didn't know about that, but she did know that most vampires were male, which meant most of them would be attracted to women.

Eve was confident in her ability to appeal to men. She knew she was pretty. Some men had even called her beautiful. Although they'd wanted to have sex with her, so she took that with a grain of salt. But there was no doubt that men paid attention when she walked by or entered a room. She had a body they liked, with full breasts, a slender waist, and curvy hips. Add in her new vampire killer outfit, with its cleavage baring neckline and short skirt, and she not only looked hot, she looked available.

Of course, her intent was to kill a vampire, not seduce him, so she'd designed a concealed weapon for herself. It was a big knife in a sheath down the center of her back, hidden beneath the fall of her long, thick hair. Her plan was to wait until the vamp was preoccupied with her nearly naked breasts and neck, then pull the blade and stab him somewhere vital. She wasn't an expert, and didn't expect that first strike to kill him. But while he was howling in shock, she'd then pull out her second weapon—a slender, but sharp and strong, stake—and stab him in the heart. She'd practiced the maneuver on a dressmaker's dummy that she'd bought at a thrift shop in Dublin, and felt good about her chances.

But tonight wasn't supposed to be about killing vampires. She was going to hunt in Dublin, where her brother's killers lived their shady lives. She'd donned the outfit without thinking, and by the time she'd realized what she'd done, she'd decided to "fuck it." Her plan had been to offer a dutiful good-bye to her mam, climb into her car, drive to Dublin, and never come back. Her mother's excessive nastiness had delayed that plan, but it wasn't completely dead yet.

"Not dead yet, Evie girl," she muttered to herself. "But it will be if you don't stop moping around this stupid Howth dock and get your ass on the way to Dublin."

Deciding to head for the city that same night, she stuck with her route along the wooden dock, since it was the quickest way back to her car, which was parked at her mother's house. She'd no sooner made that decision, however, than her heel caught between the planks yet again. Cursing as she freed the trapped stiletto, she changed her mind one more time and, walking on her toes, headed back for the sidewalk. It would take longer this way, but at least her expensive new boots would survive the trip. She was nearly there when a burly male with a scruffy beard emerged from the parking lot of a local pub and stepped directly into her path, bumping her so hard she nearly fell.

Eve stared in shocked recognition. Vampire. The thug who'd slammed into her and whose meaty hand was now holding her arm was a vampire, his fangs flashing briefly in the moonlight, before he concealed them behind a closed-lip smile. It was on her tongue to give him a curse and an elbow, and be on her way, just as she'd done with a hundred different guys before. But this was it. Her first real vampire. If she failed now . . .

Her heart was pounding, her mouth too dry to speak. She glanced around. "*Not here, girl,*" she told herself. A nearly full moon was lighting the dock, gleaming off the still waters of the harbor. And the pub behind the vampire was full of people and maybe more vamps. Someone could walk out at any minute and see what she was up to.

She smiled at her captor, making no attempt to free her arm. "Thank you,' she said breathily. "These heels are sweet, but, I swear, they're going to kill me." She smiled again, clamping down hard on the shudder that tried to rock her body.

"Where you hurrying off to, lass?" he asked, his accent strong, his voice as deep as his chest. "Come inside, have a pint."

"Oh," she breathed, leaning in so that her breasts brushed his chest. "I'd love to, but I can't stay. I'm driving back to Dublin tonight. I've a job to get to."

"Well, then, let me at least walk with you a bit. So you don't fall again," he added with a sly look.

"Well . . ." Eve pretended her indecision. Should she agree to walk into the dark with this perfect, and very big, stranger? Or decline and stumble away on her own? No decision, really. "I hate to take you from your friends—"

"They'll wait," the vampire said brusquely, then shifted his grip from her arm to her body, dropping his hand to circle her back and grip her side just below the curve of her breast. Using his hold to get her moving, he hustled her away from the crowded pub and up the hill to the deserted street.

Eve almost panicked. His forearm around her back was pressed right against her knife. What if he discovered the thick leather sheath? What if he pulled her knife and used it against her? She'd have nothing but a sharp stick with which to defend herself!

His thick fingers moved, stroking the underside of her breast through her shirt. "You're lucky I found you," he murmured. "You're far too pretty to be walking alone. Not with vampires lurking about."

Eve saw her chance. Stopping dead in her tracks, she turned to face him. "Vampires?" she asked, pretending shock. "There are vampires in Howth? Real ones?"

He laughed. "Is there some other kind?" He pulled her close and shoved her into the narrow, empty space between two buildings. The stores were all closed, the buildings dark. There was no one around to witness what he was about to do. But then, no one would be there to witness what *she* did either. He slammed her back against a rough wall, using his weight to keep her there. "I deserve a reward for being such a gentleman," he muttered and bent his head to the swell of her half-naked breasts. He licked the delicate skin along the line of her leather top, then probed even farther, digging his tongue beneath the leather to curl around her nipple.

Eve grimaced in disgust. When she'd set herself up as bait, she hadn't considered that it would mean getting up close and personal with the vampires before she killed them. And contrary to belief, not *all* vampires were swoon-worthy romantic hero types. She supposed even the pig currently rooting against her breasts would be considered good-looking, but there was the matter of personal hygiene. She fought the urge to gag and concentrated instead on figuring out a way to reach her knife. Moaning theatrically, she shoved against him, hoping he'd think she simply wanted to get closer to his slobbering mouth. As if. He bought it, though. Giving a grunt of satisfaction, he yanked her against his chest, putting a few precious inches between her back and the stone wall.

She reached over her shoulder and slid her hand beneath her hair. Her fingers closed around the hilt of the blade, and—She gasped as he suddenly yanked her top down, tearing the leather as if it was paper and baring her breast completely to the night air. Before she could voice a protest, he growled in satisfaction and closed his mouth over her nipple. She jerked at the feel of his teeth against the sensitive bud, followed hard (no pun intended) by the press of his erection against her belly. It was everything she could do to stop herself from kneeing him in the bollocks. She wasn't a good enough actress for *this*.

Closing her eyes, she sucked in a long breath and reminded herself why she was there, why her back was scraped against the rough stone, why her naked breast was hanging out for the world to see, and, dear God, why this animal had his mouth on her tit and his cock against her body.

She reached over her shoulder, closed her fingers over the hilt, and slid the knife from its sheath. She'd practiced that maneuver a million times. The blade came out smoothly and felt good in her hand. She swallowed hard. She'd never killed. Not even a chicken, much less a man.

But this isn't a man, she reminded herself. Looking down she eyed the angles. She'd have one chance to get this right. Gripping the blade in her right hand, she slid her fingers up on the leather-wrapped hilt until they were nearly touching the blade . . . and then she struck.

Something must have warned the creature in the instant of her attack, because his head came up, fangs bared, his teeth leaving a bloody furrow in her breast. Eve bit back her scream and followed through, slicing the sharp edge of the blade through the taut skin of his neck, his own movement adding pressure to the strike as he raised his head to stop her. Eve had done her homework. She needed to hit an artery, needed to see the blood pump, not gush. An instant later, she screamed as blood burst from the wound, covering her everywhere. The vampire shoved her away, a big meaty hand going to the side of his neck, as he rose to his full height, eyes glaring red fire, fangs dripping with his own blood as he glared down at her.

Eve dropped the knife, ignoring the sharp bite of pain as it skimmed over her thigh. Her hand went to a pocket sewn into the seam of her skirt, fingers closing around the sharpened stake waiting there. Her skin was too slick, too covered with blood. The vampire roared and smashed her against the wall as she wiped her hand frantically on her skirt, her fingers finally finding enough traction to grab the stake, to lift it. Twisting her hair in one hand, he slammed her head hard against the brick and yanked it to one side. His mouth came down, his fangs pierced her neck, and Eve struck with all her strength.

She stood frozen, every muscle locked, her entire body trembling in shock as the vampire disintegrated right in front of her. When she finally moved, it was to bend over and throw up, retching until there was nothing but bile burning her throat as her stomach wrenched in fear and disgust over and over. The hand she raised to wipe her mouth was shaking so hard that she crushed her lip against a tooth, opening up a fresh flow of blood.

She dropped her hand to one side, shuddering when she saw the dusting of gray ash that seemed to cover every inch of her. Stifling a horrified shriek, she began slapping frantically at her breasts and shoulders, her legs . . . her hair. She thought she'd throw up all over again, but though her stomach revolted, there was nothing left.

Fighting back the urge to curl up in a ball and sob, she forced herself to think. To move. This vampire hadn't been alone. She was sure of that. The pub had been crowded, and he'd talked about his friends . . . hadn't he? She couldn't remember. She couldn't *think*. She just knew she had to get away from there. Had to get away from this pile of dust and mud before some other vampire came along and realized what had happened. Her eyes went wide. Vampires had telepathy. What if his friends sensed he'd been killed and came after her?

That thought jolted her into action. She hurried down the quiet street, covering her naked breast with one hand, laughing at herself for the gesture. She was covered in blood. If anyone saw her, a naked tit would be the least of her worries.

Her car was parked behind her mother's house. She'd fully intended to go back inside after a walk to cool off. But that was out of the question now. Her mother would have to wait. There was nothing left to say anyway.

The lights were off in the house when she finally stumbled to her car, every muscle quivering in fatigue and aftershock. Her purse was already inside, her key fob tucked down into her boot. She retrieved it with shaking fingers and clicked it once to unlock her small sedan. It wasn't anything fancy. It was old, with none of the bells and whistles of the better models. But it had been Alan's once, the only thing of his that had gone to her. Her mother had demanded Eve turn it over, even though she had no need for a car, not even a driving license. But Eve had refused. The car was all she'd had left of the brother she loved, and she was going to need it in her quest for revenge.

A light flicked on in the house when she started the engine. Her mother. Awakened no doubt by the combination of the alarm's beep when she'd unlocked the car and the engine noise. Eve saw a curtain stir, but she ignored it and pulled away into the alley.

She was halfway to Dublin before she stopped trembling enough to consider her night's work. She'd learned a lot from this first—and what easily could have been her last—encounter with a vampire. To begin with, the sheath down her back had been a stupid idea. It looked good and felt dangerous and sexy, but it wasn't functional. All it had taken was for the vampire to put his arm around her—something that was bound to happen again—and her main weapon had been useless. Not to mention when he'd pressed her against the wall. *That* would almost certainly occur again, whether on a dark street or in a club. How many times had she seen a man press a woman against a wall in a darkened club, kissing and groping, while the music pounded? Hell, she'd been the woman against the wall more than once.

And the damn knife was too big. She hadn't considered that she and the vampire were likely to be body to body. After all, seduction was her first weapon, right? So, there was bound to be more—she swallowed hard—sexual contact. Not actual *sex*. But more touching and, *ew*, licking, like what had happened earlier. She ran careful fingers over the crusty fang marks on her breast, touched her neck which was sore and bruised around the twin puncture marks where he'd barely pierced the skin of her neck. Wounds like that were likely to happen again. Maybe worse.

Maybe the next vampire would manage to pierce her vein, to suck her blood. She shuddered, but the reality was unavoidable.

"Deal with it, Eve," she said, talking out loud in the empty car. She yawned without warning. Another aftershock effect. Adrenaline crash. Just a few kilometers more, and she'd be home. She shook her head, trying to wake up . . . and frowned. Something was weird. She reached back, wondering if she'd cut herself when she'd pulled the blade out, or maybe put it back in. Half her back felt cold, and her head was too light . . .

"Oh fuck," she gasped, her car nearly swerving into the next lane as she felt the back of her head. She brought her hand back, gripping the wheel with both hands as she groaned out loud. A bunch of her hair was gone. She could feel some of the sheared off bits now, covering her shoulders. Could this night get any worse? Her first hunt and what a fucking disaster! The only good thing was she'd managed to kill a vampire.

She frowned. Okay, so that *was* good. Very good. She nodded to herself. She could get a new knife, could ditch the stupid sheath and come up with something better. And her hair would grow back.

But that vampire—that fucking, evil monster—would never kill again.

She smiled for the first time that night. Finally, there would be justice for her brother. No, not justice. Revenge.

Howth, Ireland, present day

QUINN SAT INSIDE the small dockside café, thinking about the cold. He'd forgotten about the winters around Dublin. Sure, it got cold—fucking cold—in New England, where he'd lived and worked for the last several decades. But no one sat around cafés, sipping tea in the middle of the night and staring out at empty marinas, either. If there was any sitting around the marina, it was in a dark bar with good whiskey and a big wide-screen TV. He sighed and signaled for another pot of tea. His reasons for being in Howth had nothing to do with the weather, and everything to do with an uptick in late night boat traffic. That and gossip in the blood houses of Dublin that Lord Sorley was using Howth like a private yacht club—running shipments of guns, and even some drugs, into the seaside suburb on regular fishing boats. In fact, from what Quinn could tell from the several nights he'd sat in this very accommodating café, at least some of the boats bringing in contraband at night were being used for fishing during the day. He hadn't been able to ascertain if the owners knew about the illicit use of their boats, but he wouldn't be surprised. Smuggling paid well, and everyone could use a few extra Euros these days.

He turned to greet the lovely waitress who was delivering his fresh pot of tea, admiring the lush curves beneath her practical uniform, and giving her a smile that brought a lovely pink flush to her creamy Irish skin. "Thank you, love," he crooned. She rewarded him with a smile that belied the tiredness in her eyes. "Are you off soon?" he asked, brushing his fingers over hers on the tea pot.

Her blush heated further, and she ducked her head shyly. "Aye. Only another fifteen or so." She caught her breath. "Unless you need me to stay, sir."

"No, you go on home. I'll probably be here again tomorrow. We can talk then. And call me Quinn."

She smiled sweetly. "Thank you, Quinn. And I'm Cassidy."

Fifteen minutes later, the curvy Cassidy waved as she hurried out into the night, leaving Quinn behind in the unlocked café, as if he owned the place. And maybe he did. He'd made a variety of investments in Howth, and hadn't had a chance yet to match every one of his records with a physical building. He was winking at Cassidy as she passed the big window, when the sudden flash of a white hull on the dark water drew his attention.

With a flick of power, he darkened every light in the building, so that by the time the boat slid close enough to be picked up by the few dock lights on their skinny poles, there was nothing to draw their attention to the empty café.

Quinn waited, and right on schedule, two vampires strolled out onto the wooden dock. They were both in thick with Orrin Sorley. Not a part of his innermost circle, but definitely close to it and well trusted. Quinn's goal in Howth was to bring himself to Sorley's attention. Unfortunately for those vampires out there, the vampire way of moving up was to kill everyone who stood in your way. Lucky for them, he wasn't ready to make his move yet. They'd live another night, maybe two. But no more than that. Quinn could hear the clock ticking in his head. He had a timetable, and those two would die. But not tonight.

Outside, the vampires exchanged a few friendly words with each other, while they stood side by side, waiting and watching, along with the unseen Quinn, as the boat slipped silently past several of the marina's floating docks. Finally, the engine reversed as the smuggler slowed and turned, making it obvious which dock slip he was aiming for.

The two vampires strode down to meet it, walking right past the window where Quinn sat in the dark. He wasn't worried about being seen. For all their success at smuggling, the local vampires were very lax about security. He assumed this was because they'd bought off the local authorities, and no one else was stupid enough to challenge them. It wasn't a matter of cowardice, it was one of survival. If a local citizen challenged the vamps' right to do business in Howth, that person—man or woman—would only end up dead. Quinn never blamed ordinary people for choosing to survive. It was the authorities he criticized—the men and women who sucked on the taxpayer's teat, and who'd sworn to obey the law and serve the community, only to take bribes and look the other way, no matter how heinous the crime. Those fuckers deserved to rot in hell.

He grimaced, disliking his own thoughts. Too many years in the American legal system had jaded him when it came to the blind wisdom of Lady Justice.

He turned his attention back to the current criminal endeavor. He had an excellent view, since the boat had come into dock just slightly left of the café. Shifting his chair back from the window a bit, he put himself into a deeper shadow, lest one of the smugglers happen to look the wrong way. The two male vamps exchanged a few words with the human running the boat. A bulging envelope of cash traded hands, the captain called down below decks, and then another human emerged to begin passing sealed cases up to the two local vamps. The unloading went quickly. There were only five of the medium-sized cases, and once they were all sitting on the floating dock, the boat quickly maneuvered out of the slip and back into the harbor. Quinn wasn't at the right angle to see where it went next, whether to some other slip within the harbor, or out beyond the breakwater, but that wasn't his concern. The cases had been too small to carry enough guns to make the trip worthwhile, which meant the shipment was probably drugs. Most likely meth-amphetamine, since that was where the greatest profits lay. Quinn wanted to know where the smuggled goods went next. Did Sorley's people drive the delivery directly to Dublin, to be cut and distributed? Or was there a local distributor who dealt with Dublin's many suburbs? For that matter, was it raw product? Or already cut and packed for sale?

And when the fuck had he become an expert on the illegal drug trade? The answer to that was simple. He wasn't. Which was why he was in Howth. How to be a drug lord in three simple steps. Frankly, he had no interest in becoming a drug kingpin, but change took time. If his plan for the Irish vampire community worked out, he hoped to eliminate drug smuggling as a vamp enterprise within a decade—an instant in time for a vampire. But for now, it was an important part of the vampire economy, so he needed to know how it worked. Because the first step on his road to becoming Lord of Ireland was to insinuate himself into Sorley's inner circle by taking over what was an important part of the vampire lord's business—the Howth smuggling operation.

The sound of raised voices drew his attention outside the window, where there seemed to be trouble in paradise. The two vampires, who'd been so chatty before, now appeared to be having a difference of opinion about how best to move the newly arrived goods off the dock. The bigger of the two vamps lifted a single case, as if weighing it. And from the ease of his lift, Quinn would guess it didn't weigh much. Not for a vampire, anyway. But the vamp's buddy seemed to disagree. He clearly wanted to fetch a dolly or some other wheeled conveyance and move all five cases at once.

Quinn sided with the big guy. They were vampires, for fuck's sake. They could carry all of that in a single trip. They didn't need a fucking dolly. Maybe the question had to do with leaving one vamp alone with the drugs, while the other brought the cart. Maybe they didn't trust each other. Or were they concerned about a competitor's attack? After all, the reason they were doing this in Howth was to circumvent the gangs who controlled the drug trade in Dublin.

An unhappy thought suddenly occurred to him. Did they know, or suspect, that he was hanging around? Was that why they were reluctant to split up? He frowned. He was confident no one knew he was in the country, other than the people who'd helped him get there. But it never paid to be overconfident. He didn't know everyone who'd helped him, or who'd helped *them*. There could easily be an informant at work.

The two vamps were still arguing, and Quinn was contemplating going out there and killing them both, just to get the night over with, when they abruptly stopped arguing and turned to grin at something out of his line of sight. Quinn changed position within the dark café just in time to catch the completely unexpected arrival of a sexy redheaded female. Human, no doubt about it. And what the hell was she doing out there alone at this time of night, and dressed the way she was?

From the top of her red head to the tips of her shiny leather boots, and everything in between, she practically screamed vampire bait. The theme of the night was black leather, with a faux fur collar on her black leather jacket adding a flirtatious note to the outfit. And that's exactly what she was doing, flirting with the two hulking vampires. The woman clearly had seduction in mind, and Quinn couldn't help wondering what the fuck she was thinking. But, his two vampire thugs seemed more than willing to be seduced.

Placing a coy hand on one thuggish chest, the woman said something short and to the point, then smiled and walked away. Two hard gazes swiveled to watch the sway of her hips until she disappeared into a narrow alleyway where it headed up the hill to intersect with Howth's main street—where all the storefronts were closed and shuttered for the night. There would be no one around. No witnesses.

The two vampires clearly came to the same conclusion. Drugs forgotten, they exchanged quick grins and, all but flashing fang in their eagerness, took off after her. Oddly enough, the ease with which the two vamps had left the smuggled goods sitting on the dock reassured Quinn that Sorley's people didn't know he was in Howth and watching their every move. But his biggest concern right now was the woman being pursued by the two very large vampires. If she was lucky, they'd feed while fucking her senseless, and maybe leave some money on the dresser. If she was unlucky, they'd still fuck her, but her body would be found bloodless and floating in the harbor.

Quinn told himself it was none of his business. The woman had invited the pursuit, and even if she hadn't known the two males were vampires, they were still obviously bad news. But a moment later, he was pushing his chair back. His mother hadn't raised him to leave even clueless women to their fates. Abandoning his fresh pot of tea, and cursing himself for a fool with every step, he took off after them.

He slowed when he neared the alley. He had enough functioning brain cells for that. What he was calling an "alley" was simply a very narrow passage that climbed the steep hill between one street and the next. Stuck between two very old buildings, it was too narrow for any kind of vehicle, barely wide enough for walking, and too dark for most humans to feel safe at night. There was no light of any kind in there, no lit windows, no public lamps, just old brick walls, lots of dirt, and an overflowing garbage bin or two thrown in for good measure. He frowned. Why the hell would a woman alone walk this way? And where the hell was she?

A familiar scent abruptly wafted through the air. Blood. And something else that had his fangs trying to slide over his lower lip, uncaring of who saw. Forcing his fangs under control and out of sight, he drew a deeper breath and scowled, just as the young woman tripped into sight from the deepest, darkest part of the alley, the spiked heels of her leather boots—so impractical on the uneven streets and wooden docks—making it difficult for her to gain a firm foothold as she hurried back down the steep incline. Her gaze was focused on the rough surface beneath her feet and the shadows all around, so she didn't notice him at first. But then her survival instincts finally kicked in, and she looked up sharply, realizing that she wasn't alone. She raised a hand, and his vampire sight caught the gleam of a blade covered in blood. And not just any blood, but vampire blood, which would dust tomorrow morning in the sunlight, but for now remained very much red and wet. It wasn't the blood that drew his attention, however. It was that other scent, the one that had brought every one of his defensive instincts to high alert.

The woman was covered in dust. Dust that had been two vampires before they'd followed her into that alley.

Quinn stared. What the fuck?

Chapter Three

"OH! YOU STARTLED ME." Eve took a step back, covering her gasp with a trembling hand, as if the man's sudden appearance had truly startled her. As if. She'd just dispatched two burly vampire thugs. Her first double kill. A lone human male wasn't even a blip in her pulse rate. Still, she eyed him carefully, searching for any sign that he was other than he appeared. But there was no trace of fang, and none of the predatory arrogance that she associated with vampires. Plus, she'd never seen him before, and she knew every vampire in Howth, at least by sight. Especially the ones who hung around the docks late at night in order to greet certain sneaky boat captains.

"Sorry," the man said, stepping back politely, to give her more room. "I thought I heard a ruckus and wanted to help."

"A ruckus, was it?" Eve wanted to laugh at the word choice, but he seemed so very sincere that she didn't want to hurt his tender, knight-to-the-rescue feelings. "You're American," she said, looking up, way up, to meet a pair of remarkably blue eyes. Crystal blue, and gleaming like fine glass in the dim light from the dock. He smiled—a perfectly white, very American smile—and she felt her heart flutter. It was embarrassing, but there was no other word for what her heart was doing. He was more than handsome. He had . . . She didn't have a word for it. Some people would call it "charisma" or "sex appeal." She only knew it made her want to get closer to him. A lot closer. And maybe naked.

"Guilty as charged," he admitted. "But born in Ireland, I'll have you know."

His voice was as striking as his looks, a smooth growl that made her nipples hard. Eve stared wordlessly, trying to deal with her reaction. It had been months since she'd had anything to do with a man, other than the vampires she'd killed. And they weren't really men. She hadn't had sex with anyone in . . . fuck, it had been years not months. So, why her reaction to this guy? Sure, he was good-looking. More than that, if she was honest. His hair was styled in a longish razor cut, trimmed on the sides, longer on top, and it was the color of dark honey. The kind of blond that had probably been paler when he was young. And those remarkable eyes. His looks alone would have drawn attention, but it didn't hurt that he was such a big man. Not just tall, but broad-shouldered and firmly muscled. A man who looked like he could handle himself in a fight. A man who'd stepped up in the middle of the night to defend a woman he didn't know. She hadn't needed his help, but he didn't know that.

"You've come back to our fair country to claim your heritage, then?" She heard the flirty lilt in her voice and wondered where the hell *that* had come from.

"I don't have a heritage to speak of. No lords in my family history," he said, still smiling. He glanced over her shoulder into the shadows of the narrow passageway, but she wasn't worried. There was nothing left of the two vamps, but dust. "You're all right, then?" he asked, looking concerned. "I thought I saw two very dangerous-looking guys following you."

"Oh, them. Just a couple of lads I know. Friends of my brother, actually. They've just come in from a long run at sea and are blowing off steam. They like to talk but they're harmless."

He studied her a moment, and she wondered what he saw. Eve had a mirror. Her looks were still there, still enough to attract men, but she'd changed. The last five years had hardened her. Gone were the soft cheeks and innocent gaze of the university student she'd been before her brother died. Grief lived in her eyes now. And death. She didn't fool herself into thinking the killing she'd done was anything but murder. Sure, they were vampires, monsters. But the law recognized them as people. If she were ever caught, she'd be imprisoned for life. Assuming the vampires permitted it to get that far. More likely, the local vampire lord would lock her up in a dark room and torture her for a very long time. The possibility should have worried her, but that would mean feeling something. And she hadn't done that since her brother's funeral.

Which was why her reaction to the handsome American was so unsettling.

"Well, nice meeting you—"

"But we didn't," he interrupted quickly. "Meet, that is. I'm Quinn Kavanagh." He held out a hand.

Eve looked at his proffered hand. She didn't meet many Americans in her regular life. Her side job of doing research for grad students who had the money, or the parents, to pay others to do their work for them, sometimes included non-Irish clients, including Americans. But since her work was almost exclusively online, she rarely met any of *them* in person, either.

So, she didn't know quite what to think of Quinn Kavanagh. A fine Irish name, if it was real. And why wouldn't it be? Just because she was a criminal, that didn't mean everyone else was. She slipped her hand into his, feeling the rough skin of his palm and fingers as they closed around her much smaller, but equally calloused, digits. She practiced a lot with her knife, and it showed. She waited for the crushing handshake. So many men tended to do that, as if wanting, or needing, to establish dominance from the very beginning. As if she wasn't already aware of their greater size and strength. But Kavanagh's shake was carefully calibrated to be firm, but not crushing. It was a warm, enveloping exchange of pressure that somehow managed to be reassuring instead of overwhelming. Her heart did that damn fluttering again.

"Eve," she said simply, not offering her last name. Her heart might be smitten with this handsome American, but he was still a stranger, probably just come from the pub, and she was still engaged in some questionable behavior in her off hours.

"Can I walk you home, Eve? I wouldn't want you to run into any more of those overfriendly lads."

"Not necessary," she said instantly. "It's not far, and I can—"

"I'm not trying to insult you. I'm sure you can handle yourself just fine. But my parents raised me the old-fashioned way, and that means a gentleman never leaves a lady to walk alone on a dark street."

That sparked a real smile from Eve. "What makes you think I'm a lady?"

His remarkable eyes gleamed in a newfound shaft of moonlight. "Why wouldn't I?"

Eve blinked. There was private knowledge in those eyes. Did he know about her vampire hunts? Was he Garda, the Republic's national police force, after all? She frowned. Impossible. He was definitely American, with that accent, the perfect teeth and hair. Even his clothes were finely made, for all they were casual. Why not let him walk her home? There had to be more to life than stab, stab, stab, right? She grinned at her own tasteless joke.

He caught the grin and gestured toward the street behind him. "Which way, my lady?"

QUINN STUDIED THE woman as they walked slowly down the

deserted streets. Howth rolled up the sidewalks early on weeknights. He could still hear faint sounds from the local pub, but these were the suburbs. Families lived here, wanting away from the hubbub of the city, while still being close enough to commute to work. Not exactly Quinn's scene, but he could be anyone he needed to be. Even before he'd been turned, he'd been good at that, at showing people what they wanted to see. Lovers and girlfriends in the past had criticized him, saying he was emotionally unavailable, whatever the fuck that meant. And now? Well, hell, he was a vampire lord. He could wrap himself in power and make people see whatever he wanted them to. He wasn't putting that much effort into it tonight, however. He was simply making sure that the lovely Miss Eve of the unknown last name didn't realize she was walking home with a vampire.

She'd done him an unwitting favor by killing the two thugs, but that didn't make her innocent. Why had she done it, and how? She was an unknown. A random factor he hadn't counted on, and Quinn didn't like random. He could make her talk, of course. He could seduce her, fuck her. Hell, he'd do whatever it took to become the next Lord of Ireland.

Not that seducing Eve would be a burden. She was a beautiful woman, with moody dark eyes and long, red hair that caressed the pale curve of full breasts beneath her black leather top. Her short, tight skirt showed off legs that were slender and well-toned, and even those spike-heeled boots could only make her tall enough that her head hit his chest. Sexy as hell. Certainly the sexiest woman he'd met since arriving here. But it was more than her looks. An indefinable ping against his vampire senses was telling him something that told him that Eve was more than she appeared.

Oh, yeah, we can't forget that part, he reminded himself with an inward grin. This imminently fuckable woman had just killed two vampires and had nothing but a slightly elevated heart rate to show for it. He'd intended to kill those two himself as he moved up the chain of Sorley's command. But he couldn't ignore the fact that she'd killed them, instead. What was her role in all of this? Whom did she work for? Because Buffy didn't exist in real life. There was no organization of watchers who kept track of vampires and sent out killer cheerleaders. If Eve was hunting vampires on behalf of some shadowy organization, he needed to find out what it was and shut them down. And if she was doing it on her own, then the shutting down might very well include Eve herself.

Though, he'd really like to fuck her first.

"You live alone then?" he asked, as they turned to climb another hill. Howth was a city of hillside streets, many of them old and narrow.

"Who says I live alone?"

Quinn rolled his eyes inwardly. She was a combative little thing. "No one. That's why I asked the question," he said smoothly.

She gave a breathy laugh. "My mam lives down the way, but you're right, I live alone. It's a small place, but at least it's quiet."

Quinn smiled to himself. He could understand that. He'd loved his folks, but he hadn't lived with them since his first year of college.

"Is it safe for you to live alone here? I'm still learning this area."

"Safe enough. You're thinking about those two earlier. I told you. They're harmless."

Quinn was a damn powerful vampire. He could spot a lie as easily as breathing, and even if he hadn't already known the particulars, he'd have known Eve was lying through her pretty little teeth. He could push her to tell him what he wanted to know. Telepathy came with being a vampire. The stronger the vampire, the stronger the telepathy, and the greater the ability to use it. But he didn't want to use it on Eve. There was no urgency yet. It wasn't as if she was going to take on the entire vampire establishment of Dublin all on her own. Hell, if she tried to force her way into Sorley's Dublin headquarters, she'd be dead before she cleared the first gate, no matter how sharp her knife was. Oh, yeah, he hadn't forgotten the shiny blade she'd slipped into the sheath on her firm thigh, barely hidden beneath that tiny skirt. Nor the calluses he'd felt on her fingers when they'd shaken hands. But there wasn't a knife in the world that could stand up to a machine-gun toting vampire or two.

So, while Eve presented no real danger to his future subjects, she clearly knew more about vampires than the average citizen. And she was a native to the region. She could be useful to him, even if she didn't know it. And then there was the whole fuckable quotient. He decided to wait and see how the situation played out.

They slowed in front of an older building. Probably *much* older. It wasn't unusual in Dublin—or Ireland, in general—to find homes and other buildings that were hundreds of years old and still occupied, most with significant upgrades over the years. The block where Eve lived was the working man's version of Lucas Donlon's modernized castle.

The street was mostly unlit, but for a single pole lamp on each corner, with the rare glow from an unshaded window casting a dim square of light on the uneven sidewalk. Quinn could see well enough with nothing but moonlight, but he wondered how Eve could maneuver the uneven sidewalks on those heels. They walked side by side, their bodies close enough that she could grab his arm if she needed to, but she never did. She'd said her mother lived nearby. Maybe she'd grown up in this area and had memorized the rough streets over the years.

Eve's place was one in a line of four small units, each no more than twelve feet wide with a painted door in the middle. She stopped and turned to him, keys in hand. "Well, thanks for the escort, Kavanagh."

Quinn was amused. It had been a while since a woman had given him the brush-off, even when he'd been human. But as a vampire. . . . Hell, women tripped over each other to get to him when he visited a blood house. That wasn't ego speaking, either. It was fact.

Eve, the vampire killer, on the other hand, couldn't wait to get rid of him. Too bad for her that Quinn had no intention of being shaken off. Even if he hadn't wanted to bed her—and look at him, being all polite with his words—he'd have stuck close. If vampires were being killed, it was his business as the future Lord of Ireland, to investigate. Whether Irish vampires knew it yet or not.

He drew closer to Eve, trapping her against the door with his body, while not actually touching her. She was the skittish sort. He'd have to go slowly. "Good night, Eve," he murmured. Without warning, he dipped his head down and kissed her. It was a bare touch of his lips against hers as she sucked in a surprised breath. He didn't know if it was anticipation or fear making her heart pound, but she didn't pull away and didn't try to draw that wicked knife of hers and cut off his balls, either. He took it as a positive sign. "We'll see each other again soon," he promised, and walked away.

EVE WATCHED THE American stroll down the block, not even glancing back at her before he turned the corner and was gone. Cheeky fucker. Maybe it was the American way to kiss women you barely knew, but not in Ireland. She scowled. It obviously *did* happen in Ireland, since it had just happened to her, and she hadn't so much as breathed a word of protest. None of the local lads would have dared take such liberties. Even without her brother to defend her, she had a reputation as a cold bitch, one who wasn't afraid to leave marks on anyone who got too friendly. The question was . . . why had she let Quinn Kavanagh get as close as he had? She had a knife for fuck's sake. And if she didn't want to use that, there was always her fist. Or her knee.

Her face pinched in thought before she realized she was standing in front of her half-open door, staring down the empty street like a daft cow. Blowing out an exasperated breath, she shoved into her tiny flat before any additional cold air could get inside, then closed the door behind her.

Whatever had possessed her to kiss Kavanagh, or let him kiss her, didn't matter. She had a job to do, a brother to avenge. There was no room for midnight dalliances with handsome strangers. She locked the door with a firm click of the deadbolt, dropped to her only chair to strip off her boots, and thought about the day ahead. She couldn't afford more than a few hours of sleep. She had a heavy research workload right now—the kind of work that paid the bills—which meant it had to take priority over her vampire hunts. If she went out at all, it would be well after midnight, when she'd already done her paying research through the day and into evening. Sometimes she got lucky, catching a vampire or two on their way home. Vamps tended to pay less attention as dawn drew near. Bodies were tired, thoughts were sluggish. All of which made her hunting a lot safer. A tired vampire was her perfect prey.

She set the alarm on her mobile, hoping for an early start in the morning, then flicked off the light and pulled the covers over her head. Her eyes closed, and she saw Quinn Kavanagh's smiling face for a brief moment, before her thoughts scattered and sleep claimed her.

QUINN PULLED through the gate of his newly-acquired home in Howth, glad to see Garrick's sedan already parked near the front stairs. He let himself into the house, not bothering to call out his arrival. They were vampires. Garrick had known the moment he arrived. There was no need for a lot of unnecessary shouting.

He found his cousin in the ground floor room they were using as an office. It was the dining room, which they were obviously never going to use for that purpose. But the dining table was more than spacious enough for the two of them, the overhead lighting was good, and the room had plenty of outlets in convenient places. The table held what seemed like a lot of computers for only two vampires, but that was Garrick's doing. While Quinn had been laser-focused from his early teens on getting good enough grades for law school, Garrick had been charming the school secretary, sneaking into her office, and changing his grades in history and English to match the ones in math and science, to ensure he got into his geek college of choice. He'd graduated from that same college with a host of job offers, and had been fully and profitably employed in the early development of what would become modern personal computing, when he'd caught the eye of the vampire bitch who'd changed both their lives forever.

Boston, Massachusetts, USA, 57 years ago

QUINN RAISED HIS eyes from the contract, frustrated by language that was unnecessarily congested even by legal standards that were designed to obfuscate and confuse. He squeezed the bridge of his nose, wondering if he needed glasses, and then frowned. Why was his phone ringing? More importantly, why the hell wasn't his secretary answering the damn thing?

He lifted his head and blinked, surprised at the nighttime lights outside the windows of his high-rise office. Fuck. Now that he thought about it, he had a vague memory of his secretary bidding him "good night." He was even fairly sure he'd answered and had told her to leave the door open. But that might have been the previous night, or, hell, any of a hundred nights before that. He'd become the workaholic his mom had warned him he would become, something that had cost him more than one girlfriend.

And the damn phone just kept ringing. He looked, saw it was his private line, and hit the speaker button, expecting his cousin Garrick's voice. "Yeah. Kavanagh here."

"Mr. Kavanagh," a woman purred. He wasn't a fanciful man, but there was no other word for the sound of that voice. It made him suspicious. No one had his private line except family and ex-girlfriends. And she was neither of those.

"Yeah," he said. "Who's calling?"

"This is Marcelina Rios," she said, as if he should recognize the name. He didn't. Figuring this was his cousin's idea of a joke, he checked the calendar. Not his birthday, not April Fool's, or Valentine's.

"How can I help you, Ms. Rios?" He played along on the off-chance this wasn't a prank.

"Your cousin recommended you."

Quinn's jaw clenched. He didn't have time for this shit. "Right," he said tiredly. And he *was* tired. Fucking exhausted. He'd thought making partner at the law firm would make his life easier. "Give my regards to Garrick," he muttered and lifted his hand to disconnect.

"Mr. Kavanagh," Rios said somewhat sharply. "I no longer expect much from your kind, but simple courtesy would do."

Something about her voice—not the purr, but a sense of authority or . . . no, it was *entitlement*—made his finger freeze before he could hit the button.

"All right," he agreed. "So again, how can I help you?"

"I'm in need of legal advice. Garrick tells me you're the best."

"How do you know my cousin?" He hadn't actually seen Garrick in months, though they'd once been as close as brothers. They were still close, but like everything else in his life, Garrick had slipped away under the constant demands of his job.

"Garrick is very dear to me," she said.

Quinn frowned. What the hell did that mean? And what was it about the way she talked? It was formal, as if she had to think about each word before she said it. He considered. Maybe English wasn't a ready language for her. She had no discernable accent, or, rather, she did, but it was the accent of a person who spoke multiple languages. He'd had clients like that before, mostly older people who'd been born in Europe and had lived in the U.S. a long time. But this woman didn't sound old.

Telling himself his next call was going to be to Garrick, demanding to know what the hell was going on, he dug down for his polite voice and asked, "What sort of problem are you having?"

"So, you'll help me?" She sounded way too pleased.

"I don't know if I can yet. What's the problem?"

"We should meet."

Quinn frowned. This was the oddest conversation. "Maybe you can give me the basics first."

"It's complicated."

"It usually is. Give me the highlights."

"The highlights," she said distastefully. "A rather large corporation wants a piece of property that I've no desire to sell. It's been in my family for generations, you understand."

Quinn didn't understand *any* of this, but he said, "Yes," just to keep her talking and get this damn farce over with.

"Good. Garrick said you would."

He was going to kill his cousin. "I still don't quite understand the problem."

"They've bought off some politician or other and are trying to take it away from me by force. They're saying I have an imperfect title or some nonsense."

"And do you?"

"Do I what?"

"Have an imperfect title?"

"Mr. Kavanagh, I don't even know what that is, and I'm beginning to think this was a huge waste of my time. Garrick was obviously mistaken about you."

"Wait," he said, cursing himself in the next minute. Why the hell had he said that? But he knew why. Because of Garrick. Because he'd been a bad cousin and a worse friend over the last few years. Because Garrick, who never asked him for anything, had reached out through this admittedly odd woman, and Quinn couldn't simply blow him off. "We should meet," he said, hoping she mistook the resignation in his voice for tiredness at the end of a long day. "I don't know my calendar . . ." He paused, knowing how stupid that sounded. "My secretary—"

"Perhaps we can keep this informal," Rios suggested. "A conversation between friends."

Friends? He wasn't friends with this lady. He sighed inwardly. But . . . Garrick. "All right," he agreed. "I'll call Garrick—"

"That won't be necessary. Garrick will escort me to whatever meeting we arrange."

Quinn didn't like the sound of that. What the hell was his cousin into? But since it seemed the only way to get answers, he glanced at the display on his computer, checking the date and time. Friday. He shook his head. What the hell was he doing at the office this late on a Friday night? He was 32 years old and single, for fuck's sake. "What did you have in mind?" he asked. "I can do lunch tomorrow, or one day next week, if you prefer."

"Tomorrow," she said quickly. "But not lunch. In the evening, if you please. I have a place in the city. Garrick will give you the particulars."

"What time—" But she was already gone. He stared at the phone for a long moment, then immediately hit the speed dial for his cousin. He listened to it ring before it rolled over to voicemail.

"Garrick, buddy," he said. "I just got the weirdest call. Some chick . . . well, maybe not a chick, she sounded a bit older than that. But, anyway, she used your name and said she wants to meet tomorrow night. You're supposed to provide the particulars. Her word, not mine. Call me when you get this." He paused. "Oh, and, dude, if this is a joke? You're going to pay." He disconnected, threw the phone down, and picked up the contract he'd been working on. He stared at it for ten seconds, then dropped it to his desk. The hell with that. It was Friday, he was tired, and life was short. He was going to do something wild, something totally out of character. He was going to go home and sleep for 12 hours straight.

Howth, Ireland, present day

THAT PHONE CALL, the one that had set so much else in motion, had been 57 years ago, but the memory of it still had the power to enrage Quinn. He sometimes wished he'd kept the bitch alive, just so he could kill her all over again. He'd torture her, bring her right to the edge of death, and then let her live, knowing he'd be back to do it again the next night.

Maybe that made him a monster. But if anyone didn't like it, they could take him on, or shut the fuck up about it.

He glanced over at his cousin. While he'd been reliving nightmares, Garrick had rolled down the table and pulled up a second keyboard. The multiple computers covering the table weren't simply for Garrick's hacking fun. There was also the rather extensive security network they'd set up on a separate shielded network, in an abundance of caution. Without daylight guards, they had to rely on technical means of safeguarding their daylight sleep. They'd installed pressure plates and cameras all around the perimeter, and motion and entry sensors on every door and window, all with piercingly loud alarms. They'd also installed vastly improved locks on every door, both inside and out, and were painstakingly careful to lock them every morning. It wasn't perfect, but it was the best they could do. If someone tried to break in during daylight, the loudest alarm in the world wouldn't wake them, but it would, hopefully, scare off the intruder. And, of course, it would let them know they'd been tested.

What Quinn needed was his team of daylight guards from the U.S. They were ready and eager to deploy, but he wanted to wait until everything was in place. He would take over the smuggling op here in Howth, present Sorley with the fait accompli—thus establishing himself as a powerful ally—then slide into Sorley's inner circle, with the vampire lord unaware that he'd just invited his killer through the door. Fun times. It would be so much easier if he could just walk into the fucker's house and kill him. Hell, he'd do that, too, before the month was over. But there were steps to take first. This was a campaign, not a smash and grab.

Once he had Howth, he'd move into the Dublin house that he'd acquired some months earlier, when he'd first known he'd be moving to Ireland. At that point, he could bring in his own team. Not only the daylight guards, but his fighters, too.

He'd told Raphael, after the Malibu attack, that he didn't want to bring any American vamps with him to Ireland, that he was going to recruit locally. But that wasn't entirely true. He hadn't wanted any interference from the Western Lord or anyone else when it came to choosing the vampires who'd form his inner circle of fighters and advisers. These were the vampires he'd have to count on in the coming battles. Their loyalty had to be unambiguously *his*. But he'd seen this day coming from the first moment he'd learned what Mathilde had done to Raphael, and why. He'd known that war wouldn't be far behind. And when the European incursions had kept coming, he'd known that the only way to win would be for the North American vampires to fight back, to go on the offense, instead of standing and waiting for the next invasion.

He and Rajmund, the vampire lord who ruled the American Northeast, had discussed it at some length, and they'd known that the day was coming when the North American vamps would be forced to take the battle to Europe. A day when the call would go out for a vampire powerful enough to command the vanguard of that battle. They'd both wanted Quinn to be that vampire, so Raj had given Quinn permission to recruit a small group of vampires as his private invasion force. He'd chosen his people carefully, and they'd all trained and socialized together for months, waiting for what they believed would be the inevitable call to arms. Like Quinn, they'd all been sworn to Rajmund initially. But now that the North American lords had set their sights on Ireland with Quinn as its lord, they'd sworn a blood oath to Quinn. They'd become *his,* and they were waiting for his call.

With their strength behind him, he'd use his newfound position with Sorley to expand his own power, while undermining the Irish lord himself. After that, it would be a matter of days before he formally challenged and killed Sorley. It sounded tedious on paper—if he'd ever written it down—but he figured it would take less than a month altogether. He frowned. A month was a long time. Maybe he could skip some of the middle part. He was a fast learner.

"Garrick," he said quietly, staring at the papers on his desk without seeing anything.

"Yeah?"

"We need the house in Dublin up and running."

"Okay," he said slowly, dragging out the word.

"I know it's sooner than we'd planned, but things change, and we need to pick up the pace. I think it's time to embrace our vampire side and shed some blood."

"Thank God," Garrick said fervently. "When do we start?"

Quinn laughed. "Tomorrow night. But first, I need you to run a full background on someone. Her name's . . . Fuck," he snarled.

"You didn't even get her name? You're such a dog."

"It's not like that. I just walked her home."

"And didn't get an invite through the door?" Garrick said in disbelief. "You're slipping, Q."

Quinn balled up a piece of paper and threw it at his cousin. "Fuck you. Her first name's Eve, and I have an address. Howth's a small place. How difficult can it be to find her?"

His cousin snorted. "Give me what you have. I'll find your lost maiden for you."

"Be careful. She killed two vampires last night."

That got Garrick's attention. "What the fuck? Why's she still breathing?"

Quinn shrugged. "I didn't particularly like the two vampires she killed. She probably saved me the effort." He paused. "And she's rather fuckable."

"Fuckable," Garrick repeated flatly. "Look, I know you like complicated women and all, but let's keep our eyes on the prize, okay? We're here to seize a country, not get you laid. Besides, Dublin is full of fuckable women. Don't get hung up on one that likes killing vamps."

"I'm not hung up. I want to know who she is and *why* she's killing vamps. Hell, I want to know *how* she's killing them. She's not exactly superhero size."

"Not a vampire herself?"

"Definitely not."

"Huh. Okay, I'll find her for you. You go be a vampire lord and get us back to Dublin."

Quinn laughed and wondered what someone like Raphael would think of his relationship with Garrick. Strictly speaking, his cousin was his lieutenant. In the world of vampires, a vampire lord's lieutenant was an important and powerful position. More than one lieutenant had gone on to rule his own territory, although it was such a close and almost symbiotic relationship that many powerful lieutenants preferred to stay with the lords they served. And even the ones who left tended to maintain a deferential relationship with their lord. Quinn was reminded of Raphael again, and the way his former lieutenant, Duncan, still deferred to the powerful Western Lord, even though he now had a territory of his own. Lucas was the same. He played at being the disobedient son, but when it came down to it, Raphael's word was law.

Quinn and Garrick had a different relationship. They'd been raised together from the time they were born, had lived next door to each other most of their lives. Their families had vacationed together, spent all their holidays together. He and Garrick were more brothers than cousins, and becoming vampires hadn't changed that much. Sure, Quinn was by far the more powerful vampire, but Garrick was no weakling. He was a strong master vampire who might have ruled a nest of his own, had he not chosen to serve as Quinn's lieutenant.

But they were still brothers under the skin. In public, they played the game as well as any other powerful vampire lord and his lieutenant. But in private, they were simply Quinn and Garrick, brothers and co-conspirators, just like always.

"I'll do the bloody part," he told Garrick now. "You find the girl."

"Wait, wait," Garrick protested. "I want in on the bloody part."

"Fine," Quinn agreed with feigned impatience. "But, first you find the girl."

"Already done," Garrick said, with an exaggerated slap of a computer key. "Check your in-box."

Quinn gave him a surprised look and opened the email. "Eve McKenzie Connelly," he read. "That's a lot of name."

Garrick shrugged. "You don't have to shout the whole thing when you're coming, lad. Fact, it might be odd if you do. Just stick with 'Eve.'"

Quinn sighed, thinking it might be nice sometimes to have a proper lieutenant.

THE NEXT NIGHT found Quinn and Garrick back on the Howth docks, but there was no cozy café this time, no hot pot of tea or pretty waitress. They stood in the cold and damp, watching a lone boat slide into the darkened harbor. The boat docked, and two of the three men onboard jumped onto the pier, looking around as if expecting someone to meet them. Figuring that was their cue, Quinn and his cousin stepped out of the shadows and strode down the dock to the waiting boat.

"Good evening, gentlemen," Quinn said casually.

The men jolted into readiness. "Who the fuck are you?" one of them asked, as behind them, the boat's engine revved, preparing for a quick departure.

Quinn turned his head slowly, until the gleam of his eyes painted the cluttered boat deck with an icy blue light. Reaching out, he touched the captain's mind and stopped him from running, or anything else, until Quinn gave him permission.

"You're here to drop off a shipment," Garrick said in a friendly voice. "We're here to pick it up. Simple as that."

The man who'd spoken glanced back at the boat, his muscles tensed to hop back on-board, probably wondering why his captain hadn't reversed engines yet. He found no answers, and his next words demonstrated why he was only muscle.

"Yeah, well. I don't know you, and I ain't about to turn over the *shipment* to you or anyone else I don't know."

Garrick grinned. "I was so hoping you'd say that." He moved before the man had a chance to react, before the human's eyes had even widened in surprise. The second man was still staring at bloody ruins of his fellow smuggler when he, too, became little more than blood and flesh on the dirty dock. Through it all, the captain hadn't moved, still caught by Quinn's will. He studied the human briefly and noted a complete absence of the usual stress reactions. There was no increased heart rate, no rapid breathing, no more than the usual sweaty skin. He looked deeper and saw that some other vampire, either here or wherever he'd picked up the contraband, had put him under compulsion. The human would still feel fear, but he couldn't act upon it.

"We'll have to scuttle the boat," Quinn said.

Garrick chuckled. "Let's get Captain Ahab there to help us unload first."

"Not here." He eyed the gore splashing the worn boards of the dock. "I don't want blood all over the crates."

"Good point. Think you can convince him to move the boat?"

"Does a bear shit in the woods?"

"I wouldn't know."

Quinn laughed, and caught the captain's flinch from the corner of his eye. Interesting. The human must have some small measure of in-born resistance to telepathic control. It wasn't enough to resist whatever vampire had planted the compulsion, though, which, oddly enough, was a bit of good luck. That compulsion had saved his life. If he'd fought back when Quinn and Garrick had first confronted them, he'd be dead along with his crew. Quinn decided, in that moment, to let the human captain live. After all, he wasn't guilty of anything other than conspiring with vampires to smuggle illegal goods. And he was unlikely to go running to the authorities with that story.

With a graceful leap, Quinn was on the boat. Two long strides took him into the small wheelhouse which reeked of the captain's stale sweat.

"Relax, Captain," he said smoothly. "What's your name?"

"Bohdan," the human rasped. "Bohdan Honza."

Czech, Quinn thought to himself. Not entirely a surprise. Despite its landlocked status, a lot of young Czech men found their way to the ports of Europe and worked as crew on big cargo ships. It was a short step from that to running a small smuggling vessel of your own. "Well, Bohdan Honza," he said to the man, "this is your lucky night. Is there a place nearby where we can unload your cargo without anyone noticing?"

"Yes, sir. The other end of the harbor. No one's there this time of year, and especially not at night."

"You wouldn't be setting me up, would you, Bohdan?"

"No, sir!" the man said fervently. "It's a good place to unload. I tried to get the others to use it, but they wanted to be close to the pub."

"They should have taken your advice. Okay, let's get what's left of your crewmen back aboard, shall we?"

The captain nodded, his terror ramping up a notch now that Quinn had removed the old compulsion. He probably assumed he, too, was going to die that night.

"Don't worry, Bohdan. I've decided to let you live."

The man nodded again, though it was obvious he didn't believe Quinn's assurances. That was all right. He'd learn soon enough that Quinn was a man—or a vampire—of his word.

Quinn leaned out of the boathouse and signaled Garrick, who quickly picked up the bloody bodies of the two crewmen and tossed them onto the deck, then jumped onboard himself.

"Where we going?" he asked Quinn, as the captain backed out of the slip.

"Captain Honza has suggested a more discreet location to unload the cargo."

"You trust him?"

"Not at all. But right now, he's mine, and he's telling the truth."

Garrick grunted. "I'll have to move the car."

"The exercise is good for you."

"Good one, Q." They both laughed. Garrick hardly needed the exercise. He was something of a fitness freak. They both were, if truth be told. Vampire longevity was a blessing, but it didn't come with instant physical health. Regular vampires—those who weren't in the business of running a territory—had the luxury of being out of shape. Although between the vampire symbiote's obsession with keeping its host body healthy, and a diet of blood alone, it was rare to find a vamp who was overweight. But vampires like Quinn, and like his cousin, who thought to rise to the top, to rule a territory . . . they had to be prepared to fight for their lives on a nightly basis. And that meant rigorous and constant training in every form of combat.

Quinn turned back, his attention divided between keeping the captain from stroking out from fear and watching their progress through the still water. It was only a matter of minutes before they'd motored to the other, darker end of the small harbor, with its modern concrete dock. The lights of the busy pub were visible, but distant, with only the occasional loud laugh rising up enough to break the silence. There were no other boats in sight, and, though modern light poles arched overhead, none of the lamps were lit. Quinn thought back to what he'd learned about Howth. This part of the harbor had been upgraded for the tourist trade. It would be busy during the summer, when vacationers swelled Howth's population, but in the cold winter months, like now, there was no one around.

The boat bumped the dock. Garrick stepped off and tied it down with efficient motions. "I'll go get the car," he called softly and took off with a burst of vampiric speed.

"Let's go, Captain," Quinn said in an upbeat voice. "Shut down the engine, and help me get these crates off so you can get on with your night."

Sweat was rolling off the man's face, his eyes wild as he obediently turned off the engine and led Quinn out onto the deck, where he stared, frozen, at the bodies of his former crew.

"Don't worry about them. You can dump the bodies out at sea. You know better than I do what the best location would be." Quinn pulled back the thick tarp covering the cargo. "Just stack them on the dock. We'll do the rest," he said, lifting the first crate and noting its substantial weight. It was too heavy for drugs, and the configuration of the crate was consistent with weapons shipments. Guns, then. The only question was, what kind?

The captain tried, but he couldn't lift the crates alone. It was faster and easier for Quinn to do it himself, so he told the man to sit and rest, while he went to work. By the time Garrick returned with the car, nearly a third of the crates sat on the dock. And with the two vampires moving in unison, the rest were quickly off-loaded and stacked.

Honza's agitation seemed to increase with every crate unloaded, until he was practically shuddering with terror. Quinn eyed the man and shook his head. "Honestly, Bohdan. There's no need for this." Reaching out, he touched the human's forehead with a single finger, then gave him a jaunty salute and jumped off the boat to stand next to his cousin on the dock.

D. B. Reynolds

His foot had barely touched the concrete before the captain had the boat reversing away.

"Where's he going?" Garrick asked, watching the boat depart.

"Our good captain will travel several miles out to sea, where he'll scuttle the boat."

"He's going down with it?"

"Of course, not. I'm not a monster. He'll escape on a life raft, the lone survivor of a tragic wreck. What he does after that is up to him. But he won't remember anything of this night."

"You're sure?"

Quinn turned to study his cousin. "If you were any other vampire, Garrick, I'd take offense at that question."

"Lucky I'm me, then."

Quinn snorted. "Help me transfer all this mess to the car."

Garrick hefted the first crate. "We're going to need the back seat. It won't all fit in the trunk."

"It's called a boot, you American heathen. Do whatever's necessary, but do it fast. This place is deserted for now, but I don't want to take any chances."

EVE KICKED OFF her shoes and sat on the bed, reaching down to rub her foot. The damn heels were sexy and made her legs look great, but they hurt like hell. She wondered if the really expensive shoes, like the ones with the red soles that all the movie stars on the talk shows wore, hurt as badly. Did those beautiful women go home and rub their feet, too?

She flopped back on the bed, rolling to one side and reaching for her cell phone, immediately rolling back when the hilt of her knife dug into her thigh. She laughed to herself. That was one thing Hollywood starlets didn't have to worry about, she'd wager. Not that her knife had seen much business tonight, she thought, with a sigh. She'd gotten a late start, bogged down as she'd been on her side job, and, though she'd walked her usual patrol, the night had been eerily quiet. Almost as if some greater threat had the local vamps and other bad guys lying low. And then she wondered what kind of threat could make a vampire want to hide out.

Shit. Well, whatever it was, there'd been no sign of it or any stray vampires, either. The pub had been active, but the vamps had stuck to the crowds and each other. Looked like she'd be visiting Dublin sooner than expected, a move she'd been planning for some time. Not that she

51

expected to immediately start hunting vampires in the big city, but that had been her ultimate goal all along, and it was time for some reconnaissance. She knew vampires had a pecking order, an almost military structure of command. Vampires might not be human anymore, but they gossiped and bragged, just like everyone else, and she'd listened. She even knew the name of the so-called Lord of Ireland. Orrin Sorley. Talk about a puffed-up bastard. *Lord of Ireland.* She heard those words and pictured some fancy vampire doing a step dance across the stage while his fang-toothed soldiers cheered him on.

She laughed out loud at that, but sobered almost immediately. It wasn't going to be that easy. Ordinary vampires were dangerous and strong. But the big boys? The ones at the very top? They were something else. They had true power, almost magical abilities if one believed the rumors. And she had no reason not to. There were now entire online sites dedicated to the worship of the monsters, sites filled with first-hand accounts of people—mostly women—who'd been to their blood houses. Places like the local Howth pubs, but run by the vampire lords and dedicated to vampire needs. There were even a very few stories on one site from women who'd been taken as lovers by vampires close to the top, women who'd seen for themselves what the vampire lords could do.

Eve didn't know how much she believed of what they said, but she couldn't dismiss it out of hand. There was too much similarity between the stories, too many repeated themes. She hated the thought of going to one of those places and mingling with the monsters, of offering herself up like meat in a market. But she had to do it. The vampires who'd killed her brother weren't in Howth. They were in Dublin. And though she'd searched the Dublin streets for them, quietly visiting pubs frequented by the vamps, and lurking outside Orrin Sorley's palatial Donnybrook estate, she'd never caught a glimpse of them.

Her years of hunting had only confirmed what she'd begun to suspect early on, that the vampires who'd killed her brother were high up in Sorley's organization. She wasn't going to catch them roaming the streets or drinking in the pubs in Dublin or anywhere else. It was going to take more than that. She'd hidden in Howth for too long, telling herself they might show up. Telling herself she needed the practice, needed to hone her skills. But the time had come. If she really wanted to find the vamps who'd killed Alan, she was going to have to put her life on the line in a way she hadn't yet. And the truth was, she was scared.

"Looks like you're headed for Dublin, lass," she whispered. A shiver shook her body, and she told herself it was just the cold. She had a heater in her flat, but she used it sparingly, to save money. She got up and put on the kettle for a cup of tea, but couldn't escape the dread that sat like a block of ice in her chest. Yes, she'd managed to kill some vampires over the last few years. But she had a feeling Dublin would change everything.

Chapter Four

Dublin, Ireland

"THIS IS IT?" QUINN glanced casually through the passenger window as Garrick drove them past Sorley's headquarters in the Donnybrook district of Dublin. The big, red-brick house was half-hidden behind a wall overgrown with trees and hedges that screened most of it from casual view. He caught a glimpse of several vampires through the half-open wrought-iron gate, but since he didn't know any of Sorley's people, that gave him little more than a head count. And he didn't need to see vampires *or* humans to count their numbers. He swore softly. "We're going to have to go in there."

Garrick shot him a quick look of surprise. "Say again?"

Quinn stared straight ahead, thinking. "Look at the number of guards around the house and gate. That many vampires hanging around every night would attract too much attention, which means this isn't business as usual. It's a big meet. And what better way to command Sorley's attention than to invite ourselves in?"

"Or, get ourselves killed."

He grinned. "A little trust, please. I won't let the big, bad vampire hurt you."

"Not intentionally, anyway."

Quinn laughed, but sobered almost immediately. "Look, we need to gain Sorley's attention. If we walk in there uninvited, it tells him two things. First, we're not afraid of him or his people. An asshole like Sorley will appreciate that kind of braggadocio."

"Not if you're going to use five-syllable words like that."

Quinn made a face, but his cousin had a point. By all accounts, Sorley was over 200 years old, from a time when boys were put to work young. What education they got was from the priests, and that wasn't much. It wouldn't do to make Sorley feel as if Quinn was talking down to him. "Point taken," he acknowledged. "But he *will* be interested in the second thing our arrival will show him."

Garrick gave him a questioning glance.

"By now, he's missing both vampires and guns. If we walk in there with answers, he'll have to pay attention."

"Or he'll just—"

"He won't kill us outright. He'll want what we have, and what we know. And if it comes down to it, I can control Orrin Sorley."

"I'm taking my gun anyway."

Quinn smiled. "You're a vampire. You don't need a gun."

"It makes me feel better. Deal with it."

He shook his head. "I think we've driven past enough times. His guards are going to notice."

"Are we pulling into the yard?"

"No, I don't want the cargo to be that close."

They'd replaced the sedan which they'd driven home from the harbor in the wee hours of the previous night. The shocks had been destroyed, the vehicle almost dragging the ground from the weight of the guns they'd off-loaded from the smuggler's boat, with the crates completely filling both the trunk and the back seat. The Range Rover they'd rented instead was both heavier and roomier. It was also more powerful, faster, and generally more of a pleasure to drive, which pleased both Quinn and his cousin so much that they'd gone out and *purchased* a second one just like it. No more discreet sedans for them.

For this visit to Dublin, they'd flattened the back seat and spread the crates out through the cargo space, to prevent them from being easily visible through the tinted windows. The last thing they needed was some passing Garda to catch a glimpse and get curious before they could give Sorley his surprise gift.

"Park a couple of blocks down and on the opposite side of the street," Quinn instructed. "We'll walk from there."

EVE EYED THE gaggle of giggling women as they hurried toward the back gate of Sorley's estate. She was disgusted. They weren't allowed to enter through the front door, but were being delivered through the back like dry goods from the grocer. Two bags of potatoes and a couple dozen silly women. They were dressed nearly identically in short skirts and tops with low necklines, all tight and revealing. And there was so much cleavage on display that it had Eve checking her own neckline in comparison before she realized what she was doing.

"There's no other way," she muttered to herself, then slammed the heel of her hand against the steering wheel. Sorley's big meeting—which she'd heard of by chance during a visit to a Dublin blood house—was a total godsend, a way to get inside his estate. Maybe the only way. She'd checked into his household staff, thinking to get herself a job there. Vampires considered themselves a step above humans, and there was no way they'd be spending their time dusting a house that big. But while she'd discovered he did, in fact, employ a human cleaning service, they were few in number, and, as far as she'd observed, they worked only in daytime, when the vampires were all locked safely away, sound asleep.

So, she'd become vampire food, instead. Or at least, give the appearance of it. Despite her barely-there clothes, she had no more intention of allowing these bloodsuckers near her neck than she did the vamps she'd killed in Howth. This wasn't a suicide mission. It was reconnaissance. She wanted to search for her brother's killers, of course. But this was also her chance to observe vampires in their native setting. She'd learned enough about them to know they could be very tricky when it came to concealing their true nature. There were a few identifying characteristics she'd taught herself to look for—fangs being the most obvious—but, for the most part, a vampire could get away with pretending to be an ordinary human, and only another vampire would know the truth.

Unfortunately, in order to get inside, Eve had to put herself on the menu. Or pretend to. Blending in with the crowd any other way wasn't an option. Vampires weren't only bloodthirsty killers, they were also misogynistic creeps. There were very few female vamps. In fact, though she'd read about them online, and had even seen pictures of one or two who served close to vampire lords in North America, she'd never identified a single female vampire here in Ireland. Which left the giggling women as her only entrée to Sorley's party.

"Shit," she swore softly. Her skirt was as short and tight as any of them, with plenty of leg on display. And her shoes—a pair of Miu-Miu Mary Jane stilettos—were the most expensive shoes she'd ever worn and way out of her usual price range. She'd gotten them at a high-end thrift shop, where she'd gone looking for clothes, figuring a party at Sorley's would bring in a higher class of dinner buffet participants. She'd nearly swooned when she'd seen the Miu-Miu's in her size. She'd even felt a little guilty when she'd seen the price. But she'd bought them anyway, rationalizing that she was doing the human race a favor, and that the shoes were simply a weapon in her war against their common enemy.

Brushing aside the guilt over her fabulous shoes, she returned her thoughts to vampires and what might happen inside that house. Her only weapon was a small knife, snugged tight on her inner thigh, almost touching her satin-covered crotch. She shouldn't have allowed herself even that much, but the idea of going in there with no weapon at all had been more than she could handle. Her fingers fiddled restlessly with her sweater, fastening, then unfastening, the two top buttons, leaving the already low neckline to gape open farther and reveal the full curves of her breasts. It also left her neck bare, just as they'd expect. She was as ready as she could be, but now that the moment was upon her, she was nervous.

The women's laughter abruptly grew louder, and she looked up to see the back gate opening. It was now or never.

Sucking in a breath, she slipped quickly out of her car. The door closed and locked behind her. She wasn't taking anything into the house with her. No purse, no ID, not so much as a lipstick. She'd secured a spare key fob in one of those magnetic key holders that she'd placed in the front wheel well.

The women were nearly through the gate, their progress slowed by their number and the fact that the entrance had never been designed for such a large group. Eve hurried to join the tail end of their parade, and even managed to exchange some excited titters with the other stragglers. She stuck to the center of the pack as they shuffled through the gate, avoiding the groping hands of the guards along the edges, her attention fixed on the forbidding house in front of her. Fuck, but it was huge. She'd never been in such a house. She could still back out, could claim a headache or a sick stomach. She could probably vomit on cue because . . .

It was suddenly too late. The gate behind them closed with a hard crash of noise, and the house door ahead opened to cast a dim light on the now tightly-packed group of women.

"This is tonight's lot?" The question came from nowhere, a gravelly voice with no person attached to it.

"That's the whole of them," the guard from the gate announced.

"Well, don't stand there, you stupid bitches. The party's not in the fucking yard."

The women were suddenly moving again, crowding against one another, no longer laughing. But Eve could still feel their excitement, like live wires scraping against her skin with every contact. She let herself be chivied along, dread growing with every step.

She'd done a lot of stupid things over the last few years. But this might just top the cake.

QUINN WAITED UNTIL the courtyard in front of the house had mostly emptied, until the gate guards were once again slumped at their posts, more concerned with every burst of laughter, every roar of approval they were missing from inside the house, than with watching the street against intruders. It was shameful, really. Quinn had seen what real security looked like—at Rajmund's tower in Manhattan, or Raphael's estate in Malibu. Even his own small guard troop was trained far better than these. Guards like Sorley's wouldn't last ten minutes in that company. Hell, they'd never have been hired in the first place.

They served his purposes well, however. When he and Garrick strolled easily up to the gates, it took several minutes for the guards to realize the visitors weren't stopping, but were pushing their way inside. And by the time they'd puffed their chests out in aggression and opened their mouths to protest, Quinn had seized their minds and convinced them everything was fine. No threat, no uninvited visitors. They went back to leaning against the gate posts, their eyes on the street, ignoring the two dangerous strangers now walking toward the house.

"What's the plan?" Garrick asked quietly as they started up the stairs.

"There's a plan?" Quinn repeated, then laughed at his cousin's middle-finger salute. "It's simple. We're going to walk in there and wait to be noticed. And then I'm going to announce our intentions."

Garrick grunted his acknowledgment and pulled open the door.

Quinn led the way, striding into the gathering as if he belonged there. One thing he'd learned from his many years in the courtroom . . . confidence was 90% of the battle. Most humans were followers. Give them a leader and they were yours. The same was true of vampires, maybe even more so, since vampires were hardwired to respect power. And that was something Quinn had in spades.

He headed directly for Sorley, who was easy to find despite the crowd. He sat at the front of the room, separated from his guests by a few critical feet, and backed by four guards who were far more attentive than the two on the outside gate had been.

Quinn walked up to the invisible demarcation line and paused, staring boldly at Sorley over the intervening space. It was blatant provocation, and the vampire lord rose to the challenge. Sorley might be an asshole of cosmic proportions, but he wasn't stupid, and he wasn't weak.

"Who the fuck are you?" he demanded. His guards took notice, closing in on both sides of his chair and glaring daggers at Quinn and Garrick, abruptly aware of the strangers in their midst. Strangers who were dangerous enough to warrant their attention, even though Quinn was concealing the true depths of his power. He and Garrick would both register as strong master vampires, even to Sorley's radar, since the Irish lord had no reason to look more deeply.

Quinn tipped his head to Sorley and said, "I'm a man with something that belongs to you. Something you lost recently."

Sorley's gaze narrowed, and Quinn could feel the vampire lord testing his shields and finding no weakness. "And what would that be?" he asked calmly. He was a vampire lord in the heart of his power, surrounded by his people. He had nothing to fear from a presumptuous and uninvited intruder.

Quinn gave a slow, fang-baring smile. "Guns," he said simply.

Sorley's attention sharpened. He glanced over Quinn's shoulder and jerked his head sharply in a silent signal to one of his vamps. Quinn felt Garrick tense next to him, but he wasn't worried. He'd have detected any hostile movement behind them. Whatever Sorley had his vampire doing, it wasn't an attack. Maybe it was something as innocuous as trying to reach the two dead vampires by phone, or maybe some of the human crew from the boats.

"I'll ask you one more time," Sorley said softly. "Who are you?"

Quinn made a show of his answer, pressing a hand to his chest in mock dismay. "Where are my manners? My name is Quinn. And this is my cousin Garrick. We're new to town and recently ran into a . . . business opportunity that, as it turns out, involves you."

"American," Sorley said, practically spitting it like a dirty word.

"Guilty as charged," Quinn responded easily. "Though both born in Ireland, as it turns out. We've come back to advance our fortunes in the land of our birth."

"To rediscover your roots," Sorley said mockingly.

Quinn gave Sorley a cool look. "I wasn't aware I'd lost them."

The vampire lord stared for a moment, then barked a laugh. "I like you, Quinn. You've got cast iron bollocks. Now where the fuck are my guns?"

"Nearby," he said simply.

The vampire lord's attention went over Quinn's shoulder again, and he knew the same vampire Sorley had signaled before had returned from whatever errand he'd been sent upon. His mouth tightened perceptibly.

"Oh dear," Quinn thought. *"Bad news?"* He was smart enough to keep the thought inside his own head, but couldn't help the tiny smirk that crossed his face before his expression settled into a bland mask.

Sorley came to his feet with a growl. "No more games. What do you want?"

"The same thing we all do. Business. Money. A good life. Women to suck and fuck."

Sorley laughed again, then backed up and sat in his chair. He flicked a hand at one of his guards, who immediately produced a second chair and placed it next to Sorley's.

"Have a seat," Sorley said, making it sound more like an order than an invitation.

Quinn bowed slightly in thanks, but moved the chair so that it faced Sorley at an angle. There was no way in hell he was turning his back on the vampire lord's personal guard. He sat, and Garrick immediately took up position behind him, no doubt exchanging glares with the other guards.

"So, tell me," Sorley asked. "How exactly did you get hold of my guns?"

Quinn leaned back all casual like and began by telling him about the two vampires who'd been intended to meet the boat, and how they were dead. Eve had been the one who killed them, but he let Sorley assume it had been he and Garrick who'd done the deed. The last thing the beautiful redhead needed was a vampire lord on her tail. It was bad enough she was taking on regular vamps. Her luck hadn't run out yet, but it would, sooner or later. And when it did, she'd find herself in a world of hurt with a pissed off, *powerful* vampire.

"So, they're both dusted?" Sorley confirmed.

Quinn shrugged. "All I wanted was information. We're new to town and trying to learn the set-up. But your vamps took it badly. They attacked. We won."

Sorley pursed his lips and made a soft grunting noise. "And the guns?"

"Well, we could hardly leave the boat captain literally at sea, wondering what had happened to his contacts in Howth. So we met the boat, offloaded the cargo, and dealt with the witnesses."

Sorley stared. His eyes were cold and flat, and Quinn knew there'd be no second chances with this vampire. "You killed my boat captain?"

"He was human and, thus, untrustworthy," Quinn deflected easily. "I thought only to protect your secrets."

"Makes it harder to keep the guns flowing if you kill the fucking boat captain."

"True enough. But I have contacts of my own. Boat captains are easily replaced."

"You want the Howth import contract," Sorley said flatly, and it wasn't a question.

That's one way to describe a smuggling operation, Quinn thought. But all he said was, "Howth will be a good start."

Sorley froze, clearly picking up on the sub-text of Quinn's response. Howth was only the beginning of what Quinn wanted. Sorley's problem would be what came next. How high did Quinn want to go in the vampire lord's operation? His nostrils flared as he studied Quinn, almost as if he was literally sniffing the air for dishonesty and duplicity.

But Quinn had had decades to perfect his blank face, to control the small chemical changes that occurred when a man lied. Even before he'd become a vampire, he'd shown only what he wanted to the world, his emotions tightly contained well before he'd taken a career path that made such dissimulation a requirement. As a human, he'd been cold as ice in the courtroom. As a vampire, he'd been reborn with the power to rule, and vampire lords excelled at deceiving others.

He and Sorley were equally still as they studied each other, but it was Sorley who broke the silent tableau. He nodded abruptly. "Done." His reluctance was obvious, but it was the right decision, the only one that made sense businesswise. Quinn could almost discern his thought process, step by step. His first instinct would probably have been to kill Quinn, but he hadn't gotten to be Lord of Ireland because he was stupid. Even a surface scan of Quinn's strength would have shown that he'd be hard to kill. Not impossible, at least not as far as Sorley could tell, since Quinn was still camouflaged, but difficult. And in the final analysis, power was the one thing that vampires respected above all others. So, why waste such a potentially valuable underling? At the same time, he wouldn't want Quinn running around Dublin where he could cause problems. Much better to give him Howth, to keep him far away and under his thumb.

Not that Quinn planned to remain under anyone's thumb for long. But Sorley didn't know that.

Quinn smiled broadly, careful to make it more friendly than threatening. He wasn't ready to take on the Irish lord just yet. "Excellent. Now, where do you want your guns?"

"My lads will handle that. Where's the vehicle?"

Quinn thought quickly. He and Garrick had left nothing in the SUV but the guns. And it was the one they'd rented under one of their many aliases. The one they'd bought was safely parked at the house in Howth. "Give our new lord the keys, Garrick."

Garrick tossed the keys in Sorley's general direction, where they were caught by one of his guards.

"Down two blocks and across the street," Quinn said cheerfully. "Just click the fob if you can't find it. Oh, and, don't damage the vehicle. It's a rental."

Sorley's mouth twisted sourly, but he nodded at the guard, who immediately left the room with one other. When he looked back at Quinn, he had a grin on his face that was as false as his welcome. "Feel free to stick around, lads. The party will run late tonight. There are plenty of those beautiful women you're looking for, and there'll be no shortage of sucking *or* fucking," he added with a chuckle.

Quinn matched the grin with one of his own, then stood. "Thank you, my lord. We'll definitely be staying." His words were innocuous enough, but there was clear understanding in Sorley's eyes.

The gauntlet had been thrown. Quinn would be watching his back from here out.

SORLEY WATCHED with hooded eyes as the American intruder strolled out of the house, smiling at the women and greeting Sorley's own vamps as if he belonged here, as if he hadn't a care in the world. Bastard thought he could steal Sorley's guns and waltz in like the high king himself. He should have killed him on the spot.

He'd considered it. He'd known the moment that fucking Quinn had entered his house. Asshole thought he was so clever, masking his power. He was strong, no question of that. But Sorley was the damned Lord of Ireland. This was *his* domain. He had nearly unlimited power at his command and two centuries of learning how to use it against his enemies. And this little puppy thought he could fool Sorley? In his own lair?

Damn, but he hated everything about the American vampire, beginning with the fact that he *was* American. But his hatred went much deeper than that. Quinn might pretend he was simply an Irish-born lad come back to claim his heritage, but Sorley knew better. He had connections, too, including spies in Kildare who told him everything he needed to know about the bastard, from his Ivy League background to his time with Rajmund in the Northeast. Everything he'd learned convinced him that Quinn was in cahoots with fucking Raphael and his gang. He had no proof, no one who could confirm his suspicions, and he wasn't likely to get it. Raphael held his secrets closely and his people were slavishly devoted to him. But Sorley had been around a long time, and he could figure things out on his own, even if he hadn't gone to fucking Harvard like Quinn. The prissy son of a bitch thought he was better than everyone else.

He was about to learn different. Sorley had ruled Ireland for more than 65 years, and Northern Ireland for decades before that. He had friends and allies in places Quinn didn't even know existed. It wasn't a question of whether he was going to kill the smug bastard, it was only a question of when.

QUINN DIDN'T STAY long after his little tête-à-tête with Sorley. The Irish lord might have welcomed them publically, but everyone understood they were on probation. There'd be no sharing of secrets tonight, but then, he hadn't expected anything else. Vampire politics was a long game. Maybe it was because they lived for centuries, and so thought in years instead of days. Or maybe they simply liked to watch their prey twist in the wind. But Quinn had always planned on taking a few weeks to learn everything he needed to know, before he could challenge Sorley. Now that he was here, however, he found he had no tolerance for the long game. He was a disciplined man, but not a patient one. He figured a month at most before he lost what little patience he possessed and decided to confront Sorley and be done with it.

For now, they'd have to mingle with Sorley's inner circle, which the Howth acquisition would help him do. After all, Quinn couldn't kill every single vampire in Dublin. When Ireland became his, he'd need at least some of them to run his new territory. Vampires tended to be practical about such matters, switching their loyalty to whichever vampire provided the strength and protection they needed to go about their lives. Only those most loyal to Sorley would have to be eliminated, and they were as likely to die in the final battle, trying to defend him.

But Quinn wasn't quite ready to play Sorley's happy underling, yet. It was partly why he'd chosen Howth as his first conquest. It gave him access, but also distance and a semblance of independence. No need to kiss the ring nightly as long as he was well away from Dublin. At least as far as Sorley knew.

Before long, he and Garrick said their farewells, then retrieved the SUV keys, carefully scanning the guard's mind to be certain there'd be no unpleasant surprises. They finally made it out the front door and were just sucking in a breath of fresh air, when Quinn caught a flash of red hair disappearing along the side of the house.

He froze. Then shook his head. Impossible. How could Eve have snuck her way into Lord Sorley's lair? Sure, he and Garrick had managed, but they were vampires. She was . . . Oh fuck, she was a beautiful woman. He wondered how closely Sorley's guards had screened the "food" they'd brought in for the night, and knew the answer. Not very well.

"Wait here," he told Garrick and took off.

It didn't take long to find her. But then, she wasn't exactly hiding. She was cozied up to one of Sorley's white-collar people, a vampire who, if Quinn recalled correctly, was some sort of accountant who'd been thrilled to be invited to the night's soiree. He sure as hell didn't deserve to meet the same end as those two thugs in Howth.

He strode up to the couple and caught the vampire's attention. "Get lost," he snarled, putting a punch of power into it. It didn't take much. The vampire might be a financial genius, which made him valuable, but he had no power to speak of. Hell, he was about to be seduced by a human female. Clearly no one had taught him that it was the *vampire* who did the seducing.

The vamp's eyes gleamed briefly red, before widening in recognition. He'd been in the room for Quinn and Sorley's little sit-down. His hands came up, and he backed away several steps, before spinning about and rapidly disappearing around the back of the house.

Eve turned with a snarl that was far more vampiric than her retreating prey . . . until she saw who it was. "You," she said, giving him a confused look. "What are you doing here?"

"Yeah, that's *my* question, sweetheart. I was invited. How about you?"

"I was dinner," she answered, sounding a little defensive as she brushed her top off with nervous little jerks. She looked up suddenly and gave him a narrow look. "Wait. Why were *you* invited? You're not their usual taste."

"Cute. I'm here to negotiate a business deal with Orrin Sorley."

"Business? What kind of business?"

"None of *your* business, that's what kind."

She stared at him. "Do you know what he is? What he does?"

"Yeah, do you?"

"Obviously better than *you.*"

"I doubt that."

"Oh, really," she said. "What are you? Some kind of vamp lover?"

"I'm going to pretend I didn't hear that," he said darkly. Hooking a hand around her arm, he hustled her out to the yard where Garrick was waiting. "Look what I found," he said, meeting his cousin's curious gaze. "This is Eve. I walked her home the other night. In *Howth*."

Garrick's gaze sharpened knowingly. "Small world," he commented, then turned to Eve with a welcoming smile. "Nice to meet you, Eve. I'm Garrick, by the way, though my rude cousin didn't bother to introduce us."

Eve's entire body language changed in an instant. She was all sweetness and light as she gave Garrick a polite smile and held out a hand. "A pleasure."

"Yeah, lots of pleasure all around," Quinn said sourly. "How'd you get here, Eve?"

She exchanged a commiserating look with Garrick, as if to say they both had to put up with this rude asshole, then turned to Quinn. "Not that it's your concern, but I took the train."

"Fine. You can ride back with us." He hooked her arm, but she jerked it away.

"I have business in Dublin, and I'm not finished."

"Sure you are. The party's over." He didn't grab her arm again. He wasn't a fool or a brute. But he used his much bigger body to get her moving in the right direction.

She turned on him with a furious hiss, and he felt the sharp sting of a blade against his abdomen. He looked down in amazement at the small knife she was already disappearing into a hidden sheath between her thighs. "Did you just draw a knife on me? What the fuck, Eve?"

"It's been a long night, and I'm tired of being manhandled," she muttered.

"Come on, then," Garrick interrupted cheerfully, ignoring their hostile interaction. "It's far too late for a lovely woman like yourself to be taking the train alone, and we've plenty of room. Idiot Americans, you know. We got the biggest vehicle we could find. Totally impractical on these narrow Irish roads, but I'm a good driver. Honest."

Eve's eyes flashed a warning at Quinn, but she turned to Garrick with another smile. "You're a sweetheart to worry," she said, laying on the Irish brogue. "And me a girl you've barely met. You're much nicer than the rumors say."

"Rumors?" Garrick repeated. "There're rumors about me?"

She laughed right on cue. The Eve and Garrick Show. *What a hoot*, Quinn thought sourly, as he followed the happy couple through the gates and onto the street. Realizing he didn't know where the SUV was parked, he followed his own earlier suggestion to Sorley's vamps and pressed the key fob, following the sound of the beep to where the guards had parked almost directly in front of the house. It was an oddly reassuring location. If they'd planted a bomb inside, they'd have moved it farther away.

"Keys," he said, and tossed them to Garrick, who turned just in time for the catch, as Quinn had known he would. Vampire reflexes. "You drive, since you're so *good* at it."

Garrick grinned and went ahead to the driver's side, while Eve dropped back next to Quinn. "Seriously, Quinn," she whispered as they walked around to the other side of the SUV. "These are dangerous people you're dealing with."

"Yeah, I'm aware of that, Eve. It's kind of what I do."

"What do you mean? Are you mafia or something?"

Quinn laughed. "Mafia? You've been watching too many movies. I'm a lawyer."

"Even worse," she muttered.

"Oh, ha ha. I've never heard that one before."

"I wasn't joking."

He pulled open the back door of the SUV. "Get in."

"Why can't I ride up front?"

"Because I'm riding there. Come on, Eve. It's late."

"Obviously, you're the *old* cousin," she said snippily and climbed into the backseat with a flash of pale leg.

Garrick snickered, earning a glare from Quinn that promised payback . . . and had no effect whatsoever. Clearly he was going to have to work on his vampire lord mojo, because it was failing miserably with these two.

THE RIDE BACK TO Howth was a silent one. Eve was regretting the snap decision to lie about how she'd gotten to Dublin. Her only thought at the time had been to give away as little as possible about her investigation, which, by the way, Quinn had completely ruined. She was still fuming about that. She hadn't believed her luck when she'd realized that the vampire she'd been hustling inside the party was some big money manager for Sorley. Vampires were no different than anyone else when it came to money, especially ill-gotten money, the kind that came from smuggling and who knew what other filthy endeavors. She'd thought to seduce, or threaten, enough information from Sorley's accountant to disrupt the flow of his cash. She was no super computer genius, but she had some skill. More importantly, she also had a close friend from all the way back in primary school, who now worked for a major financial firm on the Isle of Man. One who was always willing to help a friend out for a small fee. A very small fee in Eve's case, since the two of them had raised hell together back in the day.

She'd been well on her way to gaining exactly the info she needed when super-Quinn *rescued* her. Or maybe he'd been rescuing the vampire *from* her. Either way, he'd destroyed her best chance yet to fuck with Sorley and his vampire empire. She'd actually held out hope that she could still salvage the night once she got rid of Quinn. The party had still been going strong, and while the accountant was probably running for his life, thanks to a certain interfering busybody, there were still plenty of other vamps she could hustle for information, building on what little she'd gleaned before Quinn interfered.

It hadn't even occurred to her that Quinn would offer her a ride back to Howth, or that he'd be so insistent she take it. She shouldn't have been surprised, though. He might be irritating with his attempts at controlling her, but he didn't do any of it just to be an asshole. Everything he'd done so far had been to protect her, to keep her safe. It had been a long time since anyone cared enough to worry about her. It made her want to like him, to worry about him, in turn. It also left her in a bit of a pickle. She'd either had to admit she'd lied about her car—and why the hell had she lied?—or accept the stupid ride and take the damn train back to Dublin.

Which was how she came to be stuck in the backseat with an uncommunicative Quinn sitting in front of her. The few questions she asked, mostly about Quinn's business and what had brought the two of them to Dublin, were met with few words and cool silence. He didn't seem like the criminal type, but what did she know? He was a lawyer, and everyone knew they were sneaky at best, outright criminals at worst. Garrick seemed like a nice sort, but whatever relationship the two men had, it was obvious that Quinn was the one making the decisions. She studied his profile by the dash lights of the big SUV. Garrick was friendlier and much easier to get along with, but it was Quinn who intrigued her. She'd always been drawn to demanding men, and God knew Quinn fit *that* bill. The cranky bastard. Besides, he was so big and fit. And strikingly handsome, even more so now that she had a chance to study him at leisure. When they'd first met the other night, she'd been more concerned with getting rid of him before he realized she'd just killed two vampires.

But now that she'd run into him again—at Orrin Sorley's house, of all places—she was worried about him. Worried *for* him. He didn't seem to realize whom he was dealing with in Orrin Sorley. Didn't understand *what* he was dealing with, the monster that Sorley truly was. There were few things and fewer people that she truly cared about anymore. But, for some reason, she felt the need to warn Quinn. He probably wouldn't listen, but she had to try.

She glanced out the window, surprised at the sight of familiar landmarks. She had to admit that riding back to Howth was a lot nicer in the big SUV than in her small sedan. Or maybe it was just having someone else doing the driving. She wasn't used to watching the scenery go by.

Garrick drove them to a house in one of Howth's nicer neighborhoods, an area of big homes with walled-in yards. It was smaller than Sorley's place back in Dublin, but still large by Howth standards. He pulled through the open gate and stopped. Both men climbed out, with Quinn stepping back to open her door for her, as well.

"What's this?" she said, frowning. Did they think she was going to join them in some kind of three-way free-for-all? Because that wasn't going to happen.

"I'm going to drive you home. I assumed you'd rather switch seats to ride in front, but you can stay back there if you'd like."

She scowled at the snide comment, but accepted his proffered hand as she climbed down from the SUV. It was too high, though she'd have been fine if not for the damn Miu-Miu stilettos which she'd worn solely to lure one of Sorley's vampires—a mission that Quinn had neatly sabotaged with his interfering ways. She lifted one high-heeled foot to the running board below the front passenger seat, trying not to flash Quinn in the process. But before she could do anything else, he caught her around the waist and lifted her onto the seat, as if she weighed nothing. Her heart did that flutter thing again, in appreciation of his strength and gentlemanly ways. Stupid heart. He hadn't lifted her to be a gentleman. He'd done it because she was taking too long, and he was in a hurry to get rid of her.

"Thank you," she said nicely. Just because he was churlish, that didn't mean she had to be. But then she remembered her earlier determination to warn him about Sorley and sighed. This could be her only chance for a private conversation. He might not listen, or he might brush off her concerns as craziness. But at least she could sleep at night knowing she'd tried. Well, at least as well as she ever did. She didn't sleep much after dark, too aware that any day the vampires might figure out what she was doing and come after her. She had no illusions about the odds of her survival in that case.

She waited until they'd left Quinn's neighborhood behind, with the lights of the harbor shining on their left, then said, "How about a drink?"

QUINN'S EYEBROWS arched in surprise at Eve's offer. She was up to something. She'd been cool all the way home, talking mostly to Garrick, and now, suddenly, she wanted to stop for a drink? Maybe she'd figured out he was a vampire and was plotting his demise. He wasn't worried she'd succeed, but he was curious enough to indulge her.

"Sure," he said evenly. "What's open this time of night?"

She directed him to a small, crowded pub on a side street that he hadn't even known existed. He and Garrick really should get to know the ins and outs of Howth. They'd be moving to Dublin very soon, but he'd have people staying in Howth to oversee the smuggling operation. It couldn't hurt for him to know the town better.

"Where do I park?" he asked her. The streets in this area were old and narrow, and he didn't see any signs.

"Park in front of any of the closed storefronts. There's no one to mind, and by the time they're ready to open, we'll be long gone."

Quinn figured she knew the customs, and police patrols, better than he did. And now that they were closer to the pub, he saw more than one vehicle doing exactly what Eve had suggested. He found an empty spot a block down and around a corner. Turning off the engine, he slid out from behind the wheel, then headed around the front of the SUV to help Eve out. But she jumped down before he could get there.

"You'll break an ankle doing that in those heels."

She grinned up at him. "They look good, though, don't they?"

He met her dark eyes and said with deliberate intent, "Very good." He was close enough to see her blush when she registered the double meaning in his words, hearing the compliment on more than just her shoes. Between the very short skirt and *very* high heels, she was showing off plenty of pale skin and silky smooth legs. It made him want to spread her out and sink his fangs into her thigh, while his fingers slid into the heat of her pussy, so he could feel the contractions of her body when his bite hit her nervous system. He'd fuck her after that, forcing his cock into her tight, tight body, feeling her resistance soften until she was moaning his name.

Quinn stopped himself from going any further with his fantasy. His cock was already hard and heavy, pushing at the thick fabric of his jeans almost painfully. And the more he thought about her firm thighs and luscious pussy, the more he wanted to throw caution to the wind and simply fuck her.

He reeled it in when they walked into the bar, especially when he realized there were vampires inside. Not everyone was one, not even most. This wasn't a blood house. But there were enough vampires that he knew this was a regular drinking spot for them. He stayed close to Eve, resting on a possessive hand on her lower back, just enough to make his claim clear to the other vamps, but not enough to provoke a response from his prickly redhead.

But because these were vampires who didn't know him, he also had to shut down every vamp who thought to challenge him, meeting their glares and giving them the smallest taste of his power. Whether they knew it or not, this was *his* sector now. Sorley had made it official, but it was his personal power that would make it work. Vampires led from strength, not nepotism or bureaucratic maneuvering. Every vampire he met in this new territory would test his power in one way or another. Most would be subtle, like those in this pub. They'd touch their power to his and immediately look away, acknowledging his superior strength and, thereby, his authority. A very few tried to hold his stare, but they, too, surrendered when his eyes went cold and his power grazed their hearts. Quinn made note of those, knowing he'd have to watch his back over the next few days and weeks. But first, he had a sexy woman to charm.

Eve grabbed a vacant bar stool and climbed up, smiling when she caught him looking. Quinn shrugged. He was a leg man, always had been. Sure, the neck had its advantages for a vampire, especially when you were buried deep in a woman's body. But nothing beat sinking fang into the femoral artery of a tender thigh. He remained standing while Eve swung her legs demurely beneath the bar. Right. *Now*, she was a delicate maiden. An hour ago, she'd been hustling vampires to kill.

Quinn boxed her in with one arm on the back of her stool, the other on the bar. He leaned closer, drawn by the delicate trace of her perfume, and underneath it, the delicious scent of warm blood. He wanted to lick her neck, to feel the rush of blood through her veins while her heart raced at his touch. He was hungry, he realized abruptly. Probably too hungry to be toying with Eve, especially since she didn't yet know he was a vampire. But while her blood was temptation itself, he was no ordinary vampire, not a slave to his body's desires. He was a vampire lord, with the power and discipline to do whatever it took to protect his people. Maintaining a mask of humanity tested his lust more than his strength. He *wanted* Eve Connelly, but he needed to know why she was killing his kind, and, especially, if someone had put her up to it. Needed to know if there were other hunters like her stalking Irish vampires, or training to do so. Until then, as far as Eve was concerned, he had to be just another human hustling a beautiful woman.

He drew the attention of the bartender and ordered a couple of pints, his with a side shot of Irish whiskey. Drunk straight up, he preferred scotch whiskey, but the lighter Irish sweetened a pint of ale nicely.

He raised his mug in Eve's direction. "To Dublin," he said, wanting to get her talking. She was so set on warning him away from Sorley and from vampires in general. He wanted to know why. He'd have to come up with a permanent solution for her eventually. She'd either have to stop hunting on her own, or he'd have to use his power to *persuade* her. He couldn't have a vampire vigilante roaming his new territory. But there was no reason he couldn't enjoy the time he spent squeezing information out of her. He didn't fool himself into thinking his interest was purely business, however. He was curious about her personally. Not only because she was sexy as hell, but because she'd somehow found the courage and the *strength* to take on much bigger vampires and come out on top. Yeah, it bothered him that she was killing his people, but it was remarkable that she hadn't been fucked the first time she'd tried. Literally fucked and sucked dry.

The woman and the hunter both intrigued him, and he couldn't have said which one captivated him more.

"So," he said quietly, his mouth against her ear in the noisy pub. "Vampires, huh?"

His lips warmed against her skin, and she moved away, before turning back to him with a defiant glare.

"They're real, and your friend Sorley is the head of them in Ireland."

"Softly, Eve," he cautioned, aware of the vampire ears listening. "How do you know so much about vampires?"

"Because I've seen them kill," she snarled, suddenly all flashing eyes and fury.

Quinn was intrigued by the raw emotion of her reaction. This wasn't a job for her, it was personal. But just in case, he asked, "Are you a reporter looking to break the big story?"

"Hardly," she snorted and took a sip of her ale.

"Well, you're obviously not a fan, so why hang around Sorley's place then? Why put yourself at risk like that?"

She was silent for a long moment, staring down at her finger rubbing away the wet circle left on the bar by her glass, and he thought she wasn't going to answer. But then she said so softly that he could barely hear, "Vampires killed someone I loved."

He studied her bent head. She still hadn't looked up. "Someone?" he asked leadingly.

She bit the inside of her lip, then glanced up at him and back down. "My brother, Alan."

"How do you know—" he asked, but she interrupted angrily.

"I saw them, all right? Two of them. I was meeting Alan down near the port in Dublin and . . . I saw them," she finished, almost wearily, as if she'd used up all of her anger.

Shit. No wonder she hated vampires. Quinn moved in closer, kissing the top of her head and resting his cheek there briefly, while dropping his arm from the bar stool to her back. "I'm sorry that happened, Eve. I'm even sorrier you had to see it."

She was quiet for a minute, then straightened abruptly, shoving off his arm to swing around to stare at him, her eyes wide in sudden suspicion. "Damn. You already know about Sorley, don't you? Here I was, all worried about you getting in deeper than you knew, but you've known all along what he was." Her mug slammed onto the bar top. "And you're doing business with him anyway," she said, her voice getting louder. "Why?"

Quinn held up a hand, once again urging her to remain quiet. There were too many vampires in this bar, and the fact that she didn't seem to recognize their presence made him wonder even more how she'd managed to stay alive. "Softly, lass," he murmured. "If what you say is true, you might not want to advertise your intentions." As long as he was with her, she was safe. No one but Sorley himself would dare challenge him by harming a woman he'd claimed publically. But he couldn't be with her all the time, and, besides, he hadn't truly claimed her. Yet.

She glared at him, but lowered her voice to an angry whisper. "Answer the question, then. Why do business with a bloody vampire?"

He shrugged. "You said it yourself. He's a big man in Ireland, and he controls far more than just vampires. Or maybe I should say vampires control altogether more than you think. There are certain . . . transactions in this country that go more smoothly if they're involved."

"Oh, right. You're a lawyer. You're used to working with scum."

"I think you've *definitely* been watching too many American movies."

"Not when you're sitting there defending doing business with vampires." Her eyes narrowed. "Wait. Are you one of them?"

He laughed. "I'd hardly tell *you* if I was. You'd pull that pretty knife you've got hiding between your thighs and murder me in my sleep."

Her eyes narrowed in irritation, probably wondering how he'd known where she'd hidden the knife. "Who said anything about sleeping?"

He met her eyes bluntly. "I did," he said, then grinned. "I'm a strong man, Eve, but even I can't keep it up all night long."

She sucked in a scowling breath, but didn't pull away when he bent his head to kiss her. Her lips were full and soft, and pressed determinedly together, her mouth closed. Quinn chuckled and kissed her again, teasing that firm mouth with feathering kisses, his tongue barely touching as he outlined the seam of her lips. His arm tightened around her back, his hand pressing her closer until he could feel the warm weight of her breast against his side.

He trailed a row of nibbling kisses over her soft cheek to her ear. "Kiss me, Eve," he whispered, and then followed the curve of her jaw back to her mouth. She shivered as her chin lifted and her lips opened on a tremulous sigh. Quinn slid his tongue into her warm mouth, hearing her soft moan of pleasure when her tongue wrapped around his.

Sparks flew. Quinn had never felt anything like it. He *hungered* for this woman. Not for her blood, although he knew it would be delectable. But for her body. He wanted to be inside her, wanted to possess her in a way that she'd never forget. Wanted every man who came after him to pale in comparison.

"Eve," he growled.

"Yes." She grabbed his hand and slipped off the bar stool. He barely managed to leave some money for the drinks, before she tugged him through the crowd and back onto the street. "Leave the car where it is. The shops are closed on Sunday."

Quinn blinked. He hadn't been keeping much track of the days. It didn't matter what day tomorrow was, anyway, because he'd be long gone before sunrise. But she didn't need to know that.

"Is your flat close?" he asked, pretending he didn't know exactly where they were. He'd studied the maps before coming to Ireland, and he'd studied them in even more detail since he'd been here. He'd also possessed an innate sense of direction, and always knew where he was relative to where he wanted to be. Which, in the immediate case, was in Eve's bed.

"Just around the block," she said, then gave him a condescending glance. "Think you can walk that far?"

Quinn wrapped an arm around her waist and lifted her off her feet, walking forward until she was pressed against the wall of a shuttered store. She needed to learn the dangers of baiting him too far. "Sweetheart," he said, bending to put his mouth against hers. "I could walk that far and carry you with me." And then he kissed her. There was no more gentle persuasion, no coaxing her lips open. His fingers tangled in her hair and pulled her head back as he leaned in, pressing his hard chest against her breasts, covering her mouth with a deep, slow kiss that promised all sorts of dark, erotic pleasures. His lips were sealed against her mouth, his tongue stabbing between her teeth and twisting around hers, as she strained upward wanting more. Quinn was tempted to taste her, just a small nip of her tender lip. But it was too soon for that. If he tasted her now, he'd want more when they finally fucked. He'd want to feed. Reminding himself that he wanted his true nature to remain a secret for now, he pulled back, ending the kiss with a sensuous flourish of his tongue that left her breathless when he finally released her, sliding her down the full length of his body until she stood unsteadily on her sexy heels.

Quinn wanted to laugh, but settled for a grin as she gripped his arms, her breath coming in short gasps and her heart pounding.

"Do you need me to carry you?" He couldn't resist the teasing question, which got him a narrow-eyed look that lacked her usual fire. He bent down and kissed her lips gently. "Come on, baby, I'll walk you home."

She sighed and took his hand, leaning into him as they turned the corner onto her street, not even seeming to notice that he hadn't needed her to tell him the way. By the time they reached her flat, she'd caught her breath and was no longer relying on him for support. So much so that Quinn wondered if she was going to invite him in, or if she was having second thoughts.

But she never let go of his hand as she unlocked the door, then turned and gazed up at him through her thick lashes. "You want to come in?" she asked, her fingers squeezing his in unconscious nervousness.

He pulled her closer, wrapping their joined hands around the small of her back, as he met her eyes and said softly, "I'd like that."

She blushed and tugged him over the threshold. "Come on, then."

It was all the invitation he needed to follow her into the small room. Eve let go of his hand to close and lock the door, then turned to face him. The room was lit by only a single small lamp, but he could see the gold lights in her red hair, the gleam of her dark eyes . . . and the desire when she looked at him. She backed away, dropping layers of clothing as she went.

He didn't move, simply watched her slow striptease as she continued backing toward a bed in the far corner. He glanced over as her jacket fell to the floor. It wasn't a very big bed, but it would do. His gaze slid back as she pulled her sweater over her head, baring a black lace bra that barely managed to contain the swell of her breasts. "Fuck. Me," he whispered. The outfit was pure seduction, he realized, and anger swelled, quickly replaced by fear for her safety. Had she dressed like that to better seduce the vampires she intended to kill? It was a dangerous gamble. It would be only a matter of time before her luck ran out and she was the one killed instead.

"Eve," he said, intending to warn her, but the look in her eyes stopped him.

"Not tonight, Quinn," she murmured and flicked the clasp on her bra with one hand. Her breasts were full and creamy smooth, with round, pink areolas and large nipples that stood hard and aroused, begging to be sucked.

"Christ." He was on her in two long strides, taking her mouth, feeling the crush of her bare breasts against his chest. Wanting to be skin to skin, he let her go long enough to rip his long-sleeved T-shirt over his head, then yanked her back against him, lifting her off her feet to take her mouth in a searing kiss. He demanded and she responded, opening her mouth, kissing him as hungrily as he kissed her, their teeth clashing, biting, until he tasted the first drop of her blood when her lip split. He groaned, a deep sound from his gut, as his fangs pushed against his gums, craving release. He wanted to bite her, he *lusted* after her blood. But she'd run screaming if he bit her, and he wanted her body nearly as badly. With the kind of willpower that it took to be a vampire lord, he forced his fangs back into his gums and, skimming his lips over her neck, lowered his mouth to her chest. Closing his teeth over her clavicle, he felt the delicate bones beneath her skin. So fragile. He could shatter them with a single bite. His teeth only grazed, leaving a mark without breaking the skin. Another taste of her blood would test his control too harshly. Moving downward, he took one nipple into his mouth, sucking gently at first, his tongue circling round and round, until the already firm pearl was hard and pulsing with blood. It was one more temptation that had him growling as he switched to the other breast, giving that nipple the same treatment while he continued to pinch the first into aching tenderness, hearing Eve's groan as her fingers clenched in his hair. Over and over, she cried out, hungry little moans that made his cock pulse with desire.

Her hands left his hair to tug at the rest of her clothing, searching for the zipper on her short skirt. But Quinn couldn't wait. Sliding his hands up her thighs, he shoved her skirt to her waist and removed the tiny knife she'd secured to her thigh, ripping away the silky black panties that were all she had on underneath. He felt a renewed surge of rage that she'd gone hunting some other vampire in those tiny panties, and with nothing but a fucking pocket knife for defense. His anger was quickly forgotten, however, replaced with lust as his need surged. He took a step forward and threw her on the bed, coming down between her thighs, spreading them wide with his hips as he reached down to lower his zipper and free himself. Her pussy was warm and wet, slick with arousal, as he slid the tip of his cock back and forth between her swollen lips, making sure she was ready for him.

"Do it," she whispered, reaching down to grasp his erection, lifting her hips to urge him inside.

Quinn snarled and yanked her hand away, stretching both her arms over her head and holding them there with one big hand around her slender wrists. She fought him, but his eyes met hers in a flat stare. Something she saw there made her own gaze soften, even as she gritted her teeth and said, "Get on with it then."

Quinn's teeth bared in a vicious grin. His eyes never leaving hers, he flexed his hips and slammed his cock into her body in a single stroke, not stopping until his balls slapped her ass, until he heard her scream of shocked pleasure. He held himself there for a moment, feeling her tissues tremble around him as they adjusted to his thickness, to the hard length of him. She drew a shuddering breath and licked her lips. Quinn leaned down and sucked her tongue into his mouth, kissing her slowly as he began to move, withdrawing an inch, then pushing back inside her. Doing this over and over until her tight sheath relaxed its hold on him, and Eve began make those soft, little moaning sounds again. Desire overwhelmed him as he lifted himself up, pulling his cock nearly all the way out, until only the tip could feel the wet heat of her, and then driving deep inside her again with a powerful thrust that lifted her from the bed. She moaned hungrily, her legs tightening around his waist, her hips lifting to meet his every downward thrust as he reveled in the slick heat of her pussy. He lowered his head to claim her mouth as he plunged in and out, driven by a desire he'd never felt before, wanting to claim her, to mark her as his before vampire and man alike.

When he felt his climax building, felt the tightening in his balls that told him he wouldn't be able to hold back much longer, he reached between their bodies and found the hard nub of her clit, swollen and throbbing with blood. If she'd known he was a vampire, if he'd have been free to take her the way he wanted, he'd have sunk his fangs into her neck at that moment and let the euphoric in his bite send her into a screaming climax. Instead, he rubbed the bundle of nerves between the lips of her sex, slick with arousal as he stroked it against the rough skin of his finger and thumb, until he felt it pulsing against his hold, and then he pinched, grinding it hard as Eve screamed, her hips bucking against his, her back bowed as he slammed himself deep into her pussy and stayed there, feeling his cock jerk as his release flooded her body, holding her tight against his chest as her nails dug into his shoulders.

EVE STRUGGLED TO breathe as Quinn's full weight collapsed on top of her. She wanted to say something. She *should* say something. But instead, she wrapped her arms around him and held him close, her heart sinking. She was in so much trouble here. She'd thought it would be just sex between them. God knew he had that covered. He was the sexiest, most fuckable man she'd ever met. She'd almost hoped he'd be a lousy lover, but, no. He was a fucking *fantastic* lover. He was also too smart for his own good, and sometimes even funny. And very protective, in that sexist way that assumed the man always knew what was best. He was a good guy, a nice guy. But she had a feeling he wasn't a good man. Still, that didn't seem to matter, because her poor, stupid heart was all warm and fluttery, already half in love with a man who did business with vampires. How could this happen? Her whole life lately was dedicated to getting rid of the worst of those monsters. She sighed. Quinn took it as a plea for air and immediately lifted his body off hers, rolling to one side and pulling her on top of him instead. Not only a great lover, but a considerate one. Damn him.

"Ow." It was a deep grumble as one long arm reached down and gripped her leg to stop it from moving.

"What?" she asked, and then realized she was still wearing her designer Mary Janes with their sharp, stiletto heels. "Oops." She sat up and began unbuckling the first strap. "It's your fault. You're the one who attacked without letting me get properly undressed."

"I seem to recall you joining in rather vigorously. Screaming was involved. And I'm fairly certain there's blood running down my back," he purred smoothly, his pale blue eyes half-closed as he stared down at her.

Eve shivered with remembered pleasure, heat spreading from her cheeks to her chest. She turned her face away, focusing instead on the other shoe, only to realize she was still wearing her skirt bunched up around her waist. Blushing all over again, she shimmied out of the barelythere piece of clothing, then didn't know what to do. Should she lie back down on top of him, where he'd put her? Or maybe just stretch out on her belly next to him? That would hide her sexy bits from his too-familiar gaze. But it was a bit late to be shy, wasn't it?

"Come here," he growled, deciding for her, as he first pulled her up onto his chest and then rolled her beneath him. "I'm not finished with you."

Eve felt the hard length of his penis against her thigh and her eyes went wide. She wasn't exactly experienced, but she'd been with more than one man, and none of them had recovered this quickly. Not even close. She was still digesting that fact when Quinn's cock slid easily between her arousal-drenched lips and deep into her body.

IT WAS NEARLY dawn when Quinn tucked an exhausted and very well sated Eve beneath the covers on her bed. She grumbled softly, but didn't wake, one hand reaching to hug her pillow more firmly against her chest. He stroked her soft cheek with the back of his fingers, tempted to do more. But it was late, and he didn't want to wake her. Didn't want to explain that he had to leave, had to get back to the safety of the house he shared with Garrick, before the rising sun stole his awareness.

He let himself out, making sure to lock the door securely behind, then used his vampire speed to race the short distance to where the Range Rover was parked. The drive back to the house was an exercise in control as he sped along the narrow streets, pulling into the yard just as the first light of dawn pinked the sky. Quinn had been a vampire for 57 years, a long time in a human life span, but still young for a vampire. His power gave him an edge against the sunrise, enough that *someday* he'd be able to remain conscious until the sun itself broke the horizon, but not yet.

Garrick had the door open, waiting for him with a grim look on his face. "Too close," he said harshly.

"I know," Quinn said, striding inside. "Go ahead, you can lecture me later." Garrick's resistance to the sun's rising was even less than Quinn's, and he was already stumbling as he made his way down the hall. Quinn watched his cousin go, as he secured the three locks they'd installed on the front door, knowing Garrick would have already checked the safety of the other entrances in anticipation of Quinn's arrival. That done, he hurried to the interior room they'd set up as their daytime resting place. It held two beds, a table, and a lamp, but nothing else. They didn't need anything else. When a vampire slept, he had no perception of the world around him. Nothing would wake him until the sun set. Nothing.

Garrick was already out, sprawled bonelessly on the opposite bed. Quinn pulled a comforter up over his cousin, then turned and stripped quickly—he hated waking up in the same clothes—and climbed into bed, pulling his own blankets up. He wouldn't feel the cold when he slept, but he sure as hell would when he woke.

He thought of Eve, all tousled and pink in her warm bed, and smiled as the sun took him for the day.

EVE WAS DREAMING. She and her brother, Alan, were having a picnic in Phoenix Park, sitting on the same old blanket they always used, eating sandwiches and crisps, laughing at the antics of a pair of Frisbee-catching dogs down the grassy hill. It was a beautiful day in Dublin, with blue skies and a sun so warm that she wished for the sunblock she'd left in the car. Alan applauded a particularly skilled catch by one of the dogs, then rolled over and sat up, his arms linked over his knees, his head cocked and brown eyes serious as he studied her.

He was a handsome man, her brother. Especially when he was relaxed like this, with his muscled arms bare and broad shoulders flexing beneath his T-shirt every time a pretty girl walked by on the path beside them. Eve smiled.

"You look good, Eve. It's been too long."

"Too long since what?" she asked around a yawn. The sunshine always made her drowsy.

"Too long since you looked the way you should . . . young, pretty, free."

Eve's chest constricted abruptly, as if someone was squeezing her. A cloud rolled over the sun, and she shivered, staring at her brother. "What do you mean?" she whispered, needing to ask, but not wanting to know.

"You weren't meant for this, love. It wasn't your fault, it was mine. I knew what I was getting into. I knew the risks."

Eve shook her head violently, her long hair flying as she closed her eyes, rejecting what he was saying. She didn't want to talk about that. She wanted the sun, the laughing children, the silly dogs.

"Stop, baby girl. Before it's too late. I never wanted this for you. Stop and be happy."

Everything began to pale as the dream faded. Eve cried out, reaching for his hand, not ready for their time to be over. When she woke, she was alone, with the pale light of a winter's morning adding to the chill of her small flat. Tears flooded her eyes unbidden, soaking the pillow she clutched to her face to muffle the sobs, until she drifted back to sleep.

Chapter Five

QUINN WOKE THAT night with one thought. He and Garrick needed a bigger house, if for no other reason than that he needed a *fucking* bigger bed. Not because he moved around a lot during the day—he didn't, no vampire did—but because he practically fell out of the narrow bed when he rolled over after waking up at sunset.

He caught himself before falling—vampire reflexes were good for many things—and sat up, shivering slightly. The rental house was damn cold. It had been completely renovated, including a new HVAC system, but the best heater in the world couldn't make up for thick stone walls and floors which seemed to hold on to the cold and damp no matter how much energy went into warming them. They were probably great on hot summer days, but he and his cousin would be long gone by then, moved into the new house in Dublin and ruling the territory.

Assuming they weren't dead.

On that cheery note, he headed for the shower. Garrick was still out, but he'd be waking soon. They'd been turned within only a few weeks of each other, but Quinn's greater power gave him the ability to endure more of the sun's presence at both ends of the night. It was a strength that would only grow as he aged.

He turned on the shower, letting it run to warm the bathroom before stepping inside. The hot water pummeled his sore muscles. He liked to think he was in good shape—hell, he was in *great* shape—but he hadn't exactly trained for hefting crates filled with weapons in and out of cars. Not to mention, hours of vigorous sex in a too-small bed. He was beginning to sense a theme to his life, having to do with small beds. He grinned to himself, feeling good despite the sore muscles and small beds. The sex had been great. Eve was beautiful, but he'd learned a long time ago that beauty didn't equal sensuality. He'd suspected since meeting her, however, that underneath that angry exterior was a lushly sensuous woman, and he'd been right.

He frowned, reminded of the anger that had her risking her life to kill vampires. That doused his good humor faster than a cold shower.

Quinn didn't make a habit of lying to his sexual partners. Most of the women he'd met since he'd become a vampire had known what he was from the moment they'd met. Hell, he'd met most of them in one blood house or another. People—women and men both—came to those places for one reason only. They wanted to fuck a vampire, which meant they eagerly offered a vein. It was an easy dinner for the vamp, with a side of hot, casual sex. No explanations or apologies necessary. But the women Quinn had sucked and fucked in the past always knew exactly what they were getting. Eve didn't. In fact, if she'd known, she'd have stabbed him with that wicked knife of hers instead of taking him to her bed.

He stepped out of the shower, grimacing at the thought of Eve's reaction when she discovered the truth. He didn't even consider not telling her. He wasn't that big of an asshole. The only way that would work was if he never saw her again, and he found himself surprisingly reluctant to accept that outcome. He told himself it was only because he still needed to uncover the truth behind her killing spree, but just as he'd always been honest with his sexual partners, he was honest with himself, too. If all he'd wanted from Eve was to uncover her secrets, he could have had that already. He possessed a vampire lord's skill when it came to telepathy. Of course, the deeper he probed, the harder he had to push, and the greater the potential for irreparable damage. He had a feeling Eve would require a lot of pushing, but it would take him no more than a few minutes to have her telling him everything he wanted to know. Even if he managed to avoiding harming her, though, he couldn't do it. If she ever realized what he'd done, she'd hate his guts and never trust him.

And he didn't want that with Eve, damn it.

He walked into his bedroom, which was separate from the smaller one where he and Garrick slept, and began to dress. He heard the shower come on as his cousin rose for the night. Stomping his feet into heavy duty boots, he tied them off and headed for the kitchen.

The coffee was on a timer, already brewed. Most renters might have been turned off by the small kitchen, especially if they had a family, but it was perfect for a pair of repatriated vampires. He drew in the delicious coffee scent, but went to the refrigerator first and pulled out a bag of cold blood, running it briefly under a stream of hot water, to take the worst of the chill off. The microwave would be faster, but it also destroyed the nutritional value for vampires. Normally, he'd let the blood sit in the hot water for at least twenty minutes, but he had no patience for that tonight. Drying the bag with a towel, he popped the valve and drank it down, tossing the empty bag into the trash. He then poured a cup of coffee and drank half of it to remove the taste of cold blood from his mouth, thinking about how sweet Eve's blood would taste instead. Cursing himself for obsessing over the one woman he couldn't feed from, he pulled over his laptop and began his nightly scan of the financial news. His legal work had all been in corporate litigation, which meant he'd had to be as knowledgeable in finance as he was in corporate law. That experience was serving him well now that he was on the verge of ruling a territory. Vampires were involved in all kinds of businesses, most of which were legal, despite Sorley's preference for criminal pursuits. Most vampire lords collected tithes from the various businesses under their rule, in return for their protection and, frequently, their financial backing. It was relatively common for a vampire lord to sit on the board of the larger businesses in his territory. That being the case, Quinn had made a study of the Irish economy and financial laws before undertaking to seize the territory, not to mention staying up to date on trends in the European financial markets.

He was checking one of his several portfolios when he heard Garrick's heavy footsteps coming down the hall. He grimaced, knowing what his cousin would have to say about the whole Eve situation, especially with Quinn cutting his return so close this morning.

Garrick went directly to the coffee pot. Another victim of habit.

"Sleep well?" Quinn asked. It was a joke between them, a meaningless question. There was no good sleep or bad. There was simply sleep. Although he'd heard of master vampires who'd reacted to the death of their vampire children during sleep, or, more rarely, vampires powerful enough to follow their mates during daylight, which could certainly lead to less than restful sleep. Especially if the mate was unfaithful or in physical danger. Quinn didn't have a mate and didn't particularly want one. He had his hands full right now, when it came to vampire entanglements. Not to mention petite vampire hunters.

Garrick's only response to his question was a wordless grunt. Not a good sign. He stood with his back to the room, sipping coffee, before finally walking over to sit opposite Quinn at the kitchen's center island. "Did you eat?" Garrick asked, giving him a dark look.

"Yes, Mom."

Garrick was not amused. "What the fuck was that this morning, Q? Anything could have happened—an accident, a flat tire, a fucking traffic jam—and you'd have been stuck out there all day. And that's assuming you found a bush to crawl under for protection before sunrise."

"Thanks for the visual."

"This isn't a joke," Garrick snapped.

"No, it's not," he sighed. His cousin was the only vampire who could have spoken to him like this without being on the receiving end of a violent reaction. Garrick was genuinely concerned, and, besides, he was right. It had been unforgivably stupid on Quinn's part. "I'm sorry, Gar. I lost track of the time."

"I hope her pussy was worth it."

Quinn felt a surge of heat at the crude comment. He didn't want anyone talking about Eve like that. Not even Garrick. But he forced back his anger, knowing it would only make Garrick push harder. Besides, he wasn't sure *why* the remark made him angry. The two of them had talked about the women they fucked in far cruder terms before. But this was *Eve*. And, for some reason, that mattered.

"Can I assume she doesn't know you're a vampire?" Garrick continued. "You know, given as how she didn't stake you mid-fuck, what with her being a vampire killer and all. And I'm guessing you didn't get so much as a taste of her blood despite fucking her all night long."

"What the hell, Gar?" Quinn said, his understanding finally reaching its limit. "What's your problem?"

His cousin met his gaze across the counter top. "We're about to kill a God damned vampire lord and seize his territory, which might just involve a serious battle or two. And you're off fucking some woman you should have already eliminated, before she kills you or—"

"Enough." Quinn came to his feet with a roar of sound, his power suddenly filling the small room, echoing off the stone floor and walls.

Garrick stood at the same time, watching Quinn warily, but without fear and still defiant.

Quinn gripped the island's marble counter top so hard, he felt it straining beneath his fingers, until he let go and shook his hands out. "Look," he said softly. "I'm sorry about this morning. It won't happen again. But I don't need a lecture from you or anyone else about the dangers of what we're trying to do here. I appreciate your support and wouldn't want to do it without you, but in the final analysis *I'm* the one who's going to be going toe-to-toe with Orrin Sorley. Taking down a vampire lord isn't a team sport. It's me against him. So, don't think for one minute that I haven't examined every aspect of my fucking strategy, or obsessed over every detail." He drew in a deep breath, then added, "And don't talk about Eve like that. I don't know what's going on with her and the vampire killing, but . . . she's not just a piece of ass, all right?"

Garrick regarded him somberly. "Be careful, Quinn."

"I'm always careful. You know that."

"I do. Just . . . make sure your eyes are open. This wouldn't be the first time you've been fucked over by a woman, but the stakes are a hell of a lot higher now."

Quinn stared back at him. His cousin was right. But he really didn't need a reminder of the worst time in his life, or the woman who'd changed everything.

Boston, MA, USA, 57 years ago

QUINN WOKE THE morning after his phone conversation with the strange woman, Marcelina, feeling groggy from too much sleep. Apparently, his body couldn't decide if it wanted more rest or more work. No surprise there. He wasn't sure what he wanted anymore, either. He went for a run, and when he came back, he discovered that a message from Garrick had come in overnight. He hit play.

"Hey, Q, long time and all that. Don't worry, Marcelina's cool. I'll pick you up at 7:00 tonight; we'll go to her house. You still live at the same place, I'm guessing. You didn't move without telling me, or anything, right?" His cousin laughed. "See you then."

"Well, fuck," Quinn swore, staring at the phone. "Thanks for the advance warning, asshole." He looked around his townhouse and decided he'd work at home for a few hours, then meet his cousin and get this over with. Whatever the mysterious Marcelina needed, he could probably handle it with a letter or two, maybe a phone call. And then he could get back to his career, and the work he was *paid* for.

AT 6:52 PM (DAMN digital clocks, so fucking precise) Quinn's phone rang. He accepted the call, but Garrick spoke before he could answer, saying, "I'll be there in five. Wait for me out front, so I don't have to park." He hung up before Quinn could say a word.

"Nice talking to you, too," Quinn muttered, but pulled on his jacket, flicked off the lights, and locked the door behind him. He was just zipping his jacket against the cold, when Garrick's BMW whipped around the corner. They'd both done well in life, but Quinn had the feeling Garrick was enjoying it more.

It had rained earlier and the night was cold, making Garrick's BMW skid a little on a slick patch of ice before stopping. Quinn opened the door and dropped onto the leather seat. He didn't even own a car. Traffic was a nightmare, and you didn't need one to get around in Boston. When necessary, he hired a car service.

"What's this about?" They sped away too fast on the icy road, but if he said anything, he'd have to endure his cousin's taunts about being an old man.

"It's like Marcelina told you," Garrick said. "The property's been in her family for generations, but some big developer wants it, and he's bought off the right politician. The county's trying to seize it."

"What's the deal with the title?"

"Hell, I don't know, Quinn. That's why we called *you*."

"What is she to you?" he asked curiously, mainly because he'd never known his cousin to get seriously involved with a woman, any more than he did. They both favored short, intense affairs. Good sex, no commitment.

"She's . . . special. You'll see."

He frowned. What the hell did that mean? The woman had, frankly, sounded too old to be a girlfriend. "Special, as in, you're serious about her?"

Garrick grimaced, seeming uncomfortable. "Just wait and see, all right? It's not that far."

Quinn shrugged. Whatever. He stared out the window. This whole situation was seeming odder and odder. Even Garrick was being weird. He was equal parts relieved and surprised when they turned down the long driveway of a Chestnut Hill estate that had seen better days. This was where she lived? Hell, if this was the property in question, he wasn't surprised some developer was trying to steal it. Depending on the acreage, it was worth millions. Sub-divided, it would be millions multiplied by however many homes they built. He could also understand why the city was willing to help get it into the developer's greedy little hands. The driveway was in disrepair and the house, which he could now see more clearly, had definitely *not* been kept up. He wouldn't be surprised if complaints from the neighbors had been the driving force behind the political push for the property's sale.

He frowned. The Chestnut Hill location would make things much trickier. Chestnut Hill wasn't a city in itself, but actually included parts of three separate municipalities. It could be a real nightmare figuring out who had jurisdiction, especially if the property crossed municipal lines.

"You sure she owns this place?" he asked, staring up at a big colonial-style mansion that appeared, at first glance, to be unoccupied.

"Yeah. But she's been living in Europe. She only came back to deal with all this crap."

Well, that explained the weird accent, Quinn considered. "Does she have a caretaker, a groundskeeper? Anyone charged with keeping the place up?"

"I don't know. Why don't you ask her?" They had stopped at the foot of some stairs leading to a broad, uncovered porch.

"I will." Quinn eyed the mansion as they climbed out of the car. "Anyone live here with her?"

"Not yet," Garrick said, and there was something just . . . *odd* about the way he said it. Something that made Quinn turn and stare.

"You okay, buddy?" he asked.

Garrick grinned. "Never better. Come on. Marcelina's waiting."

"Well, we can't have that," Quinn said dryly and followed his cousin into the house. He coughed the minute the door closed behind him. It was dark and dusty. If he'd had to guess, he'd have said no one had lived here in a long, *long* time, which had just added fuel to the municipality's determination to seize the property. He made a mental note to check the tax records the next day to find out exactly which municipality that was, and if there was any record of . . . His thoughts trailed off when *she* appeared.

"Quinn," the woman said in a voice that was like a thousand angels singing.

He blinked. Where the fuck had *that* thought come from? He stared at the small woman standing in an arched opening off the foyer. The room behind her was dimly lit, but a fire burned on the far wall silhouetting what he had to admit was a killer body. Her petite form was all curves, with pale breasts mounded over a corset-style top, and a tiny waist that flared to a generous swell of hips and thighs. Black pants that resembled riding breeches clung to her legs and were tucked into similarly styled boots. He found it unlikely that she'd just come in from a ride around the paddock, and so assumed the skin-tight outfit was purely for effect. He was male enough to admit it was a nice effect, but it made him wonder who this woman was, and why Garrick was so taken with her.

She stepped closer. Long dark hair curled over her shoulders and down her back. Her eyes were dark and luminous, her lips full and red. Those lips curled into a smile, and he had to fight the urge to back up. He was more than a foot taller and 100 pounds heavier than she was, and she appeared to be unarmed. So, why did he feel as though he should grab his cousin and get the hell out of there?

"Quinn," Garrick said, dropping a heavy arm over his shoulders. "This is Marcelina. My lady, this is the cousin I told you about."

Yeah, Quinn was beginning to wish Garrick had forgotten he had a cousin.

Marcelina was staring at Quinn expectantly, as if waiting for him to say something. He remained silent, still fighting the urge to get the hell out of Dodge, and he figured anything he said to her would only make things worse. Like when he was a kid and he'd ignored the monsters in his closet, because if he acknowledged them, they'd become real.

"Quinn," she said again, and he heard the disapproval in her voice, as if he'd disappointed her. "Why don't you both come sit down? We can discuss things."

He looked into the dim room beyond. "I'm going to need more light if you want me to review any documents."

She walked away, her laugh a delicate chiming sound that drifted over her shoulder.

Again with the flowery descriptors, Quinn thought. What the fuck was going on with his head? "Garrick," he muttered, pulling his cousin close. "What the hell—"

"It's rude to whisper, Quinn," Marcelina called. "Garrick, bring your cousin inside please."

Quinn frowned at the clear command underlying that delicate voice, and his frown deepened to a scowl when Garrick grabbed his arm and propelled him forward with unexpected strength. The two cousins had always been roughly the same size. When had Garrick gained the new muscle? And why?

"Come on," Garrick said harshly. "Be polite and listen."

Quinn's eyebrows shot upward, but he went along. If it meant this much to Garrick, he'd give it a shot.

"Quinn, you sit here," Marcelina said, patting the seat next to her with a delicate hand that bore sharp-looking fingernails polished a rich red.

Quinn would have preferred not to sit so close, but Garrick body-blocked him onto the short couch where she sat, while taking a satin-covered chair for himself, sitting at a right angle.

"This is nice," she purred.

Quinn noticed her perfume for the first time—something flowery and too heavy. He hated women who drowned themselves in perfume.

But then she leaned closer and touched her fingers to the bare skin of his hand. His skin crawled, and he suddenly found himself struggling against a strange fogginess that was trying to take over his thoughts . . . *Too late*.

It was the last thought he had.

QUINN WOKE TO a pounding headache and the awareness that it wasn't only his head that was hurting. His whole body felt like he'd been beaten with rubber mallets. He sat up with a groan. It was still dark, and he thanked God for small favors. There was nothing worse than having the sun drilling into his brain when he was hungover. He braced his feet on the floor and ran a hand through his hair, stopping when he realized he was still wearing his clothes. All of his clothes, including his boots. He looked around. This wasn't his townhouse. In fact, this wasn't anyplace that he recognized. And he couldn't remember drinking, either. He hadn't gotten drunk in more years than he could count.

A thrill of fear shot along his nerves, and his first thought was for Garrick. Ignoring the agony, he stood and felt along the walls until he found a light switch. He flicked it up and down, but nothing happened. Continuing along the wall, he found a door. He pulled it open and stepped out onto a second floor landing. Moonlight shone through the cut-glass panels of a front door and two side windows, and lit a wide foyer down below. Firelight flickered through a broad archway, and Quinn abruptly remembered where he was. What he didn't know was why he was still there. And why he felt so fucking awful. Where was Garrick?

Sensing the weight of his cell phone in his pocket, he pulled it out to call his cousin. If nothing else, he'd hear the phone ringing and follow the sound. But when he touched the screen and brought it to life, he could only stare. He'd lost an entire day. An *entire fucking day*. He'd come to this dusty wreck of a house on a Sunday, and somehow, it was now Monday night. He'd lost a whole day of work. His office would have been looking for him . . . He brought up the call log on his cell and found the expected list of unanswered calls. How was that possible? He never turned off his phone, never missed a call.

His pounding head suddenly secondary, he strode onto the landing and down the stairs, determined to get some answers. Marcelina was waiting in the firelit room, with Garrick standing watch over her like a guard. He gave Quinn a searching look, his gaze cautious, hesitant.

"All is well, Garrick," Marcelina said, squeezing his hand. "Quinn is with us now."

Quinn opened his mouth to demand an explanation, but before he could say a word, Marcelina pinned him with a stare and said, "Kneel."

Laughter tried to force its way out of his throat, but before he'd taken a breath, his knees hit the floor. He raised stunned eyes, first to Garrick, who wouldn't meet his gaze, and then to Marcelina, who was smiling with utmost satisfaction.

"Come here, Quinn," she said, sitting down and patting the sofa as she'd done before.

He tried to get up, but found he couldn't. It was as if his knees were stuck to the floor. He gave her a confused look.

"Crawl," she said, with a cruel edge to her soft voice.

Humiliation and rage flushed his chest and face with heat, but he found he had no choice. If he wanted to move, it would be on his hands and knees. And something was compelling him to move. *Marcelina.* He could sense the pressure she was exerting on him, as if a rope was strung between them and she was the only one pulling. He tried to resist, tried to lean back and get away from her. He should have been far stronger than she was. But that no longer seemed to be true.

She gave a yank hard enough that he nearly fell on his face. "I said, come here," she growled.

Quinn counted off every inch of the short distance between them, promising himself he'd pay her back, and storing every second of his humiliation against the day he'd make *her* do the crawling.

"So much anger." She gave a trilling laugh. "It's pointless, but you're a stubborn one. You'll have to learn for yourself. But in the meantime, you'll do what I brought you here for. This house is mine, and I intend to keep it. You need to fix it."

"What?" She wanted him to fix the place up? He didn't have any handyman skills to speak of.

"You will address me as, "Mistress!" Her voice carried a crack of power that hit him like a cane across his chest. He might have fallen if it had been possible. But she had his knees rooted to the ground, so that all he could do was sway.

Quinn stared at her. Did she want him to repeat his question?

She made a disgusted noise and looked at him doubtfully. "Maybe the turning damaged you. It happens sometimes, although it would be very inconvenient. What am I supposed to do with you?" She stared at him expectantly.

"Probably best if you release me . . . Mistress," he added with an intentional delay. "And Garrick, too."

Marcelina screeched furiously and slapped him across the face with her open hand. The blow knocked him hard enough that he fell to one side, blinking in surprise. For such a tiny thing, she sure packed a wallop.

And his much-vaunted brain finally caught up to current events.

"You're not human," he muttered, pulling himself to his knees from where he'd slumped back and sat on his heels.

"You *are* a fool."

"Maybe. But I'm right. What are you? And what have you done to me?"

Marcelina smiled then. It was a shark's grin, full of far too many teeth. Quinn squinted. Some of those teeth didn't look . . . Oh, shit.

"You're a vampire," he said flatly.

She laughed. "And so are you! I *made* you, and that makes you mine."

"The hell it does." Another blow struck him hard on the jaw, though she hadn't bothered using her hand this time. It was the same as when she'd hit his chest earlier, a strike by an invisible weapon.

"I am your Sire, boy. Your mistress. And you will respect me, or pay the price."

Quinn thought the price would be worth it. There was no way in hell he was ever going to respect this crazy bitch. But Garrick was standing there, silently pleading with Quinn to do . . . what? Go along? Just shut the fuck up? Somehow get them out of this mess? His mouth twisted with emotion. Anger. *Rage*. He wanted to lash out at someone. At Garrick for putting them in this situation, at the bitch Marcelina for thinking she could hold them here for as long as her batshit crazy mind could fathom.

But it wasn't Garrick's fault. If Marcelina could capture Quinn—and for all her deranged mind, she *had* captured him—then she'd have been able to capture Garrick, too. He didn't know the specifics, but he knew his cousin wouldn't have gone down easily. So what to do next? How did they get out of this mess?

The answer was clear, although he hated it. He'd have to play along, bide his time. There was too much he didn't know, didn't understand. Marcelina thought she was clever, thought she had them well and truly trapped. But Quinn was more than clever. He had one of the best legal minds in the city. The question was, could he play along convincingly enough to make Marcelina believe? To get her to relax and let slip what he needed to know?

He clenched his jaw. "Forgive me, Mistress," he said, every word like glass in his throat. "This is all so confusing, and I'm so hungry," he added, realizing with a lurch of his stomach that it was true. He *was* hungry, but not for food. *Damn it.* "I don't understand."

"Of course you don't," she crooned, now stroking his sore jaw. "But I'll teach you. Here," she said, offering him her delicate wrist. "Drink. My blood is stronger, and it will bind us closer together."

The last thing Quinn wanted was to strengthen his bond to Marcelina. But the scent of her blood, so close to the surface, hit him like a brick to the head. And he was suddenly ravenous. His mouth closed over her wrist, and he drank.

Howth, Ireland, present day

NEITHER QUINN NOR Garrick ever mentioned Garrick's role in recruiting Quinn for Marcelina's use. But Quinn had never held it against his cousin. Oh, maybe he had, at the very beginning. But once he'd understood, once he'd seen what she could make *him* do, he'd known his cousin hadn't been able to resist her demands. Garrick hadn't been more than a few weeks made when she'd sent him after Quinn.

The bitch had regretted her choice of playthings well enough later, when both Quinn and Garrick had grown into their power. But that was another story.

"Look," Garrick said, pulling him back from memory lane. "I usually don't give a damn who you fuck. But this girl . . . she's killing vampires. And if that's not a serious complication, I don't know what is."

"Don't worry about Eve," Quinn told his cousin. "She might prove useful. She probably knows more about the local vamps here and in Dublin than we do."

"And how useful is she going to be once she discovers *you're* a vampire?"

Quinn didn't say anything. He didn't want to think about that, but his cousin was right. Not if, but *when* Eve discovered what he was . . . "Let's forget about my sex life," he said, abruptly changing the subject. "That's not why we're here."

"Could've fooled me," Garrick said under his breath, then looked up with a bland expression, as if to deny he'd said anything at all. "You think it's time to call in the troops?"

Quinn cocked his head, thinking about his answer. The only question left was timing. Quinn hadn't brought his fighters with him right away, because he'd been reluctant to risk their lives before he'd had a chance to judge the battlefield. He wanted to *know* that he could defeat Orrin Sorley and take Ireland as his own.

He wasn't worried about that anymore. And he needed his people *here*. Every vampire lord had an inner circle of vampires he trusted absolutely. Not only to carry out his orders, but to cover his back. Once Quinn made serious moves into Sorley's business operations, whether it was smuggling or something else, the Irish lord would start paying attention. And that attention would be hostile. Quinn was working for Sorley, but he wasn't sworn to him. He owed the vampire lord nothing, and Sorley wouldn't like that. And what he didn't like, he'd try to destroy. It was the vampire way, and Quinn was going to need more than Garrick by his side.

He was also going to need serious daytime guards. The move to Dublin, combined with the arrival of Quinn's own fighters, was going to infuriate Sorley, but it would also make him nervous. And that was a bad combination in a powerful vampire. Quinn and his people were going to need better security than a few locks and an alarm system. But being the control freak that he was, Quinn had planned for that, too.

When he'd been back in Maine, running the state's vampires for Rajmund, he'd employed the same daytime security company that Raj used. It had been run by a man named Adorjan, who worked exclusively with vampires. When Quinn had begun recruiting his own fighters, the first thing he'd done was to contract with Adorjan for a daytime security force that would protect his people while they were training in the U.S., and then transfer overseas when the time came. Adorjan had taken on the assignment enthusiastically, and even planned on leading the security force himself. Quinn hadn't been surprised, since Adorjan was Hungarian and obviously a transplant to the U.S. He'd figured the man was homesick.

The surprise had come when Adorjan had approached Quinn and asked to be turned. He didn't want to lead Quinn's daylight force, he wanted something more. He wanted to be a vampire. He wanted to live forever.

Quinn had cautioned him, told him there were no guarantees. Adorjan was a powerful human, not only a big man, but one with an innate authority, a desire to lead. There was no telling what the vampire symbiote would give him, no assurance that he'd retain his natural strengths. He could wake as the weakest sort of vampire, one who essentially lived as a human.

Adorjan had been willing to roll those dice. Either way, he'd told

Quinn, he'd be going to Ireland with him. Either way, he'd fight by his side. So Adorjan had become Quinn's first child. All the other vampires in his group were sworn to him, but Adorjan was *his*. He was hardwired to protect Quinn at all costs. And fortunately, he'd been reborn as a master vampire. He was Quinn's security chief and bodyguard, and he'd be the one arranging the transfer of Quinn's people—both vampires and humans—to Ireland.

"Yeah," Quinn told Garrick now. "It'll take a few days for everyone to get here. We'll be more than ready for them by then. Why don't you give Adorjan a call, and . . . hell, what's the time difference here? Do we even share darkness with Maine this time of year?" He saw Garrick flipping numbers in his head. The guy was a math whiz. A little time zone calculation should be nothing.

"Yeah," he decided. "We can catch them just after sunset if we call in the middle of the night here."

"Good. I want everyone moving within two days. The daylight guards can fly commercial and go right to the new house. They shouldn't have any problems getting through customs. But I want the vampires on a private flight to Paris or London. Actually, make it Paris. After Raphael's visit, I doubt the French vampires are paying much attention to the airports. They're too busy staying alive. From Paris, our people can travel in pairs to Dublin—airplane or ferry, I don't care, as long as it's discreet."

"Right. I'll handle it. What about the rest of tonight? What's the plan?"

Quinn grinned. "Tonight, we're going to meet my new team of smugglers."

"Great. What do they smuggle again?"

He laughed. "Let's go find out."

"MAM? YOU HERE?" Eve called out as she let herself into the small house her mother had lived in for as long as Eve had been alive. She'd been born in this house. Her father had died in this house. Her brother had died while the family still lived there. Sometimes, she wondered if the house was cursed, and blamed her mother for not having moved long ago. She looked around and found no memories of her life here. There were pictures of her father and mother, pictures of Alan, and of the three of them before she'd been born. But there were none of her. Brigid hadn't wanted another child and made no secret of it. She'd had Alan, her beautiful boy. She didn't need a girl child slipping in and stealing a share of the love—from husband and son both—that should have been hers alone. Eve's entire life had been colored by her mother's resentment, and now her brother's death. But if her dreams meant anything, then maybe Alan didn't want her to stay that way. Maybe he wanted her to live, to walk in sunshine.

"Mam?" she called again, although, she didn't know why. There was nowhere else for the woman to be at this time of night. She never left the house after dark, and, as far as Eve could tell, the only place she ever went during the day was her bi-weekly supermarket trip, and the occasional visit to church.

"Stop yelling. You sound like a fishwife." Brigid Connelly's voice was raspy from a lifetime of smoking, accompanied by the slap of her slippers on the thin carpet.

"Good evening to you, too, Mam." She even tried to make the words cheerful. Her mother wouldn't have cared either way. "I was in Dublin earlier, and I brought some of those pasties you like." She set the grease-stained bag on the small kitchen table.

Her mother picked it up and tossed it aside. "They're cold."

"Well, of course, they're cold. It's an hour's drive." Eve had ridden the train into Dublin that morning and picked up her car, grumbling all the way on the drive back. Except when she'd been re-living her night with Quinn. A shiver of pure lust had her nipples hardening in anticipation, and she had to fight off the sensation. A visit with her mother was no time to be fantasizing about sex. Spectacular sex. *Stop it!*

Brigid fumbled in her housecoat pocket and came up with a crumpled pack of cigarettes. "Did you get my Marlboros?"

Eve sighed. "Yes." She dropped a plain white plastic bag onto the table, which her mother grabbed much more eagerly than she had the sweet pasties. The cigarettes didn't come from Dublin. Those she bought from a local smuggler to avoid the stiff taxes designed to cut down on consumption of tobacco in Ireland. All the taxes ever did was increase profits for smugglers, but since it mostly affected the poor, no one seemed to care. And the truth was that her mother would give up breathing before her Marlboro Golds. Eve couldn't bring herself to worry about it, and maybe that made her a bad daughter. But her mother had never made any secret of the fact that Eve's birth had been a mistake. "A surprise," as Brigid had politely put it, back when she'd still bothered with such niceties. Back before her father and brother had died, and Brigid had been left with no one but the daughter she'd never wanted.

"You look like a whore."

Eve blinked, still capable of being shocked by her mother's disdain. "Thanks, Mam."

Her mother made a dismissive noise, lit a cigarette, and drew deeply. She blew out the smoke and said, "You find your brother's killers yet?" It was the only thing she cared about. Eve had mentioned once that she'd seen the men who killed Alan. That had been early on, when she'd been overwhelmed by loss and had stupidly expected her mother to share her grief, even though they'd never shared anything else. Brigid's only response had been that Eve—who'd been barely 23 and a university student at the time—should "probably get on that." Eve still wondered sometimes if the only reason she hunted vampires was to somehow win the love of her mother by stalking her brother's murderers. Could she really be that pathetic?

"Not yet," she answered with false cheer. "But you'll be first to know."

She got another one of those dismissive noises from Brigid, this one laced with the scent of tobacco smoke.

Eve watched as her mother shuffled to the worn chair in front of the television and sat down, staring at some game show or other as if there was no one else in the room. "You want some dinner?" Eve asked, knowing the answer and not sure why she bothered to ask.

Brigid waved away the question with the hand holding her cigarette, never taking her eyes from the TV screen. "Like you can cook."

Eve sighed again, more deeply this time. "Okay, then. I'll be off on my whorish way. I'll let you know if I find the killers. Assuming they don't kill me first."

Another wave of the cigarette.

She stood there a moment longer, waiting for . . . she didn't know what she was waiting for. She only knew it was never going to come. Without another word, she let herself out. She'd need to take a shower and wash her hair before going hunting. Vampires' senses were much more sensitive than a human's, and it was difficult to play the seductress when she stank of cigarettes.

QUINN DIDN'T HAVE much trouble finding the gathering spot for Sorley's local vampire gang. For one thing, the boat captain had been a treasure chest of information. In fact, Quinn was sure the human had known far more about the local operation than his vampire clients had suspected. Dangerously more. It was one thing to employ humans for certain necessary tasks—like piloting a boat through daylight waters—but it was something else entirely to trust them with the inner workings of vampire business. That sort of thing would stop once he was Lord of Ireland. Sorley ran a sloppy ship—no pun intended. Quinn would not.

Apart from the captain's intel, however, was the simple fact of Quinn's power. Howth wasn't a huge city. It had fewer than 10,000 residents, with a good number of those being clustered in dense residential districts of commuters from Dublin. Vampires generally weren't found in family-oriented suburbs. At least, not the kind of vampires who ran smuggling operations. That left the small fishing village of historic Howth, which was more densely populated, and had a much smaller geographic reach. Quinn's power let him search for and identify both vampire and human life signs, and the cluster of local vampires stood out like a beacon to his senses.

"Too predictable," Quinn muttered, as he and Garrick stepped out of the Range Rover and headed for what looked like a large, weathered boathouse with light leaking around the warped doors. Admittedly, the lights were dim. These were vampires, after all. But anyone with a brain would look at that building and wonder what was going on. And now that they'd drawn closer, he could hear music—in a place where there shouldn't have been any activity at all after dark.

"Not many cars," Garrick observed.

"Maybe no one needs a car around here."

"Where do they live? You think there's a nest nearby?"

"That's what we're about to find out."

No one challenged them as they walked right up to the warehouse and opened the door. A wash of light and sound immediately greeted them, making Quinn shake his head. Had no one ever heard of a double entry system around here, with the inner door not opening until the outer door closed? It wasn't only light leakage, it was security. You couldn't force an entire troop through the entrance if they had to crowd into a tiny vestibule. Not that anyone here would notice. What if Quinn had been an enemy? One guy with an Uzi could do a lot of damage.

The warehouse they stepped into had boxes and crates stacked on both sides, some standing on the floor, some shoved onto metal shelves that lined the walls in perpendicular rows. Quinn looked around, waiting for someone to notice. He wasn't expecting obeisance, didn't even expect recognition of his power since he was shielding it from detection. But he was a stranger who'd just walked in on their blatantly illegal operation, and no one seemed to care. He was no longer amazed at

Eve's success in killing the two vamps the other night. A sexy woman, a dark alley . . . hell, it was like taking candy from a baby. Did they have that saying in Ireland? Maybe he'd teach it to this lot. He nodded to Garrick.

Putting two fingers to his lips, Garrick let forth a piercing whistle. Quinn smiled. He'd always envied his cousin's ability to do that. No matter how hard he'd tried, he'd never managed it.

The chatter cut off like a switch had been thrown, the music dying with an unpleasant electronic squawk soon after.

Seventeen vampires turned to stare at Quinn, with varying expressions of surprise and hostility. He waited. After a few minutes—the idea of one guy with an Uzi sprang to his head again, but with himself as the target this time—an average looking vamp emerged from the crowd, stepping around several much larger guys. Quinn sent out a smoke-thin wisp of a probe, testing the vampire's power, unconcerned about the local's ability to shield himself from detection. Quinn could penetrate any deception with ease, unless this guy had real power. In which case, Quinn would still be able to break through. It would simply take a bit longer. That wasn't the case, however. The local had a master vampire's strength, which he wasn't trying to conceal.

The vamp took two steps away from the crowd and studied Quinn. "Who're you?"

Quinn's lips curved in a bare smile. If this vampire was in charge, Sorley should have called to warn him that Quinn was coming, should have done him the courtesy of telling him that Quinn was now in charge here in Howth. But, of course, Sorley hadn't done that. Quinn wasn't surprised. Sorley had probably hoped the local vampires would manage to kill Quinn, thus eliminating the danger that Quinn represented to his rule over Ireland. It was a vain hope, given the disparity in power between Quinn and the local. And it was a stupid move on Sorley's part. He risked alienating some of these vampires with his willingness to let them die, and it also pissed off Quinn. Of course, he was going to kill Sorley anyway, but it was the principle of the thing.

"My name's Quinn Kavanagh."

"American," someone sneered.

"Irish," Quinn countered, without bothering to track down the speaker. "Raised in the U.S. since I was a child, but I'm home now."

"Are you?" the apparent leader asked mildly. "And what do you want now that you're *home*, Quinn Kavanagh?"

Quinn tilted his head curiously, letting just a touch of his parents'

Irish lilt flavor his words. "Are there no manners in Ireland anymore then? I give you my name, but you don't give me yours?" Whatever name the vampire gave him was likely to be a pseudonym, a nom de guerre, but Quinn needed to call him something before he killed him.

"Christie," the vampire said.

"Well, Christie, you have a choice here." Quinn let a measure of his true power leak through. Not all of it, not even close. It wasn't necessary to show his cards yet, not for Christie or anyone else he'd met so far. In fact, he wouldn't let even Sorley know the true depths of his power until the final battle, when he challenged the Irish lord for the territory. "I'm taking over the Howth smuggling operation," he informed Christie plainly.

"Says who?" someone called from the back of the pack.

"Says Sorley."

Christie's face gave away his surprise, before he managed to conceal it. "I heard rumors of your . . . *surprise visit* to Lord Sorley. So, you've got the guns."

"*Sorley* has the guns," Quinn clarified.

Christie's eyes flared briefly. "What about Jacobs and Clarke?"

Quinn considered his response. He assumed Jacobs and Clarke were the two vamps who'd been sent to receive the gun shipment before they'd had the misfortune of running into Eve. Maybe they'd even been friends with Christie. Still, Quinn had no reason to stand here and be interrogated. They were vampires, and he'd already demonstrated the only thing that mattered in their world. Power. On the other hand, treating Christie with the respect Sorley had so obviously denied him might make this transition go more smoothly.

"I never caught their names," he said smoothly, and let Christie conclude the rest.

The Howth vampire sighed, then gave the tiniest bow from the waist. "You probably want a briefing."

Quinn tipped his head. "That would be useful." He started forward, with Garrick at his back. The locals may have accepted him, but they certainly hadn't embraced him. As Quinn approached the open door of a small, glassed-in office, the music started up again. He stopped and turned around. "The music stays off permanently," he ordered. "We're smugglers, not a bunch of drunk teenagers."

He ignored the grumbling as the three of them filed into the office. He nodded for Garrick to close the door and kicked one of two chairs against a side wall, giving him a solid surface at his back and a clear view of the warehouse filled with unhappy vampires. Garrick stood across from him, one foot braced on the other wall, while Christie shuffled behind the desk and sat rather delicately, as if unsure he still belonged there.

Quinn didn't waste any time. "I'll want any records you've maintained, as well as a list of contacts and deliveries. Can you email it?"

"I can, but I'll need to scan some of—"

"The last six months will be enough. Do it now, so I have time to review it before tomorrow night. Are you the only one supervising this operation?"

"Jacobs was the one in charge. I handled the books. But now . . ." He gestured in Quinn's direction. "If you're telling me the truth . . ."

Quinn studied the other vampire as he decided whether to take offense at the sly insult. He could kill Christie with a thought, although the vamp didn't seem to realize it yet. Quinn wasn't going to reveal his power over a minor insult, but on the other hand. . . .

Christie never saw him coming. Quinn grabbed him by the throat and threw him across the room, his body shattering the window and knocking over several other vampires before he came to rest on the warehouse floor.

Brushing bits of glass from his leather jacket, Quinn stepped out of the office and into the warehouse to confront the silent group of vampires. He looked down at Christie. "I'll expect that email. Don't disappoint me." He nodded a farewell at the gathered vampires. "Gentlemen." Then he and Garrick walked out.

They continued down the street until they were well away from the warehouse, not far from the café where Quinn had spent his first nights in Howth. It was darker tonight, with no moon to add its light to the dim pole lamps. The café was closed, but down the pier a ways, the pub was still going strong, with young people spilling from its crowded bar to stand around outside, despite the dark night. Or maybe because of it, Quinn thought, seeing the furtive coupling going on in the shadows.

"That went well," he commented, pulling his attention back to the night's business. Garrick gave him a sideways look as if trying to judge whether he meant it or not. Quinn wasn't sure, either, so he added, "Better than I expected."

"Will he send the records, you think?"

"Absolutely. He'll want me to think he's cooperating."

"But you don't think he will."

"No, the quiet ones are always violent in the end."

"Do we need to worry about the house?"

"No. An attack in that part of Howth would draw too much attention. The kind that can't be bought off. They'll go for someplace familiar. An ambush at the warehouse, most likely. Tomorrow night. This is their turf, and they'll defend it."

"What about Christie?"

Quinn shrugged. "What about him? He'll have to go."

"Does he have any significant power?"

"You think he was shielding?"

"Of course, he was. Enough of the cryptic shit, Q. This is me you're talking to."

"Okay, yeah. He has enough power to control the rest of them, but nothing I can't handle. You could take him, too. But I can't afford to look weak, so it has to be me."

"Why not get rid of him later tonight? Wait 'til he leaves his boys, then take him on the street. Sweet and simple. No witnesses to know for sure."

"Because vampires don't respect sweet and simple. It has to be violent and public. Or at least, as public as a gathering of vampire smugglers can get."

"Right. We should top off our energy then. Something fresh this time." His gaze drifted to the crowded pub.

Quinn was about to respond when a familiar redhead appeared out of the darkness, her hips swaying in those spike-heeled boots, her gaze a combination of sultry and suspicious as she eyed first him, then Garrick.

"Small world," she said, stopping three feet away from them.

"Howth isn't exactly Las Vegas," he said. "And this seems to be the social center. Where else would we be on a Sunday night?"

"I don't know. Church maybe? Confessing your sins?"

"I don't believe in sins, sweetheart."

"Convenient. Good evening, Garrick," she said, giving his cousin a pleasant smile.

Garrick had been eyeing her warily, like some dangerous beast that could pounce at any moment, but he grinned at her greeting, probably enjoying the fact that she was giving Quinn a hard time. "You're looking lovely tonight, Eve." He managed to say it as if he meant it, as if he hadn't been urging Quinn to get rid of her only a few hours ago. He nodded at Eve, then turned to Quinn and said, "I'm taking off."

"Where to?" Quinn asked, lacing the question with just enough caution that Garrick was reminded of their precarious situation in

Howth. Neither one of them could afford to get too comfortable.

Garrick nodded in the direction of the pub. "Over there. I'm going to do what I do best."

"What's that?" Eve asked, before Quinn could say anything.

Garrick's jaw tightened slightly, but he played his part. "Pretend to drink hard while I sweet talk the locals into embracing our client's business. And, of course, find my own sweet lady for the night. Even sinners deserve a break."

"Especially sinners," Quinn commented quietly. "Don't be late."

"Yeah, you either," he said, with a dismissive laugh. He slapped Quinn's shoulder and took off.

Quinn watched until Garrick had disappeared into the pub, slipping his way through the crowd with remarkable ease. When he turned back, he found Eve staring at him.

"Who says I'm your lady?" she demanded.

Quinn snorted. "Who says you're sweet?"

Eve's blush was visible on her pale skin, despite the poor lighting. "What were you doing over there in that warehouse?"

"Spying on me, darling?"

"No," she insisted defensively. "I just happened to see you. And I wondered."

"Business," Quinn said simply.

"Business, my ass," she snarled. "How come every time I see you, you're hanging around with vampires?"

Quinn grinned. The snarl was cute coming from that full, pouty mouth of hers. Without warning, he closed the space between them, grabbed her around the waist, and pulled her in for a kiss. She pretended to resist at first, pushing half-heartedly at his chest. But the pushes soon turned to caresses as she gave in, her mouth warm beneath his, her tongue a silken sweep of sensation as the kiss deepened into something more, something hungry.

When the kiss ended and they both came up for air, she slapped his chest. "Answer my question," she demanded breathlessly, while doing nothing to move away from his embrace.

He studied her a moment. "Why?" he asked.

"Why?" she repeated, her voice growing louder with outrage. "Because they're . . . vampires," she finished with a whisper.

He smiled. "And don't I know that," he said, adding a touch of Irish to the words.

She squinted at him, as if trying to figure out if he was mocking her.

Or maybe he was a puzzle to solve. "Fine," she said finally, shoving away from him. "Fuck you. Do what you want, but don't get in my way. You do your business deals, but I'm going to hunt them down." She started to turn, but he stopped her.

"You're going to get yourself killed, Eve. Do it my way."

She glared at him. "*Your* way? What the fuck is *your* way? Who *are* you?"

Quinn fought to remain calm. The bagged blood had done no more than taken the edge off earlier. He needed to *feed*, and he could feel his fangs pushing for release as they responded to his hunger for this woman. If he permitted that, if he showed Eve his true face, she'd scream and run away at best, or try to kill at him at worst. Most likely the latter. He'd have to stop her either way, and he didn't want to hurt her. "Let's just say that I want Sorley dead just as much as you do," he said quietly.

Eve stared. He didn't need his telepathic gift to read the emotions warring inside her. She knew he wasn't being completely honest, knew she was somehow being played, but she *wanted* to trust him. Hell, she just wanted *him*.

He yanked her close again. "You never *did* give me a proper hello," he murmured.

"I kissed you," she insisted, her fingers caressing his jaw almost reluctantly.

"No, *I* kissed *you*."

She was Eve, so she resisted for a heartbeat or two, but then she surrendered, going up on tiptoes to meet his mouth, her arms tight around his neck as she held him against her soft breasts. "Let's go," she murmured against his mouth, sliding her hand down to take his and pull him away from the crowd and noise of the pub.

"Where are you taking me?"

She looked back at him over her shoulder. "Guess."

EVE STRUGGLED TO get the door key out of her small purse, but apparently she wasn't moving fast enough for Quinn. He was all over her, lifting her off her feet, pressing her against the wall of Mrs. Bradley's house while his mouth ravaged her, nibbling on her ear lobe, sucking her neck, his hands molding the cheeks of her ass. She wrapped her legs around his narrow hips, her body acting on its own, as if it knew what it wanted and to hell with what her brain was telling her. To hell, indeed. She struggled to think clearly, drowning in need for this man she barely knew. "Wait," she gasped, feeling the press of his erection and knowing he'd fuck her right there on the street if she didn't stop him. "Wait," she said again, tugging on his hair, swallowing a moan as his tongue swept the delicate curve of her ear.

He followed the warm sweep of his tongue with a gentle bite, but he pulled back, studying her with eyes that gleamed despite the nearly moonless night. "Wait?" he growled.

"Not here," she whispered, swallowing hard. "My flat—"

She didn't get out any more words as he swung her away from Mrs. Bradley's wall and carried her the short distance to her front door. She managed to find the right key, to scrape the key into the lock, but it wouldn't—

Quinn's hand covered hers on the door knob. He squeezed and turned the stubborn key, then shoved the door open. Once inside, he slammed her back against the closed door while his mouth devoured her with a hunger that matched her own. It was as if he couldn't get enough of her mouth, her neck. He tugged her sweater down, his fingers coasting over the soft mounds of her breasts above the lacey confines of her bra, pinching her nipples into erectness through the lace until every scrape of the fabric was like a lightning bolt straight between her legs.

Skin. She wanted skin. Reaching for his shoulders, she shoved his leather jacket back, ignoring his growl when her efforts threatened to trap his arms. With a frustrated curse, he freed first one arm, then the next, letting the jacket fall to the floor as he bent his head and took her nipple in his mouth. Eve threw her head back with a groan of pleasure, feeling the cold wood of the door on her back, and this incredibly hot man all over her front.

"Quinn," she said, tugging on his hair again to get his attention. One of his big hands slid up her thigh and under the elastic edge of her panties, and she forgot what she wanted to say. "Oh, God," she breathed when his fingers found the slick arousal between her thighs.

He slid two fingers between the swollen lips of her pussy, and she nearly came right then and there. She would have if Quinn hadn't chosen that moment to swing her around and carry her to the bed. She pounded his shoulder in frustration, and he laughed.

"Don't worry, darling Eve," he murmured against her ear. "There are plenty of climaxes in your future."

Eve blushed at the blatant carnality of his words, and then blushed more deeply at her own embarrassment. She was half naked with a gorgeous man between her thighs, his mouth on her tit, and she was worrying about him talking dirty.

He dropped her on the bed, eyeing her hungrily as he stripped off his shirt and kicked off his shoes. His pants came next, and it was Eve's turn to eat him up with her eyes, the beautiful definition of muscle beneath his smooth skin, the narrow trail of golden hair that guided her eye to the flat plane of his belly, his groin, and then his cock. Her eyes closed as desire overwhelmed her. This was more need, more straight-forward *lust* than she'd ever felt for a man. There was so much that it frightened her, making her heart pound, her lungs tighten . . . until Quinn's hard body covered her own, his strong hands smoothing along her arms and thighs, his mouth murmuring wordless reassurances in between nibbling kisses along her jaw, over her closed eyelids.

"Eve," he whispered her name with wonder, as if it held magic.

Eve speared her fingers through his hair, urging his mouth back to her breasts. She wanted the wet heat of him on her nipples, wanted . . . everything. Every part of him.

He growled, and she heard the sound of ripping lace as he pulled her bra down to bare one breast. She nearly screamed when his teeth closed over her nipple, the erotic jolt to her pussy doubled as pain fed her desire. She did scream then, biting her hand to muffle the sound, when his fingers found her pussy again and shoved inside her, when his thumb scraped over her clit in a rough caress that threatened to drown her in sensation.

She didn't remember losing them, but her panties were gone, her sex completely bare as he reached down and wrapped his fingers around her calf, bending her knee and spreading her wide for the cock she could feel lying heavy and hot against her thigh. Quinn lifted slightly, just enough to transfer his hand from her leg to his cock, then gripping his hard length, he guided the tip into her pussy. He held himself still for a moment, teasing her, meeting her eyes, watching her as he dipped the first inch or two of his penis into her body, moving slightly in and out.

Eve's eyes narrowed. "Do it," she ordered.

He smiled slowly. "Ask nicely."

"I don't have to—" She gasped as he slid in another two inches, then pulled out, holding himself tantalizingly close, the head of his cock dipping in and out, tormenting her. She gripped his shoulders, her nails digging into his flesh. "Quinn," she cried softly.

"What do you need?" he whispered, his mouth covering hers in a hungry kiss before she could answer.

"Come on," she said, hating the pleading note in her voice.

"What do you say, darling Eve?"

"Please."

He slammed into her before the word even left her mouth, his cock filling her so completely that she could feel her inner muscles stretching around him, those delicate tissues aching with strain. He began to move, fucking her, shoving in and pulling out so fast that her pussy grew hot with the friction of his movement. Her legs crossed over his hips, and she held on, her arms around his neck, her mouth crushed against his, teeth and lips smashed together until she could taste blood on her tongue and didn't know whose it was.

She closed her teeth over his shoulder, felt his skin give and the warm flow of his blood. She moaned as a fresh bout of desire hit her like a blow to the head, slamming into her from nowhere, sending shivers of sensual need skimming along her nerves, tightening her nipples until every scrape of his chest was like a caress over her clit, teasing the sensitive nub until it pulsed along with her heart. Quinn grunted as her pussy clamped down on his cock, and her womb contracted. Eve's body was out of her control, muscles flexing, spine bowed. She swallowed a scream as Quinn cursed, his body going tight as she felt the heat of his release flooding her sex, his arms holding her tightly as they rode the wave of climax together.

"Fuck," Eve swore, when she gained enough breath to speak. "What was that?"

Quinn laughed softly. "A climax, darling. I'm sure we've done this before."

"Not like that. That was . . ." She didn't have words for it.

He kissed her—soft, sweet, and lingering. She could feel his cock, impossibly still hard inside her.

"Quinn," she breathed, not sure she could take any more pleasure. Was there a limit to the amount of sensation a woman's nerves could handle before they simply fizzled out and died? Or at least slept for a while. He started to move.

QUINN BIT BACK a groan of hunger. Eve's pussy was drenched with arousal, trembling in the aftermath of her climax, hot and slick around his cock. But as good as that felt, and God knew it felt terrific, it wasn't her wet pussy that was driving him, making his cock hard, and his body ache with need. He wanted her blood. The delicious scent of it, the warm rush in her veins, the hard pulse of it against the delicate skin of her neck. His fangs pushed against his gums in relentless demand. When she'd bit him, when his blood had zinged through her system rocketing her into orgasm, he'd nearly surrendered and given his body what it needed. What it demanded. But he'd managed to hold back, to channel that desire into an almost painful orgasm of his own. He hadn't come that hard since before he'd become a vampire. Hell, he hadn't come that hard since he'd been a raw teenager, jerking off to the slightest provocation.

But, for all that, his body wasn't satisfied. It wanted blood. If he wasn't going to feed from Eve, then he'd need to feed from someone else before the night was over. It felt like a betrayal, but that was foolish. He and Eve weren't a couple. They couldn't be, as long as her hatred forced him to conceal what he was.

He pumped slowly in and out of her sweet body, feeling her arousal grow again, her nipples hard pebbles against his chest, her pussy shivering around him.

"Quinn," she cried his name softly, as if pleading for him to help her, to relieve the terrible need that had taken over her body.

He pushed her knees to her chest and thrust deeper, harder. Her pussy was swollen with need, satiny with the cream of her orgasm. Her nails scraped down his back and he hissed, drinking in the sensuous pain in an attempt to drown the hunger.

Her climax started deep, her womb flexing so hard that he felt it against his cock, rippling down his length as she screamed helplessly, her mouth shoved against a pillow to hide her cries from the neighbors. He'd fuck her somewhere private before this was over, somewhere he could hear the magic of her screams as she thrashed beneath him. The image brought his own climax roaring down his cock, joining their bodies in a moment of sheer ecstasy as his release filled her body one more time.

QUINN HELD EVE until she was soundly asleep, with the duvet pulled up to cover their sweat-cooled bodies. It was a kind of torture, lying there with a warm, willing woman in his arms. Her scent was everywhere. The tiny taste of her blood he'd gotten from her torn lip was like a drug, and he was an addict, demanding more. Cursing himself for a fool, he slid a quiet suggestion into her dreaming mind. He wanted to be sure she'd sleep the rest of the night. Not only to cover his departure, but . . . if she went hunting, he might have to stop her. Or even worse, someone else might do it for him. And he didn't want her hurt. Hell, he just *wanted* her. And how fucked up was that?

He slipped out of bed and dressed quickly. There was no denying the simple fact that he needed to feed. He could take blood from anyone. It didn't have to be a beautiful woman. He could suck a man's neck just as well. But hell if he was going to.

It was a quick walk to the pub where he'd left Garrick. The place was still going strong, though there were fewer people outside. Most of the action was now inside where a live band was playing a mix of traditional Irish and American rock covers, with the crowd cheering and clapping, and just generally having a great time. Quinn waded into the crush of people, using bare wisps of his power to clear a path, scanning for Garrick and not really expecting to find him. By now, he was probably in some willing honey's bed, fucking *and* sucking, which is what Quinn would be doing if he had half a brain.

Hunger gnawed at him as he pushed his way through all those warm, blood-filled bodies, his gaze automatically searching out and finding the perfect donors—young women, flush with health, their faces glowing with heat and alcohol. He liked the ones who were with friends, but not *with* them. The ones who stood and listened, but rarely talked. They were the easiest to seduce, surprised by his attention.

"Quinn!" Garrick's call had him heading for the back half of the pub, where the lights didn't quite reach, leaving plenty of dark corners. It made Quinn wonder if the pub owner was himself a vampire, or if he was simply a human who was aware of Howth's bloodsucking residents and offered the perfect environment as an enticement for their business. Plenty of women—and men, too—sought out places where vampires hunted their prey, lusting after the sexual high of a vampire's bite.

"Where's the redhead?" Garrick asked when Quinn joined him.

"Sleeping," he said shortly.

His cousin gave him a searching look, but didn't comment. "There's plenty of willing flesh here. It's not a blood house, but it's the closest thing to it. The ladies all know the rules, especially back here."

Quinn nodded, his attention on a curvy brunette leaning against a wide pillar that straddled the line between the front and back of the club. If she leaned left, the lights glinted off the gold highlights in her hair. But if she tilted right, she was a dark temptation, her full lips playing with the glass of amber liquid in her hand.

"You going back to the house soon?" he asked Garrick, not looking at him.

"I can wait."

Quinn nodded. "This won't take long."

Sliding through the crowd as if they weren't there, he walked up to the brunette and stood in front of her, not saying a word. She gazed up at him, her eyes wide with excitement and just enough fear to make her heart pound a little faster, which made her blood pump a little harder. Delicious.

Quinn took her hand and tugged her deeper into the darkness of the pub, not stopping until they had a private corner to themselves. Using enough of his power to make sure it stayed that way, he bent his head to her neck and inhaled the scent of her.

"What's your name, sweetheart," he murmured against her skin.

"Brenda, my lord," she breathed so softly that he wouldn't have been able to hear her without his vampire-enhanced senses.

"Brenda," he repeated, then sank his fangs into her velvety skin, reveling in the soft pop as he penetrated her vein, nearly groaning with pleasure at the taste of her blood. She was young and fresh, with a distinct bouquet of the whiskey she'd been sipping. He had one arm wrapped around her waist, the other around her shoulders, with his hand cupping the back of her head, holding her in place. Brenda moaned softly, and the scent of her arousal filled the air, until she was trembling in his arms. Quinn drank. He was so damn hungry. He'd gone too long without feeding, worrying too much about Eve. The thought of Eve made his throat clench, until he nearly choked in a way he hadn't since the first weeks of his turning.

With a silent curse, he drew hard on Brenda's vein. She jerked in his arms as she suddenly climaxed, and he ignored the flashback of Eve that threatened to invade his thoughts. Fuck Eve. He was a vampire. He had to feed.

Withdrawing his fangs, he gave sweet Brenda a final lick to sweep up a few lingering drops and seal the wound. She'd have a mild hickey in the morning, if that. But mostly, she'd have a memory of the best orgasm of her life. And, Quinn suspected, she'd now become a regular patron of the local vampires' favorite pub.

Quinn kissed the side of her forehead and eased her into a booth, where she wasn't alone. Two other women, and one man, were similarly sleeping off a vampire's bite, their bodies completely relaxed, their faces wreathed in dreamy smiles.

When he exited the pub, Garrick was waiting for him. Sunrise wasn't far off, and this was still an unfamiliar town. They had to leave enough time to secure their house before they took to their beds.

They walked the short distance back to the warehouse, where the

Range Rover was still parked. Quinn had half-expected some of Christie's vampires to vandalize it somehow. Spray some graffiti, or at least key the paint job. The absence made him suspect something worse. "We need a bomb detector."

"I don't think they carry those at the local hardware," Garrick said dryly. Dropping to the ground, he scooted under the big vehicle and searched the rear half, while Quinn did the same on the front.

"Are vampire lords supposed to do this kind of shit?" he grumbled. "Shouldn't I have a flunky or two?"

"Probably. You should make a note."

Quinn grunted and rolled out from under the SUV, then jumped to his feet and brushed off his clothes. "Anything?" he asked as Garrick did the same.

"Not that I could see, but I'm no expert."

Quinn shrugged. "If we blow, we blow. But we've got to get going."

Garrick opened the driver's door and slid inside. "Let me start it, before—"

"Fuck that," Quinn snarled, climbing into the passenger side. "You're not my canary."

Garrick pressed the ignition, shaking his head when the engine started smoothly, and nothing exploded. "You've got to start acting the part," he said with surprising seriousness.

Quinn sighed and looked away. "When will Adorjan and the others get here?"

"The daylight crew is already at the Dublin house, getting things set up. The vamp half will arrive tomorrow night."

"Good."

The rest of the short drive was silent. Garrick parked the Range Rover, while Quinn closed and locked the gates. The two of them then went through their well-established routine of securing the house against intruders, before closing themselves up in the inner bedroom with even more security precautions.

Not much longer, Quinn thought to himself, as he settled on the bed. So far, he'd managed to avoid taking on the full mantle of authority that being the Lord of Ireland would require. Sure, he'd bullied Christie and the local vamps into a pretense of cooperation. But he'd done worse than that in a courtroom while wearing a three-piece suit. Besides, it was a short-lived victory. He fully expected to receive an unpleasant welcome when he arrived at the warehouse the next night. The very fact that he was looking forward to it was oddly satisfying. Maybe he was meant to rule, after all.

On that cheery note, the rising sun's light filled the horizon, and he was out.

Chapter Six

QUINN ROSE AT sunset, ready to fight for control of Howth before the night was over. Christie had probably been on the phone with Sorley before Quinn had been gone five minutes the previous night. And Sorley, no doubt, had encouraged Christie to assassinate the usurper American who thought to waltz in and take over their business. Nationalism was always a useful tool when urging people to die for a cause, even when the people in question were vampires. But Quinn doubted Sorley's support for Christie would extend to providing any fighters. First, Sorley had seemed like the sort who'd prioritize his own safety above all others, and, second, it would be an embarrassment if he supplied fighters and Quinn won anyway. It all came down to Sorley's interests in the end, and fuck Christie if he couldn't hang on to his own town.

Garrick was already in the kitchen when Quinn joined him. "More coffee?" he asked, pouring a cup for himself.

Garrick shook his head. He had earphones on, but a glance at the cellphone sitting on the counter told Quinn he was listening to messages, not music. He hit the home button and pulled the earphones out. "Adorjan and the others will be here within the hour. They arrived in Dublin separately late last night and rendezvoused by phone. They'll meet up tonight and head this way. Traffic will be heavy, but it shouldn't take long. The last message came in about five minutes ago, and they were just leaving Dublin."

"And the daylight guards?"

"Everything's set up. They'll be ready whenever we get there."

"I'll want to talk to Joshua Bell." Bell had worked for Adorjan for years, and was now Quinn's daylight security chief. He was also mated to a female vamp who worked on Raj's estate.

"Bell's at the house and expecting your call. By the way, his wife wants to join him here, but you need to formally agree. Raj has given the okay."

"What does she do for Raj again?"

"Cooking."

Quinn looked up in surprise. "That's not usual for a vampire."

Garrick raised one shoulder in a shrug. "She was a chef before she got turned. She cooks for the daylight guards and the other humans on the estate, including Raj's mate, Sarah. She works at night, obviously, and leaves it for them to do the final prep."

"Interesting. I'll call Bell. In the meantime, we'll wait for Adorjan and the others. It could get bloody tonight."

Garrick looked a little surprised. "You think so? Christie seemed . . . resigned to the new lineup."

"Maybe. But I'm not convinced he was nothing but a bookkeeper. The two dead vamps were obviously the muscle, but there's a better than good chance that it was all an act last night, and that he's been the brains behind the operation all along. I'm not taking those odds if I don't have to. And with my own fighters on hand, I don't have to."

Garrick sprawled at the rough wooden table. "As long as we have time to kill, tell me about Eve. And why you left with her, but ended up tapping another woman's vein . . . again."

"Let it go, Garrick." Quinn understood his cousin's concerns. Hell, he had the same concerns himself. But he didn't know what he was going to do about any of them. The smart thing would be to walk away, but he didn't think that was an option anymore, although he didn't want to delve too deeply into why that might be the case.

"I can't let it go," Garrick said stubbornly. "Even if you were the only one at risk, I'd keep pushing, but you're not. We've put our faith in you, Q. Put our lives on the line. And it's not only because we know you can take the territory, it's because we believe you'll be a good ruler. And your little girlfriend puts *all* of that at risk. All of *us*. I know you. And I know if she gets hurt or killed while she's out hunting for her vengeance, you'll track down the vampire responsible and destroy him. And what will that say about—"

"I said let it the fuck go." Quinn's growl was soft, but he didn't need volume when his words rumbled with power.

Garrick stood and kicked back his chair. "And you've just made my point for me. Deal with it, Quinn. Before she costs all of us more than you're willing to pay."

Quinn could have called him back. Could have *ordered* him back. But he wouldn't do that to Garrick, and, besides, he was right. He *did* have to do something about Eve. He just didn't know what. Actually, that was a lie. He knew exactly what needed to be done. He had to tell her the truth about what he was. And, if she took it badly, then he'd have to go into her memories, her thoughts—everything that made her the Eve he knew and lusted after—and erase her knowledge of vampires altogether. Or at least the events that had set her on this destructive path of vengeance.

He wasn't naïve. He knew there were vampires who needed to be killed. But that wasn't true of all of them, and it sure as hell wasn't Eve's job to decide which ones should die. He wondered how many innocents she'd killed. Hell, he wondered how many vampires altogether. If he asked her, would she tell him? Nothing was ever simple with her. She'd want to know why he was asking.

"Fuck," he swore, tossing his coffee mug into the sink hard enough that it broke. "Double fuck." Wiping up the shards with a wad of paper towels, he tossed the whole mess into the trash, then went into the dining room, with its table full of computers. Only one of those was Quinn's, which sat on its own at one end of the big table, and he dropped down in front of it now. Checking his email first, he found a lengthy message from Christie, along with a multitude of attachments. He suspected the vamp was trying to drown him in details, but he didn't know Quinn. Quinn lived for this kind of shit. He *loved* details, loved lists and ledgers and financial disclosures. Especially the ones trying to hide something from him. He printed out every attachment, then rubbed his hands together almost gleefully and went to work.

He was still working two hours later, when the sound of more than one engine from the front yard had him coming to his feet, all of his senses on high alert. He first scanned for Garrick, finding him a moment before he heard his footsteps heading for the door.

"Garrick," he called softly, knowing his cousin would hear. When Quinn stepped into the long hallway, Garrick was already there, one hand palm down against the door, concentrating. He was strong enough, and he'd been around Adorjan and the other fighters long enough, to recognize their power signatures. A grin crossed his face as he lifted his hand and pulled the door open, then strode out into the night with a howl of greeting.

Quinn watched as Garrick and Adorjan met halfway between the cars and the house, pounding each other on the back so hard, the concussion must have been heard by the neighbors, even if the howling hadn't been. He was going to miss that when he became Lord of Ireland. That easy camaraderie, the back slapping and joking. Even Garrick would treat him differently. They'd still be friends, still joke on occasion, but there would be a new distance between them. Unbridgeable. Vampires were hardwired that way. It was necessary. He sighed and walked out into the yard, accepting greetings that were already more reserved than what Garrick had received—the back slaps not quite as hard, the occasional "my lord" slipped in.

"Sire."

Everything in Quinn responded to that simple word, and to the one vampire who had the right to call him by that title. "Adorjan," he said, turning to greet the big vampire who was his only child. They hugged briefly in the way of big men, gripping hands and slamming shoulders. "It's good to have you here, and just in time. Come inside, we'll brief you on what to expect later tonight."

"Tonight?" he said eagerly. The Hungarian accent that was his birthright was still strong after several years in the U.S., probably because he had no desire to lose it. He was a big guy, an inch over Quinn's own six foot three, with shoulder length brown hair and brown eyes. Quinn supposed he was considered handsome. Adorjan certainly never had any trouble attracting women, despite the jagged scar that bisected his right cheek, from his eye to the corner of his mouth. That scar marked him as different among vampires. The vampire symbiote could heal almost any injury, even those acquired decades before a vampire's turning. It was almost unheard of for a vampire to bear a disfiguring scar. Quinn had offered to heal him outright, rather than waiting for the symbiote to get around to it. The big Hungarian had not only refused, he'd had one of the vampire tattoo artists infuse the scar with the same combination of blood and ink that prevented the symbiote from healing tattoos. The scar was a mark of defiance against the brutal regime who'd imprisoned and tortured him. A symbol of his hatred and his triumph, too. Because he'd killed the man who'd given it to him.

And yet, this angry man who'd trusted no one had seen something in Quinn to admire. After years of working for him as a human, he'd gone down on one knee and pledged his loyalty, and only then had asked to be made vampire. Quinn liked to think he was a good man, a good leader. He'd rejected the capricious cruelty of Marcelina and patterned himself after lords like Rajmund and Raphael. They were unyielding in their power, but they treated their people fairly, demanding only loyalty in return. It mattered to Quinn that Adorjan had asked to be turned, that he'd wanted Quinn to be his Sire. It was a trust that he wouldn't betray, and it was why Adorjan was one of those vampires who would form Quinn's inner circle in the centuries to come.

"We're moving in on the local vampire smuggling operation," he explained to Adorjan. "And I expect bloodshed before the night is over."

"The others will be happy to hear it," the big vampire said eagerly. "All this flying and driving can send a vampire over the edge of crazy. Too much sitting in one place."

Quinn laughed. "Come on in, then," he said, leading the way back into the house. "Let's not entertain the neighbors. We have blood, if you need it," he added softly.

"I'm good, but one or two of the others will be glad of it. Thank you, Sire."

Quinn signaled Garrick, who got everyone moving in the right direction, and before long, they were all settled around the dining room table, with its multiple computers and, now, Quinn's neat stacks of printouts, most of which already bore his handwritten notes.

"This all came over from the master vampire who ran the local smugglers until last night."

"What happened last night?" Adorjan asked the question, even though he and Quinn had already discussed it somewhat. As Quinn's security chief, it was his responsibility to make sure everyone was briefed.

Quinn explained about Christie and the other vampires at the warehouse, while Garrick offered bagged blood in a warm water bath. Quinn moved around the table as he talked, gathering the tidy stacks of paper and moving them over to a sturdy sideboard, where they wouldn't get shuffled out of order, or, worse, dribbled with blood. He caught Garrick's bemused look, but ignored it. If being neat was his worst sin . . . but it wasn't. Never would be. He'd been one of Rajmund's warriors for decades, before Raj had become Lord of the Northeast, and he'd governed Maine's vampire community for him after that. Vampires were violent by nature, and sometimes that violence drove them too far. Quinn had killed to defend Rajmund and his rule of law, and there was no doubt that he'd have to kill again. But this time, it would be to seize and defend his own territory. And he'd do whatever he had to, kill whomever he had to, to protect the vampires who depended on him for their lives.

He thought about Eve, and the threat she posed to those same vampires. And he knew he had to confront that situation, to confront *her*, very soon.

But not tonight. Tonight was for vampires only.

They were all caught up on the plan, such as it was—basically, walk into the warehouse, trigger Christie's trap, and then kill everyone who didn't fall into line—when Garrick said, "Just one more thing." He walked over to Quinn, dropped down to one knee, and said, "I would swear to you, my lord, before we leave."

The others followed, pushing their chairs back, and dropping to their knees.

Quinn stood and stared in silence. He'd expected this at some point, but not yet. "The blood oath—"

"We all swore the blood oath months ago, and it stands," Garrick interrupted. "But the battle is upon us now, and before we go in there, I want it perfectly clear where my loyalties lie. With you. Always with you." The others signaled their agreement, some repeating the words, "with you," others simply making wordless sounds of accord.

"Thank you," Quinn said sincerely. "All of you. You honor me with your trust." He held the moment for a heartbeat, two. And then he grinned. "Now, let's go win us a territory."

The vampires rose to their feet with a roar of agreement that probably had the neighbors thinking a jet had stormed over too low, but Quinn didn't have time for the neighbors. He had a battle to win.

Dublin, Ireland

EVE LINGERED ACROSS the street from the Donnybrook mansion that was the main residence of Orrin Sorley, the Vampire Lord of Ireland. This was his "lair." That's what the monsters called it. It was the same house that Quinn had come out of a few nights ago, when he'd stopped her from questioning the accountant. Quinn still thought she'd meant to kill the vamp, and she let him think that, let him believe she was a cold-blooded killer just like the vampires she hunted.

She scowled at the thought of Quinn's attitude when it came to her late night activities. He claimed to be worried about her, but she couldn't help thinking he was more concerned about his business deal and the vampires he needed to make it happen. Asshole.

She'd considered telling him about this trip to Dublin, just so he'd know she'd be gone and wouldn't worry if he came looking for her. Yeah, she thought dismissively, in case he needed to fuck. Because that was all they ever did. It wasn't like they'd made some deep connection with each other. There'd been no flowers, no candlelit dinners. Just fucking. And, sure, she had to admit it was the best fucking of her life. The man had amazing skills and incredible recuperative powers. But her mission was more important than a good fuck. She dreamed of her brother almost every night, saw him beaten to the ground by the two vampires, heard him begging for his life while they kicked him, until he lay still and silent and dead.

She wouldn't stop until she found the vampires who'd murdered him, until they were nothing but dust in the dirt, their lives meaningless, forgotten. She knew their faces—hell, those faces haunted her dreams. And she'd learned enough about how Sorley deployed his henchmen to know that those two were probably part of his Dublin organization, just like the two she'd killed in Howth had been local only. Sorley kept his toughest warriors, his most ruthless killers, close at hand, for both his own protection and to make sure he knew what they were doing. Which was why she was moving her focus to Dublin. She was never going to find those two anywhere else.

And while she searched for Alan's killers, she'd do the world a favor and get rid of a few more of the monsters. So that some other sister didn't have to watch her brother die like a dog.

She shivered suddenly, as if the dark thoughts had brought a chill to the night. Zipping her jacket closed, she hugged herself, glad she'd thought to wear a scarf and gloves this time around. When she'd first started hunting, she'd been so focused on dressing for seduction that she'd forgotten about the hours she'd have to spend lying in wait. She'd learned since then. And not only how to dress, either. She'd fine-tuned her weapons and her technique until she'd been able to take down both of those big vampires the night she'd met Quinn. That had been the best kill of her life, but there'd been no celebration. Because of Quinn. He'd distracted her from her goal, and then, even worse, he'd made her aware, in a way she'd never been before, of the dangers of what she was doing. She hadn't killed a vampire since she'd met him. But that was about to change. She'd come to Dublin to prove something to herself, to prove that she hadn't lost her edge, hadn't lost sight of her mission.

She stilled when she detected fresh movement in the courtyard of the house. She'd established the guards' routine long ago, but this was something else. A small group of men—vampires always seemed to be men—were leaving the house, though she'd been there since before sundown and hadn't seen anyone go in. That meant this group had to have spent the day inside Sorley's headquarters, something only his inner circle ever did. At least as far as she could tell from her one time inside the house, and her many nights spent watching from afar.

She raised a pair of binoculars to her eyes, wanting details. She needed to see their faces, so she'd recognize them on the street. The binoculars were a new piece of equipment. Small and easy to conceal, but remarkably powerful.

She moved several feet down the sidewalk, careful to remain in the shadows of the tree-lined street. Between the wall and the various cars parked in the yard, it was difficult to get a good line-of-sight before they disappeared into one of the vehicles. This new group appeared to consist of three vampires, all talking amongst themselves, ignoring the guards stationed right outside the door. One of them turned to walk back inside, and she recognized him as Lorcan, Sorley's lieutenant. She'd seen him many times before, but it was the accountant who'd gotten away who'd finally given her his name and confirmed his high position within Sorley's inner circle.

Her gut tightened. If Lorcan was sending these two on a mission, then it was important. And they had to be . . . Her breath froze in her lungs. She stared into the binoculars until her eyes burned, afraid to blink, terrified she was wrong, that she was seeing what she wanted to see, not what was really there. But then one of the vamps laughed as he walked around to the driver's side of the car, and she knew.

It was them. The two who'd killed her brother. The hard reality of it finally unlocked her lungs and her legs as she raced for her car. She might have trouble keeping up with them in their fancy, high-performance sedan. But there were a lot of cars on the crowded streets of Dublin. They'd make her invisible, no matter how close she got.

Luck was with her a moment later, when the two vamps sped right past her parking space just as she began to pull out, not even slowing when they swerved around her with only an inch to spare. "Fucking vampires," she muttered. She'd noticed that about them. They were so secure in their own immortality, so confident with their enhanced senses, that they didn't give a damn about the rest of humanity who filled the city.

But they were going to learn just what an ordinary human could do. She would show them. And it would be their turn to die.

Howth, Ireland

THE WAREHOUSE WAS silent. There was no more music blasting, and only the thinnest line of dim light around the closed door of the main entrance indicated anyone might be inside. Quinn wanted to believe they'd learned their lesson from the night before, that they'd taken his admonishment about secrecy to heart. But somehow, he doubted this new security was the result of his interference. He sighed inwardly. He'd rather hoped Christie and the others would see the benefits of having a powerful vampire like himself in charge of the smuggling operation. Or, if not that, then at least recognize the opportunity to do Orrin Sorley a favor, since Sorley *had* given Howth to Quinn.

On the other hand, maybe that's exactly what they thought they were doing. Getting into Sorley's good graces by killing off a thorn in his side. A very sharp, prickly thorn named Quinn Kavanagh.

Quinn waited until all of his team were out of their cars and gathered around him, then let his senses stretch out to the building in front of him, searching for life signs, listening to heartbeats, eavesdropping on the leaking thoughts of the people inside. Most humans didn't realize just how different vampires were from the humanity they'd left behind. Vampire hearts beat stronger and faster, and their lungs drew more deeply, but fewer breaths per minute. It was their minds that set them apart, however. They sparked with a much higher level of activity than humans, their brains a constant buzz of neurons going off like fireworks in the night sky.

Not every vampire was capable of what Quinn was about to do, to scan a building and determine how many life forms were inside, how many vampires, how many humans. But for a vampire of Quinn's strength? It was as natural as breathing. "No humans in there," he said. "Fifteen vampires, including Christie." Quinn shook his head. Christie was shining like a fucking beacon, compared to the others in the warehouse. He was a master vamp, but he didn't need to paint himself like a giant target. Either he was too stupid to conceal his presence, or he wanted Quinn to sense him and ignore everyone else. Like that was going to happen.

"Rules of engagement," he said quietly. "You kill anyone who tries to kill you. No mercy. But remember, I'm here to establish my right to rule, not only in Howth, but all of Ireland. I can't start by killing every vampire I meet. So, don't kill anyone who's not a threat. I'll handle Christie. He has to die. The others—" He shrugged one shoulder. "—will be given a choice. We're vampires, not mindless thugs. You understand?"

A chorus of muffled agreement responded.

Quinn grinned. "Great, then, let's have some fun." He strode the short distance to the door and reached to pull it open.

Adorjan got there first. "Don't want to get your head blown off before you even get started," he murmured, then stepped in front of Quinn and yanked the door open.

The warehouse was empty. Or, at least, that's what they wanted Quinn to think. Did Christie really believe Quinn wouldn't have checked first? Or maybe it was much simpler than that. Maybe Christie didn't realize just how powerful Quinn was. Sure, Quinn had concealed his true strength when he'd confronted Christie last night, but Sorley had a better sense of him. He could have clued Christie in, but it would appear that he hadn't. The Irish lord seemed to enjoy playing games with other vampires' lives, pitting his vampires one against the other. Or at least against Quinn.

Christie suddenly appeared from the hallway in back, near the office where he'd met with Quinn the night before.

"Quinn," he said, smiling with feigned surprise. "And you've brought friends."

"Not friends. Advisers. Vampires with experience running a smuggling organization, or its equivalent. Where are the others?"

"Out and about. Doing whatever it is they do with their free time, I suppose. I didn't see the need to have them here for this meeting. Everything is ready for inventory," he said, sweeping his arm to indicate the warehouse full of presumably smuggled goods. "Did you have a chance to go over the records I sent you?"

Quinn wanted to laugh. Christie was so fucking smug, so certain he'd outwitted the stupid American. He didn't bother to answer the vampire's question. Without turning away from him, he addressed his own people, saying, "Make yourselves comfortable, lads," and then made as if to follow the Howth vampire into the back.

It was the tiniest noise that made him stop, the most miniscule flicker of awareness in his brain. Warning his team with a quick mental blast, he released the bonds that held his power in check. It flowed around him in a glorious nebula, invisible to most others, but a swirl of gold fire to his eyes, ethereal and fragile in appearance. But it was as hard as diamond, an impenetrable shield that he raised between his team and the vampires who suddenly materialized all around them, some coming in through a side door, others popping up from their useless concealment amid the crowded shelves.

Quinn's eyes never left Christie. He caught the look of shock on the vamp's face a moment before Christie screamed for the Howth vampires to, "Kill these fuckers!"

But it wasn't vampiric power that lashed into Quinn and his team. These were smugglers, after all. They opened up with automatic weapons, spraying round after round that crashed into Quinn's shield and fell away, until finally his patience snapped. Yes, these vampires were potentially his people, but enough was enough.

Reaching deep within, to the most primitive depths of his soul, he found the unique power gifted to him by his vampire blood. He found . . . fire.

Vampires screamed as blue flames reached out to engulf them, burning endlessly, but leaving their bodies untouched, so that the agony never ended. They writhed in pain, begging for an end, for mercy.

Don't they know? Quinn thought distantly. There was no mercy in the world of Vampire. He slowly returned his gaze to Christie, whom he'd left trapped in place, but untouched by the blue flames.

"My lord," Christie said, going down on one knee. "I didn't know."

"What didn't you know?" Quinn crooned, gliding a step closer.

"Th-that you had such power, that—"

"That I could kill you with a thought? Or let you suffer the way they are?" He gestured casually at the vampires still writhing within their prisons of the blue flame.

"My lord, please."

Quinn tilted his head curiously. "Please? Please what?"

"Don't . . ." He shot a terrified look at the screaming vampires. "Spare me."

"Ah. You believe they deserve to suffer, but you don't?"

Christie's eyes rolled in terror, until all Quinn could see were bloodshot white orbs. "Mercy, my lord."

"Very well," Quinn said idly, his gaze wandering over the trapped vampires. "Not everyone needs to die. *They* were just doing their jobs." His gaze swung back to Christie. "Doing what you told them to."

"Nooooo!" Christie's scream of denial lasted far longer than his life, as Quinn surrounded him with flames that went from blue to fiery orange in the blink of an eye, leaving nothing but a pile of dust that danced merrily as the fire consumed even that.

With a thought, the blue flames dropped from around the screaming vampires, and they fell to the warehouse floor, unconscious. When they woke, they'd remember being trapped and a vague sense of horror. But there'd be no specific recollection of fire, unless Quinn decided to make them remember. He didn't think of himself as cruel, but it was a cruel weapon. It was also very effective.

Quinn swung his gaze around to scan his people, afraid of what he'd see. They all knew what he could do. He'd made sure of it before he recruited them. But, other than Garrick, they'd never seen him burn another vampire, or any living thing, into dust.

Quinn had known early on that his power was unusual. After killing Marcelina, he and Garrick had found Rajmund, and Quinn had learned even more about his extraordinary ability. Every vampire born with the power to be a lord had a unique gift. Quinn had seen what Rajmund could do, had heard stories of Lucas's power on the battlefield. And he'd recently witnessed firsthand the unbelievable power wielded by Raphael, a power so great that he didn't know how a single vampire could contain it.

But he'd never heard of a power as willfully destructive as his own. Was there any pain greater than that inflicted by fire? He'd worked with it over the years, until he could control its effect. Blue flames to cause pain without damage to the flesh, orange to kill. There was also a paler flame, nearly white, that trapped a victim, but inflicted only terror, a wordless threat. It was all horrific. But it was his to wield, and so he'd studied it, practicing over the years, until he could not only control its destructiveness, but wield it effectively. Because he'd known even then that he had the power of a vampire lord, that the day would come when he'd want a territory of his own. That he'd have to fight to make that happen, and then fight some more to defend the people that were his. And he had to be ready.

"My lord."

His gut clenched at the formal phrase coming from Garrick. This was it. No one had forced this fate on him. Sure, Marcelina had turned him unwilling, and the vampire symbiote had given him this power whether he wanted it or not. But he'd decided what happened after that. He didn't have to be a lord, didn't have to rule so much as a nest, much less an entire territory. He could have continued his law practice, with his life only slightly altered. But he'd chosen to embrace the power he'd been given. He'd chosen to rule. And now it was time for him to step up and meet his fate, just as he'd done his entire life.

"Garrick," he said.

"What do we do with . . ." His cousin glanced at the collapsed vampires.

"They'll come around soon enough. When they do, send them home to recover and sleep out the day. But I want them back here tomorrow night. Christie had one thing right. We need an inventory, and that's going to take people and time. Anyone who doesn't show will be fair game. Make sure they understand that.

"In the meantime, I need to finish going through those records Christie sent me. He packed them with useless information to obscure the rest. He wasn't as clever as he thought, but I'll still need time to get through it all. Can I leave all of this to you?"

"Of course. Adorjan will drive you—"

"I don't need anyone—"

"You revealed your power tonight, my lord. Sorley may suspect what you are, but this will give him confirmation. Someone in this lot will talk, no matter how much we threaten. That makes you a target. Adorjan is your new security chief. Let him do his job."

Quinn stared at his cousin. "Son of a bitch," he swore softly. "All right. Adorjan," he called, "let's go."

QUINN WOKE THE next night knowing there were many more vampires in the house than there had been previously. It was more than a simple awareness of the crowd. He could sense every one of his team individually, could feel their sleeping minds. He woke earlier than any of them. He was accustomed to waking before Garrick, of course. And he'd woken before Marcelina at the end, too. But he'd never had this crystal clarity of every mind around him. He found it . . . refreshing. He'd always preferred order to chaos, precision to sloppiness. He'd driven more than one legal assistant to the verge of resigning, and had tipped two of them right over that edge. But that diligence, plus an iron will and unrelenting drive, had made him the youngest partner in the history of his very prestigious Boston law firm.

Of course, it was no longer his firm, and he was no longer a lawyer. A shame, really. He'd enjoyed the law. But now he was a fucking vampire lord, and it was time he began to act like it.

Throwing the blankets off, he got up from the bed. A single glance at Garrick told him his cousin would be waking before too much longer, just as his newfound awareness told him the others would, too. Adorjan would be the first of the new arrivals to wake. He was young, but as strong as Garrick. And utterly loyal.

Quinn took a quick shower, knowing the hot water wouldn't last long with so many people in the house. He started the coffee, but didn't wait for it to finish. He filled a single mug and, ignoring the sizzle and smell of burning coffee on the warmer, made his way to the dining room to make a few final notes on his computer. He wasn't naive enough to think he'd be able to continue doing research at this level once he became Lord of Ireland. He'd have to hire a few vampires to do it for him. New assistants to torment. He smiled at the thought. It had been too long. But still, he gazed around the room, with its neat stacks of newly organized files. He was going to miss this.

"My lord?"

He'd expected Garrick to show up first, but it was Adorjan who walked into the room behind him. "Good evening, Adorjan. How are the others?"

"Well, enough," he said, entering the room. "Happy to finally get started, after all our preparations."

Quinn smiled. "Good. Tonight we'll go back to the warehouse and establish a routine going forward. I've gone through all of this." He indicated the files with a sweep of his arm. "Christie was an idiot, but he kept good records, even if he did his best to make it look otherwise. This is an opportunity-based smuggling enterprise. Whatever they can get their hands on, whatever will make money, is what they bring in. Guns and drugs are high on the list, of course. No surprise there. This is Ireland. Guns are theoretically legal, but permits are hard to come by, with crisscrossed jurisdictions. That doesn't mean there aren't any. Lots of sport and hobby guns, especially in the countryside. The heavy hitters, the AK47s and 9mm with their 100 round mags, those are harder to find, but there's definitely a market for them. Some of the Howth operation's biggest clients are the gangs running drugs through the main port in Dublin. They need the firepower to deal with their Central American distributors. Oddly enough, the locals are bringing in their own supply of coke and marijuana on occasion, circumventing the Dublin gangs altogether. Lucky for them, and now for us, their few drug shipments are too small to concern the big boys in Dublin.

"We'll have to continue the operation as it is for now. Too many vampires depend on it for their livelihood. Not to mention, more than one human business, legal or otherwise. Even though my goal is to bring Ireland's vampires into the light, with nothing but legal ventures, that will take time, and I can't simply cut without replacing."

He looked up when Garrick joined them, coming in to stand next to Adorjan. "Garrick," Quinn greeted him.

"My lord," his cousin said.

The formality caused the same pain in Quinn's heart, but it was already fading. He'd never been a man to mourn the impossible. *No? Then what about Eve?* The thought rose unbidden, making his gut clench.

He shoved it aside. "I'm glad you're both here. Why don't we sit?"

They took seats around the elegant table, now clear since the files had been moved to the sideboard. Three young, fit men, each with a cup of coffee before him, casually dressed and sprawled back in their chairs—this didn't look much like the beginning of a coup, Quinn thought. But that's what it was.

"We're moving to Dublin tomorrow night." Their eyes widened only slightly, more in anticipation than surprise, Quinn thought. "I'll need one of the men to remain here to oversee the smuggling operation. It needs to be someone strong enough to control the local vampires, most of whom are strictly lower level in terms of their power. One or two have some strength, but nothing approaching the level of a master. They'll go along with the new management as long as it continues to make money. Which it will. One or two will think to take over in Christie's place, but they'll be gone after tonight. I'd rather leave more than one of our own to supervise, but I don't know what I'm going to face in Dublin. So, for now, at least, I want everyone else with me there. Any suggestions on who should stay behind?"

"Casey Austin," Garrick said immediately, exchanging a glance with Adorjan, who nodded his agreement. "He's strong enough, and he ran his family's farm before he was turned. His family still runs the place, and they consult frequently. He has a head for business, that's for sure."

Quinn nodded. "He was also raised by his Irish mother and grandmother after his father died, so he's fluent in Irish Gaelic. That's one of the reasons I chose him for this task force." He turned to Garrick. "Do you think he'll mind being left alone here?"

Garrick shook his head. "He has a knack for getting along with people. I've always thought there's some extra vampire magic in his blood. You watch, he'll have them believing he's always been one of them by the end of the night."

"Good to know." Quinn was thinking of the future, and the many ways he could use a vampire with a talent like that. "We'll head over to the warehouse as soon as everyone's up and ready, unless you have questions?"

Adorjan shook his head. "I spoke to Bell as soon as I woke tonight. They're ready for us in Dublin. Bell says it's a nice place. Good acreage, but too many neighbors, which is expected in the city like that. For now, we'll be keeping a close perimeter until we can build up our security forces, both day and night."

"Agreed. I'm trying to do something about the neighbors, though, and hope to have some extra acreage by the time this is all settled. We don't need any nosey humans snooping around and getting hurt, or worse." Quinn lowered his head, running through a mental to-do list. "I think that's it for now. Tell Casey I'd like to talk to him when he's ready."

THE LOCAL VAMPIRES were all waiting inside when Quinn and the others arrived, hanging around the edges of the warehouse, sitting on crates or lounging on chairs that looked as if they'd been stolen from the local pub. They probably had been. Adorjan had insisted on checking the perimeter before letting Quinn enter, looking for explosives or any other kind of trap set for the American vampire who'd so easily taken over their lives. Finding nothing, Adorjan still walked in ahead of Quinn, stepping aside when he determined it was safe, something Quinn had known all along. But the day would inevitably come when a location wasn't safe, when Quinn was too preoccupied with other matters to spare the kind of attention needed to anticipate that kind of betrayal. He'd be glad, then, that Adorjan was there to search out the danger for him. And that was why they both needed to begin *now* to establish routines for that future day.

Touching the big vampire's shoulder lightly, Quinn walked around him and into the warehouse, his gaze skimming over the assembled vamps. Everyone was here. Even if he hadn't memorized the faces—which he had—he'd counted them last night. But there was someone new in the warehouse, too. Someone hiding. Quinn sent a wisp of power around the area, searching, and found the newcomer lurking against the far wall, in the shadows between shelving units. Interesting. This night might prove entertaining, after all.

"Some of you might be worried about the new management," he said, setting aside thoughts of the lurker. "You might even mourn Christie's death." Quinn shrugged. "He had a choice. He made the wrong one. For those of you who didn't catch it, my name is Quinn Kavanagh. Orrin Sorley sent me here to take over this operation."

The lurker made his move then, striding into the light with heavy footfalls, as if trying to intimidate Quinn with his presence. The idea was laughable, but Quinn let the scene play out. The vampire was big and rough looking, with an unkempt beard and mean eyes. He marched forward until he stood in front of several others who were sitting to one side of the warehouse. And then he stared at Quinn, who gave him a glance of mild interest and kept talking.

"You can believe Sorley sent me or not. Your belief matters nothing to me. What does matter is that you *do your jobs*," he ended with a growl.

"So, you're the new management," the mean-eyed vamp sneered. "Let me break it down for you, *boss.*"

Quinn gave him a flat look. He had no time to waste on this asshole. Reaching out with his power—not his fire, he didn't need that for this piece of meat—he stopped the vamp's heart. Those mean eyes widened, going from arrogance to terror in a heartbeat. Quinn didn't give him time to beg. The asshole collapsed to the warehouse floor and, fortunately, was old enough to dust upon death. Half-deteriorated vampire bodies were a fucking mess.

"Anyone else have a problem with the new management?" Quinn asked, raking the crowd with cold eyes. "Good. Now, my read of Christie's notes says there's a shipment of guns coming in soon. How do we know when, exactly, they're coming?" He waited and eventually a vampire stepped forward.

"We don't." The vampire was older than the others. Older in age, that is, not appearance. He looked to be in his late thirties, but Quinn could feel the vamp's age in his bones. He was well over one hundred, maybe twice as old as that. But he had no power. Quinn tried to imagine living forever as an ordinary citizen. Getting up, going to work, snagging a tasty human for the night, going to sleep, and doing it all over again. Forever. He didn't think he could do it. He'd go insane and walk into the sun first.

He shook away such thoughts and focused on the vampire's words. "How's that work then?"

"They give us a call when they're a mile or two out, and we make arrangements to meet them."

"That's going to change. I don't leave things to chance. I want to know the lead time between their call and the actual delivery for every transaction over the last year. Sort it by boat captain, as well. We may have to cut loose some of our suppliers if they're not reliable. If I give you the list of deliveries, can you provide that info?"

The vampire nodded, seeming happy to be of service. "Yes, my lord. And what I don't remember, the other guys will."

"Any humans on the payroll? Other than boat captains, of course. That's unfortunate, but necessary."

"There's a handful of local humans who help out."

"Christie didn't list any on the payroll."

"He hired them as he needed them. Paid them in cash," another vampire said, standing up from where he'd been sitting on a stack of wooden crates.

"That's going to change, too. From now on, the only humans we hire are the ones we know we can trust. Mates, of course. Lovers if you plan on hanging around awhile. I don't want any vengeful ex-girlfriends leading the Harbor Police our way. Blood relatives are good, if you have them."

Quinn kept talking, ferreting out information, giving assignments as he went along. Casey had joined him at some point and was taking notes on everything. And all the while Quinn was strategizing, coming up with ways to make the Howth operation more profitable, part of his mind was mulling over this turn of events and trying to figure out how he felt about becoming a smuggler. Shit. Why had he wanted this job again?

QUINN SETTLED down early for his daylight sleep for a change. After the move to Dublin tomorrow night, there would be no more quiet nights for a while. He'd brought some financial reports to bed with him, thinking to catch up on the rest of the world, but the bed wasn't comfortable enough for reading. Or maybe it was that he couldn't relax enough to *get* comfortable. His mind wandered to Eve, wondering what she was doing. He probably wouldn't see as much of her once he moved to Dublin, either. Unless she lost her mind and decided to start hunting in the city again. He thought he'd succeeded in scaring her off, but he'd no sooner had the thought than he knew he was fooling himself. Nothing he'd said, nothing he *could say*, would make a difference. Eve was an intelligent woman with a will of iron. And she was stubborn as hell. She'd go after Sorley simply to prove that she could. And she'd get herself killed.

He was startled at the stab of pain that caused him. She was too vital, too wild, to die so young. And even knowing what he should do, what he'd told Garrick he *would* do, he wasn't finished with her yet.

The door opened, and his cousin walked in. He didn't say anything, just nodded his head in Quinn's direction, then began preparing for sleep.

"How'd it go at the warehouse?" Quinn asked.

"Better than expected. You were right about the local vamps. They just want to work. And Casey being Irish clinched the deal. They're going to make more money than ever."

"Smuggling," Quinn noted dryly.

Garrick turned to him. "For now." He grimaced, as if holding something back, then looked away and busied himself with his pillows.

Quinn watched him. "After your pillows are fluffed to perfection, maybe you'll tell me what's on your mind."

"It's not my place," Garrick growled.

"Oh, fuck that," he said impatiently. "Come on, Garrick. I get it. In front of the others, you have to play the dutiful lieutenant, but we shared a crib, for Christ's sake. I'm going to need *someone* who can be honest and tell me when I've gone off the rails, or when I'm just being a self-righteous prick. You've called me that often enough, and we both know I've deserved it. Occasionally."

That got him a bare grin from his cousin.

"Talk to me, Gar."

Garrick's mouth tightened as he sat on the other bed and faced Quinn. "All right, look. I get it. You have a different perspective on all this. It's in your blood, and your brain, too. We've always seen things differently, even before we were turned."

"Which is why I need your opinion."

He shifted restlessly. "I know you're stressed about the drug angle, and maybe the guns, too. You're not built to be a crook."

"I *am* a lawyer. Some people would say we're *all* crooks." He recalled Eve's opinion on the subject. She'd considered lawyers to be a step *below* most criminals.

"A *corporate* lawyer," Garrick clarified.

Quinn scoffed. "You think corporations aren't filled with crooks?"

"Point made. But I'm talking about you, not them."

He nodded. "And my sterling honesty is relevant how?" he murmured.

"It's not your honesty that matters, it's your inner control freak. Don't get hung up on fixing the vampire economy here in Howth. Casey's a good man. He'll do a great job, if you let him. But here's the thing. So could *any other member* of your team. But there's only one of *you*. And only you can take on the job that we've all come here for. You're a vampire lord, Quinn. That's your destiny. Not becoming the financial wizard of Howth."

Quinn smiled slightly, liking the title, even though it would never be his. "The plan all along," he said, "was to start slowly. To show Sorley what I can do, and work my way up from the inside."

"A plan you shelved a day after we got here."

Quinn sat silently for a moment, then said, "I hate it when you're right."

Garrick barked a laugh. "You always did," he said, then added slyly, "You could just walk in there tomorrow night and kill Sorley. Get it over with."

Quinn snorted. "And spend the next two years putting out fires in the lower ranks. No, thank you. It might come to that eventually, but I'll need a reason that's obvious to everyone. Even if I have to create it myself."

"Sorley will come after you now," Garrick said soberly.

Quinn grinned viciously. "Let him come. Ireland is already mine. Sorley just doesn't know it yet."

IT DIDN'T TAKE long for Quinn and the others to pack up the next night. They'd all traveled lightly, not knowing where they'd find themselves at the end of the journey. The biggest bags were filled with weapons, not personal gear. Some vampire leaders spurned modern weapons, claiming vampires didn't need them to survive and triumph over regular humans. But Quinn believed in using any assets available to him. Besides, in his world, other vampires were the enemy, not humans. An AK15 or MP5 submachine gun wouldn't kill a vampire most of the time, but it would at least put him down long enough to ensure his death by other means.

They were in the yard of the Howth house, loading the cars, when Garrick got a call. He switched it to speaker almost immediately, but Quinn didn't need the speakerphone to tell him who was calling or what he was saying.

"I've got three vamps down," came Casey's angry voice. "The shooter's stopped for now, but my guys are furious. They're on the hunt, and I didn't try to stop them."

"Any dead?" Quinn asked, stepping to Garrick's side.

"My lord," Casey said quickly. "No dead, though if the shooter had had better aim, or a better weapon—"

"We're on our way," he interrupted, then signaled to Garrick. "You and the others get over to the warehouse, make sure it's secure. This could have been a ruse to pull most of us away, and I don't want Casey left there alone."

"And you?" Garrick said quietly, for Quinn's ears only.

"I know where she lives," he said, because this had Eve written all over it. And his cousin clearly agreed. "This ends now. Go with the others. I'll take Adorjan," he added, before his cousin could object.

Garrick's expression said he still wasn't happy, but he nodded and headed for one of the other cars, leaving the big Range Rover for Quinn. He tossed the keys to Adorjan, who strode over to the vehicle and slid behind the wheel.

Quinn let him drive, but he refused to sit in the backseat like some sort of pasha who couldn't drive his own car. Rajmund had always told him it was his American upbringing—everyone equal and all that. Quinn thought it probably had more to do with endless hours spent watching TV shows about American cowboys facing down bad guys. But whatever it was, if there was going to be danger, he wanted to be in the thick of it, not rolled in bubble wrap and hidden in the trunk.

Adorjan glanced at him with a slight smile, as if following the trend of his thoughts. "Where to, my lord?"

He wasn't surprised that the vampire had figured out they weren't going to the warehouse. Adorjan was smart. Quinn wouldn't have made him security chief, otherwise.

"I don't know the address," Quinn told him. "But I can direct you there."

They rode in silence until they were almost upon Eve's tiny flat.

"Is there anything I need to know, my lord? Anything about whoever lives here?"

"It's a woman," Quinn said with no expression at all. "Human. And I suspect she's our shooter from the warehouse tonight."

Adorjan turned his head sharply and studied Quinn. "I can't let you—"

"She won't hurt me," he interrupted. He wanted to tell the vamp that he didn't need permission from anyone to do whatever the fuck he wanted. If he wanted to walk into Eve's flat and confront her with the damn rifle still hot in her hand, then that's what he'd do. And fuck the consequences. But he didn't say any of that. Adorjan was doing his job. Probably better than Quinn was doing his right now. "We'll approach together," he said as Adorjan parked. "Once you see she's harmless, you'll wait in the car until I signal otherwise."

"Yes, my lord." He wasn't happy. Quinn could feel his displeasure radiating in waves from where he sat behind the wheel.

Quinn opened the door to relieve the pressure. "Let's go."

They approached Eve's door cautiously, but with no real expectation of danger. At least on Quinn's part. She seemed to have been put on this earth to drive him mad, but he understood her. She'd gotten her shots off, taken down a few vamps, and had everyone running around. And now she'd hurried back to her hole-in-the-wall flat, thinking that made her safe. All these years of hunting vampires, and she still didn't seem to understand them very well. Vampires were predators, hunters on a scale that made her efforts seem puny in comparison. They'd track her down like dogs on a trail. Her fucking perfume alone would lead them to her front door. If Quinn hadn't sent in his people to call back the other vampires and secure the warehouse, they'd be here already.

By the time they reached Eve's front door, Quinn knew she was home. He could hear her moving around, could hear her heart pounding and the rasp of her breathing . . . as if she'd recently run a distance.

He'd been half hoping he was wrong about her, that she'd spent the night home alone, working on her computer. "Son of a bitch," he muttered, and raised his hand to knock. But Adorjan got there before him. He'd have heard the evidence of her recent escape just as clearly as Quinn. There was no way in hell he was going to let his new lord take the lead when they confronted the crazy woman who'd been shooting up vampires only minutes earlier.

"Gently," Quinn admonished. "And no fangs. We don't want to wake the entire neighborhood."

Adorjan pulled back his fist, replacing it with a two-knuckle tap that was still enough to have Eve stop whatever she'd been doing inside. But she didn't answer the door.

Quinn sighed and shook his head. Humans. They paid so little attention to the vampires among them. Eve was a hunter. She, at least, should know better. He jerked his chin toward the door, telling Adorjan to knock again. Which he did, slightly harder, but still muted, compared to what he could have done.

"Eve," Quinn said, too impatient to play her game. "I know you're in there. Open the door." He heard an audible curse, rapid footsteps, and then metallic sounds as several locks were disengaged.

Eve pulled open the door. "Come on in. Hurry," she said, her expression a combination of pleasure and concern that morphed to shock when, instead of Quinn, she found a very pissed off Adorjan glaring down at her.

She gave a little squeak of surprise and took a step back, her eyes wide with fear until she saw Quinn. Anger replaced the fear. "What the hell, Quinn? Who's *this* guy?" She jerked a thumb over her shoulder as she walked away from him and back into the room, leaving the door open.

Quinn slipped past Adorjan and caught Eve easily, getting an arm around her waist and swinging her around before she could grab the rifle lying on her rumpled bed. She obviously had a poor opinion of his deductive skills. He shifted his hold to trap her arms and stop her flailing fists. For all her struggles, however, she never screamed, confining her protests to hissed, profanity-laced imprecations. He grinned. She didn't want the neighbors hearing the ruckus any more than he did.

Adorjan reached past them to grab the rifle. "Remington, my lord." He worked the bolt repeatedly, ejecting three unused rounds. "Winchester 270s, maybe 300-yard range if a shooter knows what she's doing." He glowered at Eve. "No one else was firing a rifle in Howth tonight." He sniffed the barrel. "And this one's been recently fired."

"Take the gun and wait for me outside, please," Quinn said.

Adorjan met his gaze briefly, full of rebellion. But then his eyes dropped, and he nodded. "As you say, my lord." Taking the rifle, he strode for the front door.

"Hey," Eve protested. "That's *my* rifle."

"Be quiet, Eve," Quinn murmured as his new security chief walked outside and closed the door. "Count your blessings."

"Fuck my blessings," she snarled, writhing furiously against his hold. "What gives you the right—"

"I'm stronger than you are," he said coolly. "In human history, power has always equaled right."

"What? You're a philosopher now? Let go of me." She jabbed a sharp elbow into his gut. He barely felt it. Those training sessions with Garrick were really paying off.

"Not until you calm down."

"Fuck calming down, too. You want history? Here's some for you. Men have been telling women to calm down for centuries . . . every time we disagree with them. And we *hate* it."

Quinn chuckled. "You and I haven't disagreed on anything yet. We haven't even managed to talk."

Seeming to relent, Eve relaxed in his hold, letting her head fall back against his shoulder as she caught her breath. Quinn wasn't fooled. Eyeing the tiny kitchen, with its butcher block full of knives, he positioned himself between it and her and loosened his arms. She glared at him, then made a break for it, taking two steps toward the front door before Quinn said, "Adorjan will be waiting out there. You're better off talking to me than him."

She spun on him, her dark eyes flashing. "Who the fuck is that guy? For that matter, who are you really? And no bullshit this time."

"I told you. I'm a businessman, come to find my fortune in the land of my birth. As for Adorjan. . . ." He shrugged. "He's my bodyguard. Dublin's a dangerous place."

She snorted dismissively, rubbing her arms up and down, as if they hurt. "It's only dangerous for people who persist in doing business with vampires," she said sulkily.

Quinn saw bruises on her pale skin, and his gut roiled at this evidence that he'd hurt her. "Maybe." He took her arm with care. "Sit down, Eve. We need to talk."

"I don't want to sit," she snapped, slapping at his hands.

"Fine, then we'll stand." He took a step closer, forcing her to tilt her head back to look up at him, and finally let his anger show. The calm, reasonable Quinn was gone. He needed her to understand the consequences of what she'd done. "What the hell, Eve?" he growled. "Do you have a fucking death wish or something? You're lucky your aim is so lousy. Those are vampires down there. Do you know what they'll do if they catch you?"

"They haven't caught me yet," she said smugly.

"*I* did."

"Only because you know where I—"

Quinn let his fangs glide out, sharp points pressing against his lower lip. He didn't need to see the shocked look on her face to know what he looked like. He'd stared at himself in front of the mirror for hours when he'd first been turned, and he looked far more threatening now than he had then.

Eve tried to run again. Of course, she did. But she didn't manage a single full step this time before he stopped her, his arms wrapping her in a powerful hug, his hand over her mouth in case she tried to yell. He really didn't want to hurt her, but she fought him. Kicking, nails digging into his arms, her teeth biting his hand . . .

He pried her mouth away before she could draw blood, cupping her jaw tenderly. If she took his blood, she'd be thrown into orgasm. She'd hate that. She'd hate *him*. And he didn't want her to hate him. "You don't want to do that, sweetheart," he said quietly.

She tried to shove his arm away, taking advantage of his careful handling. But he was done pretending to be something he wasn't. He held her gently, but he didn't let go.

"You lied," she snarled, twisting around to glare at him, her eyes filled with hatred. It was nothing more than he'd expected, but it still hurt, as if she'd stabbed him deep in the chest with one of those kitchen knives.

"When?" he demanded. "When did I lie? I told you I was working with Sorley—"

"You said you wanted him dead!"

"I do. But I want *Sorley* dead, not every vampire on the fucking island. Look, I'm sorry about your brother, but not every vampire is a killer."

"What do *you* know about it?"

He laughed in disbelief. "Are you kidding? Look at me! I know a thousand times more about this than you do. Most vampires are ordinary citizens. They're shopkeepers and accountants. Lawyers, even."

"Like you? Or was that a lie, too?"

"Harvard Law, darling. Class of fifty-six."

"Eighteen fifty-six?" she asked with saccharine sweetness.

He gave her an exaggerated look of offense. "You wound me."

She scoffed and abruptly renewed her attempts at escape, with the same result. "Let go of me, you unholy bastard."

"Now that's just offensive. I'm neither a bastard, nor unholy. Stop that, damn it," he snarled, when she tried to dig her nails into his arm. "I don't want to put you out, but I will if I have to."

She twisted around to stare up at him again, wide-eyed, her chest heaving. "You wouldn't," she whispered, terror written on every inch of her face.

"Jesus Christ, Eve, what do you think I'm going to do? I just want to talk."

She went soft in his arms. He wasn't fooled this time either, but he welcomed the reprieve. "Think," he said, patiently. "If a human had murdered your brother, you wouldn't be wandering around killing random humans, would you?"

"It's not the same."

"It's exactly the same. The truth is that your brother was into something dangerous enough that it got him killed. Something illegal."

"Alan was a good man."

"And good men do bad things all the time. For money, for love, for all sorts of things. I didn't know your brother, but I'm sure he had his reasons."

"I hate you," she snarled with such vehemence that Quinn suspected he'd hit a nerve. Had the brother needed money to support their family? Was that why Eve was so driven to track down his killers? Was it guilt?

"Hate me if you want, sweetheart," he murmured. "But if you come after my people, I'll have to stop you."

"You'd kill me?" The look she turned on him this time was devastated, as if he'd wounded her deeply. It infuriated him. She was the one killing vampires, calling him a monster and fighting him tooth and nail. What right did *she* have to be wounded?

"Right back at you, Eve. Could *you* kill *me?*"

EVE STARED. SHE'D had sex with this man, had felt herself sliding into something more than just liking him. She'd even missed him when they'd been apart, wondering where he was and what he was doing. Worrying that he'd done something stupid and gotten in too deeply with his vampire business partners. Or that he'd been killed, just like her brother.

And now? She felt betrayed. Humiliated. But despite her angry words, she wasn't feeling hatred. The hell of it was, he was right. She *couldn't* kill him, despite what he was. Because she didn't want him dead. She was even still worried about him. How fucked up was that? But he just didn't seem to understand how dangerous Sorley was, or how easily he could end up dead at the Irish vampire's hands.

Tears filled her eyes. "Let me go."

His arms fell away, but he remained close to her, his size and strength reminding her of what it had felt like to make love to him, to have that beautifully male body of his between her thighs, hot and heavy, his arms bracketing her shoulders, his hips driving . . .

She closed her eyes before he could see what she was thinking. And then she remembered what he was. Vampire. He'd probably read every thought as it occurred to her, every filthy memory . . .

"No," he said. "I'm not reading your thoughts. I wouldn't. But you have a very expressive face."

"So, what now?" she asked sullenly.

"That depends on you. Can I trust you?"

"That's rich, coming from a vampire."

He sighed. "I don't have time to try and convince you of the truth. I have things to do and people who depend on me, whether you believe it or not." He ran a hand back through his hair, as if she'd worn him out. "Stop this, Eve," he said finally. "Or I'll stop it for you."

He left then. Without trying to touch her, without kissing her good-bye. And she felt stupid for the disappointment that tightened her throat.

She followed him outside, hurrying behind him as he strode for his car. "What about my gun?" she demanded.

He shot her a look over his shoulder, his handsome face creased with a half-smile. "We'll be keeping that for now."

The bodyguard stepped up onto the curb and lifted his dark gaze to her, as if he'd heard every word she'd said to Quinn inside her flat. And maybe he had. Vampires had incredible hearing, everyone knew that. He opened the Range Rover's door and positioned himself between her and Quinn, as his head dipped in a respectful nod. "My lord," he said, waiting until Quinn was out of her line of sight before turning to shoot her a deadly glare. Quinn might not be ready to kill her, but that one would do it with a smile on his face and never think twice.

Eve jammed her hands into her pockets, furious and frustrated in equal measure. The damn vampire had shoved his way into her house uninvited, stolen her rifle, *threatened* her, and then waltzed out like he was the fucking king of Ireland. Her hands fisted, the fingers of one closing around something hard and small. She fidgeted with it idly, staring daggers at Quinn while he gazed serenely back at her. The smug bastard. And with good reason. There was nothing she could do about . . . Wait. Her finger traced the outlines of the object in her pocket. Not nothing, after all. Storming up to the closed door, she smacked Quinn's window with her right hand to cover the sound of her left slapping something else entirely on the roof of the SUV. Behind the glass, Quinn smiled and winked, while Eve mouthed, "Fuck you," and shot him a one-fingered salute as they pulled away.

She watched until the vehicle's red taillights disappeared around the corner, then raced into her flat and dug around her tiny desk until she found what she was looking for—directions for the tracker she'd slapped on the smug asshole's roof. She'd bought it for her cell phone a while back and then forgotten all about it, when she couldn't find the damn thing. Apparently, it had been sitting in the pocket of the sweater she wore around the flat the whole time. *There* was a bit of serendipity that she wasn't going to complain about. But now, she needed to make sure it worked, and see how far she could track it.

"You think you're so smart," she muttered, clutching the flimsy page of directions. Walking over to her bed, she propped herself against the headboard and started to read, but. . . . Her bed smelled like him. Her eyes burned with tears she refused to shed. Hugging her knees to her chest, she wrapped her arms around her bent legs and tried to think. She couldn't believe she'd fucked a vampire. Not just fucked, but . . . hell, admit it. He'd been charming and smart, even funny sometimes, when he wasn't trying to run her life. And so handsome that it made her teeth ache. She'd *liked* him—one of the monsters who'd killed her brother. Except . . . he hadn't been a monster. Not with her.

Tears filled her eyes again and she didn't try to stop them. Frustration, sadness, and confusion all tumbled together. She hadn't cried this much since her brother had died. Hadn't been this confused in much longer than that. She'd been so focused on finishing university, so excited about going on to graduate school. And then her brother had been killed and vengeance had substituted itself for books and studying. A new focus, a new obsession. Her life for the last five years had revolved around nothing but revenge, working just enough to pay the rent, to buy food, and give her mam what she could. And there'd been equipment to buy, too. Things she'd needed in her hunt. Like the damn rifle Quinn had just stolen from her. She'd scrimped and saved for two *years* to afford it, had spent even more money going to the range, learning how it worked, practicing until her arms trembled with effort.

So stupid. Tonight was the first time she'd used it in real life. She hadn't even been trying to kill the local vamps, though she'd never admit that to Quinn. She'd been trying to wound, not kill, and she'd hit what she'd been aiming for. It had been a sort of live fire exercise. Everything she'd read about long distance shooting had discussed the careful compensation needed for wind and elevation, and even temperature and humidity. She hadn't been able to practice under the right kind of long-range conditions, hence tonight's shooting gallery.

She'd counted it as test before she headed back to Dublin and her pursuit of the vampires who'd killed her brother. She'd followed them for two nights before coming back to Howth, and she'd only come back because she had to get some side work done, to earn enough damn money to keeping going. But in the two nights she'd watched them, she'd figured out where the pair of murdering vamps lived and, most importantly, where they fed. She'd even snapped a couple pictures with her cell phone. She'd been ready for the kill, and now the gun was gone. All that money and work for nothing.

She sighed and rubbed the bruises on her arm where Quinn had grabbed her, but that only reminded her of the stricken look on his face when he'd noticed those same bruises. It *humanized* him and made her want to like him, even more than she already did. Or had, before she'd known what he was. A vampire. And not just any vampire, but one with a bodyguard. She started thinking about how he'd always seemed to be the one in charge, even with his so-called cousin. Was Garrick even really his cousin? Or was that just another farce on his part? He hadn't been faking his anger tonight, that was for sure. He seemed to consider those vampires *his*, for some reason. And he claimed to want Sorley dead. Was it possible? Had he come over from America and taken over a chunk of Sorley's business as the first step toward his real goal?

She knocked her head against the wall. She didn't know what to do now. Should she continue her crusade? But what if that meant confronting Quinn? Could she kill *him*? Could she kill someone he cared about? Like his supposed cousin, or even that stupid bodyguard who treated him like he was royalty. Someone deserving respect. Did vampires have feelings like regular people? Did they love?

She pounded her head against the wall harder this time. Damn Quinn for doing this to her. Her fist crumpled the tracker directions, and she stilled. That was a place to start. She'd follow him and find out what he was up to. And then, maybe she'd get her damn rifle back.

QUINN WAS FURIOUS at himself and at Eve, too. That wasn't how he'd wanted to tell her what he was. But then, he admitted, he hadn't given the big reveal much thought at all. He'd been stupid to think he could hide it from her in the first place, stupid to think that scene could have gone any differently than it had, no matter how he'd done it. Unless it had been over his bloody body. Or hers. He growled. No way in hell. He didn't know how he was going to swing it, but somehow he had to extricate Eve from this clusterfuck, without her getting hurt. Even if it meant bundling her up and shipping her somewhere where there were no vampires for her to kill. Except he couldn't think where that would be. Alaska, maybe. Those long summer days wouldn't be very friendly to his kind.

He glanced at Adorjan as they left Howth and headed for Dublin. The big vampire hadn't even tried to put Quinn in the backseat this time. Smart vampire. Quinn wasn't in the mood to be managed. He was usually the one who did the managing. Like now. He thought of all the people depending on him to get this right. The human security team who'd picked up and moved to Ireland on a promise. The vampires who'd risked their lives to join him in this fight. They deserved better of him. Right.

With a metaphorical slap of his hands, he put Eve out of his thoughts, shelving the problem she represented with the ease of long practice. It was all about prioritizing. He couldn't change who he was. *Wouldn't* change it, even if he could. He'd hated Marcelina for what she'd done to him. But now? He loved the fucking power of it, the new challenge that every night brought. He was going to rule a territory. Lord fucking Quinn. That's why he was in Ireland. It wasn't to fall in love. He was there to fulfil the potential of his vampire blood, to serve the unrelenting drive that had hounded him from the moment he'd awoken to discover his entire life had been turned upside down.

Boston, MA, USA, 57 years ago

MARCELINA'S FACE twisted in anger, stealing her beauty, making her look like the monster she really was. That's what ordinary humans called vampires. Monster. Devil. Spawn of Satan.

Ridiculous. Vampires were no more intrinsically monstrous that humans. History was filled with cases of serial killers, men and women who'd inflicted horrific suffering on their fellow humans to satisfy their own sick desires.

Marcelina was one of those, Quinn thought to himself. She'd probably been torturing the neighbor's cat long before she'd been made a vampire. He didn't know who her Sire had been, or why he'd chosen to turn her. He supposed the vamp had been motivated by her beauty, maybe even desire. But he could have saved the world a lot of suffering if he'd simply fucked her to death as a human and been done with it. Quinn would happily rip out the bastard's heart if he ever met him.

"Are you listening to me?" Marcelina snarled.

Quinn lifted his gaze, focusing on the beautiful psychopath who was his Sire. "I'm listening, Marcelina. I simply don't agree with you."

Her mouth opened in disbelief. "Agree? It's not your place to agree or disagree. I am your Sire. You will do what I say."

Quinn fought not to sigh with the sheer tedium of her demands. She was never going to win with this line of argument. *Ex injuria jus non oritur.* Basically, she had no inherent right to benefit from her crime against *him,* and, he, therefore, owed her no service. But he wasn't going to waste time debating entitlements with her. He was much more concerned about derailing her plans for tonight.

"If we follow your plan, we'll kill too many civilians, Marcie." He used the nickname intentionally, knowing how much she hated it. "We can't afford to go around willy-nilly killing humans."

There was so much hatred in the look she turned on him, Quinn had to smile in private satisfaction. He loved that look. It was his goal to make her regret every day of her life from the moment she'd decided to turn him and Garrick without even the pretense of consent.

"You will do what I tell you," she snapped.

"No, actually, I won't. You'd have me kill humans and put vampires at risk, for what? Because some asshole threw you over more than a hundred years ago? Get real."

She hissed like a snake. An apt comparison. "It was *sixty* years ago, and his betrayal forced me to abandon my home." She gestured around her at the rundown mansion. "I had to leave everything I knew, everyone who loved me. I was forced to run for my life in the middle of the night. I. Want. Him. Dead."

"Yeah, I get that. But here's the problem. That pimply-faced college student who dumped you is now a United States congressman. You go after *him*, you risk bringing a world of hurt on every vampire in the U.S. Besides which, the only way to get to him at night is either at a public event or in his home. Both of those venues will risk human casualties, and he has five small grandchildren who live with him. That's beyond the pale, even for you."

His risk assessment wasn't quite honest. He could think of several ways to kill the congressman and make it appear to be a natural death or an accident. But Quinn wasn't going to kill *anyone* who'd been lucky enough to escape Marcelina's clutches. He met her gaze evenly. "I won't do it."

He waited, every sense he owned attuned to Marcelina's tiniest twitch. There was no way in hell she'd let this pass. But he'd known that going in. He understood his bitch of a Sire. He'd been studying her for 12 months and 23 nights. That's how long it had been since she'd enthralled and then turned him. Oh, sure, she'd loved him at first. He was fit and strong, and, in the early throes of his vampirism, he'd been so eager to please his beautiful Sire. His eagerness hadn't survived the first month he'd spent with her, but she'd kept him in her bed longer than that. Marcelina wasn't a particularly powerful vampire, but her skill at seduction was remarkable. He'd always assumed those skills were rooted in her vampiric blood, but maybe that had only been a way to excuse his own weakness in succumbing as long as he had.

It had been more than six months since he'd shared her bed and, looking at her now, he couldn't imagine what he'd been thinking. He saw the manipulation beneath the charm, the cold calculation behind the seduction. But more than that, he saw the blackness of her soul.

Obviously, Marcelina didn't take rejection well. Witness her persistence in demanding revenge against a lover whose only crime had been breaking up with her decades ago. And, equally, her decision to send Quinn to exact that revenge, knowing full well that he was likely to be killed by the congressman's security detail, which was large and well-armed. And if he managed not to die, there was still the likelihood that he'd be identified and hunted down by the human authorities. Marcelina's escapee lover was not just a congressman, he was a *wealthy* congressman. No one who wanted to keep their job would let an attack on him go unpunished.

This mission wasn't only a potential death sentence for random vampires and innocent humans. It was intended to be a death sentence for *Quinn*. Unfortunately for Marcelina, he wasn't in the mood to die.

Her mouth twisted into a sly smile. "How are your parents, Quinn? Your father's a lawyer, isn't he? And your mother, a pretty little housewife. Niall and Maureen from Chicago. Such very Irish names. Do they know what their bonny boy is up to lately?"

Quinn's gaze hardened. He'd known this day was coming, though he might have wished for a few more months of preparation. He understood the unique vampiric gift his blood had bestowed upon him. That fire was a mark of his power, a presaging of his future strength. His control wasn't yet all that it could be, but he wouldn't accept threats against his parents. That was one step too far. He glanced at Garrick in silent apology. No matter what he did tonight, his cousin would stand by his side. Quinn just hoped he wasn't going to get them both killed.

He took a breath. He'd been practicing in private and already knew he was stronger than Marcelina. But for all his sneering disregard of her, the bond between a vampire and his Sire was *not* easily broken. It would take all of his strength to strike the first blow and shatter that bond. And then he'd have to kill her. If he'd learned one thing about vampires this past year, it was that you never left your enemies alive behind you.

Bracing himself, he gathered his power in the way he'd been practicing ever since he'd figured out what lived inside him, and what he could do with it. He pictured pulling energy from every part of his body, pictured it streaming through his veins, burning along his nerves, until it was a ball of searing, bloody power just below his breastbone. He touched his hand to his chest and held it there for a moment. Then, using all of his vampiric speed, he drew that power out of his body into his clenched fist, and threw it at Marcelina as hard as he could.

She screamed as a cloud of ethereal blue fire surrounded her. Her beautiful hair shot up in brilliant orange flames, shriveling against her head like blackened threads, while the rest of her remained untouched.

And still she screamed. The other vampires in the house, all of whom were Marcelina's children, rushed into the room. They froze in shock at first, but then, driven by the Sire bond to protect her, they ran at Quinn.

He was ready for them. Ignoring Marcelina and her agony, he swept his gaze over the charging vampires. There weren't that many. Marcelina wasn't powerful enough to control more than a dozen children, and with Quinn's defection, she'd lost not only him, but Garrick. That left only ten vampires, all weak, who rose to defend her.

"Don't," Quinn warned, his power crashing over them with that one syllable. "She's not worth it." He knew he struck a nerve with that. There wasn't a single one of her children whom Marcelina had treated gently. But the Sire bond was about more than loyalty. It was security, protection against a world that saw them as monsters. What would they be without that protection? "Get on the floor and stay there," Quinn said. "I'll protect you when she's gone."

They froze, studying him, and then one by one, Marcelina's children slid bonelessly to the floor. Some continued to watch, wide-eyed with curiosity, as their Sire twisted in agony. Others stared with eyes that burned red with hatred and satisfaction.

Quinn swung back around to face the monster who'd so irrevocably changed his life. The blue fire wasn't touching her, but the heat was. Pain marred that lovely face, straining the skin over her perfect cheekbones, drawing lush lips back over perfect teeth. Except those lips were torn and bloody from where her fangs had sliced into them, and her teeth were dripping blood onto the swell of her creamy breasts.

"Whatever shall I do with you, Marcie?" he asked with intentional cruelty.

Her mouth writhed, her lips closing to form a single word.

"Mercy?" he asked. "Is that what you think you deserve?"

She slid off her chair and to the floor, one hand reaching out in entreaty. Her hair was gone. He'd wanted her to suffer that much from the beginning, a blow to her vanity. But he'd spared her scalp, which was only reddened. Thus far.

Quinn's first instinct was to let her suffer, but he retained enough of himself, enough of the humanity his parents had given him, that he wondered what he'd become to even consider such cruelty. More important than any consideration of cruelty, however, was the simple fact that he couldn't hold the flames much longer. He was still very young as a vampire, his power far from fully mature. He had to end this.

Focusing once again on the fire inside him, he drew from the very heart, where it burned the brightest. Plucking that brilliant ember from his chest, he tossed it almost negligently at Marcelina. Her face brightened with hope at his gesture . . . and then she screamed in terror as the flames surrounding her went from blue to orange, and her body lit up like a torch. Within minutes, she fell to ashes.

Quinn sank to his knees, exhausted and panting. The fire wasn't real as most people understood it. It came from his power as a vampire, drawing on the spark of his vampire blood. When he used it, it sucked all the energy out of him, leaving him utterly drained. He hoped it would prove less grueling as he aged, and his *magic* grew stronger. Fuck. He still had a problem thinking of his new ability as magic, but he didn't know what else to call it. There were other powerful vampires out there who did know, however. Vampires beyond Marcelina's narrow little world. Maybe they had a better theory.

He was too tired to think about it now. All he wanted at that moment, all he had the energy for, was to stumble to his room and sleep for a week. But he couldn't do it, couldn't show any weakness at all. Marcelina's children might have supported his decision to get rid of her, but they were still vampires. Their instinct was to attack, especially if their target was a powerful vampire who'd suddenly become weak.

Clenching his fists to his sides, he forced himself to stand and turn around to face the others. "We've done enough for tonight," he said, deliberately including them in the overthrow, though their only contribution had been to lie on the floor and do nothing. "We're all going to need our strength for tomorrow. We have some decisions to make."

The others hesitated, but then began nodding, murmuring in agreement. "We should rest now," one of them muttered. "Dawn isn't far off," said another, his words coated with fear.

Quinn waited until they'd all gone to their rooms. He would have collapsed then, if not for Garrick, who pulled Quinn's arm over his shoulder and guided him to a nearby couch. Easing him down, Garrick said, "Do you need blood?"

Quinn swallowed, his throat dry. "Please."

"Are you okay for me to run to the kitchen?"

He nodded.

"I'll make it quick."

Quinn closed his eyes and leaned back on the couch, more exhausted than he could ever remember being. He'd played sports in high school, had kept in shape all through university and law school, had always made gym time part of his routine even when he was climbing the partnership ladder at his law firm. As with everything else, he'd been competitive as hell and played to win. But those activities were nothing compared to this. A few minutes of using his power, and he was wiped out.

"Here." Garrick's voice woke Quinn. His nostrils flared at the scent of blood, and he growled, his fangs sliding out hungrily. Grabbing the bag from his cousin, he used his fangs to slice through the plastic, not bothering with the valve, not even caring that the blood was cold enough to hurt going down. He drained one bag, and took the second that Garrick offered, this one with the valve already open. He drained that one, too, and was halfway through a third, before he slowed down.

Pausing to catch his breath, he ran the back of his hand over his mouth. "Disgusting, aren't I?"

Garrick laughed. "Your manners could use some work, but you got rid of that bitch, so I'll forgive you this once."

Quinn looked up with a bloody-toothed grin. "I did, didn't I?"

"You're the new master now. What's your plan?"

"My plan? Shit." He thought fast. The one thing he knew was that he didn't want to be responsible for this lot. "I'm going to petition Rajmund down in Manhattan and see if he'll take us on. He pays lip service to Krystof, but he runs his own city. He's reasonable and smart, and I can learn a lot from him. I'm no master of others, Garrick. I don't want it. Maybe someday, but not yet."

"Someday, though, Q. The need to rule is in your blood now."

Dublin, Ireland, present day

QUINN THOUGHT about that long ago night as he and Adorjan sped toward Dublin. Garrick had been right. The drive to rule was in his blood. It had been there before he'd become a vampire, disguised as simple ambition. His vampire blood had taken it and driven him to this place and time. Looking back, he applauded himself for choosing Rajmund as their new master. From Raj, he and Garrick had learned all the rules and basic truths of vampire society, things Marcelina should have taught them. He'd been so relieved, at first, to have gotten himself and Garrick out from under her crazy ass rule, that he hadn't given a thought to climbing any higher in vampire society. But Rajmund had seen the power simmering beneath his skin, and he'd known what Quinn hadn't—that his vampire blood wouldn't be denied. That he either had to discipline it or it would destroy him. So, he'd risen in power and skill under Raj's guidance, coming up through the ranks, learning what it meant to have the power of life and death over people who depended on you.

And then the wars had started, and he'd known his time had come.

"You know how to get there?" he asked Adorjan, completely unnecessarily. Even if the vamp hadn't memorized the route—which he probably had—the Range Rover had a nav system. Quinn hated to admit it, but he was tense now that he was making the move to Dublin. It made a confrontation with Sorley all but inevitable.

Adorjan didn't call him on the stupid question. Maybe he understood the reasons for Quinn's tension. Or maybe his loyalty didn't permit him to question even that much. He simply smiled and pointed at the nav screen. "Another twenty minutes or so, my lord."

Quinn's cell rang at that moment. Garrick. He accepted the call. "Garrick."

"My lord. I wanted to let you know that Casey's settling things down nicely, but I left Ryan Lopez with him for the next few nights, just in case. Dublin's close, but not that close. If he needed help, we might be too late."

"Good idea. You're on your way?"

"We left twenty minutes ago."

"Good. We'll see you at the house, then."

"You couldn't keep us away," Garrick said, his voice all but vibrating with excitement. "This is going to be fun."

Quinn slid his phone back into the pocket of his jacket. He drew a deep, settling breath and smiled. Fun. He could go with that.

Chapter Seven

THE NEXT NIGHT found Quinn once again seated at a huge desk—though this time the desk was real, not a dining table making do. He had a laptop in front of him and far too many piles of paperwork stacked around him. In this case, however, the files he was studying were the result of some of Garrick's world-class hacking skills . . . which meant Quinn wasn't supposed to be reading any of them. Garrick had managed to crack Sorley's security, which he'd derided as "pitiful," and Quinn now had an open invitation to peruse any of Sorley's computer files that interested him. He was making good use of it, mostly on his laptop. The paper copies were only backup, in case the Irish lord unexpectedly discovered he'd been invaded and managed to block them. Garrick assured Quinn that it wasn't likely to happen, and, if it did, there'd be no way to trace it back to them.

Quinn's deep dive into Sorley's finances was turning up what he'd expected. Sorley's businesses throughout Ireland were just as illegal as the smuggling operation in Howth. In fact, he had several other very similar ops, including a substantial smuggling business moving through Dublin's main port. Even worse, from Quinn's point of view, was that Sorley's partner in the Dublin venture was one of the city's most violent gangs.

On the good news front, the Irish lord's various businesses brought in plenty of money, even though he didn't seem to share it with the Irish vampire community at large. Sorley had to be paying his accountant a substantial bribe to keep that particular fact from the other vampires, including the lord's inner circle, most of whom lived in the big house in the Donnybrook section of Dublin. Sorley paid them a modest salary, but he could have afforded to pay them much more. He *should* have. A good vampire lord shared the wealth with his subjects. Sure, the lords lived better than regular vampires, but that was because they were the ones taking all the risks and fighting all the battles. But they also invested in their own people, their own territory.

Sorley wasn't doing any of that. He wasn't only a bad lord, he was a bad businessman. The latter indictment might have offended Quinn even more than the first. In his world, there was no excuse for sloppy financial management. His fingers itched to draw up a vicious memorandum and shoot it off to Sorley *and* his accountant, but he reined in the impulse, just as the sound of raised voices drew his attention to something happening outside.

He slid his chair back and stood, all of his senses going on alert. Sorley had given Quinn permission to take over Howth, with the implicit understanding that he would remain there. Quinn had pretended to go along, but he'd had no intention of doing that. Howth had never been more than stepping stone, a way to test Sorley's mettle. What he'd learned had moved up his timetable substantially. Sorley was weak. Not in power, but in discipline and intent. Quinn saw it, though he thought it probable that Sorley didn't. The Irish lord had spent too many decades sitting in his fancy house in Donnybrook, never venturing beyond the nearby suburbs.

But while that made him weak, it didn't make him stupid. Within the confines of Dublin, Sorley knew everything that happened. Or almost everything. He'd missed Quinn's acquisition of the Dublin Ballsbridge property, which had gone through long before he'd ever left the U.S. Though that might be because Quinn had acquired it under a false identification he'd established years ago, and Sorley didn't have the imagination to consider that possibility. Nonetheless, Quinn had known that once he moved into the house, it would be only a matter of time before Sorley himself, or one of his thugs, took notice.

Quinn sent a thread of power winding along the hall and down the stairs ahead of him, wanting to know who'd come knocking on his door. From all the yelling, he assumed it wasn't Sorley. The Irish lord wouldn't be standing in the yard arguing. He'd have blasted his way in without caring who got hurt along the way.

Garrick's voice rose above the others, and Quinn felt the blast of power as two master strength vampires squared off against each other. He quickened his pace down the stairs. Garrick could hold his own one-on-one against almost anyone, short of Sorley himself, but from the sounds of it, whoever that was out front had brought more than a few fighters with him.

The doors were already open when he reached the front of the house, and he could see his vampires lined up outside with Garrick in the middle. Giving him a telepathic whisper of warning, Quinn moved up behind his cousin and touched his shoulder. Garrick stiffened briefly in protest, as his protective instincts came to the fore, but Quinn pressed harder, and his cousin stepped aside, letting Quinn pass through to stand in front of his fighters. Vampire lords led from the front. At least, the good ones did.

Seven vampires faced him in a cluster, with one vamp braced ahead of the others. He transferred his glare from Garrick to Quinn, his look of confusion melding quickly into one of sneering disdain.

"So, you're the American who thinks he can just waltz in here and take over?" the vampire said, taking up a swaggering stance, with legs planted wide and fingers hooked into his low-slung belt.

Quinn eyed him with some bemusement. The vamp had a lot of attitude and enough charisma to get this lot to follow him. He'd observed the dynamics of the group from the vantage of the open front door, and he'd be willing to bet this bunch worked together in a kind of gang. They were probably loyal to Sorley, but Quinn's guess was that they operated independently, paying tithes to the Irish lord, but otherwise having little to do with him. No surprise there. From what Quinn had been able to deduce so far, Sorley favored that type of arrangement. It wasn't that unusual among vampires. What was unusual was that this group was apparently operating within the confines of Sorley's headquarters city.

"I'm Quinn," he said agreeably, not conceding his motivations or anything else. "And you?"

"Lon Conover, and Ballsbridge belongs to me."

Quinn tried not to smile at the vamp's arrogance. Ballsbridge was the Dublin district where his new house was located. "Does it? Odd. Sorley never mentioned you."

"I don't give a fuck who Sorley's *mentioned*. He might not be willing to fight for Ireland, but I am. And we're not going to put up with you and your fancy talk sneaking into our town and taking over."

"The last time I checked, *Sorley* ruled Ireland. *He* knows I'm here, because I *told* him. There was no sneaking involved. And, for the record, I'm as Irish as you are."

"You want to play games, smart guy? You think you can take me?"

Quinn tilted his head, as if considering the question. "Yes," he said finally. "I believe I can." He lifted his gaze with a lazy blink and let a small fraction of his power surround him.

Conover's pupils widened in involuntary shock before he could hide it, but then he moved his hands from his belt and tightened them into fists. "I beat back your boy there," he sneered, nodding at Garrick.

"And I'll beat you, too."

Quinn smiled. That wasn't true. Conover hadn't defeated Garrick. They'd barely tested each other's strength before Quinn had shown up. He didn't yet know for sure what Conover's true strength was, but he knew Garrick's. His cousin wouldn't be taken that easily. But now that Quinn was in the picture, Garrick's strength was no longer an issue. Or at least, not the most important one. Garrick and the others would back him up, but Conover had challenged Quinn's right to this place. And Quinn couldn't let that stand.

He rolled his head and shoulders, shook out his arms and flexed his hands, all the while grinning at an increasingly pissed off Conover.

"You ready there, sweetheart?" Conover taunted.

Quinn's grin disappeared, replaced by a look of utter focus as he regarded the other vampire. Sending out a wisp of power, he wound it around Conover, taking his measure. "You sure you want to do this?" he asked, giving the vamp an out as he gauged the feedback he was getting. "We could be allies instead of enemies."

The only response was a wad of spittle that landed just short of his boots. Disgusting.

With barely an effort, Quinn upped the level of power in his probe. No longer an undetectable wisp, it became a rope, thick and stinging like a swarm of tiny bees, that wrapped around Conover, trapping his arms against his body, tightening around his thighs until he could barely move.

The vampire snarled in surprise, then lifted his head with a howl and snapped the binding, freeing himself with a roar of victory as he attacked Quinn with a pummeling volley of power.

Quinn easily withstood the blow, but he was still surprised at how quickly Conover had broken free. Granted, he'd used only a fraction of his power on the binding, but he'd clearly underestimated the vamp. It was a mistake he wouldn't make again. None of that showed on his face though, as he studied his opponent, hearing the cheers and jeers of Conover's vampires, seeing the hatred in their faces, the smug confidence on Conover's. And suddenly, he'd had enough. Enough vampire bullshit, enough crazy girlfriends trying to kill vampires, enough swaggering assholes who looked at him and saw a mark. Maybe it was time to send a message to every vampire in Ireland who thought Quinn's American upbringing and Ivy League education made him easy prey.

He gathered his power, then reconsidered. He didn't need his fire to take out Conover. Hell, what he *needed* was to beat the shit out of someone. His mouth curved into a malicious grin. Without warning, he launched a powerful wave of energy, taking out every member of Conover's gang at once. They fell to the ground, bonelessly, like puppets whose strings had been cut. They weren't dead. He wasn't feeling that mean, and the only one who truly mattered was their leader. But they were out of this fight, making it a one-on-one battle between Quinn and Conover, who'd shuddered when Quinn's power had brushed past him, leaving him standing while taking out every one of his backers. He stared at the vampires lying on the ground, then spun to regard Quinn.

"What the fuck?" he demanded. "What did you do to them? Your fight is with—"

Quinn didn't let him finish. Stepping closer, he swung his fist and landed a power-driven uppercut that shattered Conover's jaw. He followed up with a jab to the gut that probably ruptured a few organs, another one to his chest that cracked his sternum, and finally a third to his throat, collapsing his esophagus. He'd been right. He didn't need fire to take down this asshole. This was far more satisfying.

Conover staggered, but tried to rally, wasting far too much energy on a magical attack, throwing a series of grenade-like bursts that splatted against Quinn's shields and burned out, fizzling to nothing.

Meanwhile Quinn stuck with the physical, grabbing Conover by his long hair and head-butting him. He grunted. Christ. That felt like he'd smashed his face into a rhinoceros, but it had been immensely gratifying. And effective. Conover's eyes literally rolled in his head as blood poured down his face, mixing with the mess of his already broken nose. The vamp staggered, and Quinn gripped his head again, slamming Conover's face against Quinn's raised knee.

"Submit," Quinn growled.

"Fuck you," Conover mumbled, the words barely distinguishable through his destroyed mouth and damaged esophagus.

"Idiot." Quinn stepped back. He had to admire the other vampire's persistence, but it was wasted. "Don't make me kill you," Quinn muttered.

Conover managed to straighten to his full height. He glared at Quinn out of one bloodied eye, the other so damaged that it was probably ruptured behind the swollen lid. "You think you can, sweetheart?"

Quinn shook his head in disgust. He was ready to finish this one way or the other. His hands ached, his knuckles were cut and bleeding, and his head hurt like a motherfucker. "Choose, Conover. Right now," he snarled. "Kneel before me, or die."

"Fuck—"

Quinn didn't let him finish. He took a single step forward, punched a hole in the vampire's chest, and ripped out his heart. His eyes locked on Conover's horrified gaze, as he loosed a tiny flicker of orange flame and surrounded the still beating organ, holding it in his palm until it disintegrated to ash, and Conover fell to dust.

Slapping his hands together, Quinn stared at Conover's gang of unconscious vamps. "What do I do with those?" he muttered.

"You want them dead?" Adorjan's deep voice snapped Quinn out of his contemplation. He hadn't been fully aware that he'd spoken out loud.

"No," he said firmly. "I'd prefer them alive, but I have to know where they stand."

"If you release them, at least some will go straight to Sorley," Garrick said from his other side.

"But some of them won't, and I don't care about the others. Sorley will find out about this soon enough, anyway." He glanced around the yard, his gaze going over the walls to the neighboring houses. The lots were big here, but still too close. "We should take this inside. You need my help?"

"No," Garrick assured him. He jerked his head at Adorjan, who immediately got the others organized to begin dragging the unconscious vamps into one of the unused garages. Garrick then turned to face Quinn, scanning him from head to toe, taking in the bloodied knuckles, the swelling knot on his forehead. "A head butt, my lord?" he asked dryly . "Isn't avoiding that sort of thing what being a vampire lord is all about?"

Quinn grinned. "I needed to vent. It's been a rough few nights."

"Eve giving you a hard time?"

"Eve hates my guts."

"You silly kids," Garrett chided.

Quinn narrowed his eyes. "Don't push your luck, asshole." He raised his hand and flexed one swollen fist. "Fuck, that hurts. No sense in fixing it before I question the others, though. We have any liquor in this house?"

"Are we in Ireland? Of course, we have liquor. There's a full bar in the den, and another one in basement."

"Good. They'll wake up soon enough," he said jerking his head at the unconscious vamps. "Make sure you maintain a guard. You know where to find me when they come around."

EVE SQUINTED through the high-powered binocs. Her eyes stung with the effort, but she couldn't take her gaze away, couldn't risk missing a single minute of what she was seeing. She only wished she could record the whole thing. She had her phone, but wasn't sure if it could catch the long-distance details, and didn't want to divert her attention to find out.

Quinn was over there. And he wasn't alone. It looked like the vampire version of the OK corral. A real standoff, like in the old American westerns her da had been so fond of. Except without guns. She'd followed Quinn to Dublin, using the tiny tracker she'd slapped on his Range Rover outside her flat. It hadn't been a car chase, since she'd been so far behind. But she'd counted on him not finding the tracker, and the tracker not falling off, before she made it to Dublin and got a fix on him through the app on her phone.

She'd expected to find him at Sorley's mansion in Donnybrook. That's why she'd followed him, hoping to figure out once and for all what his deal was with the vampire lord. Were they allies? Or had Quinn told her the truth about wanting Sorley dead?

Instead, she followed him here to Ballsbridge, to this lovely, ivy-covered brick two-story building that looked like it housed some gentleman financier and his perfect family, not a gang of ruthless vampires. But then, hadn't she thought that's exactly what Quinn was when she'd first met him? Not the family part, but he'd definitely been a gentleman. Even knowing what he really was, she'd still bet he wore a three-piece suit as well as the highest paid banker in Dublin.

When she'd first arrived at this house, she'd seen only Quinn and his gang, who'd been carrying on like they were moving in, just like anyone else would. They'd spent a good hour unloading duffle bags of gear, and boxes of who knew what. They'd probably been working for a while before she'd arrived, too, since it had taken her some time to follow the signal to this house, and then to find a good vantage point from which to do her spying.

Lucky for her, the couple across the street had gone out for the evening—based on his suit and her elegant dress—while she'd been sitting in her car down the street, wondering if she dared sneak closer. And then she'd strolled down the block, trying to look like she belonged, hoping Quinn's vampires didn't have a watch out for her specifically.

She'd breathed a sigh of relief when she'd made it to the neighbor's gate and ducked behind the thick wall that surrounded their house. They'd left their gate open, which most people seemed to do in this neighborhood. Although not Quinn, she'd noticed. His solid wood gate was closed, so you couldn't see what was going on behind it. The wall around the property was also designed for privacy, with thick blocks of stone that were tall enough to keep out all but the most determined climber. That wasn't Eve. She did, however, climb the sturdy chestnut tree that hung over the neighbor's perimeter wall. Its branches were more than broad enough to hold her and it had a trunk fat enough that she wasn't completely uncomfortable as she perched up there with her binoculars. The houses were far apart in Quinn's new neighborhood, but between the height afforded by her treetop vantage and the tree's location close to the street, she had a good view directly into his yard

And that was how she'd come to witness this incredible scene. Quinn had just killed that other vampire, but not until after he'd beaten the shit out of him. That part of it hadn't surprised her all that much. The other vamp had attacked Quinn first, and for all Quinn's gentlemanly ways, he was a big guy in great shape. He also had a temper, which he mostly hid behind that icy control of his, especially with her. But she'd known instinctively that if he ever let loose. . . . Well, that vampire—the one who'd shown up with a gang, looking for a fight— had just learned what happened when Quinn let loose. Quinn had beat the shit out of him and then punched a hole in his chest and ripped out his fucking heart! Right there before her eyes. She'd killed vampires, and she'd seen them go to dust when they died. But she'd never seen anyone, human or vampire, slam a fist through bone and flesh and tear out someone's heart.

Part of her was horrified. She was still shaking inside as she replayed the brutal scene in her mind. But another part of her was glad that Quinn was strong enough to take care of himself. Proud even. What the hell was wrong with her?

Movement snapped her attention back to Quinn's house. His vampires, including his cousin Garrick and the big bodyguard, were dragging the remaining unconscious vamps into a garage, apparently having decided they needed privacy. She was lucky Quinn hadn't done so earlier. Maybe he would have, if he'd realized how bloody the confrontation was going to get. Or if he'd known anyone was watching. She'd had a bad moment when he'd seemed to be searching for watchers in the surrounding trees. But his gaze had moved on quickly enough, and she'd started breathing again.

She waited until they'd all disappeared from sight, then scrambled out of the tree, gaining a scraped forearm for her troubles. Apparently, her tree-climbing skills were a bit rusty. She pulled her sweater over the scrape, which was oozing blood, and walked casually down the street, not drawing a full breath until she was back in her car. Her heart was racing and her breath was a little short, but mostly, she was agitated by what she'd seen. And confused. She'd been all set on hating Quinn and everything he stood for. She hadn't fooled herself into believing she could kill him, but she'd been ready to kill the others, if the opportunity presented.

But now . . . what if he'd been telling her the truth? What if he was here to replace Sorley? To change the way Irish vampires lived and conducted their business? What if he'd *help* her get the vampires who'd killed her brother?

And from the deepest part of her heart, where still lived the last remnant of the girl she used to be before her brother's death had changed everything, came a fragile whisper of hope. *What if she could go back to who she'd been, back before vengeance had become her life?*

She sat in her car, waiting for her heart to stop pounding, waiting for the unbidden tears to stop streaming down her face, and knew what she had to do. She was going to have to talk to Quinn.

QUINN STROLLED into the empty garage—empty of cars, anyway—and raked his gaze over the assembled vampires. He was still feeling mean, which didn't bode well for them. He'd confined himself to a single drink—two fingers of a very nice scotch—which had tasted fine, but hadn't helped his mood any, since booze didn't have any effect on vampire physiology. His knuckles still ached and his head hurt. What the fuck had he been thinking with that head butt? The vampire symbiote in his blood was working to heal the injuries, but the headache lingered. Quinn could have healed himself in an instant, but he didn't want to waste power if it turned out this group was going to be more trouble than he thought. Looking at them now, he knew it wasn't necessary. A quick scan told him that none of them had any power to speak of. Conover had been a strong master vampire, with enough power to be a valuable tool for Sorley. Unfortunately, he'd had ambitions beyond his abilities. When he'd challenged Quinn, those ambitions had ended in death.

But none of his followers even approached master level. Conover apparently didn't want any challengers arising out of his own clique. These six were all ordinary line vamps, nothing more. It infuriated Quinn that Conover had risked their lives in a battle that, once he'd met Quinn, he had to have known he couldn't win.

Quinn flexed his hands again, feeling the ache, and knew he had to douse his rage. Using a wash of his own power, he healed the injuries left over from his fight with Conover, and brought his temper under control. Oddly, it was the memory of Eve and their last encounter that remained a spark of discontent in his thoughts. He wanted to believe it was worry for her safety, nothing more. He would have felt the same for anyone he knew, if they were following a dangerous path, taking too many risks. But Quinn had never been one to lie to himself. He knew it was something more than that. Eve had gotten under his skin in a way none of his other women ever had. He wanted her to be more than safe, he wanted her with *him*. Wanted her clever, frustrating, stubborn self in his life. Which went to show what a twisted sense of humor the fates had. He was a vamp with a plan—organized, tidy, some would say anal. He had a checklist in his head, ticking off items as he moved toward his goal. Eve was like a mini hand grenade sent to fuck his list up. And he wanted her . . . in his life and his bed.

Fuck.

With an effort of supreme will, he shoved thoughts of Eve far away, into the back of his mind. He had other lives to protect tonight.

"Pay attention," he said abruptly. Every vampire in the garage, including Garrick and those of his own people who'd been standing guard, snapped to attention. "You have one chance, right here, right now. Swear to me or die." He let his gaze touch every one of Conover's remaining vampires, where they were seated on the floor. "Be very clear about one thing. If you leave this garage alive, your soul is mine."

One of the vamps stood defiantly. "What right do you have to demand anything of us? Sorley rules Ireland, not you."

Quinn nodded, acknowledging the vampire's point. But . . . "My right comes from millennia of vampire tradition. You challenged me, and you lost. Your life is forfeit, but I'm giving you a chance to live. Know this, however. I have more than enough power to detect lies and deceit. If you swear falsely, or if you ever betray me, your death will be long and painful."

The vampire's mouth pursed into an unhappy grimace, but he bowed his head and dropped to his knees in acceptance. The others, who'd been looking to him for guidance, did the same.

"What's your name?" he asked the vampire who'd challenged him.

"William McKeever," he muttered. "But they call me 'Numbers,'" he admitted grudgingly.

Quinn tilted his head curiously. "Numbers? Why?"

"I'm a chartered accountant." One of the other vamps snickered, and McKeever added, "And I might gamble a bit."

"Successfully?"

"Aye, my lord."

Quinn thought that might be the most interesting thing he'd heard that night. He glanced at his cousin. Garrick was good with numbers, too. Good enough that he wasn't welcome in Atlantic City. Garrick gave Quinn a smile and a small shrug.

"All right, McKeever. Can I call you 'Mac?'"

McKeever nodded almost eagerly, as if he didn't like his current nickname. "Please, yes, my lord."

"Okay, Mac, let's get this over with." Quinn walked over to where the vampire still knelt. Taking the small knife Garrick offered him, he rolled up his sleeve and cut a four-inch gash in his forearm. Blood immediately gushed from the wound, pooling in the hand that he held out.

"William McKeever, do you come to me of your own free will and desire?" he asked formally.

The kneeling vampire's nostrils flared at the scent of Quinn's blood, but he didn't answer right away. Instead, he raised his eyes and searched Quinn's face, then nodded, as if he'd found whatever he'd been looking for. "I do, my lord."

"And is this what you truly desire?"

"My lord, it is my truest desire."

Quinn offered his bloody arm. "Then drink and be mine."

McKeever—Mac—drank. Tentatively at first, as if not knowing what to expect, and then hungrily as if he'd never tasted the bounty that was a vampire lord's blood. And maybe he hadn't, Quinn considered. Not every vampire in Ireland had been turned by Sorley, or by Lord Tiegan before him.

Quinn jerked his mind back to the present, where Mac was still gorging on his blood. He had five other vampires to bind, and his blood supply wasn't endless. In fact, after tonight, he was going to need a re-supply. He hadn't had fresh blood since he'd tapped the little brunette at the pub, after his fight with Eve. He had to think back as to which fight it had been. There'd been so many. So why was she still in his thoughts?

Shaking his arm slightly, he pulled his wrist away from the vampire's eager mouth. Mac sat back on his heels, dazed, licking blood from his lips. Adorjan stepped forward and took his arm, urging him to his feet and making room for the next candidate.

One by one, the others came forward and swore, much as Mac had, each sucking down more of Quinn's blood and seeming just as dazzled by the power of it. Until the last of the six knelt before Quinn and swore . . . falsely.

Quinn pulled his arm back and stared down at the kneeling vampire. "I did warn—" But the vamp was already on his feet and racing for the exit. Before anyone could grab him, he was smashed to the ground by a hammer force of Quinn's power. He lay there, pinned to the garage floor like a bug, straining to move. Quinn strolled over and gazed down at him. "As I was saying," he said calmly. "I did warn you. I will not tolerate betrayal."

"I didn't—"

"No, you didn't. Your sin was even greater. To swear falsely on the blood of a lord. . . ." Quinn gave him an almost sad look. "Your choice. Your consequences." Pulling the sleeve down over his bloody left arm, he held his right hand out instead. With a thought, he filled his empty palm with a ball of blue fire that danced to its own music in the dim light. He raised his eyes slowly, meeting the vampire's fearful gaze. "Burn," he said simply.

And the vampire burned, twisting and screaming as he was engulfed in a cloud of blue that seared his guts and sizzled on his skin. The other vamps stared in horror, shrinking away from him as though fearing the invisible fire would spread.

Quinn watched and felt nothing. This vampire would have betrayed him, would have endangered every other vampire, and every human, in his household. One couldn't tolerate a viper in one's own nest. If anything, the foresworn bastard had gotten away too easily. Quinn only regretted that he didn't have the time to prolong the vamp's agony as he deserved.

With a snap of raw power, he increased the flame's heat until the vamp simply disappeared, incinerated in an instant, a pile of dust on the garage floor. He eyed the pile in distaste. They were going to need a private space outside for this sort of thing. Or at least, a concrete floor and an efficient means of vacuuming.

But he was done for, more tired than he could remember being in a long while. Sunrise wasn't far away and he'd bled enough for one night.

"Make sure everyone is secure for the day," he told Adorjan, then left the garage with Garrick at his side. Someone had apparently decided he needed a bodyguard, even in his own house.

"We need to accelerate work on the basement vault," he told his cousin.

"I know. We've already made it livable and private, gotten rid of the windows, reinforced the above-ground portion of the walls, both inside and out."

"We need vault doors at the stairs. One up, one down."

Garrick nodded. "With your permission, I'd like to call Lucas's man Ronan, to get a referral for the big doors."

"Lucas," Quinn said, "is a fierce fighter, and by all accounts a good lord to his people. He's also far too proprietary when it comes to this island, and he'll stick his nose in everywhere if I don't push back from the outset. But go ahead and call Ronan. Ask about the doors, but don't tell him anything else."

"I'll be careful. You calling it quits for the night? It's early enough that we could hit a local pub if you need it."

Quinn shook his head. "Tomorrow night will be soon enough. We'll go out first thing. We might as well establish ourselves in the local blood bar."

"If there's nothing else, then, I'll give Adorjan a hand."

"Nothing. I'll be in my quarters, tucked away safe and sound."

"I'd rather you be tucked in the basement."

"Later. I need privacy right now. I might come down before sunrise, but, if not, I'm secure enough."

"You're the boss."

Quinn nodded and headed down the hall alone. Garrick was right. He should be spending his days in the basement. But until it was completely renovated, he preferred his own quarters. The basement was as big as the first floor. It was one of the reasons he'd bought the house. It meant he and his vampires could have a separate and secure space for daylight sleep, behind vault-style doors, with small, private rooms for everyone, and larger rooms and suites for him and his senior staff. And after the basement was completely renovated, he'd turn his attention to privacy of a different sort. He wanted more land, more distance between him and his neighbors, even if that meant buying every property that touched his. Distance equaled safety, as well as privacy. The blood bars might be popular, but not everyone embraced the existence of vampires. There were still plenty of dangers out in the world for his people.

Including a certain redhead who was claiming far too much of his thoughts. He should walk away before he got in any deeper with her. She was a problem he might have to solve someday, and it would be much more difficult for everyone if he and Eve were still involved. The problem was, he didn't *want* to walk away. What he wanted was to sink his fangs into her pale neck, and let her sweet blood roll down his throat while he fucked her senseless. But that would be hard to do while she was dead set on killing vampires—*all* vampires.

Chapter Eight

EVE PARKED DOWN the block from Quinn's house, just as she had the night before, but she wasn't sneaking around this time. And she wasn't climbing any trees either. She'd worn a skirt and sweater, and her stiletto-heeled boots. She figured if she was going to face down a badass vampire, then she should wear her badass uniform. It might not be as effective with Quinn, since, well, he already knew what was under the clothes, but it couldn't hurt. He might not want her as mindlessly as those other vamps had—the ones she'd killed, she admitted to herself—but he wanted her. The sex between them had been flaming hot, and she hadn't been the only one feeling it.

She tugged on her skirt to straighten it, then smoothed her sweater down and pulled on her short jacket. She told herself she wasn't dithering; she was cold. But she'd never been very good at fooling herself. Shutting the car door with a muted click, she crossed the street and followed the wall along Quinn's property until she reached the wooden gate. One half of it stood open. There weren't any big vampire gang fights tonight apparently. She didn't get within two feet of the open gateway, however, before she was confronted by a pair of very dangerous-looking males. They didn't point their weapons, but they didn't conceal them either. They were both wearing matte-black machine guns on slings around their necks, their hands resting with deceptive ease on the weapons. She had no doubt they could fire and shoot faster than she could say the words. Just as she had no doubt they were both vampires. They weren't obvious about it—no fangs or gleaming red eyes—but it was dark, and they were guarding Quinn's house. After five years of studying and stalking vampires, she could make a good guess at Quinn's position in the hierarchy. He was powerful enough to have this house, even though he'd only just arrived in Ireland. Powerful enough that other vampires were trying to kill him, because they felt threatened by him. Trying and *failing*, she added. She didn't know exactly how vampire power worked, but she knew what she'd seen during the fight in Quinn's yard the night before. And that had been some serious shit.

"Hi," she said to the guards cheerfully. "I'm here for Quinn?" She said it as if unsure of her information and hoped they'd assume she was a blood whore. Or whatever they called the women who could be ordered like take-out food. Probably something nicer, like "date," maybe.

The two vampires didn't change their expressions, and they didn't say a word. They just simply stared at her. She was about to repeat her request when the front door opened, and Quinn's cousin appeared in the doorway. Giving her a long look, he exited the house and walked toward the gate, his heavy boots crunching on the thick gravel drive. Unlike the other night, when he'd claimed to be the nicer cousin, the look he was giving her held nothing but deep hostility as he came up behind the two guards.

"What do you want, Eve?"

"I want to talk to Quinn."

He snorted. "Yeah. Like that's going to happen. I know about your hobby, darling."

Eve bit back her frustration. She'd hoped Quinn had kept quiet about her hunting activities, but she should have known better. He and his cousin were close, and she was the enemy. Of course, he'd told Garrick. He'd probably told the big bodyguard, too. Or maybe not, she considered. That guy would have killed her by now if *he'd* known.

"Look," she said, trying to be reasonable. "I get that you don't like me much."

Garrick snorted again.

"Or at all. But I need to talk to Quinn. Can't you at least ask him if he'll see me?"

He stared at her a moment longer, then spoke to the two guards. "Hold her here. Don't touch her. If she makes a move, shoot her." With a dark glance in her direction, he spun on his heel and crossed back to the house.

"Bastard," she muttered, then gave the two guards a sweet smile. "He didn't say I couldn't talk."

QUINN SAT IN HIS very comfortable office, with a lovely, warm blaze dancing in the stone fireplace, staring at the facts and figures filling the computer screen in front of him. Leaning back in his chair until it tipped nearly to the wall, he switched his gaze to the gargoyle occupying one corner of the high ceiling and muttered, "Why the fuck didn't I stay in Maine? I liked it there. Raj left me alone, and the whole state was essentially mine. I could've—"

His pointless musings were interrupted by a flurry of activity out in the drive, followed by footsteps and the front door opening, then voices—all of which he recognized. The front door closed and the footsteps came up the stairs to his office.

"Come on in, Garrick," he said, before his cousin could knock.

The door cracked open a fraction and his cousin slipped inside. "Eve is here."

"I know. Where is she?"

"Better question, how'd she find this house?"

"That *is* a good question. Why don't you bring her in here so I can ask her? Where'd you say she was?"

"I didn't. She's out at the gate, where you should leave her. Or send her on her way."

"So why didn't you?"

"Because I know how you feel about her."

Quinn sighed. "Let her in. And, no, you can't search her. But I will," he added before Garrick could protest. "And you can watch, just in case she overpowers me."

Garrick studied him a moment longer, clearly unhappy and deciding whether there was anything he could do about it. There wasn't. "I'll be right back," he said finally.

Quinn waited. He thought about getting up. It was the courteous thing to do. But he was too well-versed in power plays. She'd all but kicked him out of her house. But this was *his*. Fuck courtesy.

Eve walked in ahead of Garrick, shooting a dirty look over her shoulder before turning to give Quinn a warm smile. As if she hadn't been telling him she hated him just last night. The smile dimmed a little when he didn't get up and didn't smile back.

She bit her lip nervously, and he watched, thinking he'd like to bite it himself, but he was careful to keep the thought off his face.

"Quinn," she said, hesitantly breaking the silence, "we should talk."

"So, talk." He stood and walked toward her, while Garrick stood in the doorway, watching. He'd been joking about that, but apparently Garrick had taken him seriously. "Take off your jacket," he told Eve.

"What?"

"Take off the jacket and drop the purse."

She hugged her purse to her chest. "What? Why?"

"Because I'm no fool, and you carry a knife."

Her eyes widened in shock. "I'm not letting you pat me down!"

"Why not? I've done it before. Although, this time, it will probably be less pleasurable. For you, anyway."

Her pretty eyes narrowed in irritation. "Fine," she snapped. She would have dropped her purse to the nearby table, but Garrick caught it up first. He raised one eyebrow before she could protest, then chuckled as he opened the bag and pulled out a small Sig 9mm. He held it up for Quinn to see, then set it aside and went through the rest of the purse, before tossing it onto the table.

"Your turn," Garrick told Quinn, crossing his arms with a stubborn look.

Quinn smiled. "Lift your arms out to the side, Eve. Hold them there."

She glared daggers at him, but did as he asked.

"Love this sweater," he crooned, running his hands over her back and sides, grazing the swell of her full breasts, and meeting her eyes the entire time. He slid his hands down to her hips, following the line of her skirt to her bare thighs, grinning at her outraged look when his fingers slipped briefly beneath the hem and between her thighs. "I think she's safe, Garrick," he said, speaking over her head.

"What about the boots?" his cousin demanded. "Those heels—"

"Would make a damn fine weapon," Quinn agreed. "But I like to think I could stop her before she managed to take them off. I'm not totally helpless." His voice hardened just enough on the final sentence that Garrick understood his forbearance had limits.

"As you say, my lord. I'll be nearby if you need me."

"Not *too* nearby," he said, with a lascivious wink for Eve. She made a disgusted sound, which only made him laugh. "I'll be fine, Garrick." He waited until the door closed, then walked around his desk and sat. He gestured at the chairs in front of the desk. "Have a seat."

"Can I put my jacket back on?"

Quinn gave her a careful look. "I don't think so. Who knows what you're hiding in there. If you're cold, I'll warm you up."

She scoffed wordlessly.

"I meant the fire, Eve."

Her blush was a vivid wash of color on her pale skin. "Why're you being such a wanker about this?"

He leaned back in his chair. "I don't know what *this* is."

"We need to talk."

"So you said. About what? You killing vampires?"

"Sort of. I mean, we both want the same thing . . . sort of."

Quinn couldn't help laughing. "How do you figure that?"

"We both want to kill vampires," she said, as if it was the most obvious thing in the world, and couldn't understand why he didn't see it.

"No. *You* want to kill vampires. I want certain vampires dead, but not shot from a distance or stabbed with their dick in their hand. I kill my opponents in a fair fight, and only if they refuse to submit. That's the difference between us."

"Only because you're strong enough to win. Look, I've seen you fight. I know—"

"When was that?" he interrupted, scrolling back over the fights he'd had since arriving in Dublin. There weren't that many, and none that Eve should have witnessed.

"Oh, um. . . ." She looked around, refusing to meet his gaze.

"When you said 'talk,' I assumed you meant telling the truth," he said dryly.

She scowled, as if irritated that he wasn't going to play along. Asking pesky questions and demanding answers. How unreasonable of him.

"Okay, look," she said.

He tensed. Nothing good ever followed a lead-in like that.

"I saw what you did last night. The fight and everything, I mean."

Quinn's attention sharpened abruptly. "Did you?" he asked, coming smoothly to his feet and circling around to sit on the edge of the desk in front of her. "And how did that come about, darling Eve? For that matter, how did you find this house?"

She drew a deep breath, then spoke all in a rush. "I put a tracker on your car the other night, and downloaded the app to my phone. It led me here."

He studied her. She was telling the truth. Adorjan was not going to be happy to learn he'd been outwitted by a human female. Particularly not *this* human female. Garrick's suspicions about Eve had infected the other vampire, though Quinn was confident Garrick hadn't told Adorjan about her vampire hunts. Because if he'd known *that*, Eve would be dead already.

"Spying on each other, Eve? Is that the sort of alliance you had in mind?"

"No. I only did it because you were being such a jerk about my rifle. You had no right. But then, after. . . . I started thinking about what you said, and I decided we needed to talk. So, here I am."

He settled against the desk, arms crossed. "And if I refuse? What will you do with your ill-gotten information then? Sell it to the highest bidder? Do I need to worry about some grainy video turning up on YouTube?"

"There's no video," she muttered, seeming finally to have found her sense of guilt.

"Too bad. Still, a first-hand account must be worth something to the local news. Or were you going to sell it to someone else? Sorley maybe?"

"No!" she snapped, her head coming up. "I wouldn't do anything to help that asshole. And, besides, the last thing I want is to draw attention to myself, or my connection with vampires."

"Oh, right. Because under Irish law, you're guilty of murder. Of course, there aren't any bodies, so that's convenient. Although there *is* a witness." He smiled slowly and pointed at himself. "Where do you suppose they'll put you?" he asked thoughtfully, then answered his own question. "Dóchas Centre, if you're lucky. Limerick, if they decide to send a message. Very unpleasant. You might even get out in a decade or so. Maybe less, since you were only killing monsters. Isn't that right?"

She jumped to her feet and stormed closer, her dark eyes flashing with anger when her boots hit his, and she leaned in to snarl, "They killed my brother. I *watched* them kill him and could do nothing. What was I supposed to think?"

"That the two *who killed him* were guilty of murder, not every fucking vampire in Ireland."

"And then what? Where's my justice?" she demanded.

"Justice, is it? Is that what you call murdering random vampires? Justice? You're killing *my* people. Should I now go out and kill random humans? Is that *my* justice?"

She glared at him, breathing hard, her breasts heaving, and face flushed. She looked so fucking sexy. Except for the glare, it was very much the way she'd looked after he'd fucked her.

"I saw them leave Sorley's house the other night," she said finally, speaking quietly and straightening enough that she wasn't in his face. "The two who killed Alan."

"Tell me you didn't approach Sorley about it."

"No. He wouldn't care, and I wouldn't stand a chance. I know that."

"You shouldn't be in the game at all, Eve. You're going to end up dead. If you have a problem with Sorley or any of his thugs, I'll take care of it."

"*You'll* take care of it," she repeated flatly. "Look, even if you're right about—"

"I *am* right, and you know it."

She gave him a narrow-eyed glance and continued, "—about regular vampires, *I* deserve the right to kill those two."

He studied her silently. "All right. You have IDs on them?"

"Why?"

"So suspicious. You're the criminal here, not me."

"Just answer the question, wise guy. Why do you want their IDs?"

He shrugged. "I'll round them up, and you can kill them. Face to face."

"And why would you do that?"

"Maybe I like you." He stroked one finger down her cheek.

She shied away at the gentle touch. "Maybe. But that's not the reason."

"Actually, that *is* the reason. If you keep trying to kill vampires, you're going to end up dead. I happen to like you alive."

"I'm not going to let you bite me."

He laughed. "Your loss, sweetheart. But I still don't want your death on my conscience. This is a limited time offer, by the way. Take it or leave it. But know this, Eve. I won't tolerate anyone hunting vampires in my territory, not even you."

"You won't kill me," she said with smug confidence.

Quinn leaned close. "I won't have to," he murmured.

Eve pulled back to stare at him for a confused moment as she worked out the meaning of his quiet words. Her eyes went wide. "You'd mess with my mind?" she breathed.

"If you give me no choice. . . ."

"Bastard."

He tsked. "I already told you that doesn't apply. So what's it going to be. I need an answer."

"If you're so all fired up to protect vampires, why let me kill those two?"

"Why do you care?"

She frowned. "I don't. You're right. Can I get my phone? It's in my jacket pocket."

He gave her a knowing look, then walked over and pulled her jacket off the chair. Digging through her pockets, he came up with a short, thick switchblade, which he held up for her to see, tsking loudly. Going into the other pocket, he found a pink cell phone.

"Pink?"

She snatched it from his hand. "What's your number?"

Quinn rattled off a number. It was one of several burner phones, nothing to connect it to him in case sweet Eve got a bug up her ass to frame *him* for some made-up crime.

She tapped a few keys, then waited, eventually looking around the office with a scowl. "How come it didn't ding?"

"Because it's not in this room?" he asked facetiously.

"What kind of businessman doesn't have a phone in his office?"

"The kind who doesn't want to be bothered. Don't worry, the number's good."

"Fine. I sent you pictures of the two killers. Can I go now?"

"Hey, you knocked on *my* door, not the other way around." He moved fast, wrapping an arm around her waist and pulling her close. "Unless you'd like to stay," he whispered against her ear.

She shivered, leaning into his touch before putting her hands against his chest and, after a long moment, pushing away. "I really—" She drew a deep breath. "I really have to get back."

"You could stay." As he said the words, Quinn knew he meant them. Despite everything, he wanted her to stay. He wanted *Eve*.

She looked up, and he saw the matching desire in her eyes, the remembered heat from the times they'd fucked. And for a moment, he thought she'd stay. But then she shook her head and said, "I have to go home. To Howth. You'll call me? When you know something, I mean."

He stepped away from her, both hands in the air in front of him. "Sure thing. Garrick will see you safely to your car."

"That's not necess—"

"Actually, it is. This is my world, Eve. I call the shots."

The look she shot him had a little of her fire back, which made him happier. He didn't want his Eve to be sad or confused. He wanted her pissed off and ready to rumble. As long as the rumbling didn't involve killing more vampires.

"What about the Sig? You going to steal another one of my guns?" she demanded.

Quinn picked up the gun, popped the magazine and emptied it. Then racked the slide. It was empty. "You should keep a round in the chamber, in addition to a full mag," he said as he handed her the now-empty weapon. "It gives you an extra round. And with such a small gun, you can use it."

"Doesn't do much good if you keep taking all my weapons away from me."

"Self-preservation, sweetheart." He winked as the office door opened on silent hinges, and Garrick stood there. "Make sure Eve gets to her car safely, please."

"Sure thing, my lord."

"You make your own *cousin* call you that?"

"He doesn't make me do a damn thing," Garrick snarled. "It's a matter of respect. Something you wouldn't understand."

"Garrick," Quinn said quietly, then turned to Eve. "My world, Eve."

She blushed and headed for the door, while Garrick gave him a questioning look.

"Make sure she leaves the neighborhood, then we'll talk," Quinn told him.

EVE STAYED TWO steps ahead of Quinn's cousin. He was nearly as bad as that bodyguard, Adorjan. Both of them hovered over Quinn, as if he couldn't protect himself. From *her*, for God's sake. She'd seen him take down that gang of vampires without breaking a sweat, and Garrick was worried about *her*? She reached her car and climbed inside. Granted, she *had* killed a few vampires over the last five years. But she didn't want to kill Quinn.

She locked her car doors, then turned and raised her middle finger at Garrick. Asshole.

No, she thought as she drove away. She didn't want to kill Quinn. She wanted to fuck the beautiful bastard. Fangs and all.

GARRICK WALKED into Quinn's study and closed the door softly behind him. "So?" he asked.

Quinn threw down the iPad he'd been making notes on. "She wants the vampires who killed her brother."

"And?"

"And I told her I'd deliver them, but that's it."

Garrick walked over and slumped onto one of the chairs in front of Quinn's desk. "Can I speak candidly for a minute?"

"For fuck's sake, Garrick. Talk."

"Q, you know I'll support whatever you do. Unless, you know, you become a mass murderer or something, then all bets are off."

"That's reassuring."

"Yeah, well, I just wanted to set limits before I continue."

Quinn rolled his hand in a signal to move on.

"I'm worried about this girl. We're vampires, we're territorial creatures. *You're* a vampire lord, or you soon will be, which means your territorial instincts, your *possessive* instincts, are off the charts. And when it comes to women . . . hell, we've all seen the lengths to which powerful lords will go to protect the women they love."

"I don't love Eve."

"Not yet, maybe. But you could. I've seen you with a lot of women over the years, and there's not one of them you'd have made that deal with. Any other woman would be dead by now. She's a killer, damn it."

"And so are we," Quinn said quietly. "We've both killed vampires, me more than you."

"In challenges, in defense of our lives."

"But that's what Eve thinks she doing. Defending herself and others against the kind of vampire who killed her brother."

"Except she's not, damn it. She's killing whoever crosses her path."

"Not anymore."

"If you can believe her." Garrick sighed. "So, what's the plan, my lord?"

"Don't worry. I'm not going to rush out and hunt down Eve's vamps, just so I can deliver them tied up like hogs on her doorstep. My first priority is getting rid of Sorley. As for the rest, I'm sure some of his inner circle will choose to make a stand with him. And I'm sure those two will be included in that circle." He tossed the burner phone over to Garrick. He'd retrieved it from his desk after Eve had gone. It had been in the office the entire time, just muted.

"We've met these two," Garrick said, studying the images. "Or, not met so much as seen. They were at Sorley's that first night, part of his close guard."

"They were. I'm betting they're his enforcers, which means they like beating up other people, especially people who can't fight back, like humans."

"What if they decide not to go down with Sorley's ship?"

Quinn took the phone back when Garrick offered it. "I'll be making changes once I become lord, bringing in my own people, vampires I can trust. These two don't strike me as the trustworthy kind." He lifted his gaze to meet Garrick's. "They won't like being sidelined. I expect them to protest forcefully." He leaned back in his big chair, until the springs creaked with strain. "Ireland will soon be mine, Garrick. Every vampire on this island will live by my sufferance. Or they will die."

Chapter Nine

THEY HAD A VISITOR the next night, soon after sundown—a messenger bearing a summons from Sorley. Quinn was in the front yard with Adorjan and Joshua Bell, the head of his daylight security detail, discussing improvements necessary to make the house secure. The wooden gate stood half-open, enough to admit foot traffic as there was a lot of work going on in the garages, as well as the house. The previous owners hadn't used the garages at all, and the door mechanisms had gone to rust. Quinn liked elegant cars, and he intended to put the garages to their intended purpose.

He and the others turned when a sleek motorcycle roared up to the gate, bearing a black-clad vampire. The vamp gunned the bike's engine, as if demanding admission. The gate guards regarded him impassively, not moving, even though one of the guards was from Conover's gang and must have recognized the biker.

"You recognize him?" Quinn asked Adorjan.

"Not offhand." He looked around and called over another of Conover's people who was supervising a crew working to restore the garage doors. The vampire looked up when Adorjan called his name and came running over.

"My lord?" he said, bowing his head to Quinn.

"Do you recognize our visitor?"

The vamp studied the biker. "One of Sorley's flunkies. He's probably a messenger, though he can't be trusted." Adorjan thanked him, and the vamp returned to his duties.

"Let him in," Quinn told Adorjan.

"My lord—"

"Let him in, Adorjan. He'll report back to Sorley on everything he sees here. Let's make sure it's what we want him to see."

Adorjan's mouth pinched, but he nodded his agreement and signaled the gate guards, who widened the gate opening enough for the bike and rider to pass through. The messenger would have rolled his motorcycle right up to Quinn, but Adorjan stepped into his path, forcing him to brake hard. The bike spun in a half circle, but the vamp held onto it. Kicking it to a standstill, he shut down the engine, jumped off, and stormed over to confront Adorjan, ignoring the fact that Quinn's security chief was nearly twice his size.

"What the fuck, asshole?" their visitor demanded. "Sorley's going to hear about this."

Adorjan regarded him with silent amusement. "What shall I do with him, my lord?"

Quinn bit back his grin and said, "Let's get this over with. Let him by."

The rider—who seemed to have let his position go to his head—bristled at Quinn's casual disregard, but he held his tongue. It was one thing to tell off one of Quinn's subordinates, but, apparently, it was something else entirely to show disrespect to a vampire powerful enough to warrant a personal message from Sorley.

Adorjan stepped aside. The rider stomped past him and stopped in front of Quinn. He half-bowed from the waist and held out an old-fashioned message tube. "From the Lord of Ireland," he said briskly.

Quinn took the tube and flipped it in his hand, spinning it around like a baton, testing it for magical residue. He wouldn't put it beyond Sorley to use the archaic piece as a trap to assassinate Quinn before he could become a serious rival. The messenger stared at his treatment of the tube with such horror that Quinn thought his suspicions must have merit. But he didn't sense anything and quickly realized that the vampire's shock was due to Quinn's irreverent treatment of the message, rather than some murderous plot. He'd known Sorley was a self-important bastard, but this exceeded even his estimations.

Finally, Quinn handed the message tube to Adorjan, who popped it open with intentional disregard, letting the end cap drop to the gravel drive, before pulling out the single piece of rolled paper and passing it to Quinn unread.

Quinn scanned it quickly, half-expecting it to be calligraphic, given the pomp of its delivery. But it was a simple typed message from Sorley, demanding he present himself that same evening for "reassignment." Whatever the fuck that meant. Obviously Sorley knew he'd taken up residence in Dublin Ballsbridge, rather than remaining in Howth. But then, Quinn had made no attempt to hide that fact. His presence in Dublin, by itself, didn't change his status in Howth. Although, his status *had* changed, something Sorley clearly understood. This summons was a test. And since Quinn wasn't yet prepared to challenge the Irish lord directly, he would answer accordingly.

He looked at the messenger who was waiting expectantly. "You can leave," he said bluntly.

"Lord Sorley—"

"You're done here," Quinn interrupted. "Adorjan."

His security chief stepped between Quinn and the messenger, but instead of using his imposing size, he used his power to give the vampire a backward shove, moving him several feet, until he almost tripped over his own bike. It was a blatant show of force, and the vamp's eyes went wide with shock. He scrambled back onto his bike and gunned for the gate, which, fortunately, the guards had left open. Once on the street, he hit the throttle so hard, the bike rose up on its back wheel before hitting the street with a crunch and zooming out of sight.

"Twitchy little bunny," Adorjan commented, as he signaled the guards to close the gate.

"I suspect he's more accustomed to fear and reverence," Quinn observed. "Not for himself, but as a speaker of sorts for Sorley."

"You really plan to go there?"

"Of course. It would be rude otherwise," Quinn said, with a grin.

"I'll arrange a security team to—"

"No, I'll take Garrick."

Adorjan's gaze was steely. "My lord—"

"If I show up with a bunch of guards, Sorley might feel threatened and take action. It could easily come to a fight, and I'm not ready for that yet. He already knows Garrick. The two of us will go." He smiled at Adorjan's grimace. "I *can* defend myself, you know."

"I know," Adorjan agreed. "But you shouldn't have to."

GARRICK DROVE THE Range Rover to Sorley's. Adorjan had made a final argument in favor of him going along, too, but Quinn had vetoed it.

"We'll be back soon enough. I suspect that whatever Sorley wants, I'm going to need my own people before the night is over."

They rolled through the gates of Sorley's Donnybrook estate, with its mature trees and ivy-covered walls. If Quinn's house looked like the home of a nouveau riche investment analyst, then Sorley's place should have been occupied by the third or fourth generation of some ancient Irish nobility. Although Quinn doubted there was a single drop of noble blood in Sorley's veins.

Garrick again parked on the street, not wanting to risk getting trapped behind Sorley's wrought iron gates, or end up carrying a bomb on the Range Rover's undercarriage. Quinn wouldn't put it past the Irish lord to use this opportunity to get rid of the American interloper who was already an irritant and was quickly becoming a genuine threat.

They ignored the guards—who ordered them to wait for word from Sorley before passing through the gates—and walked right up the short set of stairs and into the house. Surprised silence greeted their arrival.

"Gentlemen," Quinn said, breaking the silence. "And ladies," he added, when a group of women were ushered in from a side door. He scanned the group, looking for red hair and, not finding any, said, "Looks like I'm in time for dinner." He winked at the women who giggled happily, not at all offended.

"They're not for you." Sorley's lieutenant, Lorcan, appeared in an open doorway on the side opposite the women. He gave Quinn a sour look up and down. "He's waiting for you."

"Lovely. Lead the way."

Lorcan scowled, but apparently Sorley really was waiting, because he pushed open one of the doors and gestured for Quinn and Garrick to go ahead of him.

Quinn shared a chuckle with Garrick at that. "I don't think so," he told Lorcan, letting amusement flavor his words. "*You* go first."

"Americans," Lorcan growled. "Fucking uncouth."

Quinn shrugged. In *his* world, Lorcan would have *insisted* on going first, rather than permitting a vampire whom he clearly distrusted to precede him into Sorley's inner sanctum. But maybe they did things differently over here.

They followed Lorcan into an ordinary office. It was on the small side, with two bookshelves on the left and a single leather visitor's chair beneath a painting that looked old, but that Quinn didn't recognize. He'd taken art history several decades ago, in his sophomore year at Princeton, but only because he'd been dating a pretty blonde Fine Arts major. He'd broken up with the blonde before the semester ended. He'd still gotten credit for the course, but he didn't remember much about it.

Directly in front of him, centered between two tall windows, was a desk behind which sat Sorley in a leather chair that was too big for his modest stature. If he was trying to make an impression, he should have bought a smaller chair. But then, he didn't need a chair to impress anyone. For all that Quinn intended to kill the Irish lord, he didn't make the mistake of thinking him an easy target. Sorley was old, wily, powerful enough to have unseated the previous lord, and had held onto the throne for 65 years.

"Lord Sorley, you rang." Quinn didn't bow, or even dip his chin, but his greeting was respectful, if not traditional.

"I didn't *ring*, and I didn't ask for *him* at all." He flicked his fingers in Garrick's direction, then jerked his chin at Lorcan, as if ordering him to get rid of Garrick.

"He stays," Quinn said, his voice hard. He would play the game only so far.

Lorcan reached for Garrick anyway.

Quinn lifted his gaze to Sorley's lieutenant and *shoved*, using just enough power to get the job done. Lorcan stumbled backward with a surprised yip of sound, then immediately growled as if to cover up the embarrassing noise. He started forward angrily, but Sorley stopped him with a raised hand.

"Let it be, Lorcan. If Quinn here is too afraid to face me alone, I'll leave him his nanny."

Quinn smiled, unfazed by the intended insult. If anyone had shoved *his* lieutenant around, that person would be writhing on the ground. Either Sorley didn't value Lorcan, or whatever he wanted from Quinn was important enough to ignore the offense.

"I have a task for you," he told Quinn, steepling his fingers on the desktop in front of him.

"I assumed as much."

Sorley scowled at the interruption, but continued. "It would have been Conover's responsibility, but you fucked that up."

Quinn shrugged. "He came to my home and challenged me. He lost. It's the vampire way."

"Con was ever ambitious, but good at his job. Which is now yours," he added smugly.

When Quinn didn't comment, he continued. "One of his duties, the one he should have been doing instead of getting himself killed, was keeping an eye on the human gangs here in Dublin. We move a lot of product through the main port, most of which is controlled by one gang or another. I don't get involved in their endless battles. If they want to butcher each other, it's no matter to me. But when they try to fuck with *my* business, I *do* get involved."

"That's happening now?" Quinn asked, as much to move along Sorley's explanation as to express polite interest.

Sorley nodded. "One of the gangs has been handling my drug

imports for years, but now they want guns. Not to sell, to use. Probably against some other gang. They tell me, no guns, no drugs."

Quinn raised an eyebrow. He had plenty of guns coming in through Howth, and Sorley knew it. Was he suggesting Quinn give the guns to his human allies? That was a double-edged sword.

"I don't give a damn what they want," the Irish lord said, as if in response to Quinn's unvoiced question. "Don't mistake me. I use humans when it suits me, but they are not allies. They're animals who'd be just as happy killing every vampire in Dublin, and I have no intention of giving them the weapons to do so."

"Then what?"

"I want you to kill the lot of them. Every single gang member. Once they're gone, others will step in to fill the void, and they'll know to show proper deference to their betters."

"I see."

"Do you?"

"It's not that complicated," Quinn said dryly. "I'll need whatever you have on the rebellious gang and its members. My on-the-ground intel isn't yet established in this country."

"I should hope the fuck not," Lorcan muttered from behind them.

"You'll have it," Sorley said. "I'm assuming you have whatever personal weapons you require."

Quinn grinned. "That and more." It was a taunt of sorts, since, strictly speaking, the weapons which had come in through Howth belonged to Sorley. Not that Quinn intended to let them go, which was something Sorley surely suspected by now.

But that was a fight for another night. For now, he had to figure out how to co-opt this human gang of Sorley's into working for *him*. And without killing anyone. Or at least, as few as possible. Sorley might despise the gangs he worked with, but Quinn didn't. Human allies would be needed just as much as vampire ones as he built his power base in Ireland. These gangs knew the city far better than he did, and his vampires would have to work with them. They were *necessary*, for now, at least. And, oddly enough, that made the humans *his*, just as much as his vampires were, whether he liked it or not.

"YOU SHOULD LET me call Adorjan and bring in a few of the guys," Garrick said stubbornly. It was the second time he'd made the request since they'd left Sorley's, but he received the same answer.

"I don't need an entourage to deal with a bunch of humans," Quinn said absently. His mind was on the coming confrontation, but not the physical part of the fight. He wasn't being arrogant in refusing to bring in Adorjan or any of his team. Quinn honestly didn't need them, and the humans would respond better if only he and Garrick showed up. No need to overwhelm them with vampire muscle. According to Sorley— and he sure as hell couldn't be trusted—the leaders of the human gang had previously agreed to a meeting tonight to discuss their demands. The vampire lord hadn't said, but Quinn imagined the humans were expecting Sorley himself to show up, as a matter of respect. That also meant the humans might be planning an assassination attempt, because what better way to get what you wanted than to eliminate your rival. Sorley had probably reached the same conclusion, which explained his decision to send Quinn in his stead. If the humans killed Quinn, it would get him out of the way. But it would also give Sorley a justifiable reason to go in heavy after the gang. Win-win. The wily fucker.

Quinn didn't have Sorley's contacts in Dublin, but he had both the brains and the power to derail whatever twisted scheme the Irish lord had in mind.

"I want to talk to these humans, not kill them," he told Garrick. "If I call Adorjan, he'll bring at least a few of his fighters, and the whole thing will balloon into a giant, murderous clusterfuck that will serve no one's interests but Sorley's. And I'm not here to make that bastard's life easier."

"All right, so what's the plan, my lord?"

Quinn laughed at the many ways his cousin had of saying that two-word honorific. And the many emotions he could convey. "The plan is simple. You and I walk into the meeting as Sorley's reps and walk out with the humans in *our* back pocket, instead of his."

"Well, why didn't you say so." He swung the SUV onto a street that took them right past the main entrance to Dublin Port. Even late at night like this, it was a busy place, with passenger cars dwarfed by the huge container trucks that rumbled in and out at all hours, and bright lights spotlighting the giant cranes that were loading and unloading the multi-colored containers. Some of those, probably more than anyone knew, carried the same illegal goods that Sorley was after.

Garrick drove them past the port and into the Sheriff Street neighborhood, a poorly lit section filled with blocks of so-called council houses, the Irish equivalent of the "projects" back in the U.S. They were side by side attached homes, some with lights shining through the windows, and some fewer with brightly colored flowers blooming in window boxes. Quinn had Googled the neighborhood while Garrick drove, and so he knew that twenty years ago, it had been much worse. There was a gentrification of sorts going on now, with the old council houses being torn down and new high-rises being raised in their stead. Skeletons of building cranes were silhouetted against the skyline almost everywhere he looked. The streets were clean and neat for the most part, although some of the buildings bore gang graffiti that could easily have been spray-painted on a wall in any big city back home.

He caught himself at the thought. *This* was his home now. He had friends back in the U.S., but his parents were both long dead and, with Garrick here, Ireland was as much of a home as any he'd had.

"There's the place," Garrick said quietly, as they turned down a narrow street. He didn't have to say more. The dark-clad men hanging around the small house, some with weapons carried in the open, others with suspicious bulges beneath their jackets, gave it away. Quinn hadn't noticed any police presence since they'd entered the neighborhood, so either they stayed away from the more dangerous streets, or they'd been bought off. Either way, the result was the same. A high-level meeting between humans and vampires that had the potential for considerable bloodshed was about to happen right under their noses.

Garrick parked around the block from the meeting house. That way, if everything went sideways, the Range Rover had less of a chance of being shot up. Out of sight, out of mind. Although, hell, if worst came to worst, Quinn and Garrick could simply outrun the humans all the way back to the south side of Dublin.

Walking side by side down the middle of the street, they turned onto the block they wanted. They were big men, and the sidewalks were too narrow to give them room to maneuver. And then there was the possibility of enemies hiding in the shadows. They slowed when they neared the meeting place, which Quinn suspected was the gang leader's home. It was brightly lit behind closed shutters, and when Quinn and Garrick stopped in front of the house, the front door opened, shining even more light onto the street.

Quinn blinked slowly. If they'd thought to startle him, they were going to need more than a sudden wash of bright light. He waited silently. He'd already clocked every single human in a two-block range, from the families hiding behind closed doors and drawn curtains, to the multitude of armed guards on the roofs and behind the windows of surrounding buildings. The humans either didn't know or didn't consider the fact that he didn't need to see the guards to know they were there. Their heartbeats alone would have given them away, but he didn't need even that. He was a powerful vampire. He'd sensed their life forces just as he would have if they'd been vampires.

A human male finally appeared in the doorway, silhouetted against the bright light. Quinn thought it was a stupid show of arrogance. Sure, he was appearing like a space alien out of the white light, but he was also setting himself up as the perfect target if any enemies lurked nearby. Quinn shrugged. If the guy wanted to die, it wasn't his concern.

"I was expecting Sorley," the human said as the light behind him clicked off, leaving him backlit by nothing but ordinary lamplight. He wasn't a big man. Maybe five feet, eight inches tall. Slender but with muscles in his arms and shoulders that revealed a wiry strength.

"Sorley rarely takes meetings," Quinn replied. "And never if it means traveling to someone else's lair."

"So, he sends you into the danger zone, is that it? Into my *lair*. He must not value you very highly."

"On the contrary, my value is such that he'd like to be rid of it." He grinned to emphasize the shared humor. "Rest assured, I'm at least as capable as Sorley, and far more willing to compromise, for all that I come as his representative."

The human pretended to study him for a moment. Quinn doubted he could see much on the dark street. Rather the man was using the time to absorb what Quinn had said, and what he hadn't.

"My name is Neville," he said finally. "Let's talk."

Quinn exchanged a quick look with Garrick. "*Be ready.*" He sent the message telepathically knowing his cousin would get it, since they were both strong telepaths and had the added advantage of a blood relationship.

Garrick gave an infinitesimal nod. He didn't trust the humans any more than Quinn did. Neville gave the appearance of being perfectly rational and accommodating, but it could be nothing more than a mask hiding his true intent. There were a lot more humans inside that tiny house than could possibly be living there.

The two vampires followed Neville inside. One of the guards seemed intent on searching them before they entered the house, but a single dark look from Quinn had him backing away quickly enough.

"Matt," Neville said, shaking his head. "That's not necessary, lad. These gentlemen are our allies." He continued down the hall with them at his back, as if he hadn't a care in the world. "We've a conference room of sorts back here," he explained as he walked down the narrow, dark hall. "Nothing like yours, I'm sure. But it works well enough."

Quinn didn't say anything. His attention was focused on the number of humans waiting in the supposed conference room and the stench of gun oil and metal. *"Guns,"* he silently said to Garrick, although his cousin had probably come to the same conclusion. All vampires had enhanced senses of smell. *"I'll enter first."*

Garrick's rejection of that was so powerful that it reverberated in Quinn's mind.

"Softly, please, cousin," Quinn responded. *"That hurt. And, yes, I'll go first. If it's the trap we believe, I can take them all down in an instant. You cannot."*

Garrick's growl filled the hallway. It was intended for Quinn, but it was just loud enough that Neville's head swiveled from side to side, as if expecting a wild animal to leap out at him. He didn't stop walking, though, heading for an open door on the left, at the end of the hall.

Quinn quickened his pace just enough to put himself in front of Garrick when they hit the doorway. The lights were dim, which was suspicious. It was more than bright enough for vampires, but not nearly enough for the humans who waited for them.

"Watch your eyes," he 'pathed Garrick a moment before the lights were suddenly flipped on, beaming hot, white light, from row after row on the ceiling. Vampires weren't sensitive to light, but coming from the dark street, walking down the dark hallway, the abrupt wash of light would affect them as it would a human, making it difficult to see while their eyes adjusted. Quinn couldn't have said what the lights looked like—if they were normal household lights, or brighter spotlights—but it didn't matter. He'd read the intent in the humans' minds and shaded his eyes before the switch was thrown.

What he did know was exactly how many humans were in the room and where they were standing. Before a single one of them could bring a weapon up, Quinn buried their minds in a wave of power that shattered conscious thought and seared painfully along every nerve in their bodies. They screamed almost as one, dropping whatever weapon they'd been holding in favor of clutching their heads in a vain attempt to stop the pain. One or two were on the floor retching, while at least five had passed out completely. Quinn could have simply knocked them all out, but this demonstration of his power and control made a stronger statement.

Don't fuck with me.

Garrick entered behind Quinn, went immediately to the multiple light switches on one wall, and flipped off everything, except for one row of low wattage incandescent lights. He then walked around the big table that took up most of the available space in the room, shoved past chairs that literally filled the room from wall to wall, pushed aside humans and chairs alike, and didn't stop until his back was against a solid wall, and he was facing the open doorway.

Quinn glanced down at Neville, who was on his knees, doing his best not to throw up.

"Shall we get down to business now, Neville?" he inquired, then went to the end of the table where Garrick stood and pulled out a slightly larger chair. It was the only such chair in the room, and this was clearly the head of the table. Quinn sat, then lifted his gaze to meet the human leader's, daring him to protest. Neville cast a look around at his men—some of whom were still struggling to their feet—then took the chair next to Quinn.

"I had to try," he said quietly.

"Of course, you did. But now that that's settled, let's talk."

BY THE TIME Quinn and his cousin were heading back through Dublin on their way to the Ballsbridge house, he and Neville had achieved a meeting of the minds. Or as much of a meeting as a human could have with a vampire who could read his mind. Quinn hadn't confessed that latter detail to Neville. He'd already demonstrated his superiority convincingly. Why rub it in?

Basically, the agreement Quinn offered boiled down to, "Work with me or die." He'd phrased it more diplomatically, though. He was, after all, the product of years of legal wrangling. He knew how to tell someone to go fuck themselves in the nicest way. But Neville had gotten the message. He'd also betrayed a quickness of mind that told Quinn why he'd risen to the top of one of Dublin's most violent gangs. Neville had understood right away that Quinn was angling for Sorley's job, and that he expected to get it. And that Quinn intended to make changes to their business model that would serve everyone's interests, including future generations of Neville's neighborhood. And since that was what Neville wanted, as well, they'd reached a quick agreement.

"I want to visit Howth tomorrow night," Quinn told Garrick as they crossed the invisible line between North and South Dublin.

Garrick glanced at him. "You think that's a good idea?"

"It's not to see Eve," he lied. "We've a lot of guns in the warehouse. I want to see about moving them out. I don't want Sorley getting any ideas."

His cousin grunted. "All right. Who's going?"

"You and me."

"Adorjan is *not* going to like that. They already tried to kill you once down there, and he doesn't trust your girlfriend, either."

"She's not my girlfriend. As for Adorjan, I don't give a fuck what he likes. It's Saturday night. I want some blood, and I want to fuck, and I don't want him looming over me like a giant gargoyle."

"As you say, my lord."

Quinn didn't realize he'd let his power swell along with his irritation until he heard that dutiful response. He pulled back his power, angry with himself for letting it get out of control like some new-made vamp.

Garrick shot him a careful look. "I'll have a talk with Adorjan."

Quinn had to bite back the urge to "hmpf" like a disgruntled old man. Even if he was one.

"WELL? DID THEY handle it?" Sorley glared at the kneeling human he'd sent to spy on Quinn's supposed negotiation with the human gang. He'd have rather sent one of his vampires, but Quinn would have spotted a vamp without even trying.

"The meeting was . . ."

Sorley's attention snapped to his spy, drawn by the man's reluctance. What the fuck? "Well?" he demanded. "Speak up, you idiot."

"I wasn't in the room, my lord. But Neville and Quinn appeared more as allies than enemies by the end, and Quinn left the meeting unscathed. I was told by more than one reliable source that they've reached an accommodation."

Sorley stared at the trembling human. "Get out." The man scrambled to his feet and scurried from the room, as if expecting to be shot in the back. Not that Sorley would need a damn gun to kill a puny human rabbit. In this case, however, the rabbit was safe. The man was dependable, even if he didn't always deliver the news Sorley wanted to hear. If he was going to kill anyone, it would be that bastard Neville. The human gang leader had agreed to their plan to kill Quinn, so what the fuck had happened? What could Quinn possibly have offered him that Sorley couldn't? The damn American was fresh off the boat, and he'd done nothing but cause trouble. First with the guns in Howth and now the drugs through Dublin Port, which were far more profitable.

And what the fuck was he doing in Ireland, anyway? It was that stupid bitch Mathilde's fault. She'd started all this with her ill-conceived plan to take out Raphael. *Raphael!* She couldn't have started with someone she actually had a chance in hell of killing? And then, instead of learning from her mistake, her European friends had followed in her bloody footsteps. They'd gone and riled up every vampire in North America, and now Ireland had to pay for their fuck-ups, even though he'd had nothing to do with their stupid invasion.

Sorley watched his human spy slip through the barely opened door. He could still kill the bastard. He thought about it. But, no. The rabbit wasn't the one he wanted dead. It was time to get serious.

"Get Kelan in here," he told Lorcan.

His lieutenant gave him a sharp look along with a bow, then strode out of the room. Some communications were too sensitive for anything but face-to-face contact.

Sorley acknowledged, to *himself*, that he may have underestimated Quinn. Oh, he'd recognized his power easily enough, but he hadn't thought the uptight bastard had the balls to use it. Turned out he was wrong. That buttoned-up exterior of Quinn's was hiding the gut instincts of a real killer. He might have admired the asshole if he didn't hate him. Or if Quinn hadn't been trying to steal everything Sorley had worked so hard for. There could be only one response to that. It was time for Quinn to die.

Chapter Ten

Howth, Ireland

THE WAREHOUSE looked empty and unused when Quinn and his two bodyguards arrived the next night. Yes, two bodyguards. Both Garrick and Adorjan had insisted on accompanying him.

He sighed, while thinking that at least the unused appearance of the warehouse was a good sign. You couldn't tell it from the outside, but a vestibule had been added to the warehouse entrance as a security measure. There were now two doors, one three feet behind the other. In order to open the interior door the outer door had to be shut. It limited the number of people who could enter at once, and also provided a few minutes' advance warning of a potential intruder. It wasn't much, but a few minutes was all a vampire needed.

Quinn was aware that a new shipment of guns had arrived in the wee hours of the previous night. Casey had met the boat and discussed the new arrangements with its captain. The man hadn't cared who took the guns or what they did with them, as long as he got paid and was left alive to spend it.

That was all good. But regardless of what Quinn had told Garrick, he wasn't in Howth to check on the warehouse or the guns. Casey could handle the damn smuggling operation. He was here for Eve. There'd been no more random shootings of vampires, at least none he was aware of. So, he assumed she'd been telling the truth when she'd claimed to be reassessing the morality of her killing spree. But he was honest enough to admit that her vampire hunts were only part of why he wanted to see her. He missed her. She was a pain in his ass and a danger to his people, and he missed her. Not just to fuck, although thinking about her lying beneath him, with his cock buried in her slick pussy, those little moans she made before she climaxed, her frustrated cries when he slowed down, withholding her orgasm until she begged so prettily. . . .

Fuck. He was hard as a rock. He jerked open the Range Rover's door and stepped outside, easing the pressure on his cock while he shoved thoughts of Eve's silky body out of his mind. He was usually better than this. Always in control. But something about Eve had thrown him off from the very beginning. It was a damn good reason to walk away from her. As long as she stopped killing, he could leave her behind and get on with the business that had brought him to Ireland. Right? He sighed.

"My lord?"

Adorjan's deep voice interrupted his personal motivation speech. "Yeah. Sorry. Thinking about something else. Let's go."

He ignored Garrick's knowing glance and started for the warehouse, automatically scanning ahead. There were only four vampires inside, which wasn't unexpected, and yet . . . something was wrong. He couldn't put words to what he was feeling, but alarms were going off in the part of his brain that had come alive ever since he'd awakened as one of those rare vampires with true power. He considered his options in the instant between one step and the next. He should warn Adorjan and Garrick. But they'd insist on wrapping him in cotton batting and stowing him safely in the Range Rover while they dealt with the danger. They kept forgetting that he was the vampire lord, the baddest of the badasses, not some fragile egghead good only for sitting behind a desk and thinking about shit. Christ, if he'd wanted to sit behind a desk, he'd still be a lawyer.

Besides, if he couldn't fuck Eve, then he'd just as soon beat the shit out of whichever vampires had taken over *his* warehouse and now, apparently, thought to ambush him. He'd made his point in Dublin, when he'd destroyed Lon Conover and made Conover's people his own. And he'd made it again with the human gang leader, Ennis Neville, stealing the port gang away from Sorley and making *them* his own, too. But he clearly hadn't done enough here in Howth. That had to change.

Quinn entered the code on the outer door's new keypad lock and shoved the door open, ignoring Adorjan's hurried protest when he came up behind him. Quinn turned with a wink. "Sorry, one person at a time." The outer door closed, and he took a moment to do a deeper scan, wanting to know more about the four vampires inside and, specifically, what the hell had happened to Casey. The vamp had been part of the planning for this Irish venture from the beginning, but Quinn had only been in his head once. That was when they'd first met, and he'd needed to make sure that Casey wasn't a spy from Sorley or anyone else. He'd done the same mental scan on every member of the team. But he didn't know if that was enough to recognize the vamp now. On the other hand,

Casey had sworn a blood oath to Quinn just as the others had, which would make it much easier to pinpoint his location and well-being.

These thoughts passed through his head in a matter of seconds, the time it took for the outer door to close and his fingers to input the distinct code on the inner keypad. He couldn't afford to stand in the vestibule and contemplate the problem. Whoever was waiting would only become suspicious and make Quinn's job more difficult.

He touched on each of the four vamps inside. One was deeper into the warehouse, his presence muted as if in sleep. Casey, he realized. Either injured, unconscious, or both. Two others were very much awake, their thoughts a jumble of determination and being scared out of their minds. Yeah, Quinn could take his time with them. But it was the fourth vampire, the one lurking just inside and to the right, a position that would put him behind the door as Quinn entered. His mind was clear as a bell, cool and confident. This was a vampire accustomed to killing.

Sorley had apparently decided he didn't like Quinn's deal with Neville, after all.

He tapped the final number on the keypad and walked through, shoving the door hard to the right. The waiting assassin was far too skilled for that little trick. He stepped out from behind the door and placed a gun to Quinn's head, but before he could pull the trigger, every nerve in his arm went dead. Quinn spun, grabbed the gun with one hand, catching it before it could hit the floor. With his other hand, he sank his fingers into the vampire's throat and lifted him from the ground.

"A gun, asshole? Does no one in this town understand what it means to be Vampire?"

The assassin made a gurgling noise, which Quinn ignored, focusing instead on the buzz of the door opening behind him.

"What the fuck?" Adorjan roared and would have snatched the assassin from Quinn's fingertips.

"Stop," Quinn snarled. "This one's mine. You get the others. Garrick," he said, as his cousin rushed inside. "Check on Casey. He's in the back."

"As for you," he said to the would-be assassin, "you're going to tell me everything you know."

"I will not betray—" The vampire's words were cut off as he screamed in agony.

"Of course, you will. It's only a matter of how much pain you'll have to endure in the meantime." Quinn squeezed his fingers tighter, displacing divots of flesh. "Feel free to hang tough, by the way. I'm in a crappy mood, and this is incredibly therapeutic."

The vamp stared at him. "You're insane," he managed to whisper.

Quinn frowned. "Hey, I wasn't the one lurking behind the door with a gun, asshole."

Adorjan emerged from behind some of the stacked weapons' boxes, dragging the limp bodies of the two vampires Quinn had sensed hiding earlier. "These two were both at the meeting the other night and swore loyalty to you. They admitted to betraying their oaths, but insisted they had no choice and beg for mercy." He glanced down at them. "I got tired of their begging," he said, which explained their unconscious state.

Quinn met Adorjan's gaze and nodded grimly. He'd warned them. There was only one punishment for betrayal in vampire society, and that was death.

Adorjan dropped the two unconscious vamps to the floor, then walked over and broke apart a wooden chair, snapping off two of its legs and leaving the rest. He then came back to the unconscious vampires and, without ceremony, slammed a leg into each of their hearts, one after the other. The two vampires dusted in an instant. They'd made the wrong decision, and they'd paid.

Quinn didn't give them another thought. "What about Casey?"

"Garrick's with him. He took a bullet to the head." The big vampire's gaze slid sideways to glare at Quinn's prisoner. "That one likes guns."

"Is Casey all right?"

"He will be." Adorjan grinned. "He's got a hard head."

"Secure the doors. I'm going to question our gunslinger, and I don't want any interruptions."

QUINN'S MOOD WASN'T much better when they left the warehouse just over an hour later. The assassin had cracked far too easily. Apparently, his usefulness as an assassin had less to do with vampiric power, and more to do with his very human skills with weapons and skulking about. He'd been a hired killer with the Russian mob before he'd been made a vampire. Sorley had met him somewhere in Europe, decided a professional killer would be a useful tool, and turned him the same night. No questions had been asked or permission sought, though the Russian hadn't minded all that much. He'd happily fallen in with Sorley's plan to take over Ireland, and become his number one assassin.

The situation had worked great for both of them until Sorley had made the mistake of sending his pet killer after Quinn. The Irish lord had to know how powerful Quinn was. He wouldn't have been threatened enough to kill him otherwise. But he'd clearly underestimated Quinn's fondness for violence, mistaking his law degree for a preference for following rules. What he didn't understand was that the only rules Quinn had to follow anymore were the ones of his own making. And any vampire who tried to kill him or his was fair game. Death was a certainty. The only question was how much he'd suffer first.

The answer was not much. Sorley's pet killer was a classic bully. He loved hurting others, but had a terrible fear of his own pain. He'd caved like a snowball on a sunny day, every secret he owned spilling out so fast, it was hard to keep up with him. You'd have thought a coward like that would welcome death, but it seemed death was even more terrifying to him than pain.

Whatever. Quinn didn't care. He'd squeezed everything there was to be had from the vampire and then executed him with the third leg of Adorjan's chair. He could have ripped the assassin's heart out, but he didn't want to get that bloody. Too much clean up, and there wasn't even a shower in the building.

After they locked the warehouse, Adorjan took Casey back to the Howth house, while Quinn and Garrick left the Range Rover where it was and headed to their favorite pub. Quinn didn't mind the down time, but more than anything, he needed blood. He was using a lot more energy than usual lately, and it had been nearly a week since he'd fed from the sweet, little brunette at this same pub. Maybe she'd be around again tonight. It would make things easier. He could avoid all the foreplay involved with a new woman—making it clear what he wanted, making certain it was what *she* wanted. He wouldn't mind going right to the biting and fucking part of the night. He hadn't actually fucked the brunette last time, because Eve had been in the picture, but the brunette had certainly been willing and probably would be again. If not, he'd find someone else. Attracting women had never been a problem for him, whether human or vampire.

Quinn knew Garrick was feeling protective after the assassination attempt, but he wasn't in the mood to be babysat. He'd just have to make sure his cousin was distracted. The pub was as packed as he'd expect for a Saturday night, the inside so full that the crowd spilled out into the patio, and beyond that, onto the dock itself. Some of those revelers seemed in real danger of taking a dip in the icy waters of the harbor, but that wasn't his concern.

He could barely move through the mass of people as he headed inside. Crowds like this had a certain dynamic, a living energy that he could feed from almost like blood. But he didn't have the patience for that tonight. He wanted the real thing. Hot, sweet, and silky, right from the vein. Using just a touch of his power, he cleared a path, the mostly happy humans making room for him without even realizing they were doing it. More than one female cast a welcome glance his way as he moved deeper into the pub, but he could feel Garrick at his shoulder, his protective scowl practically cock-blocking him with every step.

Fortunately, Garrick was hungry, too. Even more fortunately, he had a type, and Quinn knew what it was. He searched as they maneuvered through the crowd, until he found the right female. Blond and willowy, with average breasts and a lost look in her big eyes that said she didn't do a lot of pub crawling. The look of a woman who needed saving. Perfect.

Quinn knew he shouldn't do it, but sometimes the end justified the means. Or so he told himself. He reached for the woman's mind and, using the gentlest of touches, steered her attention toward Garrick. His cousin had no more trouble than Quinn attracting women, so once the blonde's attention was focused on Garrick, it took no more interference from Quinn to get her moving in their direction. A slight bump of his shoulder sent Garrick stumbling into the woman at the right moment. A blush on her pale cheeks, a startled look from those Bambi eyes, and Garrick's arm slid protectively around her waist.

Quinn grinned. "Looks like love," he said in his cousin's ear.

Garrick shot him a matching grin, then frowned. "I should—"

"Don't be daft," Quinn said, cutting him off. "I'm heading for the shadows and a bite. I'll be perfectly safe while you rescue yon maiden."

Garrick shot the blonde a lustful look, then back at Quinn. "If you're sure."

"Go."

He was almost insulted at how quickly his cousin disappeared into the crowd. Maybe he hadn't had to work so hard to set him up, after all. But he wasn't going to waste the opportunity. Doing as he'd said he would, he pushed through into the unlit depths in the back of the pub. This place was the closest Howth had to a blood house. The smell of blood and sex was blatant to his vampire senses. And if that wasn't enough, the soft cries of ecstasy, punctuated by the occasional deep growl of conquest, made it perfectly clear what was happening. Quinn sharpened his gaze, and his vampire-enhanced sight pierced the shadows. Not all of the fucking going on involved vampires. Some of the human locals were taking advantage of the darkness to do some fucking of their own. Quinn's mouth twitched in amusement, as he searched for his brunette, finally finding her in a small group of women, all of whom seemed to know each other, if their lively conversation was anything to go by. His girl was on the quiet side, but not a wallflower. She smiled and laughed, and made the occasional comment, but mostly seemed simply to enjoy being there.

Quinn remained in the shadows, reluctant, now that the moment was here, to claim the lovely woman. What the hell was wrong with him? He needed blood, and she was willing. He frowned. Unlike a certain redhead who wanted to pick and choose which parts of him she accepted. She wanted the human, but not the vampire. Well, fuck that. He was a package deal, and he wasn't going to pretend to be anything less than he was. Not even for Eve.

Using a small amount of power, much as he had on Garrick's blonde, he drew the brunette's attention. Her head came up, and her eyes widened, as her tongue slid out to moisten lips he knew were pillow soft. He smiled and crooked his finger. She sucked in a breath, said something to the woman next to her, and then hurried toward him.

It was a struggle to remember her name. Quinn felt bad about that, but, in his defense, he'd never expected to see her again, and there'd been a lot going on. It hit him just in time.

"Nora," he said, all vampire dominance as he grabbed her hand and pulled her closer until they were toe to toe. Her perfume was an enticement, her breasts brushing his chest, as her breath rushed a little too fast, betraying her nerves. "Relax, baby," he murmured, adding a small push to be sure it worked. The last thing he needed was for Nora to pass out before they got to the good part.

"My lord," she whispered. She'd done that the other night, too. Used the vampire honorific, as if he expected it. He couldn't remember if he'd told her his name. Or if he'd erased it before he left her. It didn't matter. Theirs was purely a relationship of convenience. Nora wanted an experience she could tell her friends about, and he wanted blood.

"Come here," he murmured and put an arm around her waist, guiding her over to the row of booths lining one wall. There were only four of them, and they were all full. Quinn caught the attention of the two vampires currently occupying the booth in the very corner, and jerked his head. The two vamps immediately grabbed their human companions and scooted out from behind the table, disappearing into the crowd as Quinn handed Nora onto the bench seat and started to follow her.

"What the fuck is this?"

Quinn turned at the sound of Eve's voice. She was standing behind him, looking for all the world like a jealous girlfriend. Except that she didn't have the right to claim either of those things. It made him angry that she'd try.

"Eve," he said with forced calm. "I wouldn't have thought this was your scene."

"Same goes."

"Really?" He laughed. "Look around, sweetheart. These are my people." He took Nora's hand and pulled her out of the booth, thinking a little privacy might be better for what he had planned. "Let's go, baby," he told her. "I'll bring you back, don't worry." He closed the fingers of one hand over her hip, then pushed her in front of him, and began moving through the crowd toward the outside. He still had a room at the house, or there was the warehouse, which was very close and very empty. He'd take her there, in more ways than one.

EVE WATCHED IN disbelief as Quinn pulled the other woman out of the booth and headed for the front door. He was going home with another woman? What the fuck? They had a . . . a *thing* going on, didn't they? Sure, they'd hit a rough patch or two . . . She choked back a bitter laugh. Right, because discovering your lover was a vampire was a fucking *rough patch*. But, she'd thought—after their conversation the other night, when she'd admitted he might be right about her vampire kills, and she'd asked for his help—she'd thought they'd reached a meeting of the minds. They were obviously hot for each other. The two times they'd had sex had been off the charts sizzling. But there was more to it than that. She *liked* him, and she'd thought he liked her.

So why was he walking out of the pub with some other girl he was clearly planning to fuck? Oh, shit. He was going to take that woman's blood. Eve's chest was tight with unexpected emotion. It *ached*. She hadn't known that Quinn Kavanagh had the power to make her feel that much. The realization made her angry. Because anger was better than hurt.

Striding after him, she shoved her way through the packed back room where she'd *known* she'd find him that night. *And what had you expected would happen when you found him, you idiot?* she asked herself. Had she thought they'd go back to her house and have some more human style sex?

Yes, she realized. That's exactly what she'd thought.

"Hey!" she called, reaching out to grab the back of his jacket. He spun with a snarl, and Eve belatedly thought that grabbing a pissed off vampire from the back might not be the best idea. She held up both hands. "Just me," she said quickly. "Can we talk?"

He blinked lazily, but his eyes were anything but. They were sharp and unwavering, and, for the first time, she saw that they glowed from within. It was a cool white gleam that radiated like cracked ice through the crystalline blue of his irises. "More talk, Eve? I didn't come here to *talk*."

She swallowed back the nasty retort that leapt to her lips. No, he'd clearly come to the pub tonight to suck and fuck. What pissed her off was that he hadn't even thought to call and see if she was in town. Or available. Wait. *Was* she available? Fuck.

"I know," she said fighting for calm. "But this will only take a moment."

He nodded his head once, then pulled his snack close and whispered something in her ear. She gave him an adoring look, then hurried across the room and rejoined her friends.

Eve wanted to ask what he'd told her, but didn't want him to know she cared. "Can we go outside, where it's quieter?"

He shrugged, as if he didn't care either way, then headed for the exit, without even bothering to make sure she followed. Bastard. He was going to make this difficult.

The minute they were through the door, he spun, grabbed her by the waist, and pulled her around the side of the building where it was definitely quieter. It was also dark and cold, and utterly empty of other people. He didn't give her a chance to react, however, just pressed her up against the wall, holding her there bracketed between his muscled arms as he braced his hands to either side of her. He was so close, she could feel his warmth, could smell his skin. She wanted to rub herself up and down that big, beautiful body. She'd had dreams of him last night and had woken up wet and empty with longing. She ran her hands along his sides, then looked up and met his too-knowing eyes. She dropped her hands.

"What is it, Eve?" he murmured, leaning in to dip his head into the curve of her neck.

Now that she had him, she didn't know what to say.

"Come on, sweetheart. Let's *talk*." He continued his exploration of her skin, nibbling her neck from just below her ear, pushing aside the open collar of her sweater to kiss the dip of her throat, and then shoving the soft wool even farther to bare her collar bone. He took it between his teeth and bit down until she could just feel the pressure of his bite.

She jumped in surprise, and then shivered.

Quinn made a disgusted noise. Stopping at once, he lifted his head and put space between them. "Why are you here, Eve?"

"I live here," she said, having to force the words through a throat that was all but crushed beneath the pounding of her heart. "I just stopped in for a pint," she lied, not wanting to admit she'd been looking for him.

He stepped back. "Then don't let me keep you. I have a friend waiting."

"A friend? Is that what you call her? Why are you being such an arse?"

"Me? Let me explain how this works. I'm a vampire. When I come to a pub like this, it's not to join the debating society. I want blood, and I want to fuck. Those two things frequently go together with my kind."

Eve's temper was rising. She'd tried being reasonable. It hadn't worked.

"So, my darling Eve, you either give me what I came here for, or I'll go back to someone who will."

"That's it?" she demanded. "You just whore yourself out to a random stranger for blood?"

His eyes had that icy glow again. "Tread carefully, Eve. My patience is not unlimited."

"Your patience? *Your* patience? What am I supposed to do while you're fucking the flavor of the night? Hang around and wait for you to finish up?"

He gave her a disbelieving look. "I don't care what you do. We're not a couple. You can't handle the truth of what I am, and you've made it clear that you're unwilling to give me what I need. So, there, you wanted to talk? We've talked." He slammed a fist into the side of the building, then straightened and turned to leave.

Eve grabbed the front of his jacket with both hands, more furious than she could ever remember being. She yanked him close, knowing he had to be letting her do it. "Fuck you!" she snarled.

He gave her a tiny smile. "That's the idea, darling."

"I hate you," she hissed, then tightened her fists in his jacket, intending to pull him closer. She was slammed against the wall instead, his body crushing hers, his mouth coming down on her lips.

They ate at each other as if starved for the taste, their teeth clashing and tongues fighting for dominance. She tasted blood and didn't know if it was his or hers, until he groaned in sensual pleasure. She shivered in the knowledge that a tiny taste of her blood had elicited such a powerful response. It thrilled and terrified her in equal measure. But she didn't stop.

He grabbed her hips and lifted her higher, slipping a thigh between hers until she wrapped her legs around his waist, and his hands dropped to cup her ass. She was rubbing herself against him, the thick seam of the jeans she wore pressing against the hard ridge of his cock. Her fingers reached for his belt buckle, but he flexed his hips away from her touch.

"Not here," he growled.

"Where?" She barely recognized her own breathless question.

"Your place."

Eve gave a tiny scream of frustration, but knew he was right. They couldn't fuck against the back wall of the pub, for Christ's sake. She wasn't even wearing a skirt. She'd have to get practically naked to make it possible.

"Fine," she snapped. "Let's go."

He lifted her higher and demanded another kiss. It was just as fierce and out of control as the first one, but there was a *knowledge* to it. Because they both knew that the next time they kissed, it was going to end with his cock in her pussy. And his fangs in her neck.

EVE DIDN'T EVEN remember getting to her flat. They must have walked, because she'd walked to the pub, and she'd have remembered if they'd taken Quinn's SUV. But the only thing that registered was practically falling through her front door, his hands on her ass, their mouths tearing at each other, until the door closed, and they began ripping at each other's clothes instead. Quinn threw her on the bed and pulled off her boots, then stripped her tight jeans and panties together down her legs and off. She tore her own sweater over her head and was working on her bra clasp, when Quinn gripped it in one hand and snapped the thin band. Some part of Eve's brain registered the knowledge that she should protest the damage, but the rest of her body only knew that it wanted to be naked as quickly as possible. And speaking of naked . . .

She went up onto her knees and attacked Quinn's belt and zipper, while he yanked his long-sleeved T-shirt over his head and toed off his boots at the same time. Eve shoved his jeans past narrow hips, noting the absence of underwear as his cock sprang into hard and glorious view. She stroked her fingers up and down the thick shaft—once, twice—and bent to take it in her mouth, but Quinn stopped her.

"No," he said simply, then hooked her under the arms and tossed her higher on the bed, shoving his hips between her thighs and his cock into her pussy with a single, masterful thrust. They both froze for an instant, their eyes meeting in shock at the sheer intensity of the connection between their bodies. Eve's breath stalled in her lungs, and her heart seemed to stop for a moment before resuming a stuttering beat. Quinn stared at her, his penis buried deep, his hands cradling her face. He held motionless for a heartbeat, then bent his head and kissed her. It was almost tender at first, as his hips began to move in short strokes, his cock pulling out no more than an inch before sliding back in. It didn't last long, as his kiss deepened, and the hunger between them roared.

QUINN WITHDREW his cock and held it there, waiting for Eve's eyes to open, to know that it was *him* she was fucking. She made a tiny noise and lifted her hips, searching for him, before her eyes came open.

"Quinn," she whispered, staring up at him. Her hands on his chest, she closed her eyes briefly, then opened them again. "I don't hate you."

"I know." He moved then, plunging his cock deep into her body, her cry of pleasure a sweet sound as his hips began pistoning in and out, his groin grinding against her clit with every new thrust. Eve was clinging to him, her strong fingers digging into the muscle of his shoulders as she tried to hold on, her small moans of desire riding panting breaths as he fucked her hard, angry that she'd rejected him, that she'd tried to deny this connection between them, a connection that went deeper than flesh. Blood deep.

He hooked his arm behind Eve's knee and pulled her leg higher and wider, opening her even further to his demands, his claiming. She cried out as the first tremors of climax shuddered through her body, her abdomen clenching beneath him, her inner muscles shivering in anticipation. Quinn reached between them and stroked his thumb once over her clit, that tiny nub of nerves reacting as if a switch had been thrown, as she exploded into a trembling, thrashing orgasm. Her teeth closed over his shoulder, and he reveled in the pain, his cock growing impossibly harder as her pussy flooded with heat and cream, making her passage slick and welcoming his renewed assault.

Quinn growled low in his chest and bent his head, his mouth going to her ear. "It's time, Eve."

She shivered once, but her pussy clenched around his cock at the same time, letting him know it was desire, not fear, that caused the reaction.

He twirled his tongue along the curves of her ear, then slowly licked his way down to her neck. Her vein was plump and eager when he drew it into his mouth, sucking hard enough that her pale skin would bruise. He wanted her marked, wanted no doubt that she'd been taken. She was his.

"Last chance," he murmured against her skin.

She trembled, but arched her neck, inviting his bite.

Quinn's fangs slid eagerly from his gums. He was more than simply hungry for blood, he was hungry for *this* woman's blood. His fangs sliced through her silky skin, encountering the slight pressure of her vein, before piercing that, too. Blood flowed. As sweet and thick as fresh honey, it rolled down his throat in a velvet wave of sensation. He swallowed over and over, a growl of satisfaction rumbling in his chest, as Eve suddenly began to tremble beneath him.

"Quinn?" she asked in a tiny voice. And then the euphoric in his bite slammed into her, and he had to cover her mouth with his hand to smother her scream as she soared into a second orgasm, this one far more powerful than the first, her slight weight bowing against him as her muscles bucked and rippled uncontrollably.

Quinn lifted his mouth from her neck, managing to lick the wounds closed, before he surrendered and rode the wave of her climax, her pussy clamping down on him so hard that the pulsing of her sheath was like fingers gripping and releasing his cock in rhythm. He groaned, then lifted his hand from her mouth and kissed her, as heat filled his balls and roared down his cock, and they crashed together into a final, utterly out of control, orgasm.

EVE LAY CRUSHED beneath Quinn's heavy body, not feeling trapped, but some other emotion that she didn't want to examine too closely. She didn't want to think about that other thing either, but no one had ever accused her of being a coward.

Sex with a vampire. Yep, that was the thing she didn't want to think about. She'd just had sex with a vampire, most especially including him biting her neck. She shivered, remembering it, and had to tighten her arms around Quinn when he noticed and started to shift his weight off her. If he moved, she might fly apart.

"No," she murmured, holding on to him. "Stay."

"What am I, a dog?" he muttered. But he said it with humor and settled his full weight on top of her again, his only concession being to lower her leg from where it had been hooked over his arm. Smoothing his big hand along her thigh, he massaged the strained muscles and would have straightened her leg completely, but Eve wrapped her leg around the back of his thigh instead. He made a rumbling sound of pleasure and flexed his hips, his very firm cock reminding her that vampires had much faster restorative powers than humans.

Good God.

If Eve hadn't already figured out why women lined up to have vampires suck on them, she sure as hell knew now. Quinn had already given her the most mind-blowing climaxes of her life, and that was *before,* when she'd thought he was an ordinary human. But this last orgasm, the one they'd shared after he'd taken her blood, had positively fried her brain. And he was ready to do it again. She didn't think she'd survive it, survive *him.* Because the truth that was settling into her heart and making her lungs catch was the creeping knowledge that this was more than great sex. This might be . . . Shit. She couldn't even think the word.

Quinn kissed the side of her neck, right where he'd bitten her. The skin was tender, but not raw and bleeding the way she'd assumed it would be.

"I have to go, sweetheart."

Eve's stomach plummeted. "You don't have to," she whispered, knowing it was going to hurt when he left.

He kissed her forehead and rolled to the side, taking her with him. "It's late, and we're driving back tonight."

"You could stay here."

"An enticing offer," he murmured, taking her mouth in another luscious kiss. "But I have enemies." He slipped his arm out from under her and stood, taking all that heat and desire with him.

Eve watched him get dressed, unsure what she was supposed to think about that last statement. He had enemies. And so. . . . What? Was he implying she could be bought? That she'd give him up to those enemies? Or maybe it was that he didn't want to put her in the path of the people—vampires?—who meant him harm. Maybe he was worried about her safety, rather than his own.

She could ask him. But he might not tell her the truth, and she wasn't sure she wanted to know which one it was, anyway.

Fully dressed, Quinn bent over and pulled the covers up to her chin, then kissed her again. The kiss was still delicious, but some of the explosive anger between them—the very thing that had triggered their earlier passionate collision—had returned. He bit her lower lip as he pulled away, tugging it between his teeth just enough to hurt.

"Be good, Eve."

"I will if you will," she responded, eyeing him uncertainly.

"You'll hear from me," he growled, and then he was gone, using that damn vampire speed of his that didn't even give her the satisfaction of throwing something at him.

QUINN *MOVED*, USING his vampiric gifts to get away as far and as fast from Eve's flat as his considerable power allowed. It wasn't only that he needed to meet up with the others and get back to the Ballsbridge house. It was also to escape the overwhelming temptation of Eve herself. For the first time since he'd been made a vampire, he'd considered remaining in his lover's bed through the day. It was insane and dangerous. Even if he'd been able to trust her, and he wasn't yet certain that he did completely, her tiny flat wasn't equipped to provide him with a secure daytime resting place. He'd never seen her place in the daytime, for obvious reasons, but he doubted the pale curtains on the main window blocked the sunlight, and the door was so flimsy as to barely qualify.

Garrick would knock his lights out for even thinking about it. Even Adorjan might be tempted to set aside his respect for Quinn's position and whack some sense into him.

Reaching the now-deserted pub, he was happy to see the Range Rover still standing in the parking lot, looking like a metal and glass indictment of his poor judgment. At least according to Garrick. Striding over to the vehicle, he dug in his pocket, then realized he didn't have the damn key. Even if his cousin had left it unlocked, he couldn't—

"Looking for this?" Garrick strolled out of the pub, dangling the key fob from his fingers.

Quinn winced privately, but reminded himself *he* was the vampire lord here, not Garrick. "Great, you're here. Where's Adorjan?"

Garrick studied him for a moment, then drew a deep breath. "He's waiting at the house. You want to stay here or—"

"No, we're going back to the city, and we'll have to ignore the speed limits to do it," Quinn said, sliding into the passenger seat.

His cousin joined him, punching the ignition before he was fully seated. "I'll let Adorjan drive. He's been dying to break the law ever since we got here."

Quinn thought that they'd already broken more than a few laws. Murder, for one. Smuggling, criminal conspiracy, racketeering . . . He could go on. But all he said was, "Good. Because we're going to be breaking a few more very soon."

Chapter Eleven

Dublin, Ireland

QUINN WOKE IN THE security of his new private suite in the Ballsbridge house. It was nice to finally have a safe place to spend the day, but all he could think was that it would be even nicer if a certain hot redhead was waking up next to him. He quashed that thought before it was fully formed. Sure, he was attracted to Eve. What man wouldn't be? She was gorgeous and sexy and as fiery as hell . . . and if any other man laid a hand on her, he'd kill him.

His eyes flashed open. Christ, where had *that* come from? He couldn't get involved with Eve or any other woman. He had a challenge to win and a territory to run. Hundreds of vampire lives depended on him. He didn't have time to worry about a woman, other than as a source for blood. And if spectacular sex went with it, all the better.

He sat up, and his senses automatically spread through the rest of the house, touching every living person—human or vampire. He sensed Garrick and Adorjan rising to wakefulness, as more of the others began to stir with every minute that passed. By now, his vampires were all well-rested and well-fed, a strong fighting force that would be tested over the next few nights.

It was while he was showering that he sensed another presence on the estate. One who couldn't match a vampire's strength, but who was powerful all the same.

"Damn it, Eve," he muttered, toweling himself off quickly. "What the fuck are you doing here?"

"DAMN IT, EVE, WHAT the fuck are you doing here?" she muttered to herself as she watching the closed gate through her binoculars, waiting for the almighty Quinn to grant her entrance. The human guards who'd been there when she'd first parked down the street were being replaced by vampires. The two groups were consulting, giving a shift report, she supposed, as if this was some ordinary corporate headquarters instead of a vampire's lair. It shouldn't have surprised her. Quinn was a bossy guy. He probably *did* run his vampire empire, or whatever they called it, like a corporation. She'd like to see *that* board meeting. Did they serve warm blood in flasks, instead of water? Did vampires drink water? They drank booze, so why not?

Forcing her thoughts away from such trivial considerations, she continued her surveillance. She was there to talk to Quinn, to settle, once and for all, what this thing was between them. And, also, she admitted grudgingly, to finish their discussion about her vampire killing. Whatever else happened between them, she knew she couldn't go on as she had. Now that she'd gotten to know—and, er, fucked—Quinn, and after meeting his cousin, and even Adorjan, she couldn't justify killing every vampire she met on a dark street. Yeah, sure, Adorjan was a scary motherfucker, but that didn't mean he deserved to die. There were plenty of scary humans, too. Some of whom were even involved in the kind of crimes that had gotten her brother killed.

And that was the other truth she'd had to face. Her beloved brother, the most important person in her life, had been involved in a criminal conspiracy dirty enough that it had gotten him killed. It destroyed a little piece of her soul to admit that. The same man who'd soothed her skinned knees and cheered her football games, who'd screened her dates and yelled louder than anyone at her graduation, had been a criminal. She didn't know why he'd done it, or even what he'd done to make his criminal bosses angry enough to murder him. But Quinn was right. Alan hadn't been an innocent mowed down by evil vampires. He'd put himself at risk and paid the price. But had he considered the price *she'd* pay if he died? Not the vampire hunting—that was on her. But what about the empty spot in her life that no one else would ever fill?

She sighed and rubbed her eyes, telling herself she was tired, not crying. When her eyes blinked open, she saw that the gate finally had been rolled back. Not all the way, but just enough to—

A knock of her window startled her into a high-pitched shriek. She glared at the man standing outside her car door, looking in. Not a man, she realized, catching the glint of red in his eyes, but a vampire. Of course. She buzzed the window down just enough to hear him.

"What?" she demanded. "This is a perfectly legal parking spot, and—"

"Lord Quinn has invited you to join him."

That's what he said, but what he clearly meant was that Quinn had ordered him to drag her inside kicking and screaming, if he had to.

"Fine," she said and buzzed the window back up. She'd hoped to force the vamp to jump back in order to keep his nose from being squished, but the damn window didn't move fast enough. He gave her a smug look, which she ignored. She'd intended to go in and see Quinn anyway, so what difference did it make how she got there? She *was* curious to know how they'd spotted her. She was well down the block, under a tree, with no lights anywhere.

Shoving the expensive binocs inside her pack, she hefted it onto her shoulder and climbed out of the car, closing and locking it behind her. The locks wouldn't stand against vampire strength, but they might deter crooks of the human variety.

"Lead the way," she told the vamp, but he shook his head.

"I don't think so." Something about the way he said it made her think he knew how she'd spent the last few years and wasn't willing to give her his back. On the one hand, *yay her!* for having a big bad vamp afraid of her. On the other hand . . . shit, maybe she'd killed one of his friends. Maybe even someone he loved.

This whole "vampires are people, too" thing sucked.

The vampire guided her all the way into the house, then up the wide stairway with its exquisite crystal chandelier. The first floor—what Americans, and probably Quinn, called the second floor—was a long hallway, with subtle sconce lighting that hadn't been there the other night. Or maybe it simply hadn't been turned on. With the extra light, she could see details. The dark wooden wainscoting consisted of panels that were lovingly detailed, probably antique, and the raw silk wallpaper above them would have cost more than all her belongings combined. It was all terribly beautiful, and it all fit with what she knew of powerful vampires. They had money. Sorley's house wasn't as tasteful as this, but it was stuffed with priceless antiques, and the house itself was in one of Dublin's most exclusive neighborhoods. If she'd once doubted Quinn's determination to rule Ireland—not his singled-mindedness, but the practicality of such a goal—she didn't anymore. Not after seeing how he was settling into this house. And not after witnessing his ruthlessness the other night, or the way the vampires around him treated him like royalty.

She looked up to find Garrick standing outside the open door to Quinn's office, giving her a death stare. She might have won over Quinn, but his cousin still hated her. She smiled brightly, but his expression didn't change.

"I've got this," he told the vampire who'd brought her this far.

She turned to watch as the vamp didn't say a word, simply spun on his heel and headed back downstairs.

"Lord Quinn is waiting for you," Garrick said, drawing her attention.

She noted the formal address, figured it had some meaning for him, but didn't know how she was supposed to react. She gave him another bright smile and said, "Thanks," then walked past him into Quinn's office, head held high.

"Close the door, Eve." Quinn's voice from behind her sparked a shock of remembered lust, her breasts seeming to swell as an ache settled between her thighs.

She had to draw a careful breath before she turned to meet his bright blue gaze, knowing he'd see the desire in her eyes if she wasn't careful. It would be a mistake to let him have that much control. He was already arrogant enough. He gave her a knowing look, and Eve swore inwardly.

Standing near the discreet bar tucked against one wall, he lifted a beautiful crystal decanter filled with dark gold liquid and poured himself a drink. The dark, peaty scent of Irish whiskey filled the room as he held up the decanter. "Drink?"

She shook her head. She'd never been much of a whiskey drinker, for all that it smelled divine. A half-pint of ale was more her speed, and she rarely finished even that. "Did I interrupt something?" she asked, fighting to keep the snark out of her question. "Your cousin didn't seem happy to see me."

"Well, you've been killing vampires, lass, and he doesn't want me dead."

Eve couldn't stop the jerk of surprise that had her eyes going wide and her mouth opening in shock. "I'd never hurt *you*," she breathed.

Quinn gave her a bemused smile and settled behind his desk, studying her.

She knew it was stupid, but her feelings were hurt. She hadn't expected a soliloquy of everlasting love, but a hello kiss would have been nice. After all, they'd practically attacked each other last night, as if they couldn't get enough. He'd even taken her blood! And now, he was treating her like an annoying neighbor.

Fine. Who cared?

Too restless to remain still under that careful gaze, she wandered over to the window, which mostly looked out over the side yard, with its winding path and carefully manicured shrubbery. If she looked left, she could just see the detached garages, which hummed with activity. Lots of coming and going, though she didn't know what for.

"Why are you here, Eve?" Quinn asked.

She swung around and tilted her head curiously. "How did you know I was here in the first place?"

He shrugged. "I always know where you are."

"What does that mean?"

He gave her a vague look. "I'm a powerful vampire. I keep track of the people who matter to me."

She experienced a moment of pure, feminine satisfaction at that admission. She "mattered" to him. But then she frowned. Damn him. What did that mean?

"I have a question," she said abruptly.

There was that bemused smile again, as if he found her entertaining.

"Is this real?" she blurted out. She'd never wanted anyone the way she wanted him. No matter how cool he pretended to be, he'd been just as hot for her as she'd been for him. And that had never happened to her before. So she needed to know. "Are you doing something to me? To us? Making me want you the way I do?"

The elegant crystal tumbler thumped to the desk, and she thought for sure the glass would shatter under the crushing grip of his hand. "Fuck, Eve," he snapped. "I thought we were past this." He threw the glass at the empty fireplace, breaking it anyway.

The office door popped open almost instantly. Garrick took a half-step into the room, his gaze sweeping over her, before landing on Quinn.

"It was just a glass," Quinn said quietly, glancing at his cousin. "Thanks, Garrick."

Garrick gave Eve a careful look, said, "My lord," and ducked back out again, closing the door.

Quinn waited a moment, then stood and leaned over his desk to say tightly, "No, I'm not *doing* anything to you. No one's *doing* anything." He gave her a look that was hot with more than just anger. "I want you. But I'm not going to live with this constant suspicious bullshit. You either deal with what I am, once and for all, or go find some nice Irish lad, have lots of boring sex, and pop out a bunch of babies."

It was Eve's turn to be pissed. Hell, she had a *right* to be pissed. He *wanted* her? Well, then, why the fuck hadn't he acted like it when she'd walked in? And what the fuck was up with the, "I'll be in touch," line when he'd left her this morning? That wasn't something you said to a person who mattered.

She stormed around his desk, ready to get in his face, only to find him giving her that damn bemused look again. She tightened her hand into a fist and swung at his smug face, but he caught her hand with ease.

"No hitting," he said, laughing.

She ground her teeth so hard, she could hear the noise. "For the record," she growled. "I don't want some nice Irish lad, and I sure as hell don't want a swollen belly."

He raised one eyebrow. "What *do* you want?" he purred.

She glared at him, then sighed in resignation. "For some reason, you fucking American bastard, what I want is you."

Quinn reached out, wrapped his hand around the back of her neck, and pulled her in until she bumped against his chest. "That wasn't so hard, was it?" he murmured, his whisper a warm brush of air against her ear.

Eve felt her temper rising again, since *he'd* been the one being an arse about things, but he didn't give her a chance. Twisting his fingers in her hair, he tugged her head back, met her eyes, and said, "Good evening, Eve." And then he kissed her, melting away her anger and destroying any thoughts she'd had of resisting.

"Damn you," she whispered, when they came up for air. His arms tightened and he kissed her again, deeper this time, his big hands sliding down her back to cup her ass and press her against his erection. Eve moaned softly, pushing her breasts against his chest and shivering with perverse pleasure when her tongue caressed his fangs.

Lifting her easily, Quinn swiveled to place her on his desk, then stepped between her thighs and pushed her legs wide, until the thick bulge of his erection was nestled against her sex. Hips flexing, he rubbed over her swollen clit until she found herself grinding against him, her arms twisted around his neck to keep him from moving away. She leaned back to tug his shirt out of his slacks, and he took advantage, slipping two fingers into her blouse and popping the buttons one by one until he bared her bra, and then twisted the front catch open on that, too. The bra fell away to either side, spilling her breasts into his waiting hands. Leaning forward, he drew the tip of one into his mouth, stroking her nipple with his tongue, sucking it to a stiff peak before biting just enough that she could feel it, and then grazing his fangs over the soft flesh until he drew the smallest trickle of blood.

Eve groaned as the stinging pain traveled like an electric shock, shooting down through her abdomen and groin until it plucked at her clit, until she'd have sworn she could feel the stroke of his tongue on the throbbing nub. Quinn licked away the small bit of blood from her breast, his tongue sliding over and back to twirl around her nipple, as he reached beneath her skirt and slid his hands into her panties to cup her bare ass. Eve shuddered with pleasure when he moved his teasing mouth to the other breast, tasting and biting in turn, taking his slow time while she grew more and more frantic with desire.

Sliding a hand between their bodies, she gripped the hard bulge of his erection through the fabric of his jeans. It was Quinn's turn to groan as she slid his zipper down and reached into the opening to wrap her fingers around his thickness. His penis was all hot velvety skin and steely hardness. She closed her eyes, loving the feel of him, wanting him deep inside her. She scooted closer to the edge of the desk and would have slid herself right onto his cock, but he went suddenly still, his arms tightening around her protectively a moment before a knock sounded on the office door.

"We've got trouble, my lord."

Quinn cursed silently at his cousin's voice. There was very little privacy in a house full of vampires. Garrick knew what Quinn was up to with Eve and wouldn't haven't interrupted him if it wasn't serious.

For one minute, he considered fucking her anyway. She was ready for him, her pussy hot and soaking wet where she'd been grinding it against his cock, her arousal like the sweetest perfume. It was nearly as enticing as the rush of her blood, its delicious scent so close beneath the satin beauty of her pale skin. Her breasts were full and lush, narrow trails of blood betraying the mark of his fangs, her nipples as hard and ripe as berries, and just as succulent. She was still rocking against him, whispering his name like a plea over and over again . . .

Quinn shut his eyes and stepped back, pulling the two sides of her blouse over her beautiful breasts. "Rain check, sweetheart."

Eve blushed in hot embarrassment and began hurriedly putting herself back together, slapping away his hands when he ran the backs of his fingers over her breasts while pretending to help her fasten the bra. "Is it always this busy?" she asked quietly, her fingers shaking as she slipped the tiny buttons into their holes.

"No," he muttered. "Only when I'm trying to seize a country."

She chuckled, then looked up to meet his eyes and realized he was serious. "Oh. Right."

He reached for the lowest button on her blouse, his fingers

ridiculously large for the narrow button holes.

"I'll do it," she said brushing his hands away. "You take care of your own self." She nodded at his raging hard-on.

Fuck, Quinn thought viciously. Or not. That was the problem, wasn't it? Stepping away from her seductive heat, he zipped his jeans and shook his hips, trying to get his unruly cock to loosen enough that it didn't look like an animal trying to break free. Which was what it felt like right about now.

He eyed Eve, while she tried to get everything covered, and decided he didn't want anyone else to see her like that. She was his, in all her enticing, frustrating, irritating as hell, sexiness.

"Stay here," he ordered and walked over to the door, opening it enough that he could slip into the hall without making it look like he was hiding anything. His cousin knew better, but Garrick did no more than cock a cynical eyebrow.

"What's happened?" Quinn asked.

"Got a call from that human gang leader at the port—Neville. He says there's a bunch of Sorley's people down there making trouble. He wants to know what you're going to do about it."

"Shit. Sorley has a mole somewhere, probably in Neville's gang. He knows about our deal and doesn't like it, so he's decided to fuck it up." Quinn looked to the side, thinking. "All right. Who knows about this?"

"No one. I took the call and came directly to you."

"Good. I want this kept quiet. A small group—you, me, and maybe three more. Only people we can trust absolutely, vampires from our original team. We leave in ten minutes."

"Yes, my lord." Garrick strode away without another word, taking the stairs quickly, but without any evidence of urgency. Anyone seeing him would see nothing out of the ordinary.

Quinn watched him go, then opened the door behind him and slipped back into his office.

"I have to go," he said, walking to the wall behind his desk and pressing a hidden panel. A door popped open to reveal a collection of weapons—guns and knives mostly, but there were a few grenades, and even a small crossbow. He'd bought the latter on a whim and had never had a chance to use it. Even the guns were only for backup purposes. He wouldn't have much credibility as a vampire lord if he had to rely on human weapons instead of his own power.

"Whoa!" Eve's reaction to the arsenal was one of undisguised admiration. "Nice. If you had all this, why'd you have to steal my rifle?"

Quinn shot her a frustrated look over his shoulder as he selected a Colt 1911 and donned a leather shoulder holster to carry it. "I didn't steal your rifle. I saved you from being hunted down by a bunch of furious vampires."

"Please. Like I've never evaded your kind before." She strolled over and began picking up and putting down the weapons, one at a time. "So where're we going tonight?"

"We? You're staying right here where you won't get into trouble. I'm going to take care of some business."

"The kind of business that ends up with dead vampires? I'm in."

"The hell you are."

"News flash, *my lord*. I don't need your permission. I'll go wherever the fuck I want."

He grabbed her around the waist and slammed her up against his chest. "This isn't a joke, Eve. I want you here, where I know you're safe."

She placed a hand on his chest and gave him a sweet smile. "I haven't been safe since my brother was murdered five years ago," she explained. She shoved away hard, surprising him into letting her go. "I won't stay here. You're going to the docks—"

"How do you know—"

"Well, goodness, Quinn, I have ears, don't I?"

"You eavesdropped?"

"Of course, I did." Her eyes lit up when she saw the crossbow. "That's a beauty. I'll just borrow this against that rifle you stole."

Quinn grabbed her wrist, as if he'd stop her, then said, "You go with me, and you do what I say."

She snorted. "If I take my own car, I can do what I want."

"Eve," he said, more exasperated than he'd ever been. Everything was a battle with her, even sex. Which admittedly was incredibly hot. But *this*. "Why are you being so difficult?"

She shrugged. "I'm not the problem, lover. You are. You're so all fired up to control everything and everyone that you're ignoring how useful I could be in a fight."

"I'm not using you as fucking *bait*," he snarled, thinking of her previous hunting techniques.

"You sure as hell aren't. But I make a damn good sneak. I can go places you can't."

Quinn didn't need anyone to sneak around for him. His power let him scan his enemies and take them out far more effectively. But it was obvious that Eve wasn't going to remain behind. If she was with him, there was at least a chance he could keep her alive. Plus, at least then she wouldn't fuck up his own plans.

"You're going with me. Take or leave it. And, Eve?" He met her gaze directly, letting his power rise until he could see its silver-blue glow reflected in her dark eyes. "I'm not like those other vampires you seduced into falling on your knife. If I wanted you to stay here, you'd damn well be doing it."

Her eyes were solemn when she looked back at him, her face set in defiance. But underneath all that determination, her heartbeat was jumping, and her scent was flavored with fear. Even so, her tone was full of snark when she said, "Message received, my lord. Now can we gear up and get out of here, before the bad guys all go home?"

He studied her a moment longer, then glanced at her spike-heeled boots, shook his head, and said, "Do you have more practical shoes?"

She gave him a smug look. "In my car."

THEY TOOK THE TWO Range Rovers. Quinn rode in the second vehicle with Adorjan driving, Garrick in the passenger seat up front, and Eve sitting next to him. The three other vampires—all people he'd brought from the U.S., since he couldn't be sure who Sorley's spy was, were in the first vehicle.

"Do you have a plan?" Garrick asked, his manner slightly stiff. He hadn't been happy with Eve's inclusion. Quinn couldn't blame him, but he wasn't going to let his cousin tell him which woman he fucked, or even if he armed her to the teeth and brought her into battle. Eve was right. She wasn't some fainting maiden. She'd been in enough fights that she could be useful, and she could also take care of herself, to a certain extent. What she couldn't do for herself, he'd damn well do for her.

"My plan," he answered Garrick, "is that we walk in, size up the situation, and then kill the bad guys."

Next to him, Eve covered her mouth to conceal her snort of laughter. She wasn't stupid. She knew Garrick didn't like her, and he wouldn't appreciate her laughter.

"Great," Garrick said insincerely. "Do you mind if I call Neville and see if he has any useful info before we go charging in?" His question was almost as snarky as Eve's had been, and Quinn wondered, not for the first time, if there was something about *him* that attracted snarky people. He grinned, thankful his cousin wasn't paying enough attention to notice.

"Go ahead," he said. "Call."

Garrick finished his call to Neville as they rolled through the main port gate with no problem, despite their lack of credentials. "Persuading" gate guards and police officers, among others, was a basic talent that many vampires possessed, especially those charged with driving vampire lords around.

"What's the word?" Quinn asked, eyeing the towering containers. They all looked the same to him, but Adorjan seemed to know where he was going. It would be incredibly easy to set up an ambush in here. Maybe not for him, but certainly for human targets, like Eve's brother, or the members of Neville's gang who'd been trapped that night.

"Neville has a dozen or so men on the dock, but some of them are down. He's not sure how many."

"He's not there?"

"No."

Quinn shook his head in disgust. Say what you would about vampires, but they damn well led from the front, not the cozy safety of their cottage. "Does he have any detailed intel on Sorley's vamps?"

"Nothing new, except for the number. Five or six, he says."

That sounded about right to Quinn. He'd have sent the same number, if he'd decided to kill a few humans and throw a wrench into the gang's smuggling operations. They should have been more than enough, except that Sorley hadn't counted on Quinn.

Adorjan abruptly swerved around a short stack of containers and skidded to a halt. The second SUV drew to a stop next to them, being careful to leave room for the vehicle doors to open. Quinn threw an arm across Eve's legs, stopping her from opening her door. "Keep your earpiece on," he said, referring to the Bluetooth bud he'd given her that matched the ones his team wore. "And remember what I told you. You do what I say, or I'll take you down myself."

She gave him a narrow look. "Yes sir, my lord, sir."

He gave her a smacking kiss on the lips. "You're finally learning." He watched her climb out of the SUV and disappear between two stacks of containers, then he opened his own door and slid out.

By the time he joined his vampires on the dock, any trace of amusement was gone, leaving only deadly purpose. He glanced around, using all of his senses to evaluate the location. The port was a noisy place, even this late at night. The deep-throated whine of heavy cranes and the clang of metal containers never seemed to let up, and the air was cold as hell and wet with more than the usual ocean mist. Quinn thought about Eve's bare legs and how icy the metal containers would be, and he wished he'd told her to do more than change her shoes. At which point, he reminded himself that she was a grown woman who was fully capable of choosing her own wardrobe, and that he had better things to think about.

"Five vampires and . . ." He cocked his head. Humans could be difficult to pick up, especially if they were injured. "Neville's dozen are still alive, but some are hurt badly enough that they're probably out of commission." He glanced at his vampires. "Shall we, gentlemen?"

They started forward with deceptive casualness, strolling around the intervening shipping containers as if they were touring the docks and just happened to come upon the confrontation between Sorley's vamps and the human gang members.

"Keep walking, boyo, this is out of your league," one of the vamps sneered, when Quinn's first vampire rounded the last stack of two containers. He caught sight of Quinn, and the sneer disappeared, replaced by rage. "What the fuck? Does Sorley know you're here?"

"I don't report to Sorley," Quinn said mildly. He eyed the three fallen humans, one of whom would die if he didn't get help soon. Quinn hoped Neville had a good doctor on his payroll. "Adorjan, call Neville. Tell him to come get his people out of here."

One of the standing humans stared at him suspiciously. "Who are *you?*"

Quinn didn't answer, only waited while Adorjan made a brief call. He gave Quinn a discreet nod and slipped his phone into his pocket, just as the human's mobile began to vibrate in silent mode, making a buzzing noise that was easily detectible to a vampire. Quinn nodded at the man to answer. The human did so, his suspicious stare never leaving Quinn, who personally thought the man should be a tad more grateful. Quinn had probably just saved his life.

He gave the human a full-toothed grin, fangs gleaming, and the man finally seemed to understand. This shit was about to get bloody. If the humans stayed, the only thing they could do was die.

He watched silently as Neville's people gathered up their wounded and surrendered the field, then he turned to Sorley's vampires, giving them a look with just as much fang, but a lot less grin. "It's just us now."

"Yeah," their seeming leader scoffed. "There's just one problem. We belong here. You don't."

Quinn regarded him quizzically. "No, actually, *I'm* the one who belongs. Sorley sent me out here the other night to deal with a problem.

I dealt with it. That makes all of this mine."

"That's not how it works, asshole. I don't know who the fuck you are, but—"

"Quinn," he said. "Quinn Kavanagh, but there's no need to be formal. And you are . . ."

"I'm the last face you're ever going to see—"

"Oh, please, we're resorting to movie clichés now? Are we vampires or bit actors?"

"What the *fuck* you talking to him for?" one of the other vamps snarled at their leader. "Come on, Barrie. Let's smoke these fuckers and get on with it."

Quinn's gaze swung back to *Barrie* with a lazy grin. The impatient vamp might not understand, but Barrie did. Quinn was still camouflaging most of his power, but Barrie must have known about Quinn's mission to meet with Neville for Sorley, as well as the outcome. It followed, then, that he knew he'd been sent here tonight to fuck up Quinn's plans for a private alliance with Neville. He'd probably even expected a confrontation with some of Quinn's people. But he clearly hadn't expected Quinn himself to show up.

"You know who I am," Quinn said quietly, trying to push Barrie's decision along. "You know what will happen here."

Unfortunately, Quinn knew what was going to happen, too. Barrie wouldn't back down. He *couldn't* back down without losing face, and it appeared he was one of those vamps who'd rather go down bloody, than walk away from the fight.

"I don't give a fuck who you are," Barrie growled now, so very predictably. "This is Sorley's territory, and his word is law. Not yours."

Quinn shook his head and tsked. "Not for much longer, Barrie." He released his power with a rush, exhilaration sweeping over him with near-orgasmic pleasure. God *damn* that felt good. "I'll take Barrie," he told his people calmly.

EVE SLIPPED AWAY between the metal containers, grabbing the first ladder she came to and climbing upward. The metal was cold and wet, sometimes rusted, rough against the bare skin of her legs. It scraped her thigh as she took the final high step to the top, and she reminded herself to wear leggings next time she decided to join in on one of Quinn's adventures in vampire land. She knew the only reason he'd brought her was to keep her from going off on her own. Lord knew he didn't need her to help him fight. She had seen what he could do, one on one. Even more, she'd seen what he could do without so much as lifting a fist. He'd sent her up here as a lookout of sorts, watching for enemies trying to sneak up from behind. She doubted he needed that, either, but she kept an eye out anyway, wanting to believe she was helping.

The sound of voices drew her farther away from the vehicles. Walking as softly as she could, she snuck across the tall containers, jumping over a three-foot gap at one point, coming to a freezing halt when she landed for fear the vampire audience below had heard. But it seemed the interminable racket from the port covered up whatever noise she'd made. And besides, the vampires down there seemed much more interested in each other than anything she was doing.

She drew the little crossbow—her new favorite weapon—and crept closer to the edge, sacrificing the skin on her knees to lie flat and spy on the proceedings.

Quinn was down there. She heard him before she saw him, his deep growl sending shivers up her spine, reminding her body of sensual pleasures that had no place in this setting. She scooted the last few inches, bringing the players into view. There was Quinn, looking all badass and sexy, with his people spread out behind him. And facing him was—

Eve sucked in a harsh breath. She knew the vampire facing off with Quinn. She'd spent months looking for him, days following his every move. His name was fucking *Barrie Meaney,* and he'd been one of the vamps who had killed her brother. She stared. She'd waited so long for this moment, and now that it was here . . . a loud drumming filled her ears and her muscles seemed locked in place. She tried to breathe and realized the sound in her head was the racing of her heart, pounding against her ribs. She heard Quinn saying something in her ear and blinked in confusion before remembering the tiny earpiece he'd given her.

" . . . take Barrie."

What? Eve couldn't make sense of the message, but she didn't care. Heat flooded her muscles, ice filled her heart, and her thoughts were suddenly cool and calculated. She'd trained for this day. She'd spent five long years waiting for it. She raised the crossbow and fired.

QUINN HAD NO sooner given the order than the low whisper of a crossbow string sounded, and a thick bolt struck Barrie in the chest. The vamp staggered, but didn't go down right away. He was too old and too strong. Quinn growled his anger over the comm. He knew exactly who'd fired that bolt, just as he knew it wouldn't be enough. He sent a lance of power slicing into the vampire's chest, melting the aluminum bolt and destroying Barrie's heart, finishing what Eve had started. He'd demand an explanation for that later, but it would have to wait.

For the moment, Barrie's abrupt dusting had shocked Sorley's vamps into stillness, but that wouldn't last. Quinn was of a mind to let his people fight it out. He had confidence in their abilities and knew they'd win, and the occasional battle served as a necessary relief valve when it came to vampires. Especially those strong enough to serve in a lord's trusted inner circle. But he'd no sooner made that decision than he became aware of the humans working all around them on the docks, and of the many human minds suddenly turning their way.

"Too many eyes on us, lads," he murmured over their Bluetooth comms. "Everyone back off a bit. You, too, Eve." He heard a feminine splutter of outrage over the line, but sent a needle sharp shot of power at her position on top of a double stack of containers to his right. He sensed as much as heard her shrieked curse, but she'd deserved more than a tiny electrical jolt for shooting Barrie the way she had, for acting without notice and violating his orders. Quinn had reacted quickly enough to mitigate the fallout, but under other circumstances, with a more powerful vampire, for example, it could have spelled disaster.

He didn't have time right now to lecture Eve, however. His vampires were pulling back as ordered, already heading for their vehicles. They knew what was coming, but Barrie's followers didn't seem to realize it. They were still watching the retreat with expressions of triumph when Quinn reached out with a sweep of destructive power and reduced all four of them to dust in an instant.

"Let's go." Only Garrick and Adorjan remained, waiting for him. The others were already in their vehicle and on their way to the port gate. He was about to start searching for Eve, when she raced up to the Range Rover and jumped into the backseat, slamming the door. Quinn slid in from his side and wrapped an arm around her, pulling her into a rough embrace as their vehicle caught up with the first, and the two of them zoomed through the jungle of containers and away from the port, slowing only long enough to zap the security cameras as they passed through the gate.

No one said a word until they'd left South Dublin and were on their way home. The rain had grown heavier, becoming a silvery curtain of concealment as they headed for the Ballsbridge house.

Quinn kissed the top of Eve's head. He was still pissed as hell, and they were definitely going to have a talk before the night was over. But for now, he was glad she and the others were safe and sound. Because it wasn't going to last. Quinn didn't fool himself into thinking he could get away with killing one of Sorley's enforcers without the vampire lord knowing who'd done it.

He hadn't planned on killing Barrie. Hell, he hadn't even known whom he'd be confronting on the dock that night. But once the conflict unfolded, there'd been no question of how it would end. It had been Eve's crossbow that had started the killing, but he'd never intended for Barrie or any of his people to leave the port alive.

Quinn's original plan might have involved more time, but it wasn't going to work out that way. He'd probably been a fool ever to think otherwise. Sorley would already be gathering his forces, preparing for the challenge he knew was coming. It would be days yet, before they faced each other. But the final battle for Ireland had begun.

For tonight, however, he and his people were safe, and he had a warm woman he intended to spend the rest of the night making love to. *Assuming she'd still be in his bed after he finished reading her the riot act for firing that damn crossbow,* he amended. Or maybe the riot act could wait until tomorrow night.

"YOU'RE WITH ME," Quinn told Eve, when they arrived at his place. He hooked his hand around her arm and walked her all the way through the house and out the back, heading for what looked like a completely separate wing. He was being pushy about it, and she was sure he was pissed because she'd shot that bastard Barrie. But she'd do the same thing all over again, given the chance, and once Quinn stopped dragging her around and *listened,* she was sure she could make him understand.

At the time, her brain had been so jumbled, so filled with *noise,* that only one thought had managed to make itself heard. Kill Barrie Meaney. She could no more have pulled her shot in that moment than turned the bow on herself. It simply didn't compute.

But now, looking back, she saw details. Like when she'd first seen the gang of humans facing off against Sorley's vampires, trapped between them and Quinn. She'd been sure the humans were done for, because she'd fully expected Quinn to side with his own kind. But Quinn had protected the humans, instead of killing them, especially the ones who'd been injured. He'd stood guard over their retreat and had been turning to confront Barrie when . . . She winced at the memory, knowing she'd rushed things when she'd killed the bastard, but she wasn't sorry. She just wished the other killer, Cillian, had been there, too.

She hoped Quinn would understand. *Needed* him to understand how important this was to her. But underneath all of that emotion was something else—the thrill of victory. The excitement, the sense of vengeance fulfilled after all this time, of knowing one of her brother's killers was dead, was thrumming in her veins like the best drug imaginable. She wanted to scream to the world, to shout at the heavens. She wanted to *fuck*. All she could think about was stripping off Quinn's clothes and jumping onto his cock. She grimaced. Okay, *that* sounded painful. She'd slide slowly, deliciously onto his cock instead. She shivered in anticipation, riding her adrenaline high, as they reached the entrance to the separate house wing.

Quinn tugged her up a short set of stairs, keyed in the door code too fast for her to catch, then pulled her inside and shut the door. She looked around, curious despite her impatience. The décor was much the same as the main part of the house—moneyed elegance—but it was obvious that this wing had been built decades later. The door jambs were all straight, the floor was even, and there wasn't that indefinable scent of age that pervaded even the best-maintained old homes. She knew, because every place she'd ever lived had been at least a hundred years old. From the small house she'd grown up in, and where her mam still lived, to her Dublin flat during university, and now the tiny place she called home in Howth. The main part of Quinn's house had that same feel, despite the money that had been spent to modernize it. But this place was newer. She could practically smell the new lumber, the fresh paint. Although, that might just be because Quinn and company had painted recently.

"Does this connect to the main house?" she asked, looking around and running her fingers over the too-smooth plaster walls. They were in a wide hallway, with three widely-spaced doors to the right, and two to the left.

He didn't answer her question. "These are personal quarters. The rest of the house is for business."

"You have a business?" she asked, half joking.

His response was perfectly serious. "I'll soon be running a good part of Ireland, Eve. So, yes, I have a business. This way." He gestured down the wide hall to the left, frustrating her curiosity.

She glimpsed a very modern bathroom through the first door. More evidence that this wing was newer. Quinn didn't offer her the facilities, didn't even slow, but simply propelled her to the door at the end of the hall. It opened without a key, which she found curious. Shouldn't personal quarters be locked?

She had time to see that the room was a huge bedroom, saw the gleam of a gorgeous mahogany bed, and then Quinn was on her, one arm around her waist, the other hand twisted in her hair, dragging her head back to look up at him. "What's it to be, darling Eve? Shall we talk, or. . . ." His eyes were shot through with shards of light, his mouth a sinful temptation as he bent to kiss her.

Eve didn't even try to resist. He was an addiction, and she wanted more. Straining upward against his grip on her hair, she put her mouth to his and kissed him, her lips pressed hard against his, her tongue sweeping in to invite more. He pretended to hold back, letting her do all the work, despite the erection she could feel rubbing against her belly with every move she made. Her teeth closed over his lower lip and bit down hard.

He cursed and yanked back, but not fast enough. Blood flooded into her mouth, but she wasn't worried. Vampirism wasn't contagious. She knew that much. Creating a new vampire involved the complete exchange of blood.

But that wasn't the only effect of a vampire's blood.

QUINN SAW THE moment his blood hit Eve's nervous system, the moment her brain reacted to its presence with an endorphin rush that piled onto her adrenaline high and shot her straight into an orgasmic bliss so intense, she collapsed in his arms, crying out in helpless pleasure. He scooped her up before she could hit the floor and laid her on the bed. He'd intended to have her there anyway, but not like this. Every encounter they'd had so far had involved tearing off each other's clothes, and fucking hard and fast. He'd planned a slow seduction for tonight, his mouth on every inch of her delicious body, and her mouth on his cock . . . after which he'd spank her cute ass for shooting Barrie, and then fuck her again.

But then she'd bitten him and the die was cast. He couldn't resist the sight and feel of her climaxing in his arms. Her body writhed against his, her breasts rubbing against his chest, her nipples so hard, he could feel them despite the layers of clothing. Wanting more—her breast in his mouth, her nipple against his tongue—he shoved up her sweater and pulled down the sheer cup of her bra. Her breast burst free and he took it, sucking half the warm globe into his mouth, his tongue rasping over her nipple, while he freed the other breast and kneaded it with his fingers, until he switched breasts and gave the other one the same treatment. Pulling back, he bracketed her slim torso in his hands and admired his handiwork—her full breasts shining wet in the golden light of the overhead, her nipples swollen and flushed with blood. He leaned forward again and took a delicious nipple between his teeth this time, hearing her cries, her fingernails scraping his scalp, as he bit down and tugged lightly. And then he did what he'd been dying to do all evening, ever since they'd been interrupted by Garrick and had to rush into battle.

His fangs slid out from his gums, and his hunger surged. Opening his mouth over the swell of her breast, he bit her again, harder this time, as he ever so slowly pulled away, letting his fangs scrape along her flesh, tasting the thin line of blood he left behind. Eve moaned and pressed the back of his head, asking for more. Quinn lapped up the droplets of blood and looked up, reading the desire in her dark eyes, as she thrust out her chest, angling her other breast into his mouth.

He growled and slid his fangs into her flesh, triggering the euphoric in his bite, savoring her screams when she was thrown into another climax hard on the first. Dropping his hand between their bodies, his fingers slid under her skirt, over the silky skin of her thigh, until he felt the wet heat of her pussy through her panties. He tore the thin fabric impatiently, ripping it away from her hip to shove two of his fingers inside her at once. She was already so slick with arousal that she took his intrusion easily, her sheath still trembling with orgasm as it stretched to accommodate him. He began pumping his fingers in and out, while she tore at his shirt, yanking it over his head, until he had to slide his hand out of her sweet body in order to get the rest of it off.

Eve took advantage of his distraction, rubbing his erection through the fabric of his jeans, sliding down the zipper and freeing him from the painfully tight confinement. Shoving him hard over, she switched their positions and tried to straddle him, but he was stronger and had other plans. Rolling her beneath him, her skirt around her waist, her sweater pushed up with her breasts bare over the cups of her bra, he shoved his hips between her thighs and slammed his cock into her pussy as deeply as he could go. One long, hard stroke and she was his, her sheath trembling around him, her legs gripping his hips as she lifted hungrily to meet his thrusts.

"Fuck," he swore, taking her in a demanding embrace, crushing her lips beneath his, his tongue claiming every inch of her mouth. She met the demands of his kiss, just as she did his cock, vying for a control that he wouldn't surrender, until her twisting tongue scraped his fang, and he groaned. Her blood was the sweetest confection, so unexpected from the fierce fighter she showed to the world. He sucked on that bit of blood, and his hunger roared. He wanted more. He could scent the warm seduction of her blood so close beneath her pale skin, could feel her veins plump and begging.

"Eve," he breathed. His lips skimmed the curve of her jaw, dipping briefly to the elegant sweep of her clavicle, licking the slick saltiness of her skin, before kissing his way up to her neck and the swollen line of her jugular. He was hungry. He'd used a lot of power over the last few days, and while he'd had a taste of Eve's blood from the vein, he hadn't *fed*. "Eve," he said again, her name coming out on a growl as his control fractured.

"Quinn," she whispered, turning her head to one side and baring her neck in invitation. "It's okay."

It was everything he could do not to rip into her neck and feed. But he was a vampire lord. Discipline and control defined him. He waited until her arousal soared again, until she was once more on the verge of climax, with her pounding heart matching the thrust of her urgent rocking against him. And then, with his cock sliding in and out of the warm, wet cleft between her thighs and her whispers a constant, soft plea in his ear, he sliced through her skin, felt the slight pop as his fangs sank into her vein, and then groaned in pleasure as her blood poured down his throat.

Eve gave a low, moaning scream, her back arching against him, as the surge of chemicals hit her blood stream. Fangs still buried in her neck, Quinn clutched her to his chest, one hand on the back of her head and the other low on her hips, crushing her already sensitive clit against his groin every time he drove into her, going harder and deeper, until he felt her hot, slick channel clamp down, rippling along his length as she screamed his name. His own release surged, spilling into her body in a rush of heat, as he lifted his head and snarled, bloody fangs glistening. Only one word filled his head. *Mine*.

THE RAIN WAS STILL coming down hard when Eve woke to Quinn's voice telling her to sleep. Her bleary smile became a frown when she realized he was kissing her good-bye, tucking the blanket around her and climbing out of bed. She sat up, clutching the sheet over her naked breasts. "Where are you going? Did something happen?"

He turned back, his eyes alight with that eerie shattered ice glow as they skimmed over the sheet she was gripping so tightly. He didn't move, simply smiled, slow and seductive. Eve's body remembered that smile, remembered what came after. Her nipples hardened and warmth pooled between her thighs, which were already sticky with arousal.

Damn, she thought, not for the first time. *No wonder women throw themselves at these guys*. Hard on that thought was the image of women throwing themselves at *Quinn*. She didn't like that one at all.

"Sunrise is near," he murmured, right against her ear, having somehow crossed the room to sit next to her, while she'd been having murderous thoughts about other women.

She turned to study him, only inches away. Her body was urging her to grab him. To tumble him back to the bed and slide him into her body one more time. His words registered belatedly. She stared at the heavy drapes over the only window, then turned back to him with a frown. "What does that mean?"

His head tilted, and he gave her a puzzled look. "Are you awake, sweetheart?"

She scowled. "Of course. What does that have to do with—"

"I'm a vampire, and the sun is about to rise. I'm going to sleep, whether I want to or not."

"Okay," she said, still not understanding. "So, get back in bed!"

"My daytime sleep is taken elsewhere. Stay as long as you want. The daylight guards know you're here, and they'll help, if you need anything." His eyes went blank for an instant, as if his thoughts were far away. When his eyes focused again, he said only, "Time is short. I'll see you tonight."

And, just like that, he was gone. No kiss good-bye, no explanation of *why* he had to sleep somewhere else when he had a dark room with a perfectly good bed right there, and with *her* in it. Bastard. He still didn't trust her. Her lips twisted. She *supposed* she could understand why, but at some point, he was going to have to put the past behind them. Or walk away. Her heart ached at the thought. She didn't want him to walk away. Didn't want him to be *able* to. She already knew *she* couldn't do it. How the hell had she gone from a hardened vampire killer to falling in love with one of them instead? And not just *any* one of them, but a vampire lord. The future ruler of all Ireland's vampires, if he was to be believed. *He* sure as hell believed it, which meant she did, too. She'd never met a more determined man than Quinn Kavanagh, vampire *or* human.

She sighed. So what to do now? She'd already slept a few hours after being fucked into unconsciousness by a certain vampire. She could stay in this room for a while, this *very* nice room with an intensely masculine vibe—heavy mahogany furniture that gleamed with deep red highlights, a central chandelier that was a fucking piece of art and sure as hell hadn't been picked up at the local IKEA. The drapes were a heavy, deep-burnished gold, the bed linens a shade darker than that.

But as nice as the room was, she didn't feel like hanging around all day doing nothing. She didn't even have her laptop with her, which meant she couldn't get any work done. And she'd spent enough hours spying on Quinn's estate that she knew the place closed down tight during the day. There was no activity at all, except for the daylight guards and their conscientious routines. She was going to be bored out of her damn mind.

"All right, Eve," she said, speaking out loud because everything was just so *quiet*. It was never this quiet at her flat. "Get your ass out of this bed, and get going. Right," she added, as if answering herself. She threw the covers back and padded over to the most luxurious bathroom she'd ever seen. She'd seen the guest bath at Sorley's mansion, which had a more prestigious address than Quinn's. It had been nice enough, but the style had been old and fussy. Full of elaborate gold fixtures and mirror frames, with heavy, flocked wallpaper. It had all cost a fortune, she was sure, but it had none of the clean lines and welcoming luxury of Quinn's. His was the kind of bath that made you want to fill the tub and soak for an hour. Maybe light some candles and drink a glass of wine while doing it.

Of course, all that would be better if she had Quinn in the bathtub with her. Stupid vampire.

She settled for a hot shower and clean hair. She didn't have her hair dryer and couldn't find one anywhere in the bedroom or bath, so she braided her wet hair away from her face instead. It would still be wet by the time she got home to Howth, and maybe she'd dry it then. Or maybe she wouldn't bother. From the looks of things, she'd be spending more time facing down enemy vampires than enjoying romantic dinners over candlelight. At least, for the next few days.

When she went to get dressed, she realized her panties were gone, courtesy of Quinn's impatience, and her skirt was short. Nothing she could do about that. On the other hand, her car was still parked down the block, so at least she didn't have to worry about some pervert staring up her skirt while she sat on the train. Wearing her Nike trainers, which simply didn't belong with the skirt, she made her way down the wood-floored hallway, noticing that all the other doors were closed, and the entire wing was perfectly silent. Did vampires sleep behind those other doors? A wicked voice inside her head told her to peek in and see, but she squashed that idea with little effort. Even if it was true, it struck her as beyond rude, more like a taboo or an intolerable perversion, to spy on vampires while they were helpless in sleep.

She opened the outside door to a wet, winter's morning. The rain had let up only a few minutes ago, but the grey sky and heavy clouds told her it could start again at any moment. Taking that as a sign she should get her ass in gear, she tightened her jacket and walked quickly towards the front gate.

It took a few minutes. Quinn's house was big, and she'd had to go all the way around. The main part of the house, which Quinn had referred to as a business office, was locked up tight, so she couldn't cut through. There was a lovely path along the side yard, but it was meant for sunnier days meandering around. Still, she didn't have much choice, and she walked along the path until she finally reached the front. One of Quinn's guards was waiting for her when she emerged from the side yard.

"Ms. Connelly."

She smiled, feeling awkward. There was only one reason for her to be slipping out with the sunrise, and that was because she'd been fucking one of the vamps the night before. The guard knew her name and probably which vampire she'd spent the night with, too. What was it the Americans called this? The walk of shame. Except she didn't have anything to be ashamed about. She was young, single, and free, and she could fuck *anyone* she wanted, for *as long* as she wanted.

"My car's down the block," she explained.

"I know. Would you like some breakfast first?"

Eve's stomach growled at the mention of food. Come to think of it, she hadn't eaten dinner last night, because she'd been with Quinn. The downside of dating a vampire? You couldn't count on regular meals together. "You have breakfast here?" she asked him.

He nodded. "For the daylight crew. Come on, I'll show you." He started walking back the way she'd just come. "My name's Bell, by the way. Joshua Bell."

"I'm Eve, but you probably know that."

He nodded and turned up a short walk to a side door on the house. "Lord Quinn put your name on the visitors' list."

Eve eyed him shrewdly. "And I bet you ran me."

"Of course, I did," he said unapologetically. "The safety of everyone on this estate, including Lord Quinn, is my responsibility."

"What'd you discover?"

He led her into a very modern kitchen and yanked open one door of the biggest refrigerator she'd ever seen. "Everything's fresh. Eggs, fruit, fruit juice. There might be yogurt, though we don't get much call for that. There's frozen stuff down below, mostly breakfast and snack types. We have a cook who comes in to prepare fresh lunch and dinner. My guys have big appetites." He closed the refrigerator and opened a double cupboard next to it. "Baked goods. Pastries, breads, and bagels. There might be some scones left. Coffee machine and electric kettle." He pointed to those devices on the countertop. "Coffee pods and tea in the cupboard just above it." He finished with a flourish and a grin. "And that's it."

Eve was a little overwhelmed, so she said the first thing that came to mind. "You didn't answer my question. What'd you discover when you ran me?"

He regarded her steadily. "You received better than good grades all through school. You were admitted to Trinity College, graduated with honors, and were accepted into their graduate program, when"—he paused and met her eyes —"your brother's death ended all that. You dropped out and began doing private research on the side, writing thesis papers and dissertations for other people, instead of finishing your own. All of which produces just enough income to support yourself and your aging mother."

Eve looked away, uncomfortable with such a flat distillation of her life, even though it was accurate, as far as it went. She was hardly going to insist he include her nighttime hunting habit. "Anything else?"

"Nothing of note," he said, although she had a feeling he wasn't being completely honest with her. And why would he be? For all his friendliness, his loyalty was to Quinn, not her. "Any questions?" he said, waving a hand to indicate he was talking about breakfast.

She considered. "I do have a question."

He gave her an inquiring look.

"You know a lot about guns, right?"

He seemed to relax, as if he'd expected something a lot more difficult from her. "That's putting it mildly."

"Good. I have this gun." She started to pull it from her purse, but thought better of it. "I'm taking it out now, okay?"

He nodded, but she saw that his eyes followed every move of her hand as she pulled the Sig out of her purse and placed it on the counter.

He picked it up, popped the mag and set it aside, then racked the slide and removed the chambered round. "Sig P938," he said, laying it on the counter. "6 round mag, plus one in the chamber if you're smart, given the small magazine. You have a question?"

She blinked. He'd handled the gun with the same competence as Quinn. She didn't want to look like an idiot, not knowing more about her own gun, but on the other hand, she really wanted an answer. "Okay, I bought this for self-defense a while back. I was feeling jumpy after Alan was murdered. I didn't know why they'd gone after him, and . . ." She saw the sympathy on his face, and looked away, feeling guilty about lying. She cleared her throat nervously. "Anyway, everyone says"—she was careful not to admit she had any personal experience on the subject— "that the ammo I'm using isn't any good against a vampire. But I've heard there's something else out there—"

"Wait," he said, holding a hand up to stop her. "You want my advice on how to *kill* vampires?"

She frowned. "Not *every* vampire, obviously. But I was with Quinn last night when he faced off against some of Sorley's vamps, and it seems like that's likely to happen again in the near future. It would nice if I could do more than stand around wringing my hands."

He eyed her carefully. "Can you shoot?"

She nodded. "I have over 100 hours on the range. I know that's not much," she hurried to add. "But I go whenever I can, and . . . and I'm good," she finished defiantly.

"It's enough. I'll tell you what. I've got some work to do first, but if you meet me here in, say, four hours, I'll take you to the range myself, and check you out. If you're as good as you say, I'll get you the ammo you need."

She gave him a huge smile. "Thanks! Um. Here? Like, the kitchen, or—?"

"In the front, near the garage. We'll go to the range, then grab lunch on the way back, and you can explain some of this Irish food to me."

"Great! I need to run home first and change. But I'll be back in time." She grabbed a fruit pastie, took a big bite, then wrapped the rest in a napkin, and headed for the door. If she left now, she'd have plenty of time to get to Howth, shower and change, and pack a few things, just in case she spent another night with Quinn. No more short skirts without panties for her.

"You sure that's all you want to eat?" Bell asked, following her outside.

She swallowed and said, "Gotta save room for lunch."

"All right, come on, then. I'll walk you to your car."

"Oh, that's not necessary," she dismissed. "This is Ballsbridge not Balleyback. Besides, it's sunrise. All the bad guys are asleep in their beds by now."

He smiled. "All the same," he said calmly. "I'll see you there safely."

Eve rolled her eyes where he couldn't see it. Quinn had clearly left marching orders where she was concerned. She wasn't going to waste her breath.

Bell walked her the short distance. Taking her keys, he unlocked the car and inspected it inside and out, before stepping back, and handing the keys to her. "Drive safely now."

"I will. And I'll see you later."

EVE WAS HALFWAY home to Howth when her cell phone rang, startling her. She checked her dashboard clock and saw it read 10:05 am. Hanging around with vampires was screwing with her sense of time, but sunrise was between 8:30 – 9:00 this time of year, so that had to be right. She'd somehow thought it was later. She couldn't imagine who would be calling her this early. Most of her clients were graduate students and didn't crawl out of bed before noon.

Grabbing her phone, she risked life and limb long enough to check the display. She winced. It was her mother. Probably calling to complain about Eve not having come by in days. She'd be full of tales of prescriptions gone unfilled—they weren't—and bare food shelves—they weren't either. Brigid Connelly walked to the store every damn day, mostly for the gossip, and the pharmacy was right next door. But she wouldn't stop calling until Eve answered.

She accepted the call. "Good morning, Mam. You're up bright and early."

"I can barely sleep anymore with these hip pains."

Eve knew better than to respond to that.

"Where are you?" her mother demanded.

"Dublin," she lied. "I've been doing some research for a client."

"Another cheater, you mean."

"Yeah, well, those cheaters provide me a nice income. I should get back to it."

"When are you returning to Howth?"

Eve grimaced. "I'm not quite sure. If there's something you—"

"There's something we need to discuss. Tonight will do."

"Mam, I'm not sure—"

"Alan was always so good to me, so attentive. If he were still alive—"

Eve cut her off. She'd heard it all before, how Alan had been the perfect son—which he had been—and now he was dead, which was somehow all Eve's fault, and Brigid was left with only her ungrateful daughter to care for her.

"I'll be there tonight. I'm not sure what time."

"It's no matter. I've nowhere else to be."

Christ, she was really laying it on thick this morning. One of the local biddies must have scored points on the gossip scoreboard. A daughter who'd married well, or a son who'd struck it rich, or, the gold medal of gossip, that same son asking his mother to come live with him, so he could take care of her.

"See you then," Eve muttered. "I've got to go." She tossed the phone down. For a day that had started in Quinn's bed, this one was sure going downhill fast.

QUINN LEANED AGAINST the open doorway, watching as Eve walked back and forth in the back garden, sometimes talking to herself in a way that sounded like an argument. The garden was lit, courtesy of the small pathway which led along the side of the house and then meandered over a manicured lawn, before ending in a rose garden. The lawn was where Eve paced, debating with herself. According to Joshua Bell, she'd been gone for a few hours this morning, but had returned in time for Bell to take her to the range and make sure she knew how to shoot that gun she was carrying around. Bell had also confided that Eve was after some ammo with enough punch to kill a vampire and had asked if Quinn wanted her to have it. The thought of Eve in possession of vampire-killer rounds was rather terrifying. On the other hand, if she was going to follow him into fights among vampires, as she had last night, it would be better if she could at least defend herself. So he'd told Bell to go ahead.

Since she'd gotten what she wanted from Bell, Quinn was trying to puzzle out what might have brought on the pacing and arguing. His security people told him she'd spent much of the hour before sunset, sitting quietly, seeming to enjoy what was forecast to be only a brief break in the wet weather. The pacing and arguing had only commenced once the sun had set, which was a giant hint that it had something to do with him.

"You could have waited in here," he said, the words a low murmur that his power sent whispering directly in Eve's ear.

She spun, expecting him to be right behind her, then spun again when she didn't find him there. Her gaze lifted to search the yard, eventually seeing him where he stood backlit in the doorway to the residential wing where he, Garrick, and Adorjan had their personal quarters. He smiled at the irritated look on her face, a look she'd smoothed over by the time she'd marched across the lawn and stood looking up at him. He reached down, wrapped an arm around her waist, and drew her up the three steps to the house entrance, pulling her flush against his chest.

"Good evening, Eve," he crooned and gave her an intentionally seductive kiss. He wanted her to remember what they'd had the night before, when she'd been trembling in his arms after multiple orgasms, and still pleading for more.

He was satisfied to see that she was flushed and breathless when he finally released her, her heart racing and her arousal scenting the air. She licked her lips. He followed the movement, struck by the sudden desire to suck her plump lower lip between his teeth and bite down. Hard.

"Stop doing that," she gasped, sounding utterly flustered.

"Doing what?" he whispered against her ear.

"Looking at me like—"

He straightened so he could see her face. "Like what, sweetheart?" He gave her an innocent smile.

"Pfft. Never mind. Can we talk?"

"Aren't we talking already?"

"Not like this," she insisted. "Not . . . out here where anyone can listen. And not like"—she waved a hand between them—"*this,* with you being all sexy and trying to seduce me."

He grinned. "I'm not *trying,* Eve."

"Like *that,*" she snapped.

His grin became a laugh, but he slid one hand down her arm to clasp her hand and tug her inside and down the hall to his suite.

Once there, he closed the door, then crossed to the sidebar and poured himself two fingers of Irish whiskey, which was beginning to grow on him. He raised the crystal decanter in Eve's direction, asking if she wanted some. She shook her head. He'd noticed she didn't drink much. Probably a matter of control, which he could understand well enough. He'd have done the same if he wasn't a vampire who could drink the whole fucking bottle with no effect.

"Water, if you have it," she said.

Quinn opened the small refrigerator and withdrew a chilled bottle of water. "Glass?" he asked.

She shook her head again. "The bottle is fine. That way I know what's in it," she added defiantly.

He chuckled. "Eve, darling, I don't need drugs to seduce you."

She blushed hotly. "It's not nice to gloat."

He walked over and handed her the bottle, making a show of twisting the cap so she could hear the plastic tabs breaking. As she took the bottle, he leaned in and kissed her cheek. "I'm sorry," he said, but layered it with so much seductive power, she shivered.

"No, you're not," she muttered and took a long drink of water, as if trying to douse the heat of his presence.

He took a sip of whiskey and sat on the short sofa near the windows. "So, what are we talking about, then?"

Eve walked over and sat on the opposite end. She seemed nervous, avoiding his eyes, which made him intensely curious. He'd never given her any reason to fear him.

"Okay, first . . ." She paused, and gave him a narrow-eyed look, as if expecting him to say something sarcastic. When he didn't, she grimaced and said, "You were right."

She made it sound like an accusation. If this was supposed to be an apology, she sucked at it.

"About the vampires, I mean," she explained. "How most of them are just ordinary people going about their lives, and if my brother had been killed by a man—a human, that is—I wouldn't have gone out and started shooting random humans."

He opened his mouth to respond, but she wasn't finished.

"But I didn't actually kill random vampires, either. I may have . . . *overstated* the scope of my hunts when we first met. For all I knew, you were just one more Sorley thug, and I needed to make you believe that I was no easy prey. But I was never out to kill *every* vampire, Quinn. Only the ones who worked closely with Sorley, the ones bollocks deep in his personal crime syndicate. Those are the ones I went after because I thought they'd lead me to the two I was *really* after. The ones who murdered Alan."

Quinn tilted his head, studying her, waiting to see if she was finished. When it seemed she was, he said, "What about McKeever?"

She scowled. "Who?"

"Numbers. The accountant you were about to kill before I stopped you outside Sorley's that night."

"Oh, come on," she said in disbelief. "I was never going to kill *him*. I just wanted information. He does all of Sorley's books, you know. He knows everything."

"Yes, I know. As for the others . . . Eve, just because a vampire, or a man, works for an asshole, that doesn't mean he's an asshole, too."

"Well, I know *that*. But I told you, I was careful."

Quinn sighed. They were never going to agree on this. "All right, then, tell me. What does this epiphany of yours mean for the future of my vampires?"

"*Your* vampires?" she repeated, confused. "I've never attacked any of—"

He raised an eyebrow.

"Oh, for God's sake, I told you, the rifle was a test. If I'd been trying to kill someone, they'd be dead."

"A test where you used *my* people for target practice. What if your aim had been off?"

"It wasn't. Don't be such a baby."

The look he gave her was definitely not amused.

"Fine. I won't do it again."

"Because I have your rifle," he said dryly. "But let me get this straight. I'm right about your vengeance hunt against vampires, but it doesn't matter, because you've only ever killed bad guys, and, besides, sometimes you weren't really trying to kill anyone, anyway. Is that about it? Oh, and I *think* somewhere in there is an apology. It's hard to tell."

She gave him the bored look of a teenager, but then sighed deeply and admitted, "There *is* one other thing."

"I can hardly wait."

"You know that vampire I shot last night? The one with the crossbow?"

Quinn scowled. "Ah, yes, Barrie. The one you shot without my go-ahead and nearly—"

"He's one of the vampires who killed my brother. I had to kill him. There was no choice."

"Look, Eve, I get it. But you very nearly fucked up that whole situation. *My* people could have been hurt, because you couldn't follow the one, *simple* order I gave you."

"You think *he* was following orders when he kicked my brother's head in?"

"Yes, actually, I do. Barrie was one of Sorley's enforcers. You can bet he was doing exactly what Sorley told him to."

She drank a sullen swig of water, then took her time replacing the plastic cap. "I'm not sorry I killed him."

Quinn snorted a laugh. "You *didn't* kill him. *I* did. Barrie was far too powerful to be killed by a single bolt to the chest like that. It's too clean. A strong vampire can recover, especially if that's his only damage. You've killed vampires, I'll give you that. But you've never come up against one with real power. If you'd used that crossbow on someone like Sorley? Like *me?*" He leaned toward her. "I'd make you eat that bolt for dinner, sweetheart. And then I'd drain you dry and make you *love* it." He straightened and said soberly, "And so would Sorley. Don't doubt that for one minute. He's the fucking Lord of Ireland, Eve. You don't get that far by playing nice."

EVE PUSHED HERSELF as deep into the plush sofa as she could, wanting distance between her and Quinn. He was so angry about this. She'd admitted he was right, what more did he want? And for him to laugh and say *she* hadn't been the one who killed that evil fucker, Barrie Meaney? Not to give her even that much, when he had to know what it meant to her? Or maybe he didn't. Maybe he was so lost up there in his super powerful vampire universe, where all he had to do was lift a finger and his enemies died, that he could no longer understand what it was like for everyone else. Well, fuck him. She didn't care what he said. She knew she'd killed at least some part of Barrie. Maybe hers hadn't been the last, fatal blow, but she'd weakened him. She'd been part of the precious *team* that had killed him, and she was going to kill his buddy Cillian, too. Because her brother's death demanded vengeance, and she needed to *finish* it, so she could finally just stop.

She looked up to find Quinn eyeing her far too closely, as if he knew what she was thinking. He didn't, though. If he had, he'd have been locking her up until this was all over. Or he'd have tried, she thought defiantly.

Across the room, a mobile phone buzzed angrily on a tabletop. Eve patted her pocket, finding her phone there. Quinn stood with an impatient noise and crossed to the sideboard, where he must have set it down while he was preparing his drink.

"Yeah," he said, answering the call. "Really. All right, put him on."

QUINN STUDIED EVE while he waited for the call to be switched over. She was hiding something. Her emotions, to begin with. Building walls between them. He wouldn't permit that. She was his, whether she knew it yet or not. He could be patient, give her time to come around, but he wouldn't let her deny what was happening between them. Call it chemistry, fate . . . call it what it was, fucking combustible attraction. But what it *wasn't*, was something she could ignore. He wouldn't let her.

A man's voice on the phone said, "Sir. My name is—"

"What's the message?" Quinn cut off the plummy sounds of Sorley's flunky. The vampire claimed to be calling on behalf of the vampire lord and had insisted on speaking to Quinn directly. Quinn didn't need his name or particulars. All he needed was the message he'd been ordered to convey.

The vamp sputtered a moment or two, then pulled himself together. "Lord Sorley requests your presence this evening. He said only that there are matters to discuss. I am not privy to—"

"Okay," Quinn interrupted again. "Any particular time?"

"At your convenience, sir."

"Great. We'll be there."

"But, sir, Lord Sorley said only you—"

Quinn disconnected and called Garrick. He was sure Sorley had ordered Quinn to come alone. But Quinn wasn't suicidal, and he didn't take orders from Sorley. Garrick answered on the first ring. "My lord?"

"We've been summoned. Or rather I have, but I think we both know what this really is."

"You think he'll challenge you so soon? I mean formally? He seems more like the sneak attack sort."

"I agree. He won't want to give me much of a warning, so there'll be no formal challenge. The only question is how much willing support he's mustered among his people. It could be every vamp in the city. Hell, maybe the county. I doubt it goes much beyond that, but he can draw on the whole fucking territory, if he's willing to kill a few vampires. And I think we both know he's willing."

"So, why agree to show up at all? Why not do it on *your* terms. You're the challenger, not him."

"Yeah, but I'm tired of the game. I want this part of it over with, so we can start rebuilding what he's broken."

"All right," Garrick agreed instantly. "What's the plan?"

The plan was simple enough. There wasn't one. Without knowing what they'd face at Sorley's, he had to fall back on tradition and hope it had become tradition for a reason.

When he disconnected, Eve was watching him with a glint in her eyes. "I want to go."

He didn't respond immediately, but just walked over and sat in the chair facing her, rather than beside her on the sofa.

"I'm serious, Quinn."

"You don't know what you're talking about."

"I know that something big is going down tonight, and I know it involves Sorley. I want to go."

He pretended to consider it, but tonight's challenge was vampire business. Humans had no place there. If Sorley had a mate, she might be there. The same went for any other vampire who trusted his mate to hold her own in what was certain to be a violent battle. But he and Eve sure as hell weren't mated. He didn't even know how she felt about him, other than as a good fuck. And there was also the feeling he had that she was holding something back, that she had some other reason for wanting to go to Sorley's. And until he knew what it was, he couldn't trust her not to do something like she had the other night with Barrie. That had turned out well enough, because he'd been ready to kill the vamp anyway. But he was reminded that there was a second vampire out there who'd been responsible for killing her brother, a vampire who almost certainly worked for Sorley. If Eve spotted him and pulled a surprise like she had with Barrie, vampires would die. *His* vampires.

And then there was simply her safety. Because, regardless of how she felt about him, she was *his*. And he wasn't going to risk her getting hurt or, even worse, killed. This was a vampire challenge. It would be fought with vampire weapons, which would certainly be fatal for his redheaded lover.

"Sorry, sweetheart," he said. And he *was* sorry, but only to disappoint her. "This is vampire business, no humans allowed."

She studied him intently, searching for the lie in his words. She wouldn't find it. Quinn had perfected a blank face long before becoming a vampire.

"All right."

He stilled. He hadn't known Eve long, but he knew this wasn't like her. She never gave up without a fight. He made a note to have their vehicles checked for bugs, and to assign one of his vamps to keep an eye on her while he was gone. It would have to be someone powerful enough to control her, but who at least *seemed* harmless enough not to set off her radar.

"I don't know how long we'll be gone, but you can wait for me here," he said, more as a test, than anything else.

She shrugged. "No. I'm going home tonight. To Howth," she clarified. "I haven't been by to see my mother, and she's gotten after me about it."

Losing patience, he stood and pulled her to her feet. "Don't do this, Eve."

"Do what? I don't know what—"

He took her mouth in a hard, commanding kiss, his teeth clashing against hers, his tongue winding around hers, demanding a response.

Eve held out for a heartbeat or two, pretending not to care, not to feel anything, but the chemistry between them couldn't be denied. With a deep groan, she melted into his embrace, her arms tightening around his back.

Quinn fisted a hand in her long hair, tipping her head back as he deepened the kiss, until one of his fangs tore the tender flesh of her lip, and the sweetness of her blood filled his mouth. He squeezed her against his chest, his arm a band around her lower back as he straightened to his full height. Taking her with him, he strode for the bed. He didn't have time for this. His vampires were waiting, *Sorley* was waiting. But if he was going to die tonight, then he was going to have one final taste of his Eve.

Her legs were crossed behind his back when they reached the bed, pulling him tight against the heat between her thighs, her kisses as demanding and ravenous as his own. Her ass hit the mattress and her legs loosened as she reached for his belt, nimble fingers making quick work of the heavy buckle. Smooth leather slid easily through the constraining loops, before she slid his zipper down and wrapped her fingers around his cock. Leaning forward, she took him into her mouth and sucked him deep, her cheeks hollowing with the effort.

Quinn groaned, his hand on the back of her head, urging her forward. He wanted his cock buried in her sweet pussy, but her mouth was so damn hot and wet, and it felt so fucking good. Ripping her blouse open, he snapped the band on her bra and bared her breasts, squeezing the succulent flesh, weighing them in his hands as he flicked her nipples into flushed and swollen peaks.

Eve moaned around his cock, the sound a delicate vibration along his shaft that had him shuddering with desire as she took him deeper and deeper. He could feel her throat muscles working, struggling to swallow, the constriction caressing his full hard length. He pumped in short strokes, in and out, fucking her mouth. She looked up at him, raising only her eyes, while her lips remained wrapped around his dick. It was incredibly erotic, and he nearly climaxed at the sight. But he wanted her pussy, wanted to come deep inside her body.

Tightening his hand into a fist around her hair, he pulled her off his cock, her mouth coming free with an audible pop as he dragged her higher up onto the bed. Ripping her jeans and panties down her legs impatiently, he tugged one shoe off so he could yank the constricting fabric over her foot to make room for his hips between her thighs. Eve gasped, but spread her legs wide in invitation, her pussy glistening with arousal, the outer lips swollen and flush with readiness.

Quinn snarled as he slammed his cock into her tight channel, gliding through the creamy wetness of her sheath. He stretched her wide, one hand cupping her ass, tilting her higher and opening her up to him even more. Plunging deep into her sweet body, he began rocking back and forth, the hard pearls of her nipples scraping against his T-shirt clad chest with every movement. Eve was making hungry little noises, swallowing her screams with every thrust, until finally her pussy clamped down on his cock, and she shattered around him, holding him deep inside her as her climax went on and on, her inner muscles flexing and squeezing his length, while her nails scraped bloody furrows into his shoulders.

Quinn fought his own climax as long as he could, loving the feel of her hot, tight body around him, the sight of her lost in orgasm as his cock thrust back and forth. But, finally, it was too much. He drove himself as deep as he could go and climaxed hard, his release pumping into her sex, until he collapsed on top of her, one hand still twisted in her hair, the other cupping her delicious ass to hold her close.

They lay there together, breathing, until finally Eve muttered, "You weigh a ton."

Quinn laughed and rolled away, pulling her up onto his chest, with one possessive hand still petting her naked butt. They stayed that way until their hearts slowed and their lungs were no longer gasping, and then Eve patted his chest. "I've gone and drained you now, before your big meeting."

"It's not that big of a meeting," he lied.

"Still, I don't want that huge bodyguard of yours blaming me for making you weak in front of Sorley. Do you need blood?"

Quinn smiled at the eager note in her voice. Apparently, his Eve had decided she rather *liked* being bitten, after all. But he'd already spent more time with her than he should, and the others would be waiting. Why the fuck did Sorley have to pick this night to play his games?

He shook his head in regret. "I'm sorry, sweetheart. But as much as I'd love to sink my fangs into your pretty neck, and as delicious and tempting as your blood is, it's not necessary. I'm strong enough that I don't need to drink every night, and *you* need your blood, too."

She sighed in regret, then stretched out her entire body, rubbing against him in pure sexual enticement. The witch. She sat up abruptly, her legs straddling his hips, as she fingered the tatters of her shirt. The buttons were gone, but there were no tears. Her bra, on the other hand. . . .

"Will you be late tonight?" She didn't look at him, pretending to be casual, but he could feel the fine tension in her body as she waited for his answer.

He stroked his hands over her smooth thighs. "It depends on what Sorley wants, but whatever it is, I suspect it will take longer than it needs to. He prides himself on being a pain in my ass." His hands tightened, holding her in place. "Will you sleep overnight in Howth, or come back here?"

"Here?"

He nodded. "My guards have you on their list, even if I'm not back."

"Is it good to be on this list?" she asked, grimacing in disgruntlement.

"It's a very short list of people who are welcome in the compound, smartass."

She laughed, a sweet, almost childish sound that he hadn't heard her make before. He smiled.

"Well, just as your night depends on Sorley," she said, leaning over to prop her elbows on his chest. "Mine depends on my mam, and I suspect I'm in for a lecture."

"Lecture?"

"About what a bad daughter I am. I'm overdue for a reminder."

He eyed her solemnly. "You could just stay here, you know. Give her a call instead. I'm sure the lecture would be just as effective."

She shook her head, then stretched up to kiss him. The kiss started sweet, but went on and on, until it threatened to spark the passion that lived between them. As if she sensed the same danger, she broke away and sat up, breathing heavily. "Thanks," she said after a moment. "But I have to make a personal appearance this time."

"I'll send someone with you, then. Things are too unsettled right now. I don't want you going there alone."

She gave him a disbelieving look. "Don't be ridiculous. I've been making this drive alone forever. I'll be fine."

"Maybe. But I'm not taking any chances."

"Quinn, I don't—"

He cut off her objection with a kiss. "Don't waste your breath. I'll make it someone you know. Come on." He started to sit up, but she stopped him.

"Call me when you finish tonight, okay? So I know you made it out alive." She said it as a joke, but there was fear in her eyes. For him.

Quinn hauled her close and kissed her again. Deeply, passionately. A long, lingering kiss meant to brand himself onto her heart. "I'll make it back, Eve. I'm not finished with you yet."

"Quinn," she breathed, as her eyes filled with tears. "I'm serious. Sorley's a sneaky bastard. He'll do anything to win."

"So will I, sweetheart. Sorley's not the only one who can fight dirty." He sat up then, taking her with him, until they both stood by the side of the bed. He turned her toward the bathroom and smacked her ass. "You get first dibs on the shower. Make it quick."

She stared at him for a moment, her gaze serious as it met his.

"I'll be fine, Eve. I promise."

Nodding, she toed off her jeans and panties from the other leg, bent over to retrieve them from the floor, and then hurried to the bathroom.

As soon as the door closed, and he heard the shower running, he called Garrick. "Is everyone ready?"

"Waiting on you, my lord."

"Ten minutes, Garrick. And then we'll go give the vampires of Ireland a new lord."

Chapter Twelve

"YOU THINK THIS is it?" Garrick's question was sub-vocal, meant for Quinn's ears only. It was difficult to have a completely private conversation in a vehicle full of vampires. Garrick sat next to Quinn in the back seat, with Adorjan in the front passenger seat and Casey driving. Quinn had called him back from Howth with the sunset, knowing the final confrontation with Sorley was near. When it came, and Quinn suspected it would be tonight, he'd need all of his American team at his back. They were the ones who'd sworn to him from the very beginning, not knowing what the future held, but believing in Quinn, in his strength and ability. Their loyalty had brought them to Ireland—a place where most of them had never set foot—to help him take and hold a territory of his own.

Quinn didn't have to think about his answer for Garrick. "I think it is." His gut was telling him that tonight was, indeed, *it*. Either Sorley would confront him openly, or he'd do something that would force Quinn to issue the challenge. Probably the latter, since Sorley was the kind to let others do the dirty work and take the responsibility if it failed.

Quinn didn't intend to fail.

Sorley's house was mostly dark when they arrived, his guards sharply alert when they opened the gates to admit Quinn's two SUVs. A pair of guards tried to slow them down as they drove through, harassing him simply on principle, it seemed, since there was no other reason to do it. It wasn't as if Sorley wanted a public battle in the middle of Donnybrook.

Casey ignored their demands and plowed through, followed bumper-to-bumper by the rest of Quinn's team in the second SUV. The two vehicles came to matching tire-squealing stops, and the doors flew open to disgorge Quinn's team. Everyone except Quinn, that is. Even Garrick jumped out to join the security cordon around the first SUV and hold Sorley's people at bay. Quinn seethed silently, once again hating the necessity that had him sitting in safety while his people put themselves at risk. For him. But it was part and parcel of being a vampire lord. Not because the lords couldn't take care of themselves, but because vampire society was old and rooted in tradition. It was expected that a vampire lord would have a retinue of guards who surrounded him whenever he ventured out. It seemed contrary to logic, but the absence of such a cordon would make him seem weaker, not stronger.

So, he sat and waited until Garrick opened the door for him to exit. And when he climbed out, he didn't protest as his vampires closed in to form an impenetrable circle around him. Sorley's vampires glowered at the show of force, but no one tried to stop him, or even approach, until they entered the large, marble-floored foyer of the house.

"Quinn." Lorcan approached on his right, a friendly and completely fake, smile on his face. "You brought friends," he said, eyeing the six vampires behind Quinn, including Garrick and Adorjan.

"Sorley's message was short on details. I thought I might need a few fighters," Quinn said blandly.

"This is more than a few."

Quinn shrugged. "My people are protective. You understand." He gave the other vampire a cool look that stopped just short of a challenge. He wasn't about to be derailed by a confrontation with Sorley's lieutenant. He'd wipe the floor with the vampire, but it would be a waste of time and energy. Or maybe that was the point. Maybe Sorley had sent Lorcan out as a sacrificial goat to weaken Quinn. He was a vampire lord's lieutenant, after all. He'd put up a good fight. But Quinn wasn't falling for it. "I'm assume Sorley's in there?" he asked, gesturing at the double doors to the vampire lord's throne room, behind which he could very clearly detect Sorley's power like a simmering volcano.

Lorcan gave Quinn an absent glance, probably telepathing with Sorley, getting permission to proceed. Quinn didn't wait. Gesturing for his people to remain close, he started forward, not even breaking stride when Adorjan shoved the doors open with a slap of his hands, hitting them so hard that they crashed back against the inside walls.

Lorcan hurried to get between them and the dais, signaling the four vampires who surrounded Sorley as he strode ahead to join them at the vampire lord's side.

That damn dais will be the first thing I get rid of, Quinn thought to himself. Then hard on that, *why bother?* He wouldn't be keeping the house anyway. Sorley had probably booby-trapped half the rooms, either as a defensive measure, or for guests he wanted to get rid of. And the décor was a bit overdone. Rather like the long, fur-lined cloak the Irish lord currently had draped over his shoulders. Quinn wasn't sure what kind of fur it was—nothing from Ireland, he was sure of that. Ermine, maybe. A fur reserved for royals and the nobility, once upon a time. How very apt. Quinn wouldn't have known where to find such a cloak, even if he'd wanted to. And why the hell would he?

He came to a halt a good distance back from Sorley, refusing to crane his neck to look up at the Irish lord. "Lord Sorley," he said formally, refusing to use the alternate honorific of "my lord," since Sorley was not, nor would he ever be, Quinn's vampire liege. "I received your message, although the context was unclear. Nevertheless, here I am."

Sorley glared down at him, hatred in every line, every nuance of his body. He'd probably known why Quinn was in Ireland soon after his arrival, had probably seen through the cover story early on. But the cover had never been more than a delaying tactic. Sorley was smart enough, and his spies good enough, to have dug out the truth as soon as Quinn started making waves in Howth. If they'd been *very* good—or if Quinn and his allies had been worse—the Irish lord would have known about Quinn before he'd ever set foot on the island, and they could have stopped him before he reached Dublin. It would have attracted far less attention and caused fewer headaches for the Irish lord. Not to mention the ramifications of having his rule challenged in the open like this. Even if Quinn lost—which he wouldn't, but if he did—the simple fact that Sorley had been challenged would be seen as evidence of his weakness. He'd be forced to fight off several more competitors before he finally re-established himself. And it was always possible there was a powerful vampire lurking somewhere in Ireland, just waiting for his chance to rule.

Too bad that hypothetical vampire hadn't stepped up when he had the chance, Quinn considered. Too late, now.

Sorley leaned forward. "I ordered you to present *yourself*, not bring this rabble along with you." He gestured at Quinn's very efficient and well-ordered team. Hardly rabble.

"As I said," Quinn responded coolly. "Your message was unclear."

"Well, it's clear now. Get them out of here," he called over Quinn's head, addressing the two vampires who stood by the now-closed doors.

"I don't think so," Quinn said. "They're my people, not yours. I'll determine whether they stay or go."

Sorley stood, his rage a physical thing that tore through the big room like a wild animal, crashing into furniture and breaking everything it touched. "I am the Lord of Ireland," he snarled, his lips drawn back over his teeth. "You *and* your people belong to *me,* as long as you're on *my* island."

Quinn considered his possible responses, but there was really only one choice. It was why he'd come to Ireland, after all. "Then maybe it's time you stepped aside," he said quietly.

EVE HADN'T BEEN fooled by Quinn's blithe dismissal of his meeting with Sorley, but there wasn't much she could do about it. She'd witnessed plenty of bloody fights during her days of stalking the vampires who'd been responsible for her brother's death. She'd known vampires were violent creatures, even before she'd seen Quinn kill everyone who came up against him.

But, even though Quinn's ultimate goal was to kill Sorley and take over his empire, she didn't think that challenge was going to happen tonight. A fight like that, a battle for all of Ireland, would require more planning and preparation. If nothing else, they'd need a location where they wouldn't risk a bunch of human witnesses. Vampires might have come out of the shadows in the strictest sense, but they didn't exactly advertise how they conducted their society *or* their business. It was one thing to have paparazzi publishing glamorous photos of sophisticated vampires and their beautiful women, but it was something else entirely to have pictures of a no-holds-barred, bloody battle plastered everywhere, complete with exploding bodies that left nothing but piles of dust on the streets of Dublin. She didn't think either Sorley *or* Quinn wanted that kind of a fight made public.

So, while she wasn't happy at being cut out of the night's festivities—was even a little pissed to be honest—she wasn't worried about Quinn's safety. He'd said the night's meeting was vampire business, so it was probably just secret vampire stuff. They had to have plenty of those—secrets, that is—since they'd been around for a very long time, and most of *that* had been in hiding. Hell, for all she knew, Quinn and Sorley were deciding on the rules for when they finally got down to it and fought the big challenge. Was it some kind of duel? Like a cage match? Okay, probably not that. Quinn didn't strike her as a cage match kind of a guy, although he would look *fine* stripped to the waist and battling it out. . . . She pictured Sorley as his opponent and the fantasy lost its edge. He was good-looking enough, but the whole evil vibe destroyed his appeal. The challenge had to be something like that, though. She'd sure like to find out what it was. Maybe she could persuade Quinn to let her come along for that one. Although, she'd probably have to be sneaky and just follow him instead.

That idea cheered her up immensely, so she was grinning when she left Quinn's house and started across to the wooden gate, which was always closed these days. There were still plenty of guards around—more evidence that the big battle wasn't tonight, because surely Quinn would have taken all of his fighters—and someone had brought her car inside the wall. It sat off to one side looking like the poor relation to every other vehicle there. The two big, black Range Rovers were gone. She'd noticed that Quinn always took those, since they had room for him and all his guards.

"Good evening, Miss Eve."

She swung around at the familiar voice, blushing guiltily when she saw who it was. Numbers. Sorley's former accountant, whom she'd semi-seduced, while trying to learn some of Sorley's secrets. Not the vampire kind of secret, just the rich asshole kind. Like where he kept his money and what he did with it. Unfortunately, Quinn had caught her before she could pump Numbers for much information. He'd assumed she meant to kill the accountant, and she'd let him believe it, since it added to her tough hunter image. But then he'd laid on the guilt trip, and she'd confessed. Honesty was a pain in the ass sometimes.

Numbers was one of Quinn's people now. He'd sworn some kind of blood oath that was apparently foolproof. If a vampire tried to fake it, Quinn would know and, well, things wouldn't go well for the vamp.

"Hey, Numbers," she said, smiling as she headed for her car, juggling her keys in one hand. How had they moved her car without the keys? Why did she even bother to ask these questions?

"Mac," the vampire said, as he moved in to walk beside her. Not threatening, just companionable. It was odd how he managed that. He wasn't as big as some of them, but he wasn't small either. Maybe five feet, nine inches or so. But he was still a vampire, still stronger and faster than even the strongest human would ever be.

She glanced up at him, confused.

"Lord Quinn calls me 'Mac.' I like it better."

"Oh. Okay. 'Mac' it is."

He walked to the other side of her car and stood there, as if waiting for her to unlock the door.

She looked at him over the roof of the car. "Um. You need a ride somewhere?"

He returned her look with one of surprise and a little embarrassment. "Didn't Lord Quinn tell you?"

"Tell me what?"

"I'm, uh. . . . That is, he asked me to keep you company tonight."

"Keep me company," she repeated stupidly, a moment before it hit her. Quinn thought he was *so* funny. Of all the people he could have chosen, he'd picked Mac, aka Numbers, to keep an eye on her. The vampire she'd tried to seduce, or at least pretended to. "Look, you don't need to do this. I told Quinn I don't need a babysitter. I'm just going to see my mam."

But he was shaking his head. "It's not like that, Eve. He's not worried what *you'll* do. He's worried someone will try to hurt you."

"I've been taking care of myself most of my life." Although, really, only since her brother had died, but the last five years had felt much longer than that. "I think I can handle it."

"I *know* you can," the vampire said fervently.

She blushed at this reminder of their prior meeting.

"But Quinn worries," Mac continued. "It's kind of hardwired into his nature. That's what vampire lords do, they worry about things."

"Not Sorley," she countered.

He shook his head. "Even Sorley. His priorities are different, as are his methods for dealing with it, but he worries all the time." He pulled open the unlocked passenger door. "Come on, Eve, what can it hurt for me to go along?"

"I'm going to visit my mam. Trust me, you don't want to be there."

"So, I'll wait outside and keep you company on the drive back."

"I might not drive back if it's too late. I'll just stay in Howth."

Mac shrugged. "I can stay at Quinn's house there. No problem."

Eve sighed. Clearly he wasn't going to give in. He'd been given his orders and nothing else mattered. If she didn't let him ride with her, he'd probably grab a car from the garage and follow her. "All right," she said reluctantly. "Get in. But you're in for the most boring night of your life."

"I doubt that," he said cheerfully, sliding into the small car. "I'm an accountant, remember?"

Eve had to admit that Mac was good company. He'd been Sorley's accountant for decades, but he was also an inveterate gambler and had the stories to prove it. Turns out, there were definite advantages to being a vampire when it came to certain kinds of gambling. Eve knew about vampire telepathy, and how some vamps were stronger than others, although she was beginning to understand that she'd assumed *every* vampire had far more telepathic ability than they actually did. Some vampires were amazingly powerful, like Quinn. But the scale for the rest of them varied. Some could push a human to open the main Dublin Port gate, as Quinn's bodyguard had the other night. Others were only slightly better than a persuasive human.

Mac, for example, couldn't *push* a mind very hard, but he could *read* them like an open book. Particularly if the human was intently focused on something, like the cards they were holding in a poker game. Unfortunately, he explained, he loved gambling more than he loved winning. So, most of the money he won at cards went to pay his bookie, with whom he bet on everything from horse racing, to football games, to really stupid stuff, like the sex of the next royal heir, or who'd win the latest talent show or film award.

Eve thought he was crazy for throwing away so much money. But it didn't seem to bother Mac at all. He just loved the game of it.

"Whatever," she said, finally giving up on convincing him to change his life. They were nearly in Howth, driving up Thormandy Road, so she grabbed her mobile from the center console and called her mother. It rang four times before she answered, which made no sense. Her mam's house was tiny. It was no more than a dozen steps from one room to the next, not even counting the fact that she always kept her mobile in her housecoat pocket. Her mam was convinced that hooligans were waiting on every corner, and she'd need the phone close when they broke in.

"It's about time you called." Brigid's greeting was as loving as always.

"I'm in Howth," Eve said, not bothering to respond to the implicit accusation. She'd learned long ago that it was pointless. "I'm stopping at my flat for some things, but then I'll be by, if you'll be there."

"Of course, I'll be here. Where else would I be in the middle of the night?"

It was hardly the middle of the night, but that was another argument not worth having. If she hadn't asked, if she'd assumed her mother would be home, that would only have generated a different snide remark. "I'll see you soon, then," Eve said, and rang off without waiting for a response.

Mac glanced at her sideways. "You two get along?"

Eve was embarrassed, reminded that he'd have heard both sides of the conversation. "She hasn't been the same since my brother died." That much was true. He didn't need to know the rest of it.

"The brother who was killed by a vampire."

She shot him a quick look, surprised he knew about that. "Yes," she said. "It was two vampires who killed him. I took out one of them the other night on the dock. Well," she added reluctantly, "Quinn did. But I helped."

"I heard about the fight down at the port. I didn't know about your brother's killer being there, though."

She didn't know what else to say about that and didn't particularly want to say *anything*, so she changed the subject. "You sure you don't want me to drop you at the house first?" It was the house where Quinn's vampires stayed when they were in Howth, doing whatever it was they did. Smuggling mostly.

"No," he said. "Lord Quinn would want me to stick with you. Don't worry. Mothers love me."

"Not mine," she muttered. "She never liked a single boy who came round to see me."

"She'll like me."

Eve shot him a sideways look. "Don't go pulling any of that vampire shit on my mam."

He laughed. "I won't."

She didn't quite believe him, but let it go. Hell, maybe he could change her mother's mood for an evening. Make her civil, at least. "I'm stopping at my flat to pack a few things, then we'll go."

The street in front of her flat was predictably short on available parking. She drove past once, then continued around the block, optimistically hoping someone would have freed up a space. Mac caught what she was doing. "Go ahead and double park. I'll stay with the car."

"You sure?"

"It's that or watch you circle the block a few more times, so, yeah."

Eve grinned and pulled up directly in front of her flat. "I'll be fast," she promised and jumped out. Mac came around to switch places with her, sliding in behind the wheel. "In case a copper comes along," he explained.

Once inside, Eve grabbed underwear and toiletries, along with an extra pair of jeans, a short skirt, and the boots that had driven Quinn wild. Life couldn't be work, work, work, all the time, right? She also gathered her research work materials, since it seemed she'd be spending much of her time in Dublin for a while. She had her laptop at Quinn's, and much of her research was done online, but there were certain texts that she referred to over and over again, and she preferred to have those on hand.

Mac was waiting patiently when she walked back out again. Throwing the two bags in her trunk, she took the passenger seat instead of making him switch.

"So, where am I going?" he asked.

Her mother's place was close, only three streets over. She gave him directions, then asked, "You sure about this? I can still drop you off somewhere fun. The pub's open."

He shook his head and made the first turn. "I'm good. Stop worrying. I won't upset your mam."

"I'm worried about you, not her."

He smiled. "Is the parking better at her place?"

She nodded. "She has her own space in the alley behind her house. It's small, but doable."

A few minutes later, she was showing Mac where to pull in behind her mother's place. "I'll get out first, and that way you can park right next to the house." Eve couldn't understand why she was so nervous about this visit. It couldn't be because Mac was with her. She'd stopped caring about whether her mother liked her friends a long time ago. But there'd been something odd in Brigid's voice earlier. She was never pleasant, not to Eve, but there'd been a note of . . . satisfaction? . . . in her tone. Odd. But then, Eve had never been able to figure out what made Brigid the way she was.

Once Mac finished parking, they walked down the side of the house, bypassed the back door that her mother never let her use, and knocked on the front door. Mac gave her a questioning look. She didn't blame him. How many daughters had to knock on their mother's front door like a stranger?

The door opened and her mother was there, dressed in her usual housecoat and slippers, her dark gray hair cut short and curling around her head. It was a nice cut, and her mam had great hair. It had been red once, just like Eve's, and still showed copper glints in the right light. But her mother didn't keep it short because it looked good. She did it because it was easy to care for.

Brigid Connelly looked at her only surviving child. "You're late."

"A little bit," Eve admitted. Anything else would become an issue, and she wanted this visit to go as smoothly, and quickly, as possible. "There was traffic."

Her mother looked beyond her to where Mac stood at her back. "Who's that?"

"Mam, don't be rude," she said quietly. "This is William. He's a friend."

"He the bloodsucker you're fucking?"

"Mother!" Eve was genuinely shocked at her mother's language, and her rudeness, too. Was this what they'd come to?

Brigid only gave a dismissive shrug and turned away, walking down the short hall to what she referred to as the parlor. It was a small sitting room that was only used for visitors. Eve didn't count as such, but maybe Mac did, despite the lack of welcome.

Eve crossed the threshold, then turned and said, "Come in, William. You're welcome." This might be her mother's house, but Eve had grown up there and lived there, even after Alan died, until she finally couldn't take it anymore and had switched to her flat. She'd hoped her welcome was still valid and breathed a sigh of relief when Mac entered the house without a problem.

"Sorry," she muttered under her breath, starting down the hall toward the parlor.

"Don't worry yourself. Families are complicated things."

Eve agreed with him, but she still wasn't ready for the huge complication waiting for her in her mother's parlor.

Chapter Thirteen

HER MOTHER WAS already seated on the faded settee and had already lit one of the cigarettes that would probably kill her someday. She blew out a stream of smoke. "Tell me, Eve. How do you live with what you're doing?"

Eve paused in the archway, waving her hand against the cloud of smoke, thinking maybe she should open a window in the kitchen on the other side of the parlor. "What is it I'm doing, Mam?"

"Fucking the same bloodsuckers who killed your brother, that's what."

Eve wanted to respond, to use the same argument Quinn had used on her. That not all vampires were the same, that, just like humans, some were killers, some weren't. Of course, Quinn was a killer, too. He was just more selective in whom he killed, which was mostly other vampires, though Eve was sure he'd killed a human or three in his time. But it didn't matter, because, when it came to Brigid, the argument would have fallen on deaf ears. The only thing her mother wanted to hear, the only thing she cared about, was that the vampires who'd killed Alan were dead.

"One of them is dead," Eve told her. "I killed him." Her mother wasn't likely to quibble over the details of who struck the final blow.

Her mam's lips tightened into an unhappy line. "And the other?"

"I know who he is. I'll get him soon."

Brigid grunted wordlessly, took another drag on her cigarette, and looked away. Eve stared at her in sudden realization. Her mother hadn't looked her in the eye once. Not even when she'd opened the door. It was almost as if she was hiding . . .

"Mam," Eve asked in sudden urgency. "How did you know I was dating a vampire?"

"Is that what you call it? Dating?"

"Answer the question. How'd you know?"

Her mother took her time, drawing in another lungful of smoke and blowing it out, picking a piece of tobacco off her lip from the unfiltered cigs she preferred. "Two of the local boys came around. They saw you at the pub."

Eve was feeling a little sick. "Local boys. Who were they?"

"They said he'd probably infect you. That I should call next time you came around. For my own protection."

"Eve." Mac's voice was taut. "We should go."

She nodded, but she already knew it was too late. Some instinct had her backing out of the small parlor, and into the hall where she'd have more room to maneuver. A heavy footstep sounded from the kitchen a moment before Cillian, her brother's second killer, emerged from his hiding place. But he couldn't have been there all along, because Mac would have sensed him. Which meant her mother had given him an invitation to use the back door, something she'd never let her own daughter do.

"Mam," Eve breathed. "He's a vampire. He killed Alan."

"Don't be ridiculous," her mother snapped. She was saying more, but Eve had stopped listening. She stared at the monster who'd kicked her brother to death, her head filled with conflicting advice, telling her what to do, how to kill him, how to escape.

"Out of the way, Eve." Mac's voice broke through the noise. He gripped her shoulder to pull her out of the way, but Cillian was faster, and so much stronger.

"*You* get out of the way," Cillian growled, baring his fangs at Mac. "Fucking traitor." He grabbed Eve's left arm, twisting it behind her back until it hurt. "It's the pretty human I want. She'll be a handy bargaining chip for Sorley to use against Quinn. And when that's done, she'll have . . . other uses," he said, almost a caricature of a leering villain as he stared down at her.

It was Quinn's name that got her frozen brain functioning again. They wanted to use her against Quinn. Which meant the meeting he'd been called to with Sorley wasn't a meeting at all. Sorley was going to challenge Quinn, but first he'd hobble him with threats against Eve's life.

No. The word resonated in her head with crystal clarity. She didn't know if Mac had enough power to do anything against Cillian. She didn't know if Cillian had *any* power or if he was just a thuggish tool. What she *did* know was that he wasn't paying any attention to her. She was just a human female, after all, only good for food and rape. His attention was all on Mac, who was staring at Cillian with death in his eyes and pink sweat rolling down his temples.

Cillian suddenly tightened his grip on her left arm, maybe in reaction to whatever Mac was doing. But Eve was right-handed. Her heart was tripping with fear, adrenaline singing in her veins. She reached into her jacket pocket and wrapped a hand around her Sig pistol, now loaded with its new 9mm Hydra-Shok ammo. The ammo Joshua Bell had told her would work. Hoping he was right, she sucked in a breath, pulled the gun out of her pocket, pressed it against Cillian's left chest, and pulled the trigger. All in one motion—five shots, point blank, in rapid succession, saving two bullets, just to be safe.

She held her breath, still not sure . . . until Cillian dusted right before her eyes.

Somewhere in the background, she heard her mother scream once, and then nothing, but there was no time to investigate as a second vampire surged forward. She raised her weapon, but he moved faster than she could follow, grabbing her right arm and knocking it aside before she could fire. This was it, she thought, until a slender knife flew over her shoulder and into the vamp's throat. The vampire roared and blood gushed as he instinctively raised a hand to staunch the flow. Eve pulled her aim back and fired her last two bullets, stepping up until the barrel of her gun was no more than two inches away from his burly chest. The vampire—she didn't even know his name—gave her a startled look, and then he was gone, adding to the pile of dust in her mother's hallway.

Eve stared at the place where the vampires had been, her entire body shaking with the after-effects of an adrenaline rush like she'd never had before. Not even when she'd faced off against her very first vampire. This was her mother's house. The only place she'd ever called home. A place that was no longer hers.

"Eve."

Mac voice shook her out of her stupor. She stared at him over her shoulder. "Nice knife throwing," she said vaguely, hearing the tremulous quality of her own voice.

He touched her cheek. "We have to get back to Quinn," he said, meeting her eyes. "He needs to know about this."

Eve blinked. "Right." She looked down at herself. She was covered in blood from the nameless vamp's gusher, and wearing a fine coating of dust. "I need fresh clothes."

"Change in the car, lass. There's no time."

"Right," she said again. She shook herself, then turned to find her mother leaning against the parlor wall, looking pale, but otherwise uninjured as she stared daggers at Eve.

"*You* brought this into my home. You and that vampire you're fucking."

Eve met Brigid's eyes and turned away. "Let's go," she told Mac. She didn't bother saying good-bye to her mother. Whether or not she'd known the two "local" men were vampires didn't matter. What mattered was that she'd set Eve up to be . . . what? Kidnapped for her own good? Her mother had trusted strangers instead of her own daughter.

She walked out, closing the door behind her in more ways than one. The two vampires who'd murdered her brother were dead. She'd fulfilled her promise to Alan, and to herself. She was done with the past. Now, she had to save her future.

SORLEY BARKED A laugh, staring in disbelief at Quinn's challenge. "You think to challenge me? *You*? Raphael and his friends aren't going to bail you out this time, boy. You're on your own."

Quinn tilted his head curiously. "I'm not aware of Lord Raphael ever *bailing me out*, as you say."

Sorley's eyes went cold with hatred. "You think you're so clever," he growled. "Well, so am I. I know all about Raphael and his scheme to steal what's mine. Do you know how old I am? How many years I've had to hone my power? You're a puppy compared to me."

Quinn smirked. "I've been a vampire for 57 years, which is 399 in dog years, so . . . hardly a puppy. But then"—he lifted a taunting gaze at Sorley—"some of us are *born* to rule. While others require more tutoring."

Sorley seemed to swell with his anger, the hatred in his eyes swinging from cold to searing hot in an instant. Throwing aside the ridiculous fur cape, he strode to the edge of the dais, knocking aside his own guards, moving incredibly fast, his speed taking even Quinn by surprise as he launched an attack. Every vampire lord had a talent, and it seemed Sorley's involved speed.

Quinn staggered as Sorley's first strike slammed into him with little warning. The Irish lord didn't have only speed on his side, he had power. The blow hit him like a crack of lightning, driven by a magic that bit into every inch of exposed skin and sent him skidding back several feet. Quinn snarled and dug in his heels, furious at himself for being caught off guard. But before he could recover, he was bombarded by a series of smaller, but still powerful, blows that pummeled his head and body like a crazed fighter determined to intimidate a weaker opponent with speed before he could so much as raise a fist.

Quinn was aware of Garrick and the others stepping up to surround him, but he waved them back. This was between him and Sorley. He could draw on his people for power, just as the vampire lord could, but in the end, it came down to the two of them. Sorley had struck the first blow, but Quinn wasn't weak, and he sure as hell wasn't intimidated. Drawing on his own power, he raised shields, which should have been in place the moment he'd walked into this damn relic of a house, and began lobbing powerful bombs of his own—small, fire-driven attacks that struck with a deceptive ease that had Sorley laughing in derision. Until the small bombs split open, releasing a lava-like fire that clung to everything it touched, burning skin, hair, clothes. It was hungry and it *ate*. Sorley's laugh turned to an outraged bellow as the fire dug into his flesh and refused to let go.

Furious, fangs bared and jaw clenched against the pain, he spread his legs like tree trunks and threw everything he had at Quinn, trying to break through his shields, to douse the flames along with Quinn's life.

Quinn endured, standing strong against Sorley's attack as his flesh bruised, bones cracked, and tendons tore. Internal organs ruptured under the massive blows, and his chest cavity filled with blood, until he could hardly breathe and his sight began to gray from a lack of oxygen. In a moment, one of his lungs would collapse and he'd be done for. He could no longer *endure*, he needed to do more, or he would die and his people would die with him—his friends. Garrick. Eve.

Taking a single step backward, ignoring the look of triumph in Sorley's eyes, he reached over and grabbed Garrick's belt knife, rammed the blade deep between his own ribs, and twisted. It hurt like hell, but blood poured out, and the pain disappeared beneath a wave of relief as his lung expanded and his vampire blood began to heal the injuries that had caused the collapse in the first place. With his first full breath, Quinn reached for the deadly magic that was his alone. Letting his power swell, he fed the fire that lived in his soul from an ember to a searing flame, letting it grow until it was eating him alive, hungry for fuel, and demanding to be set free.

Sorley had switched out his attack, withholding his magic, which used far more power, and substituting a physical assault instead. Furniture, wall hangings, and elaborate works of art flew through the air in a whirlwind of debris as Quinn strode closer, Sorley's eyes widening in surprise at the speed of his recovery.

The debris stopped as Sorley changed his tactics yet again, pausing as if to regroup and gather his strength, before Quinn could renew his attack. But it was too late. Stopping two deliberate steps away, Quinn reached deep, and freed the ravenous flames building inside him. Fire spilled from every pore, surrounding him, caressing him like a lover, before stretching out its fingers to feed. Whatever, whomever, it touched, burned. Sorley's guards, caught up in the maelstrom, screamed, batting at flames that wouldn't go out, while the fire leapt from chair to cloth to curtain, threatening to take the entire house along with it.

Quinn was lost in the beauty of his power, the elegance of the flames as they swirled around him in a deadly dance. He was aware of Sorley stumbling backward, staring in horror as the deadly flames swayed closer. Until a new troop of vampire guards arrived with a raw shout of defiance. Rushing in to protect their master, they formed a barrier of flesh and power between Quinn and Sorley, as the vampire lord ran.

Quinn hated killing vampires like this, fighters who were merely doing their duty. But he had to get to Sorley before the old lord could escape and regroup. If that meant going through these guards, he'd do it. He made an effort to pull back his power, to dampen the flame so it would injure but not destroy, until, one by one, he and his fighters took out or immobilized every vampire who stood in their way.

Finally racing down a long hall and out through a side door, he threw back his head and howled when he found Sorley gone, along with at least some of his strongest warriors, Lorcan probably among them.

Quinn's furious howl sent a whirlwind of power roaring through the neighborhood. Trees bent, branches cracked, and car alarms went off up and down the street as he stormed back into the house, searching for someone who could tell him where the vampire lord had gone. This was Sorley's territory, his land. He could have a bolt hole anywhere on the damn island, where he could draw power to help him heal and strengthen himself for the next battle.

Aware of the flames still licking at his soul, Quinn forced himself to take it down a notch, before he burned one of his own people in a fit of frustration. He was still focusing on dousing the fire, when Garrick approached, dragging a burley vampire by one arm. The vamp was badly burned, half his jaw nearly gone, but his eyes gleamed red with the power of a low level vamp, and they were filled with rage as he glared at Quinn.

"Who's this?" Quinn asked.

"Guard Captain," his cousin provided. "I caught him and these others trying to sneak a car out of the garage." He jerked his head sideways, indicating two other low-level vamps, both of whom had their hands bound behind their backs with heavy-duty cuffs that only worked because the vampires were injured.

"Captain," Quinn said slowly. "It seems you've been abandoned by your master. Where'd he slither off to, do you think?"

"Fuck you," the vamp captain snarled.

"Wrong answer." Quinn slammed a fist into the vampire's chest and ripped out his heart, squeezing it between his fingers with a sizzle of power, before dropping it to the floor and turning to the next vampire. "You're next. Where'd Sorley go?"

The vamp was visibly trembling, bloody sweat rolling down the sides of his face from his forehead. "I don't know, my lord, I swear."

Quinn narrowed his eyes in frustration. The vampire was telling the truth, as was the next one, when the question was put to him. A different sort of fire burned in Quinn's gut as he fought to keep his temper under control. Sorley was *not* going to walk away from this. If he escaped tonight, he'd hide somewhere in the countryside, rebuilding his base, harboring his strength until he was ready to attack again. He had an advantage over Quinn. He knew Ireland better, knew the small towns, the secret backroads and hideouts. Places he could rest and recuperate, gathering his supporters until he was ready to reclaim his throne. It could be days, weeks, even months. And it was intolerable.

As long as Sorley lived, even in hiding, Quinn couldn't seize the territory. It would tear Ireland's vampires apart if he tried to rip them from Sorley's living hand. That wasn't the way he wanted to begin his reign as Lord of Ireland.

"Fuck!" He kicked a delicate table, shattering its spindly legs and splitting the rest into so much kindling for the flames.

A sudden squeal of tires, along with shouts among his fighters, had him spinning for the front door, ready for a fight. But it wasn't an enemy who stormed up the stairs. It was the redheaded hunter who'd stolen his heart.

"Eve? What are you doing here?"

"QUINN!" EVE WAS so happy to see him standing there, all strong and healthy, that she wanted to throw her arms around him in relief. But mindful of the situation and their audience, she pulled back, her arms stiff and her hands fisted with the effort to restrain herself. Walking right up to him, she nearly missed a step at the sight of his blood-soaked shirt. Her eyes met his. "Are you okay?" she whispered.

He nodded grimly. "I handled it. What are you doing here?"

She winced, suddenly unsure. "I came to warn you."

He scowled. "About what?"

"About all of this." She gestured helplessly at the vampires running around in controlled chaos of the big house behind them. "Cillian was waiting for me at my mother's house."

Quinn frowned. "Who's Cillian?"

Eve grimaced. She probably should have mentioned this before. "He's the other vampire who killed my brother. Him and Barrie Meaney."

Quinn's eyes narrowed, as he closed his hand over her nape and pulled her close. "We'll talk later about your tendency to keep secrets. Are you all right? And your mother?"

Eve let her head fall forward to hit his shoulder. She'd be strong again in just a minute, but for now. . . . She let herself lean on him for that instant of time, soaking up the heat and strength of him, feeling his other arm come around her, feeling safe for the first time in longer than she could remember. A single tear rolled down her cheek, soaking into his bloodied shirt.

"Eve?"

There was concern in his voice, but also a gentle reminder of where they were and who was watching. She nodded her head and pushed away from him, ending the moment. "Cillian's dead. So's the vamp he had with him." She shrugged. "I don't know his name. Mac—"

"Dead . . . what the fuck happened?"

"They knew I was going to be there, and—"

"Who's *they*? And how the hell—"

"My mother," she said simply, trying to keep the emotion from her voice and knowing she failed when Quinn grabbed her hand and dragged her into the house, turning into the first open room and slamming the door behind him, leaving the two of them alone. Quinn didn't hesitate, didn't ask permission or give her a chance to resist. He simply wrapped her in his arms, and held her so tightly, she couldn't have broken free if she'd wanted to. Which she didn't.

"Talk to me, sweetheart."

"I don't know where to start. I just—"

"Tell me what happened. Start at the beginning."

He was still holding her, his words a warm rumble against her ear, her own muffled by the hard muscles of his chest. The blood-stiffened fabric scraped against her cheek, and she frowned, shoving him away, running her hands over his chest, pulling his shirt up over what should have been an expanse of ridged muscle and smooth skin, and finding a mass of bruises instead. "What the hell? What is this?"

He grabbed her wrists to stop her, then ran his hands up to hold her arms. "I'm fine," he insisted. "Sorley and I did each other a lot of damage, but when he realized he was about to lose, he threw a bunch of vampire guards at me and ran. We're trying to find him, so I can finish this. Now, tell me what happened, Eve. Is your mother safe?"

"Safe." She bit off the word with a bitter laugh. "You know . . . I'm *barely* welcome in her house, her own daughter. But she invited that murdering bastard in, the same vampire who killed the son she claims to have loved so much."

Quinn shook his head, as if to clear it. "I don't. . . . Eve, you're not—"

"They claimed they were local lads—Cillian and some other vampire. They pretended to be worried for her safety since, as they said, I was fucking a vampire and you'd probably turned me by now. They told her that whenever I came for a visit, my mam should call them, for her own protection," she ended bitterly.

"Did your mother know Cillian personally? Why would she—"

"No. I think that must have been the other vamp, the one Cillian brought with him. He looked familiar, but I didn't get a good look at him before. . . . Well, it doesn't matter now. They're both dead."

"And your mother?"

"Oh, she's alive and well. But dead to me."

"I'm sorry, Eve. I swear I didn't know they'd try—"

"Of course, you didn't," she interrupted. "That was the whole point. They were there to kidnap *me* to use against you. Not great planning on their part, since all of *this*"—she gestured around them—"was apparently going down at the same time. But all I could think was that we had to get back here to—"

He grinned. "To warn me. You were worried."

Her eyes narrowed. "So, fine," she snapped. "I was worried. For nothing, as it turns out." She twisted out of his arms. Or at least she tried to.

Quinn held on tight, forcing her to look up at him or be suffocated against his stupidly gorgeous chest. "It wasn't for nothing," he said, meeting her gaze. "Thank you. And, Eve,—" He waited until she was looking up at him again, meeting his eyes. "I love you, too."

Tears flooded her eyes turning everything into a blur of crystalline images. Furious with herself, she thumped a fist against his chest and wished she could tell him he was full of shit. That she didn't love him any more than he really did her. But damn if she could say it.

"I'm an idiot," she whispered. "Falling for a damn vampire. What kind of life can we—"

Quinn was smiling, completely missing her point. Didn't he understand? He was going to live forever, while she'd grow old and wrinkled. How much would he love her then? And how long could they possibly have before that happened? Ten years, maybe less, before he wanted a younger woman, someone fresh and new. Not one whose skin was beginning to sag, who had to work twice as hard to keep her muscles firm, had to dye her hair against the encroaching gray . . .

"Eve, darling, you're thinking way too hard. We'll talk vampire lovers later. Right now, I have to find Sorley. Like yesterday. My people are spreading out over the city—"

"Doolin," she said in sudden realization. "Doolin," she repeated, seeing Quinn's puzzled look. "I followed him there several times when I was looking for Barrie and Cillian. I didn't know their names, yet, but I knew they worked for him, and . . . and don't give me that look. I'm still alive and in better shape than you, I might add."

Quinn scowled, but made a rolling gesture with his hand, telling her to continue. "What about Doolin? Where is that, anyway?"

"Southwest of Dublin, near the Cliffs of Moher on the west coast. You've heard of those?"

"Right. Okay. Why the hell would Sorley go there so often?"

"Well, shit, Quinn. I don't know. I couldn't exactly ask around about him, could I?"

He gave her dark look. So much for the lovey-dovey stuff.

"I think he has family there," she admitted. "You should ask Mac. He might—" But Quinn was already gone, yanking the door open and shouting for someone to find Mac.

"YES, MY LORD," Mac told Quinn. "Lord Sorley, that is, er—"

"I don't give a fuck about titles," Quinn snapped. "Just tell me what you know."

"He has family in Doolin. His mother's people, I think. And a house. He sends money once a month to cover expenses, and they make sure it's ready whenever he wants to visit."

"Why go there at all?"

"I can't say for sure. I was only his bookkeeper. But . . . I think he keeps a woman in Cardiff."

"Cardiff?" Quinn repeated in surprise. "Well, fuck, that makes no sense. Doolin's hardly the best jumping off point for Wales."

"No," Mac agreed, "but if he wanted to keep his absence from Ireland a secret . . ."

Quinn pondered the idea. "Maybe. He goes to visit family and sneaks away for a quickie in Cardiff. Shit." He scowled, thinking. "Is there an airport near—"

"He has a helicopter, my lord."

Quinn regarded Mac silently. "Way to bury the lead. Where's he keep the chopper? Dublin? Fuck. He might already be—"

"No, my lord, in Doolin. He'll have to drive that far, but once—"

"Once he's in Doolin, he can hop on his helicopter and be off to who knows where," Quinn finished grimly. "How far to Doolin from here? How long?"

"At this time of night, two and half hours? Maybe three if they want to avoid getting nicked for speeding."

"Garrick!" Quinn shouted, "Get Lucas's man Ronan on the line. It's time for him to choose."

Five minutes later, Garrick handed him a phone. "Ronan, my lord."

Quinn nodded grimly and took the phone. "Ronan. I need a helicopter. Now."

"My lord, I don't—"

"Bullshit. You have one hidden in that big barn on the edge of your property, and you have three different vampires on staff who can fly it. I need it in Dublin."

"When?" Ronan asked, with a resigned sigh.

"If you want this takeover to succeed, you'll have it here five minutes ago."

"I'll need to call—"

"Don't bother. I'll call Lucas myself. You get that thing in the air." He disconnected and handed the phone back to Garrick. "Find Lucas for me. As a courtesy," he added.

Garrick laughed, then turned away and started punching in numbers.

"You're going to Doolin?"

Eve's voice had Quinn spinning around, taking her hand, and pulling her with him as he strode out to one of his two Range Rovers. He opened the back cargo door, yanked a small, black duffle closer, and began rummaging inside it. "That's where Sorley is," he said.

"I'm going with you."

Quinn lifted his head and drew breath to argue with her, but then, seeing her determined glare, he crooked his lips into a half-smile. "Okay," he agreed and had to swallow a laugh at her look of surprise. "You're the one who figured out where Sorley would go, and you're decent with a crossbow, even if—"

"I don't need a crossbow anymore. This works much better." She pulled a 9mm Sig from a pocket in her jacket, checked the safety, and then expertly flipped the weapon around to hand it to him butt first.

Quinn examine the gun quickly. Bell had told him about the weapon. It was small, probably considered a micro-compact, but a good fit for Eve's smaller hand. He popped the magazine. "You re-loaded," he murmured. "Good girl." He laughed at her look of outrage over his comment and handed the gun back. "Have you been holding out on me, Eve?"

"No," she said defensively. "I've had the gun awhile, but I never used it except on the range, because I couldn't get the right ammo until—"

He raised one eyebrow. "When?"

"I don't want to get anyone in trouble."

"No one's in trouble," he said patiently. "Just tell me."

"Well, the other day, after we . . . um, anyway. You went off to do your vampire sleep thing, and I was talking to Joshua Bell, and he . . ." She scowled at him. "Well, what did you think? That I was going to hang around eating bonbons all day? Maybe read poetry in the garden?"

Quinn fought back a grin at the image. "Hardly," he said dryly, enjoying her description too much to admit that Bell had cleared it with him before he'd supplied Eve with the ammunition. "Can you shoot that thing?"

"Absolutely. How do you think I killed Cillian and his buddy?"

That image drained away every ounce of humor he'd found in the situation. "All right. Do you need more ammo?"

She shook her head. "I have my own supply."

Quinn grabbed the back of his bloody and torn T-shirt, yanked it off over his head, and tossed it into the cargo compartment. Next, he grabbed a bottle of water from his duffel and poured it over his chest, using a towel to wipe away the worst of the blood and dry himself off. His side ached a little, but that wouldn't last much longer. Digging out a clean T-shirt, he pulled it over his head and turned to find Eve watching with an appreciative gleam in her eye.

Pulling her in for a quick kiss, he said, "Hold that thought," then nodded over her shoulder at Garrick who was walking toward him with cell phone in hand.

Lucas, Garrick mouthed.

Quinn took the proffered cell phone. "Lucas," he said brusquely. "This is a courtesy head's up, from one lord to another. I've requested the use of your helicopter on an urgent matter. It's already in the air."

"Good evening to you, too," Lucas growled. "Ronan already called. My people are loyal."

"Funny," Quinn snapped. "So are mine."

Lucas laughed. "Can't we all just get along?"

"I will if you will. Thanks for the chopper. I'll let you know how it turns out." Quinn handed the phone back to Garrick. "I could hate that fucker really easily."

"You're not alone. He gets on people's nerves. But he runs his territory well, and the other North American lords seem to like him. Especially Raphael."

"Yeah, I saw that. There's something more than mutual respect between those two. I'd put money on Raphael being Lucas's Sire."

Garrick nodded. "That's the rumor, but the official line is that it's neither confirmed nor denied."

"Which we both know means it's true. What's the status on the chopper? And where's it landing anyway?"

"Dublin Castle," Garrick said, sharing Quinn's look of surprise. "Apparently, it has a helipad that's used by visiting dignitaries."

"And departing vampires, at least for tonight. Let's go." He grabbed Eve's hand. "You're with me, sweetheart. I have to make sure you're only shooting the bad guys."

Chapter Fourteen

Doolin, Ireland

QUINN HAD NEVER been to this part of Ireland. It was a short-coming on his part, he thought, as they flew through the night. Lucas's helicopter wasn't one of those five passenger sightseeing types, but a full-on troop carrier. Quinn appreciated it, even as he wondered how the hell Lucas had managed to slip it into the country. Apart from Sorley, who would surely have kept a close eye on Lucas's property, there was the scrutiny of the Irish government, who would have plenty to say about a private citizen bringing in a piece of heavy military equipment like this. It made Quinn wonder if Lucas's sights hadn't been set on ruling Ireland, after all. He shrugged. If so, it was a dream Lucas would have to put aside, because Ireland was Quinn's now. Or it would be very soon.

"How long?" he asked the pilot, who was one of his own people. Lucas's pilot had offered to stay on, but Quinn had declined, promising he'd return the chopper in good order and before the night was through. Probably not in time to fly it back to Lucas's estate in Kildare, however. He frowned. They'd have to hide the damn thing somewhere. Immediately on that thought, he laughed at himself. He had much bigger worries than where to hide a helicopter. Like getting rid of Sorley once and for all.

"Fifteen minutes, my lord."

Lightning flashed in the night sky, followed three beats later by a crack of thunder so loud that it pressed on his ear drums. The thunder was still echoing through the night, when it began to rain in thick sheets.

"We're going down," came the pilot's warning.

Great, Quinn thought. He was going to die in a helicopter crash only minutes away from achieving the pinnacle of vampire society. Vampire Lord. A title owned by few and always claimed over the blood and dust of one's predecessor. And it had nearly been his. His skin tingled with goosebumps as the helicopter dropped . . . and he realized that the vamp had been letting him know they were landing. Not crashing. He looked around carefully. Vampire night sight, notwithstanding, it was dark enough in the chopper that no one should have noticed his two-second look of doubt. Next to him, Eve squeezed his hand, and when he glanced over, she winked. Okay, so none of his vamps had noticed, at least.

The skids of their helicopter brushed the ground a moment later, the wash of its navigation lights spotlighting another helicopter powering up about a hundred yards away.

"That bird's too light to lift off in this weather," his pilot informed him.

Taking that as the good news it was, Quinn didn't wait for his chopper to settle on the wet grass. He pulled the door back and jumped out, searching the area for any sign of Sorley. If the vampire lord hadn't been able to leave by air, then he had to be running on the ground. But where? And how? Almost too late, he remembered whom he was chasing, *what* he was chasing. Sorley was a *vampire lord*. He burned with not only his own power, but the power of all those who were pledged to him. The power of almost every vampire living in Ireland was tied in to his.

Quinn stopped searching with his eyes and began searching with the power that made him something *other*. The power that made him not simply Vampire, but a vampire *lord*.

Like a shutter flipping open, he saw the night filled with an array of lights, representing the life forces of the people around him. His vampires were solid flames, with Garrick and Adorjan burning visibly brighter, reflecting their greater power. And in the distance . . . the beacon that was Sorley, beaming like a spotlight against the dark sky . . . and moving away fast.

"He's there." Quinn pointed and started running. "In a fucking car." He'd never catch up on foot. They needed a vehicle of their own. But this part of Doolin wasn't exactly high density. And even if they managed to find a car or truck, grand theft auto wasn't exactly one of his—

"Here, my lord!" Adorjan's shout was punctuated by another booming crack of lightning, following only seconds later by the rumble of thunder.

Quinn spun around and spotted his security chief sitting behind the wheel of an older model Ford sedan, using his fists to smash the steering column. Two minutes later, he'd done something with the ignition and the engine sputtered to life. Quinn exchanged a look with Garrick as they piled into the passenger seats, privately hoping the old car had enough life left to fulfill its mission tonight. Quinn would buy its owners a brand new fucking car, as long as this one lasted long enough to catch up with Sorley.

Adorjan drove, speeding after Sorley, trying to stay on the road as he followed Quinn's directions. The black night was absolute, broken only by repeated lightning strikes that threatened to blind, instead of lighting the way. Quinn could still follow the vampire lord's blazing trail, but unfortunately, magic didn't care about roads or physical obstacles. It said, "over there," and left the rest up to Quinn, which was a pain in the ass. He'd managed to overlay his inner vision on the physical reality, but between the disorientation of seeing two views at once, and the rapid twists and turns in the rickety car, he found himself wondering if vampires could still vomit.

"I can't see a thing!"

Quinn was startled to hear Eve's voice coming from the back seat. How the hell had he missed her jumping into the car with them? And what the hell was she doing there? He had no time to worry about it, however, as Sorley's power signature took a sudden dive. Was he blocking? But, no, it reappeared a moment later, just as their own car skidded down a short incline, and Quinn realized the road had entered a series of short dips and valleys.

"Fucking coward. He's a damned vampire lord," he muttered, holding on as Adorjan fought the car back under control. "He should act like it."

"Where does he think he's going?" Garrick asked, as confused as the rest of them.

"He's not thinking at all," Quinn said. "He's just running."

Sorley's power signature abruptly stopped moving. It was sudden enough that Quinn closed his eyes, wanting to get rid of the physical, so he could concentrate on his vampire senses alone. A second later, he opened his eyes, just in time to yell, "Stop!"

Adorjan spun the wheel frantically. The ancient car and its nearly bald tires skidded in a full circle before coming to a shuddering stop only a few yards away from a fifty foot drop into the Atlantic Ocean.

"Fuck," Eve breathed, and Quinn's heart nearly stopped at the reminder of her humanity. He and his vampires probably would have survived the fall, albeit, not without significant damage. Enough to let Sorley escape, at least. But Eve . . . she would almost certainly have died.

Quinn shoved his door open and rounded the car to where she was climbing out from behind Adorjan's seat. "Stay here," he ordered, then bent to give her a hard kiss. "Please." He didn't know if she'd pay attention, but there was no time to argue. Sorley was out of his vehicle and running for a long, low building to one side. Quinn didn't know exactly where they were, or what the building was, but he wasn't going to give Sorley another place to hide.

Quinn stopped chasing after Sorley long enough to lob a concentrated beam of power directly in front of Sorley, cutting him off and forcing him to change his trajectory, away from the building.

Good, Quinn thought viciously. The last thing he wanted was to chase the coward through miles of corridor. For one thing, it would leave too many questions for the human authorities, but, more importantly, it would be too fucking time-consuming and an even bigger pain in his ass than this damn car chase.

Quinn finally brought the craven vampire lord to ground, high on a grassy cliff, with nowhere else to run. Sorley spun into a defensive crouch, knees bent and hands curled into claws. His face bore no signs of humanity, the sophisticated mask torn away to reveal the monster within—fangs bared, gleaming brightly with every crack of lightning, and eyes burning a sickly green with his power. The color was muddled, as if it had once been a pure emerald, but had been overtaken by something dark and unnatural.

Sorley sneered as thunder roared and the rain grew impossibly heavier, icy cold needles that threatened to slice every inch of exposed skin. "Can't use your precious fire now, can you, boy?"

Quinn laughed and loosed his power completely, holding nothing back. Pale blue flame blossomed all around, surrounding him with a power that screamed with the joy of being free. It had been locked away for so long. He couldn't remember the last time he'd fully embraced the glory of what he was. Vampire lord. Born to rule. And, by God, he was going to fulfill that destiny or die.

He filled one hand with the bright, blue flame and made it dance, twirling it around and through his fingers, smiling when he looked up and caught Sorley's look of dismay. "It's not fire, you fool," Quinn called. "It's magic." And then closing his hand around the flame, he lifted it in a blindingly fast move and threw it at Sorley, laughing when the vampire ducked.

Sorley snarled his rage and attacked, moving with that incredible speed of his, spinning to one side an instant after he launched a pounding series of attacks on Quinn's shields, pummeling the same spot over and over again, as if hoping to weaken it enough to break through. It wasn't a bad strategy. The smallest hole in a vampire's shield could be fatal. But Quinn hadn't wasted the last few years. He'd practiced and honed the use of his power until it was second nature for him to shift energy around, to reinforce the point of attack, and launch a counter-attack of his own. He'd also designed a fluid defense, one that could take his opponent's strategy and use it against him. Having witnessed Sorley's speed only hours ago in their first battle, he now did exactly that.

Fashioning his power into liquid flame, he threw it ahead of the fleeing vampire, then used Sorley's speed to bend it around, until it engulfed him in sizzling magic. Sorley twisted and screamed, too lost in agony to *think*. If he'd taken a moment, he'd have known it wasn't true flame, and he could have countered it with magic of his own. But the fear of fire was written in the deepest strands of human DNA, and while vampires might consider themselves a higher evolution, they were still human at the core.

And so Sorley fought fire, not magic. He rolled on the wet ground and raised his arms to the pouring rain, to no effect. Quinn's power was unrelenting, trapping his opponent in a seamless cocoon of flame that slowly turned from agonizing blue to a killing orange that took hold of Sorley and burned away first his clothes and then his skin, blackening his bones while the vampire lord still lived. Quinn watched longer than he should have, relishing Sorley's torment, even while recognizing the cruelty of it and knowing it made him less human. But then, he wasn't human any longer. He was Vampire.

Finally, he walked over to the blackened mass that had been Sorley and, reaching through a fire that had no power to harm him, he plucked the vampire lord's heart from between his crumbling ribs. Holding the beating heart in his hand, he dug deep within himself and brought forth a final reservoir of power, a pure, white flame so bright that it cast everything around it into shadow. Quinn cloaked Sorley's beating heart in that flame, until it, too, blackened and disintegrated into ash, to be washed away by the cleansing rain.

Quinn didn't notice when the rest of Sorley's body dusted into nothingness. He slumped to the ground as his magic was sucked back into his body, compressing it into a hot core that was always there, but lay quiescent for now, seeming as exhausted as he was. He welcomed the cold rain, his eyes closed, every muscle loose with relief that the battle was over. And he'd won. He was the Lord of Ireland, ruler of all her vampires.

He smiled despite his weariness and gathered his strength to stand, when a force heavier than any he'd ever encountered crashed into him, slamming him back to the ground as a thousand voices all crying out as one overwhelmed every sense he possessed.

"Quinn!"

He heard Eve calling his name, heard her arguing with Garrick who was holding her back. What the hell was . . . oh right. The damn territorial mantle. Forcing himself to focus amidst the cacophony of screaming demands, he insulated himself from the *others,* the vampires who were now his to defend and protect, vampires who relied on his strength for their very lives. This was the burden that came along with the power of being a vampire lord.

Pulling his awareness back until their demands were a unified hum, instead of a thousand or more unique voices, he gathered his strength and said quietly, "Enough. I'm here. Ireland is safe. Go back to your lives, and . . . *shut up.*" He added that last in utter exasperation with their whining. Fuck.

He opened his eyes and looked up, meeting his cousin's gaze with a nod that said, "We did it." Garrick grinned and released Eve, who raced over and caught Quinn when he would have toppled over, what little strength he'd had after the battle having been consumed by the struggle to subdue his new subjects.

Eve's arms felt good around him. She was his humanity. Her heart beat strongly, blood pumping beneath warm, soft skin, as she murmured love and encouragement, stroking him as one would an injured child. The image made him grin as she struggled to help him stand. He was a foot taller and far too heavy, but that didn't stop her. Nothing stopped his Eve when she set her mind to it. Not even physics.

Garrick and Adorjan stepped in to help, dragging him back to his feet, half-carrying him back to their rickety car while Eve held his hand.

"The pilot wants to wait out this weather," Garrick told him from the front seat, when everyone was finally back inside. Quinn's head rested on Eve's shoulder in the backseat, her arm around him, her soft breasts pressing against his arm. "He says he *can* fly, but he'd rather not. And Sorley's house is empty. We can hang there in the meantime."

Quinn laughed. "It's my house now."

His cousin and Adorjan both joined the laughter, but Eve said, "Wait. Won't his heirs get—"

"Not in the world of vampires," Quinn told her, hearing his words slur with exhaustion. "What was his is now mine. And that includes everything."

"Ugh. Even that awful Donnybrook house? You're not going to live—"

"No," he said around a yawn. "Later," he mumbled, his eyes closing. He was aware of Eve kissing his forehead, and then nothing.

Chapter Fifteen

Ballsbridge, Dublin, Ireland, six months later

QUINN STOOD ON the narrow balcony outside his office window, watching as the high wall between his house and the next was demolished. The huge, yellow backhoe was relentless, smashing into the wall, section by section, until it was nothing but a pile of concrete blocks. A second machine joined in on the destruction, gathering up huge loads of the concrete and hauling it over to a big dump truck, which would take the debris . . . somewhere. Away. That's all Quinn cared about. The job was noisy and dirty, and Quinn kept telling himself it would all be worth it. He'd wanted more space between him and his neighbors, and he'd needed more room—more sleeping quarters, more living space for his growing crew of vampires and guards. So, he'd made an offer that was too generous for the owners to refuse, and now the neighboring house was his.

"Are you standing out here again?" Eve's teasing voice was accompanied by the sweet scent of her perfume, as she slid under his arm, and put her head on his shoulder. "It'll be okay, baby. A few more days, and you won't know the wall was ever there."

"Uh huh. And then they'll start renovations on the house. More noise and destruction."

She laughed. "Come on. It's cold and wet out here, and this stupid balcony is going to collapse. It's not even a real balcony, you know."

Quinn tightened his arm around her and turned them both back into his office. "So you keep telling me. You should probably stay inside anyway. The cold's bad for your aging joints."

She pulled away and punched his ribs. He barely felt it, but he made an "oophing" noise for her benefit.

"Enough with the aging jokes!" she scolded. "How was I supposed to know your blood was a fountain of youth?"

Quinn pulled her against his chest, and twisted his hand in her long hair. Tugging her head back, he demanded a kiss. Her mouth opened beneath his, her lips soft and warm, her tongue tangling eagerly with his. "You know I love you, don't you, Eve?" he asked against her lips.

"I know," she whispered.

"And you know, if you leave me, you'll immediately shrivel up like a leaf in winter."

Her laughter spilled into his mouth, lightening his soul. "You're awful."

"But you love me anyway."

"Aye. I do love you."

"We should get married, then."

Eve's brown eyes were suddenly shiny with tears. "Was that a proposal, Lord Quinn?"

"It was."

"Then, I say, 'yes.'"

Epilogue

Somewhere in the Highlands of Scotland

"IT'S CONFIRMED," Fergus McRae said. "Auld Lord Erskine won't admit it, but the American, Quinn Kavanagh, defeated Sorley of Ireland. Dusted him complete is what I heard. Washed away in a rain storm like yesterday's dirt."

He spoke in a subdued tone, as they all did. The house where the three vampires sat around a simple wooden table was safe ground. It had been in the McRae family for generations upon generations. But they'd been born and bred in the Highlands. Long before they'd become vampires, they'd been fed superstition along with their mother's milk. And one never knew who was listening on the wind.

"Who's yer source?" It was Lachlan, the largest among them, who asked the question, though he spoke softly enough. Dark in body and soul, his power was a humming presence beneath the skin, always there, waiting to pounce. If they were going to fight for Scotland's vampires, it would be Lachlan who'd lead the challenge to become the next Scottish vampire lord.

"'Twas Taskill who told me," Fergus responded. "But I don't need a source to know Sorley's gone. I can feel it in my bones."

"Aye, we all felt something," Munro agreed. He was the third of their number. "Quinn's rightly the new Irish lord, but, even so, I heard it was Raphael's support that made the difference."

"Oh, aye, going in, maybe," Fergus agreed. "But even Raphael would nae interfere in a territorial battle. This Quinn guy had to have won it on his own."

Silence then, as the fire crackled, and they all contemplated the territorial changes so close on their own borders. Once again, it was their leader, Lachlan, who broke the silence. "What does that mean for us?" he asked quietly, his voice almost lost in the wind pounding the walls. "Must we reach out to Raphael, as well? Is he now the arbiter of vampire challenges worldwide?"

The others frowned at the idea. Vampires were a fiercely independent lot, violently territorial. It didn't sit well that anyone outside Scotland would tell them who should rule.

"I've never heard of such a thing," Fergus said. "But I'm thinking it couldn't hurt to reach out. Casual like."

"Right," Lachlan agreed somberly. A deep frown marred his broodingly handsome face. "Fuck. You think he's listed in the phone book?"

They all laughed at the ridiculousness of that, then Fergus brightened. "I think I can get a number for that mate of his, Cynthia Leighton."

Lachlan gave him a glance that carried all sorts of meaning, most having to do with what a bad idea that was. "It's probably not wise to cozy up to Raphael's lover," he said, just in case his cousin hadn't gotten the non-verbal message.

"Oh, aye, and I was born yesterday," Fergus responded. "I'm not cozying up to anyone. You're forgetting our wee cousin Catriona, and that fancy French school she went off to. And who do you think was there at the same time?"

"Leighton?" Lachlan asked, suddenly intent.

"The same."

They all straightened in their chairs, as if understanding that this one moment could change their lives forever. They looked from one to the other, each of them nodding in turn.

"It's time, lads," Lachlan said. "Let's do it."

To be continued . . .

Acknowledgements

As always, I want to thank my editor, Brenda Chin, who does such a fantastic job of making sense of what I write. Sincere thanks to Debra Dixon for bringing Quinn to such beautiful life on the cover, and to her and everyone at ImaJinn and BelleBooks who do so much on my behalf.

Most of 2017 passed in a confused blur for me, but, as always, my writing and my readers kept me grounded and kept me going. My trip to Dublin, Ireland was a very bright spot. It made Quinn a better book, but it also gave me a much-needed break that recharged not only my writing, but my life. There are so many people in Dublin that I need to thank. Alan Bradley of Touristy Ireland spent an entire long day driving me from place to place, answering my questions, checking off my long list of locations and things I needed to see, and giving me a history of Ireland that filled page after page in my notebook. Bryan Murphy provided a wonderful tour of Trinity College, including a close-up look at the magnificent Book of Kells, and the magical Long Room library. Tony from Extreme Ireland hosted an informative and joyous journey across Ireland to the Cliffs of Moher. But the highlight of my trip was a rainy Saturday afternoon at a hotel bar in Dublin with Tracey Nugent, Beryl Nugent, John Nugent, and Ruth Weal. It's a day I'll never forget! Thank you all.

Many thanks also to Connie Pokoyoway who won my Valentine's 2017 contest and gave me the wonderful character of Adorjan, who keeps Quinn safe despite himself.

Thank you from the bottom of my heart to author Angela Addams, who lives too far away, but who's the best friend and sounding board a writer, or even a regular person, could ever have. Hugs to Karen Roma for her tireless efforts to make my books better, to Annette Stone whose invaluable assistance frees my time to write, and to authors Steve McHugh and Michelle Muto who have shared this journey from the very beginning,

And, finally, I'm so thankful for my family. This was a rough year, and the pain doesn't seem to end, but I couldn't keep going without the love and support of my large and extended family. Love you all.

About the Author

D. B. REYNOLDS arrived in sunny Southern California at an early age, having made the trek across the country from the Midwest in a station wagon with her parents, her many siblings and the family dog. And while she has many (okay, some) fond memories of Midwestern farm life, she quickly discovered that L.A. was her kind of town and grew up happily sunning on the beaches of the South Bay.

D. B. holds graduate degrees in international relations and history from UCLA (go Bruins!) and was headed for a career in academia, but in a moment of clarity she left behind the politics of the hallowed halls for the better paying politics of Hollywood, where she worked as a sound editor for several years, receiving two Emmy nominations, an MPSE Golden Reel and multiple MPSE nominations for her work in television sound.

Book One of her Vampires in America series, RAPHAEL, launched her career as a writer in 2009, while JABRIL, Vampires in America Book Two, was awarded the RT Reviewers Choice Award for Best Paranormal Romance (Small Press) in 2010. ADEN, Vampires in America Book Seven, was her first release under the new ImaJinn imprint at BelleBooks, Inc.

D. B. currently lives in a flammable canyon near the Malibu coast. When she's not writing her own books, she can usually be found reading someone else's. You can visit D. B. at her website www.dbreynolds.com for information on her latest books, contests and giveaways.

Printed in Great Britain
by Amazon